# FINAL DESTINATION 2

Black Flame presents the novelization of Final Destination 2 – the New Line Cinema hit movie. En-route to a weekend getaway with her friends, Kimberly Corman watches helplessly as a truck careens out of control and loses its payload, causing an accident that leaves twisted metal and dead bodies in its wake.

Moments later, Kimberly finds herself still stuck in traffic, with a line of commuters she saw die moments before, trailing behind her. Shocked into action, Kimberly blocks cars from joining the traffic as her premonition starts to unfold. Death tears up the highway in a massive pile-up, with those left on the onramp narrowly escaping with their lives. Death won't be cheated so easily and this random group of strangers, who were all meant to die in the freeway disaster, must join her in a thrilling race against time to stay alive.

*More Final Destination movie novelizations from Black Flame*

**FINAL DESTINATION**
Natasha Rhodes

**FINAL DESTINATION 3**
Christa Faust

*Final Destination further adventures from Black Flame*

**DEAD RECKONING**
Natasha Rhodes

**DESTINATION ZERO**
David McIntee

**END OF THE LINE**
Rebecca Levene

**DEAD MAN'S HAND**
Steven A Roman

**LOOKS COULD KILL**
Nancy A Collins

# FINAL DESTINATION 2

A NOVELIZATION BY NANCY A COLLINS &
NATASHA RHODES

BASED ON THE MOTION PICTURE

STORY BY J MACKEYE GRUBER & ERIC BRESS AND
JEFFREY REDDICK   SCREENPLAY BY
J MACKEYE GRUBER & ERIC BRESS

BASED ON CHARACTERS CREATED BY
JEFFREY REDDICK

**BLACK FLAME**

**A Black Flame Publication**
www.blackflame.com
blackflame@games-workshop.co.uk

First published in 2006 by BL Publishing, Games Workshop Ltd., Willow Road, Nottingham NG7 2WS, UK.

Distributed in the US by Simon & Schuster, 1230 Avenue of the Americas, New York, NY 10020, USA.

10 9 8 7 6 5 4 3 2 1

Copyright © MMVI New Line Cinema. All Rights Reserved.

Final Destination and all related characters, names and indicia are trademarks of New Line Productions, Inc. 2006. All Rights Reserved.

Black Flame and the Black Flame logo are trademarks of Games Workshop Ltd., variably registered in the UK and other countries around the world. All Rights Reserved.

ISBN 13: 978 1 84416 318 2
ISBN 10: 1 84416 318 0

A CIP record for this book is available from the British Library.

Printed in the UK by Bookmarque, Surrey, UK.

No part of this publication may be reproduced, stored in a retrieval system, or transmitted in any form or by any means, electronic, mechanical, photocopying, recording or otherwise, without the prior permission of the publishers.

This is a work of fiction. All the characters and events portrayed in this book are fictional, and any resemblance to real people or incidents is purely coincidental.

# PROLOGUE

There is a theory that if a butterfly flaps its wings in Brazil, it will cause a tornado in Texas.

Of course, this is impossible.

Or is it?

The scientists amongst you could argue over the reasons for the evolution of the butterfly, the biological and geographical pressures that led to its colonization of Brazil, and the wind-speed vectors that would make a change in air pressure in one continent snowball enough to change weather patterns in another. It *might be* possible, you may doubtfully concede, but only under remarkable, one-in-a-million circumstances.

Trouble is, in an infinite universe, every second of every day there are a billion million-to-one coincidences.

The Butterfly Effect is a major component of Chaos Theory, and came out of an attempt to to predict weather patterns, but is more commonly used by students, and anyone left in the bar after closing time, to drop at random into their conversation and try to make it sound as though they aren't talking complete and utter garbage. Chaos Theory is essentially a rather feeble attempt by many people to predict how tomorrow will turn out, by looking at all the tiny variables and events and coincidences of today, and projecting them into the future.

The less scientific among us might call those coincidences *Fate*. Fate affects everyone among us, from the youngest to the oldest, from the emperor sitting on his golden throne to the whacked-out hobos sniffing meth and raging blindly at the sky down on skid row. Fate is the ultimate leveler, and the butterfly theory and the science surrounding it is simply a tidy way of summing up an age-old question that has plagued man since the dawn of time.

The question is simply this: do I control my own fate?

Look a little deeper, and you'll find your answer. Not in the shadowy foothills of ancient texts and bygone civilizations, but in the everyday world around you. There is no religion devoted to studying Fate, no devout sect that calls for its believers to throw themselves upon the mercy of Fate and beg for its forgiveness. No one ever sacrificed themselves for their belief in Fate, for its effect is as mechanical and as certain as the next sunrise, if somewhat less predictable. It is mankind's nature to need something to believe in when faced with uncertainty, and you can't get much more uncertain than Fate.

So, if we want real control over our lives, perhaps the real question we should ask is this: why did the butterfly flap its wings in the first place?

To arrive at your final answer, you'll have to look a little deeper. Now turn your attention to our universe, a collection of billions of suns and worlds, all rotating together in a complex dance started trillions of years ago by forces beyond our imagining. Look closer, down through the glare caused by the deadly radiance of countless suns, until you see our galaxy, and in it our solar system, a collection of tiny worlds made of gas and ice and rock. Focus in on that one lucky planet, Earth, a world that, through its unique balance of chemicals and gasses and temperatures, made life possible.

Look closer. See the clouds part and the far-off landscape of cities and towns and fields spread out before you, their lights twinkling cozily in the darkness. Now focus in on the right-hand corner of the country we know as America, zoom in on New York, and take a look around its outskirts for a small town containing a street called Western Avenue. Don't ask a local cab driver how to get there; he won't have a clue and will drop you off in Western Central some thirty miles away, then overcharge you for the privilege.

Aren't you glad you bought that Thomas Guide map now?

On that street is a house, and in that house is a girl. Her name is Kimberly, and she is about to find out that sometimes, Fate doesn't need to cause a tornado to kill you.

# ONE

Thunder grumbled outside the window as Kimberly drew her curtains and hurried around her brightly lit bedroom, pulling handfuls of clothes out of her closet and dresser drawers as she did so. Picking her way around the teetering piles of belongings strewn in colorful drifts all over the floor, she placed the clothes in neat piles at the foot of her bed, next to her brand new, open suitcase.

Tomorrow—or rather later that day, since it was already past midnight—she and her best friend, Shaina, were going to drive down to Florida, along with a couple of old buddies from high school. Kimberly was so excited that she knew she would have trouble sleeping. She had stayed up late packing to stave off the inevitable tossing and turning and staring at the ceiling, and now she was kind of wishing she hadn't.

This was to be her first Spring Break as a college student, and her first non-family road trip. When she was younger, she and her parents had always gone somewhere over the summer, but that was back when her mother was alive. As it was, it had taken a great deal of fast-talking to get her father to agree to let her go on this trip. He had always been overprotective of his only child, and the events of the last year had made him even more so.

However, when she reminded him that she was nineteen, had been working her ass off at college in order to make the Dean's List and really, really needed a vacation, he had finally relented and given the trip his blessing. Kimberly had been counting the days 'til the trip for what seemed like forever, but now that the day was finally upon her, she realized that she was hopelessly unprepared.

She adjusted the volume on the retro Nineties silver stereo perched precariously on her dresser, currently pumping out the Ramones at full volume, and stepped back to regard the mess on her bedroom with good-humored bewilderment. Her usually tidy room was awash with a flood of multi-colored clothes, jewelry and cosmetics that spilled off the bed onto the floor, sorted into piles of various sizes that overlapped one another and blended together to create a tangle of possessions, as though there had been an explosion at Macy's department store. In fact, her father had put it best when he'd come into her room earlier and had told her it looked like her closet had thrown up.

Looking at the mess that now filled her room, Kimberly couldn't help but agree with him.

Yawning, she poked at a pile of leaky sunscreen lotion bottles with the toe of her scuffed sneakers and tried to remember whether her dad had a second suitcase he could lend her. There was no way all this would fit into just one case, but she'd sorted through it five times and there was nothing else she could weed out. It was all essential stuff. She really should've started packing days ago—what if she arrived at her destination and found out that she had forgotten something vital, like her lip gloss?

It was clearly time to get organized. Kimberly picked up her spiral-bound Hello Kitty notepad and studied the list she'd written to help her pack, checking the items off one by one as she placed them in the suitcase.

Toothbrush and toothpaste: check. Clean underwear: check. Bikini set: check. SPF 50 sun block: check. Sunglasses: check. Condoms: check. Flip-flops: check.

As she stood there, pen poised thoughtfully over her pad, there was a sudden gust of cold wind from the half-open window behind her desk, making the curtains billow into the room. A roll of distant thunder followed.

Kimberly looked up, distracted. Then reality kicked back in and she set down her paper and pad, and moved quickly to close the window before the rain started. Last thing she needed was an inch of rain soaking her carpet and drenching her carefully chosen lingerie.

Yanking down the sash, she secured the old-fashioned clip latches and stood back, gazing thoughtfully at the darkness outside her window. The temperature in the room seemed to have dropped by several degrees. She shivered and gave her chilly upper arms a brisk rub. There was a great deal of difference between spring weather along the Hudson River Valley and Central Florida. It was hard to believe that in less than twenty-four hours she would be sitting on a sunny beach, soaking up the rays and ogling cute guys in board shorts. As it was, she'd definitely be dressing in layers tomorrow morning, or she would, in all likelihood, die of hyperthermia before she hit the city limits.

Of all the ways there were to die, that was not how she wanted to go.

Kimberly threw a couple of pairs of fashionably ripped Lucky jeans into the suitcase, decisively closed the top and hauled it off the bed with an effort. Enough with the packing; it was time for some relaxing. She was far too keyed-up for her own good. After turning down the volume on her stereo, she clicked on the television on top of her dresser and channel-surfed until she found CNN. Hey, there was an idea. Maybe if she watched the news channel for a bit she'd get bored and be able to fall asleep.

Stripping down to her T-shirt and panties, Kimberly stretched out luxuriously on her bed, hugging her pillow to her. It was still a little cold in the room, so she wriggled further over onto the bed and hooked her cold feet underneath the soft cotton of her scrunched up comforter to warm them.

*Perfect.*

Snuggling down, Kimberly watched the talking heads droning on about Capitol Hill insiders and Wall Street closings, and soon she began to yawn. The soporific sounds of the air conditioning humming overhead lulled her into a trance, and she could feel her limbs relaxing as her eyelids grew increasingly heavy. Her body felt as though it was made of lead, sinking down into the black tides of unconsciousness.

After drifting in and out of a light doze for a while, Kimberly rolled over and fell into a deep sleep.

Unaware they were speaking to an oblivious audience, the talking heads continued to drone on and on, the images on the screen flickering and rolling, disrupting into bursts of static as lightning from the approaching storm arced across the midnight sky. When the signal finally straightened itself out, it revealed the opening credits of a late night live talk show. Garish neon titles rolled as the talk show host, an older man with a shaved head, glasses and a graying goatee, smiled slightly and nodded his head in polite acknowledgement of his applauding audience.

"Good morning, America, and welcome to *Midnight Report*. I'm your host, Carter Randolph."

In the studio, several hundred miles away from where Kimberly lay slumbering, Randolph turned and directed seventy-five percent of his best smile at the camera, his eyes narrowing slightly as he squinted myopically at the autocue. Thirty years in the TV industry had destroyed his eyesight to a point where he needed to wear glasses just to put his contacts in every morning. Every relentlessly glaring studio spotlight, every crappy low wattage autocue just made things worse.

Although less than fifty years of age, Randolph had the anxious, "please don't fire me" look of an industry professional who knows his useful days will soon be up. Being relegated to the graveyard slot on the news channel was just the final kick in the teeth, but for now, he was willing to take anything that paid enough to keep up the payments on his wife's new cherry-red BMW. He hadn't the heart to tell her that he was no longer getting the generous monthly wage from the news network that he used to command, and only prayed that she never came across his glassily grinning face adorning every month's issue of 'The Randolph Report,' the news magazine for the under twelves that was currently paying for three-quarters of their monthly mortgage.

Life, as Randolph saw it right now, basically sucked.

Randolph cleared his throat and straightened his tie, hoping that his mother wasn't watching this. "Tomorrow—or should I say today, since it is already past the witching hour—marks the one year anniversary since Volare Flight 180 exploded and crashed shortly after take-off at JFK Airport. It's a disaster that's affected many; none more so than Mount Abraham High School, which lost forty students and four faculty members in the crash. But it was the events after the crash that turned this tragic story into something even stranger. The survivors, who managed to get off the plane before it crashed, died soon after in a series of mysterious and bizarre accidents."

The autocue rolled on, but Randolph paused, directing a seething glare at the studio's Floor Manager, who was busy hustling an academic-looking man in an unwashed white shirt and ill-fitting charcoal pants into the chair opposite him. The cheap pine floor vibrated as the operators rolled their cameras in toward him, ready for an introductory close-up.

Randolph shook his head, resigning himself to his fate. He still couldn't believe some of the losers the Head Honchos at the studio hauled in for him to interview. Last week there had been that guy who believed that aliens were responsible for the wave of missing pets down in Colorado, citing a cat's collar found in a tree by his house as conclusive evidence that his little Fluffy had been spirited off into the sky by ETs from another dimension. A couple of weeks before that he'd interviewed a woman who, although normal in every other respect, firmly believed that she could communicate with birds, thus sharing the secrets of the animal universe with mankind. She had even brought a bird into the studio to demonstrate. That one had kept the guys in the newsroom sniggering for almost a month, and Randolph had briefly become an inadvertent star when the video clip of the pigeon pooping on his jacket had become the most requested download for two weeks running on the newsroom's internet site.

Randolph straightened his glasses and gave his new interviewee a tight smile. Dreading the backlash on this one, he turned his gaze back to the flashing autocue.

"Now, to some, those deaths were just tragic coincidences, but to others they were an indication of more sinister events taking place. That's the contention of tonight's guest, Mr Chris Welles."

As Randolph turned to his guest, the camera pulled out to show the thin, weedy-looking man with the pallor of a computer nerd seated in the chair opposite him. "Thanks for joining us."

"Thank you for having me," Welles replied, with every indication of sincerity. He was in his early thirties, and the way he squirmed in his seat and glanced fitfully at the camera every few seconds suggested that he was unused to being on television.

Randolph disliked him instantly.

"And I appreciate your using the word 'sinister,'" Welles went on. "Most people say 'supernatural,' because they think I'm talking about ghosts and witches, and stuff like that."

"Well, here's your chance to set the record straight." Randolph was having difficulty keeping his own face straight, let alone the record. He poured himself a cooling glass of water, and surreptitiously popped two Valium pills into the corner of his mouth while pretending to gnaw an already bitten thumbnail. In his book, the sooner this freak show was over, the better.

Welles twisted uncomfortably around in his chair as he glanced anxiously at the winking red light of the camera beside him. Under the harsh studio lights, his pale, pinched face looked almost like a skull, his eyes hiding in two pools of ugly shadow that, even now, the lighting guy was scrambling to fix. "I believe that there's a sort of force, an unseen malevolent presence that's all around us, every day. I believe it determines when we live and die. Some people call this force the Devil. I believe that the whole religious thing is bogus. I prefer to call it 'Death Itself.'"

Randolph's brow furrowed as he tried to understand what his guest was saying, even as he felt the Valium start to kick in, soothing the worst of his irritation. "So, I'm surrounded by Death?" He snorted, amused and yet slightly disconcerted by the thought.

"Absolutely. Absolutely." Welles nodded, becoming more excited as he spoke. "Every day, everywhere, all the time, and that's what I want people to understand. Death has this grand design that we all fit into. So when Alex Browning got off that plane and took the other survivors with him, he basically screwed up Death's plan, and that's what I'm trying to warn people about."

The furrows across Randolph's forehead grew deeper. "And the fact that all the survivors have died is your evidence of this?"

"Well, it's not so much that the survivors died, but it's the *way* they died." Welles leaned forward in his chair, his eyes burning with the fervor of a zealot. "I mean, there were so many weird, seemingly random things about the way they died, it just didn't seem to make sense, and *that's* the proof that there's something out there."

As the voices on the TV set droned on, Kimberly's fingers twitched in her sleep. She was dreaming: half-formed, foggy images of sun-kissed boys with laughing eyes and bronzed muscles cavorting through her young, slumbering mind. She lay sprawled on the bed half-under the sheets, her full lips parted slightly as she breathed shallowly, the soft light from the lamp on the landing draped in pretty curves over her perfect porcelain complexion. In sleep, Kimberly's face looked much younger than her nineteen years, still smooth with youth, yet bearing the hallmarks of adulthood in its high cheekbones, curving eyebrows and wide, generous mouth. She was a pretty girl, and she was going to grow up to be a beautiful woman. Those who knew her would be surprised at how peaceful she looked right now, cocooned amid the folds of her comforter like a fairytale princess. The only sign of life was the light, regular rising and falling of her chest, and the occasional twitch of her lips as the muscular hunks in her dreams whispered sweet nothings to her.

As she lay there slumbering, a sudden breeze blew across Kimberly's sleeping face, fluffing up her dark hair and slipping icy fingers down the front of her thin cotton T-shirt. She frowned in her sleep, and a moment later she twitched and her eyes suddenly snapped open.

Startled, Kimberly sat up with a jolt, uncertain as to what had caused her to wake, but knowing that it was something important. She had a strange, nagging feeling that she had just heard someone call her name.

She looked around the room, her vision still blurry from sleep. Her bedroom was illuminated by the yellow light from the hallway, spilling into the room through the half-open bedroom door. The dozens of snapshots plastered over every inch of wall space beamed down at her: happy pictures of herself, Shaina and a giggling gaggle of other teenage girls, posed sprawling crazily over the bonnets of fast cars, on the beach, at the mall. The sight of them reassured Kimberly. Her attention moved on, caught by a flickering blue light, and her gaze finally came to rest on the television. She licked her dry lips and tried to focus in on the screen, still slightly dazed from her nap. The volume on the TV seemed to be turned up too loud, but she was too warm and comfortable to get up and turn the set down.

Stifling a yawn, Kimberly settled back to watch.

Back in the studio, the furrows on Randolph's forehead had turned into ditches as he interviewed his unwanted guest. "Wait a minute, that's not proof," he was telling Welles, who sat back in his interview chair, arms folded, glaring at the host. "That's just your interpretation of events, but they can't be proven in order to support your ideas."

Welles's voice took on the petulant tone of someone unaccustomed to having his opinion questioned. "You should be more open-minded about possibilities."

Randolph shook his head, rolling his eyes as he spoke. He couldn't believe this guy! He was almost as bad as the pigeon woman.

"Mere coincidence would have one or two of these kids die, but not all of them, including their teachers," Welles continued.

"Yes, but people die all the time. Why should this be any different?"

Welles made a steeple with his fingers and peered over the top of imaginary glasses like a disapproving school teacher. "It forced people to question these so-called every day coincidences. What if they were something more? What if you could do something about it?"

Randolph gave a humorless half-laugh. This was quite plainly bullshit, and if he had even one iota of self-respect left, he wasn't going to just sit here and let this guy yak on without interruption. "Please! Are you listening to yourself? This is crazy. You're saying we should be on guard *every* morning as we leave the house?"

Kimberly jumped as the door to her room suddenly slammed shut, jolting her from her cozy reverie. Darkness fell across the room as the light from the hallway was cut off. She glanced behind her cautiously, and then slowly turned her gaze back to the screen. This guy on TV was freaking her out, making her jumpy. He was obviously a loon, but at the same time, there was something oddly compelling about him. He seemed utterly convinced he was speaking the truth.

Kimberly's liquid brown eyes narrowed as she curled up on the bed and stared at the screen, transfixed.

"That's *exactly* what I'm saying. Exactly that," Welles said, leaning forward in his chair, a weird gleam in his eyes. "And in order to survive... the *only* way to survive... is to look beneath the visible world. Because, in the end, *no one* can escape Death."

He turned his gaze on the camera and looked straight into the lens. "And today may be *your* day to die."

As the host opened his mouth to reply, the picture broke up as a wave of magnetic interference from the approaching storm swamped the signal. The picture rolled once, twice, and then finally went down for good as the TV show disappeared into the ether in a burst of white static. A loud hissing sound came from the speakers, underpinned by a strange noise—a dull, resonant bass throb, like a slow-motion growl.

Kimberly blinked, then reached over and grabbed the remote. She clicked the channel button repeatedly, but the signal was gone for good. Her pretty mouth twisted into a pout. Damn! She was just starting to get into that!

Disappointed, she shut off the television and slid down off the bed to close the window, which she suspected must be open for the door to have blown closed. She shuffled over to the window that faced the street, only to find it was already shut. She frowned as she rubbed her bleary eyes.

Man, she was losing it.

Puzzled, she stared at the window for a long moment and then remembered that she had closed it before she lay down. So what caused the door to slam shut, if not the wind?

As Kimberly stood there pondering, a bright flash of lightning lit up her bedroom as brightly as daylight, momentarily revealing the dozens of grinning faces in the photos on her walls and searing them into her eyeballs.

Then the room fell dark again.

Kimberly blinked, rubbing her eyes to dispel the ghostly after-images that danced across her retinas. A peal of thunder ripped across the sky, making the wooden puppets hanging in her bedroom window dance, and the clouds finally opened up, loosing sheets of gray rain upon the world outside.

Kimberly backed away from the window as lightning struck the ground outside, feeling an odd sense of foreboding shoot through her.

The storm had finally arrived.

# TWO

It was seven in the morning when Kimberly hauled open the back of her red Tahoe SUV, a folded roadmap clamped between her teeth. She was vibrating with excitement, and for once in her life had managed to get out of bed without an alarm clock.

It was finally road trip day! She just knew this was going to be one of the best weekends of the whole year, and she fully intended to make the most of it. It was a shame about the weather, but they'd be in Florida soon enough. The driveway was still wet from the heavy thunderstorms that had moved through the area just after midnight, and the early morning air was crisp enough for her to wear her light blue warm-up jacket over her striped tank top and low-rider jeans.

Kimberly placed her suitcase in the cargo area, let the map drop from her mouth and caught it in her free hand as she turned to face her father. "Thanks, Dad. I'll call you."

Her father, Ambrose Corman, stood in the driveway with his shoulders hunched and tried to look like the thought of his daughter leaving for Spring Break wasn't worrying the hell out of him. He was a tall, good-looking man in his early forties, with just a touch of gray at his temples. Thinking about his daughter in Daytona, in the company of her best friend Shaina and two boys, was sure to add a few more gray hairs over the coming weekend.

Although Kimberly and Shaina had been friends since first grade, Mr Corman had always had his reservations about their relationship. Over the years, Shaina had turned into something of a wild child, getting herself mixed up with the wrong kind of crowd without seemingly caring about the effect it was having on her GPA. He had always seen her as a bad influence on Kimberly, but he had always deferred to his wife when it came to the situation. Even now he could hear her voice in his head, telling him to quit worrying and just be glad Kimberly had a friend.

In a way, he had to admit that she was right. Kimberly was doing a heck of a lot better than he was. When his wife died, he had shut himself off from their circle of well-meaning friends, turning into something of a recluse. It wasn't intentional. He just couldn't bring himself to accept her death, and until he did, nothing in the outside world would make any sense to him. Kimberly was the only thing in his life that held meaning for him now, the physical end result of his love for his wife. Now that she was growing up, he felt like he was losing her too. It was all very hard for him to take, and seeing Kimberly hanging around with Shaina was particularly difficult for him, as he knew the kind of crowd she was part of. Just the thought of his daughter being around those kinds of people filled him with fear.

Still, he had to admit that Shaina had really been there for Kimberly over the last year. Despite her personal failings, he knew she would sooner die than let anything bad happen to Kimberly.

"You sure you have everything, Kimberly? Credit card? Cellphone? AAA Card?" Mr Corman asked, trying to keep the anxiety out of his voice and failing dismally.

Kimberly laughed as she tossed back her long brown hair. Her father had always been protective of her, but during the run-up to this trip he was starting to drive her just a little bit crazy. She smiled up at him, her eyes sparkling with amusement. She loved her father, and only wished that he would lighten up a bit. "Relax, Dad, its Daytona, not Somalia."

"Fix-A-Flat?" Mr Corman continued doggedly, doing his best to defuse the discomfort he knew they both shared. He rocked back on his heels, thrust his hands deep in the pockets of his comfy gray pants, and gave her a sheepish grin. "Road flares? Sun block? Mace?"

"Condoms? Whips? Chains?" Shaina Gordon added with a saucy smile as she strode up the Cormans' driveway with her bags. Mr Corman glanced up as Kimberly nodded a greeting to her blonde, leggy friend, and raised an eyebrow at his daughter.

"Sheesh," Kimberly muttered under her breath, her cheeks flaming red with embarrassment.

"Just kidding, Mr Corman," Shaina said sweetly, flashing him a teasing smile as she stepped smoothly around him, just close enough so that he could feel her body heat and smell the sweet candy-scented perfume she always wore. As she slung her high-fashion Roxy duffle bag in the back with Kimberly's things, Mr Corman couldn't help noticing that under Shaina's jean jacket, he could clearly see the surgical steel ring glinting in her exposed navel, breaking up the smooth lines of her tanned skin with a wicked flash of silver. He sucked in his breath and averted his eyes. If Kimberly came back with a pierced tongue or something equally horrendous, he'd know exactly who to blame.

Shaina glanced at Mr Corman. Jeez, this guy had tension spilling off him by the bucket load. She could practically feel it. She gave him a pleasant smile, wondering if Kimberly knew how hot her dad was. "Don't worry, I'll keep an eye on her," she assured him, then shut the back of the SUV and climbed merrily into the front passenger seat.

"Thanks. That makes me feel a *lot* better," Mr Corman called back, his voice heavy with sarcasm. Then he turned and smiled awkwardly at his daughter, who threw her arms around his neck and kissed him on the cheek.

Kimberly held her father close, hoping to somehow squeeze the worry out of him. "I know this is the first time we'll be apart after what happened... but everything's going to be okay," she said in her best reassuring voice.

"I know, honey." Mr Corman sighed. "It's just— your mother would have been so proud of the way you've handled yourself through all of this."

Kimberly's smile widened, even as she fought to keep her lower lip from trembling. He always knew what to say to her to make her not want to leave him. She hugged her father tighter, breathing in the familiar smell of him. "I know, Dad."

"Can we go get the guys?" Shaina called out loudly from the cab of the Tahoe, shattering their sweet little father-daughter moment. "I'm getting *horny!*"

"Great," Mr Corman said, rolling his eyes heavenward. He let go of Kimberly and jerked his head at the car with a small smile. "Go on. Get out of here."

Kimberly gave her father one more quick kiss and hurried toward the driver's side door. "I'll call you," she promised him.

Mr Corman shook his head ruefully. He would just be glad when this little trip was over and

Kimberly was back safely with him, where she belonged.

Kimberly opened the driver's side and slid in behind the wheel. Slamming the door shut behind her, she gave her friend a dirty look. "Whips and chains? That's nice."

"Whatever," Shaina said with a laugh as she cranked up the radio. "Besides, your dad's cool."

As the SUV pulled out of the driveway in a blast of loud rock music and a gale of girly laughter, Mr Corman cupped his hands around his mouth and shouted, "Buckle up!" There was no reply.

He stood and anxiously watched the vehicle roar off down the wet street, waving until it was out of sight.

As he turned to go back into the house, a stain left on the driveway's surface caught his attention. Curious, he knelt and dipped a finger in the fluid, then held it up for closer inspection. The liquid was as red as newly spilt blood.

A frown darkened his face as he felt a pang of worry go through him. Kimberly's car was leaking.

Oh great. Something else for him to worry about...

Route 23 was a winding, divided freeway with two lanes of traffic going in each direction, one eastbound and the other west. It was the main traffic artery between Interstate 87 and Interstate 88 for northern New York State, not to mention the various suburban bedroom communities of

Albany and Schenectady, such as Mount Abraham. It was always busy, especially during the morning rush hour, and today was no exception. Now that the rain had stopped, the going was a little quicker, but to Kimberly, it still felt infuriatingly slow.

Kimberly sighed and drummed her fingers on the wheel as she waited her turn to merge onto the busy highway from the on-ramp. She just wanted to be there already. Up ahead was a traffic light that allowed two cars at a time onto the freeway. Since it was the middle of the morning rush hour, the flow of traffic seemed to be getting slower by the minute. After crawling through town, she wanted nothing more than to put her foot down and get up some speed.

She glanced in the rearview mirror at her backseat passengers and a smile quirked her lips. Originally she and Shaina had planned to go down to Daytona by themselves, but of course her father had put his foot down about that. He insisted that they take at least one male companion with them, for safety's sake. Kimberly had initially laughed at him—the idea of anyone even trying to mess with her while Shaina was in the car was just funny—but then she had seen that he was serious. So at the last minute, and more to humor her dad than anything, Kimberly had invited Frankie Arnold along for the ride.

The Arnolds had lived across the street from the Cormans for years. Frankie was a "nice boy": polite to adults, eager to please and a tad dorky.

He'd had a crush on Kimberly since they were in the third grade together, all those years ago. While he was a sweet guy, and kinda cute in an Emo-band-lead-singer kind of way, she saw him more like a brother than a potential boyfriend. He wasn't really her type, but hey, her dad was happy, and so she was too. She knew that Frankie was too overawed by her to ever try to put any serious moves on her. The guy blushed every time she so much as smiled at him, so she knew that in all likelihood, he would behave himself on this trip.

All in all, she didn't mind the idea of traveling on a twenty-four hundred mile round trip with Frankie.

Unfortunately, the same could not be said of the fourth member of the crew, Dano Royale. Shaina and Dano had been heavy-duty party-pals back in high school, and the guy had changed very little in the time since. Dano was still a slacker-ass stoner, who was too busy doing bong hits to worry about his grades, or indeed, anything other than getting high and having a good time. Kimberly couldn't say that they were the best of friends, but Shaina seemed pretty enamored with him. In all likelihood he was supplying her with free weed in return for party favors, so he had been invited on the trip too. Rumor had it that his family was loaded, so all he had to do was pretend to go to college and live off his trust fund.

In short, life was good for Dano.

Kimberly watched him now in the rearview mirror as he glanced furtively around to make sure nobody was looking at him, and then reached quickly into his jacket pocket and pulled out a plastic ziplock bag full of weed. Fumbling in his other pocket for some papers, he started rolling himself a sneaky joint. Kimberly shook her head in bemusement. The drug scene had never really interested her, and the amount of effort Dano put into getting and guarding his stash never ceased to amuse her. She'd warned him not to light-up before he had sat in the car

The light switched from red to green and the line rolled forward another fifty feet. Kimberly put the car into drive and tapped the gas pedal, easing it forward. Finally, some movement! At last she was next in line to enter, after the 1989 Buick Regal ahead of her. Kimberly gazed reflectively through the windshield, peering through the back window of the Buick. Hey, was that a limited edition Captain Crash doll on the back seat? She hadn't seen one of those in years...

"Watch it," Shaina yelped, as the SUV nearly hit the bumper of the car in front of them.

Kimberly gasped, startled from her thoughts, and quickly slammed on the brake, causing her passengers to jerk forward in their seats. Kimberly tightened her grip on the wheel and grimaced in embarrassment. "Sorry, guys."

"Whoa! Easy, Kimmy," Dano said with a bemused laugh as he pulled a silver lighter out of his jeans pocket and clicked it open. "This your first year of driving?"

"Want me to take over?" Shaina asked, glancing at Kimberly in concern.

"No, I'm good," replied Kimberly, trying to smile despite the sudden feeling of ill ease that swept through her. She gazed down at her freshly painted pink nails, chewing on her lip. Something had been niggling at her ever since they had set out, and she couldn't for the life of her identify what it was. She had a weird, cold knot of fear in her stomach, and the further away from home she drove, the more it seemed to be growing. She couldn't be homesick already, could she? God, she hoped not. That would be the last thing she needed.

A hand slapped against Kimberly's window, causing her to glance around, startled. An old woman was peering into the car window at her with chilling intensity. Kimberly stared at her, transfixed. The woman looked like she was at least sixty years old, although her face was so wrinkled and weather-beaten it was hard to be sure. She wore a filthy, woolen cap pulled down over a shock of grayish yellow hair, which stuck out in all directions like a tattered dandelion. The hand she had used to slap the car window to get Kimberly's attention was encased in a battered, red leather glove, the fingers of which had been cut off. In her other hand, she was holding up a plastic string bag that had in a previous life been used to transport oranges, but was now filled with crushed aluminum cans and other recyclable refuse. As the old crone glowered at Kimberly, she shook the sack vigorously, causing the cans to rattle.

"*Ew*! Let's go!" Shaina pleaded.

"Get lost, you fucking freak," Dano muttered.

Kimberly smiled apologetically at the woman, who stared back unflinchingly, her sea-green eyes hard and cold. Kimberly frowned. Despite the fact that she had quite clearly lost her mind, Kimberly could've sworn she saw recognition flare in the depths of the old woman's eyes. Not that she recognized Kimberly, exactly; more that she recognized something *in* her that she knew…

The plastic bag the old woman was holding suddenly gave way, spilling its contents into the road with a clatter. The homeless woman glanced downward, a sudden look of confusion on her sad, lined face, and awkwardly bent down to retrieve them.

Kimberly couldn't help feeling a little bit sorry for her. As she watched the old woman scrambling to reclaim her spoils from the roadside, she found herself wondering who the woman was, where she had come from, what had happened to her to cause her to get into this state. She wondered whether the woman had any family left, and if so, if they knew that she was living like this. She tried to imagine what it would be like to be sixty and homeless, grubbing for cans to swap for pennies to buy herself a paltry crust of bread each day, and suddenly her own life didn't seem quite so bad.

"Hey, Dano," Frankie said, leaning across the back seat to dig his friend in the ribs. "Shouldn't we go back and help your mother?"

"Blow me," Dano sneered as he flipped Frankie the bird. "You're fucking hilarious man. You're not gettin' *any* of my weed, man." He waved the bag of grass for emphasis. "*None* of it."

"Whatever." Frankie chuckled. He gazed out of the side window for a moment, then stretched his arms above his head and yawned hugely. "So, what are we gonna do in Daytona?"

Dano grinned, his fit of pique forgotten, and sat up in his seat with a sudden burst of excitement. "Oh, man. We're gonna see lots of honeys there. We're gonna get drunk, we're gonna smoke some huge spliffs on the beach, we're gonna have this awesome fucking party."

As the traffic light turned from red to green, Kimberly pulled the SUV out onto the highway. As Dano continued to drone on about the "fucking awesome time" they were going to have in Daytona, Kimberly noticed a large electronic sign on the side of the road that flashed: "WARNING: CONSTRUCTION NEXT 180 FEET."

Again, something niggled in the back of her head. The sign seemed significant to her in some way, but she couldn't for the life of her figure out why.

As Kimberly merged into the traffic, gazing at the sign, she nearly collided with a speeding school bus. She reflexively jerked the wheel to the right and realized she was heading straight toward the orange road construction barrels in the slow lane. She swerved back into the left lane, just behind the school bus. She blinked rapidly, swallowing a sudden knot in her throat, trying to ignore the odd looks the others were giving her. Jeez, what was wrong with her? She had to get a grip on herself. That old woman had spooked her out big time. She had to get her head together, concentrate on more important things, like all the boys she was going to meet on this trip.

Giving the car a jolt of gas, Kimberly pulled around the bus, the side of which was draped in a brightly colored homemade banner that read: "DEMOLISH THE MUSTANGS—Smoke Their Butts!" Inside the bus, she could hear the high school football players chanting in unison: "Pile-up! Pile-up! Pile-up!"

The knot of worry in Kimberly's stomach seemed to grow bigger. That wasn't the kind of thing she wanted to be hearing while driving at sixty miles per hour on the freeway. In an effort to distract herself, Kimberly reached down and flicked on the radio, hitting auto-seek to scan the stations. After a moment, a newscaster's smooth, trained voice spilled from the speakers:

"A candlelight vigil to mark the one year anniversary of the crash of Flight 180 will be held at 8pm tonight at the Mount Abraham Municipal Auditorium…"

Kimberly grimaced and quickly hit the seek button on the car radio. The chorus of AC/DC's "Highway to Hell" filled the car at an ear-splitting volume, causing both Kimberly and Shaina to jump. With an apologetic expression, Kimberly reached to lower the volume. She hit the seek button and changed stations again, this time landing on "A Grisly Car Crash" from Nervous Norvus. A chill crept over her and she quickly flicked the radio off, deciding to just concentrate on the road.

"Christ, is this 'Tribute to Princess Di Day,' or what?" Dano chuckled, and went back to constructing his mammoth joint. Kimberly glanced anxiously at him, but said nothing.

As they continued along Route 23, their SUV pulled up alongside a black Trans-Am traveling in the slow lane. The vehicle had a red and gold firebird painted on the hood, and chromed hubcaps and headlamps. Linkin Park blasted at full volume from the onboard sub-woofer system. Kimberly glanced idly at the driver, a good-looking young guy in his early twenties with short, blond hair and blue eyes. He was wearing a brand new black and orange leather racing jacket. He turned his head to flash a cocky yet somehow creepy smile at Shaina, and revved his engine loudly.

"Oh my God!" Kimberly laughed. "Jesus, all the crazies are out today."

"A Trans-Am?" Frankie snorted, trying not to sound jealous, but failing miserably. "That shit went out with New Kids on the Block."

"Yeah, who does he think he is? *Knight Rider*?" Dano sneered as he gave his joint a final twist.

"Who?" Frankie looked puzzled.

"You know, Hasselhoff before he did *Baywatch*," Dano explained.

Kimberly shook her head in disgust and shot her best friend a disparaging glance. "What's the chance of finding a nice, mature guy once we get to Daytona?"

Shaina shrugged and grinned. "How does a nice, mature fuck sound?"

Kimberly laughed until a cloud of blue smoke wafted past her head from the back seat. She instantly recognized the pungent smell of weed in the smoke and twisted around in her seat, taking her eyes off the road just long enough to confirm that Dano was indeed smoking a joint in her car, directly behind her.

Kimberly scowled. She'd told him not to light up in the car! If the smell got into the upholstery she'd never get it out, and then that would be the end of her driving privileges. "Hey, I told you guys no drugs in the car! My dad's gonna freak!"

Dano and Frankie exchanged looks. "God, what a geek," Dano muttered out of the corner of his mouth.

"Calm down, Kimmy. It's not drugs, it's weed," Frankie added.

"Yeah, you should have specified," said Dano, between tokes.

Kimberly turned to Shaina, pleading silently her with her eyes for her to do something. Shaina took the hint and turned around in her seat to glare at Dano. She opened her mouth to speak.

Suddenly the hands-free cellphone, which was mounted on the speaker system below the dashboard, began to ring. Kimberly hit the speaker button and her father's voice filled the cab of the SUV.

"Kimberly? It's Dad."

Kimberly glared at Dano in the rearview mirror. Talk about weird timing. It was as though her father could smell the weed from across the miles that separated them. "Hey, Dad, what's up?"

"Your car's leaking transmission fluid," said Mr Corman, anxiety tightening his voice. "I want you to have it checked as soon as possible."

Kimberly gave a small smile, even as Shaina rolled her eyes in the seat next to her. "I got it, Dad. I'll call you if I have a problem."

"I *mean* it. Take care of it," crackled the phone. Kimberly recognized the firm, "do as I say!" tone in her father's voice, and inwardly smiled. There was no arguing with him when he used The Voice with her. It was the same voice he used to use to order her to go to bed when she was little, and it still had the same effect on her.

As Dano chuckled behind his hand and leaned over to hand Frankie the joint, he glanced out of the rear passenger-side window, into the slow lane. A customized black Harley motorbike drew up alongside them, easily keeping pace with the speeding SUV. A chunky outlaw biker, wearing a studded jacket and a skull and crossbones bandana, was seated in the saddle. Despite his age and overall lack of physical fitness, the biker had a blonde hottie riding behind him.

The motorcycle mama noticed Dano looking at her and cheekily lifted her flame-striped Harley-Davidson T-shirt, flashing a pair of perfectly formed—and perfectly naked—breasts. Dano thumped his hand on the seat and gesticulated wildly in the direction of the window, choking on the pot smoke in his lungs.

Beside Kimberly, the phone cracked. "Is that someone coughing?" asked Mr Corman, his tone heavy with suspicion.

"No, Dad. Don't worry about the car. I'll take care of it," Kimberly said, trying her best to hurry her father off the phone. "Bye. Love you."

"Bye, honey," Mr Corman sighed as he hung up.

Beside Dano, Frankie finally turned his head to look out of his window, but he was too late. The biker chick had already pulled her shirt back down, so all Frankie saw was the biker glowering back at him. Noticing his attention, the heavyset man scowled and flipped Frankie the bird with a heavily ringed finger as he gunned his hog, pulling away from the SUV.

Frankie looked back at Dano, baffled by the biker's response. "What did you do to piss that guy off?"

"Dude, look at those titties!" Dano howled at the top of his lungs, now that the coast was clear, exhaling a huge cloud of pot smoke. He pointed a wavering finger after the Harley.

Kimberly glanced over her shoulder at her semi-hysterical passenger. "Shut up, Dano."

"Didn't you see that?" Dano said to Frankie as he passed the joint back to him, beside himself with excitement. "You missed that? Aw, that's too bad!"

"Kimberly's right, man," said Frankie in a monotone. "Shut the fuck up."

Shaina glanced sideways at Kimberly, her pretty elfin face creased into a frown. "Um, your dad's not going to call, like, every ten minutes, is he?"

Before Kimberly could answer, Dano suddenly jumped in his seat, kicking Kimberly in the back. "Aw, shit! Fuck. There's a cop right behind us." As Kimberly glanced around in annoyance, Dano craned his head around to look out of the window. His eyebrows pinched together in fear as he quickly lowered the joint and shoved his bag of weed into the front pocket of his pants. "Pull into the other lane, *now*!"

Kimberly did as she was told without thinking, only to be startled by the blast of an air horn as a black flatbed semi hurtled past her at high speed, so close she felt a sideswipe of air rush in through her rolled-down window. The semi was hauling an immense load of giant, freshly-cut logs, which were secured to the back by long lengths of iron chain. The semi was already in the lane she was trying to join, and had accelerated to stop her from cutting in front of it. Kimberly was forced to swerve to avoid colliding with the back of the flatbed, which was kicking up a considerable wake of spray from the rain-slicked freeway. Her wheels skidded as they fought to keep a grip on the treacherous wet asphalt.

"Look first, idiot," Dano yelped.

Shaina turned on the radio and leaned across the front seat. "Ignore him," she told Kimberly, tossing her hair.

Kimberly glanced into the rearview mirror and turned pale. The state trooper had pulled into the slow lane behind her, almost as if he could sense the presence of weed in the car with some freaky cop sixth sense. Visions of having to call her father from the police station to bail her out flashed across Kimberly's mind, and she turned around in her seat and glared at Frankie. "Put that thing out *right now*," she snapped. "I'm serious."

"Get rid of it!" agreed Shaina.

"Okay," Frankie said, moving to toss the joint out of the open window next to him.

"No, man, hold up." Dano snatched the still-smoldering joint from his friend. "They look for shit thrown onto the shoulder." He lowered his head below the back of the seat for one last, quick surreptitious toke, and flicked the incriminating evidence out of the back window and into the fast lane.

The joint sailed through the air, leaving a trail of glowing sparks behind it, and bounced onto the windshield of a Ford Expedition in the lane to their left. The wind caught it and sent it rolling into the space between the windshield and the hood of the car, where it came to rest amid a litter of dried leaves trapped behind the Expedition's windshield wipers. The leaf litter ignited with a flare as the wind fanned the sparks, creating a sizeable flame.

Inside the Ford, Kat O'Brien was too busy talking on her hands-free phone headset while trying to light a cigarette to notice the burning joint land on her windshield. She glanced down at her watch as she lit up, mentally calculating the exact number of minutes she had left to get to her business meeting and still leave time for a sneaky stop at the low-carb food bar on Main Street. Dinner last night had been a coffee and a hastily snatched stale croissant from the office's communal fridge, eaten on the run between three back-to-back Power Performance seminars, most of which she had slept through. Her stomach had been grumbling for the last twenty-five miles, and she was feeling tired and light headed with hunger. It was not a good combination when you had a schedule like hers to contend with.

She shifted her cigarette into her other hand, listening intently to the barking voice in her ear. "No, I'm stuck on jury duty, so I won't be able to pitch the campaign. Let's get Silverstein to come in and—what the hell?" Kat was surprised to see a small campfire burning merrily on the other side of her windshield. "No, not you," she quickly reassured her coworker on the other end of the line. She flicked on the windshield wipers and squirted a dash of wiper fluid onto the screen, successfully putting out the tiny blaze, although her wipers smeared ash and dirty water all over the windshield. That meant a stop at the car wash, taking precious minutes off her breakfast stop.

Fuck!

Irritated, Kat glanced over to her right and saw a red Tahoe in the lane next to her, slightly ahead of her. The back window was open, through which she could see a slightly pudgy Phish-wannabe sitting in the back seat, looking extremely nervous. The moment he noticed Kat glaring in his direction, he gave her a pleading look and put a finger to his lips. Then he glanced pointedly over his shoulder at the state police cruiser riding the Tahoe's bumper.

Getting his meaning, Kat flashed the worried stoner a condescending smile and gestured at the cop car with her cigarette as if to say "he'll get you for that, you know." Dano gave her a limp grin in return, and went back to trying to figure out how to put on his seat belt while simultaneously stuffing the last of his weed down his pants without attracting the cop's attention.

Back in the SUV, Kimberly took her eyes off the police car in her rearview mirror as the dashboard "check engine" light began to flash orange.

*Ding... ding... ding... ding...*

Great, now the car was yelling at her.

Kimberly glanced over to the side of the road and saw a roadside sign that read: "Next Service

23 Miles." She bit her lip in worry. Maybe she should listen to her dad after all. If the car really had sprung a leak, the last thing she wanted was for it to break down in the middle of some lonely highway late at night, with only the trees and the axe murderers to keep them company. She could just see the headlines now.

"I think we should pull over and check the car," she said, anxiety flaring in her voice.

Shaina sighed and rolled her eyes, pushing her long blonde hair off her face. "Kimberly, stop it!" She turned to face Kimberly and gave her a wide, reassuring smile, speaking in a voice she usually reserved for small dribbling children and demented old people. "The *car's* gonna be fine. Your *dad's* gonna be fine. *You're* gonna be fine. Okay?"

Kimberly glanced over at her unhappily, then exhaled and nodded sheepishly. Shaina smiled, relieved that her friend was finally starting to relax. What was her deal? She had never seen her wound up so tight, but she knew a good way of fixing that. Shaina smiled to herself. If she didn't finally get Kimberly laid on this trip, there really was no hope for her.

She glanced back at Dano and Frankie, who were still trying to pretend they weren't keeping an eagle eye on the police officer on their bumper. "So? What's the cop doing? Did he see that?"

"I'm not sure," Frankie said, his eyes flicking to the rearview mirror and back, "but I don't think he saw us."

"I dunno, man," Dano said anxiously. "I think he's on his walkie-talkie. What if he's radioing up ahead?"

Shaina glanced over at Kimberly's suddenly tense expression, and shook her head in despair.

Thomas Burke frowned at the large, red Tahoe SUV directly ahead of him. The bright color of the car really wasn't helping his hangover. He supposed he should overtake, but right now, he just didn't care. He'd be back at the station soon enough, and then he'd find a nice, quiet, dark room to lie down in for ten minutes to soothe his aching brain. He'd had some hangovers in his life, but this one was a real doozy.

He groaned and reached for his sunglasses. If he'd known that going out for a "quick drink" with Drake after work last night was going to mean the pair of them staying up till 3am in some sleazy downtown bar, downing tequila slammers and trying to calculate to the nearest decimal place exactly how many laws the bar was violating by letting them stay there drinking so late, he would've passed and gone home to watch *The X-Files* on the TV instead.

Yawning loudly, he picked up the radio mike mounted on the dash and twisted the flex around his hand, wishing that the sun would stop being quite so bright. "Hello, Dispatch? This is Burke, Car Five-Oh. I was supposed to be off today. How did I get screwed?"

"Hello, Car Five-Oh. This is Dispatch. Drake called in sick."

"Copy that," Burke said, scowling in disgust as he switched off his mike and returned it to its holder. A vivid memory popped into his head of his young and annoyingly handsome partner sitting on the bar last night, conducting an impromptu seminar on the importance of not drinking and driving, watched by an eager crowd of young, impressionable girls who were, later on, more than happy to offer a stranded police officer a lift home. Officer Thomas still couldn't figure out quite how Drake had ditched him between the bar and the parking lot, but he fully intended to take the thirty bucks his own cab fare home had cost him out of Drake's paycheck.

He was a cheeky son of a bitch.

"Go on, sleep it off, Drake," he grumbled under his breath.

Rubbing his bleary eyes, the young police officer reached over to the Dunkin Donuts bag in the front passenger seat and removed a Styrofoam cup full of coffee. He lifted the steaming cup to his lips, but it was still too hot to sip out of comfortably. Without thinking, he placed the container on the dash and reached into the bag for a donut, hoping that the sugar would wake him up a bit.

On the dash of the patrol car, the hot liquid in the coffee cup shimmered from the vibrations of the car. After a couple of seconds, the cup started sliding forward, moving closer and closer to the edge of the dash.

Back in the SUV, Dano was still staring nervously over his shoulder at the squad car. Frankie laughed, shaking his head. "Relax, dude. We're home free. Nothing bad is gonna happen, okay?"

In the front seat, Shaina glanced over at Kimberly. She was sitting ramrod-straight in her seat, gripping the wheel tightly and staring out of the front window. Despite the fact that she outwardly appeared calm, Shaina could see the two tiny furrows just above the bridge of her nose that indicated Kimberly was trying very hard to look like she wasn't worrying. Judging by her frequent quick glances in the rearview mirror, she could see that Dano obsessing over the cop was freaking her out.

Shaina tapped her finger to her perfectly made-up lips, thinking. It was time to change the mood in the car, and she knew just how to do that. She turned around in her seat so that she was facing both Kimberly and the boys in the back. "Hey, did you know in Daytona it's five guys per girl?"

"I can live with that," Kimberly said, returning Shaina's wicked grin with one of her own.

Frankie popped his head in between the two girls, a hopeful smile on his face. "Hey, Kimberly, where does that put me?"

"In the back seat, Frankie," Shaina laughed, pushing him away playfully.

The foursome laughed, and the atmosphere of worry between them was broken. Shaina smiled, pleased with herself.

Suddenly, Kimberly yipped as a large white van in the fast lane swerved directly across their path into the slow lane, toward the breakdown shoulder. Kimberly pumped the brake and swerved just in time to avoid an accident, as the van hit its brakes and pulled back over in the fast lane. Shaina gave the van a "what the fuck?" glance, and went back to drumming her fingers to the beat of the radio. The sooner they were in Daytona, the better.

As the van passed them once again, Frankie stuck his head out of his window and shouted at the woman behind the wheel. "What's your problem? You on fucking crack, baby?"

In the driver's seat of the white delivery van, Isabella Hudson struggled to regain control of her vehicle as she choked back sobs that threatened to tear her apart. Tears streamed down her face, blurring her vision as she fought to stay in the lane, gripping the steering wheel with one shaking hand. The heavily pregnant woman clutched a cellphone in her free hand, into which she was currently screaming at the top of her lungs. "How could you *do* this to me, Marcus? I'm about to have our baby! Is that not enough for you?"

Isabella swallowed a sob, and then her face froze. Her pretty brown eyes widened in disbelief and shock. "The doctor said WHAT? I have to come in to test for STDs! *Goddamn* you, Marcus!" Isabella dropped the cellphone onto the floor of the vehicle and pounded her fist against the steering wheel as she pulled the delivery van back into the slow lane. This day couldn't possibly get any worse.

In the back of Isabella's van, the dozens of white roses and funeral wreaths destined for the Flight 180 memorial service bobbed gently as the van accelerated down the freeway.

Two lanes away, Eugene Hooper gunned his shiny black Kawasaki ZZR1200 as he moved in and out of traffic, the engine buzzing in his ears like an enraged hornet. He'd had a late start that morning, thanks to the weather forcing him to wear his new riding leathers. He normally didn't wear them as they took way too long to put on, but the chill, damp morning air would freeze him to the bone at sixty miles per hour if he didn't wear something a little warmer than his usual jeans and T-shirt.

He glanced down at his watch, half hidden by the thick, insulated sleeve of his leather jacket. If he didn't want to be late for class, he was going to have to really step on it. His face creased in amusement inside his helmet. Seeing that he was the teacher, he doubted he'd be able to get away with arriving late and slipping in at the back like he used to do.

Eugene checked his mirrors and twisted the throttle, cutting in front of a white delivery van and pulling away from the little knot of vehicles traveling together at the same speed. That was odd—why was everyone sticking to the speed limit? There must be a cop around. He glanced in his side mirror as he struck out toward the center lane. Yup, there it was; that distinctive flash of red, white and blue that put terror into the hearts of otherwise decent citizens. Eugene nodded sagely to himself and glanced down to check his own speedometer.

Dead on sixty mph: he was safe.

As he approached a flyover bridge, a discarded plastic bag was kicked up from the side of the road by a white van exiting the lane in front of him. It whipped toward his face. Instinctively, Eugene swerved his motorcycle to avoid the road hazard. His path took him into the adjacent lane, where he slowed as he felt his bike start to wobble beneath him as the high-speed maneuver disrupted the Kawasaki's center of gravity. Eugene shifted his weight forward to compensate and eased off the gas a little until he felt the big bike stabilize.

He breathed a small sigh of relief. That was close. You had to be so careful when the road was wet like it was today. One moment's inattention at this speed and you'd be hamburger meat quicker than you could say "Oh, crap!"

"Oh my God," Shaina cried in disbelief, pointing at the vehicle in the fast lane beside the Tahoe. "Look at that guy!"

Kimberly glanced over and saw a giant beer delivery truck with "Hice Pale Ale" stenciled onto the cab's doors. As she watched, the truck driver hoisted one of his company's fine products to his mouth and took a hearty swig, completely oblivious to the fact that he was being watched.

"He's drinking a beer," she cried, shocked. As the beer truck passed the SUV, she could see that it had a sign painted on its side that read: "Drink Responsibly."

"Oh, yeah, that's *real* responsible," muttered Kimberly as she reached back and pulled on her seatbelt, pressing the metal tab into place with a click. She could hear Frankie and Dano laughing at her from the back seat, but she didn't care. She'd had her fair share of close calls already this morning, and they were barely half an hour into their trip.

Her dad's voice rang in her head—he'd told her to buckle up, hadn't he? She suddenly remembered all the lurid stories he'd told her about pretty girls who forgot to put on their seatbelts, and then got their faces ripped off going through the broken glass of their own windshields. Kimberly shivered. Okay, so perhaps that wasn't a good thing to dwell on right now, but hey, her dad was only trying to protect her. So what if the others thought that seatbelts were for losers? If anything happened, she'd be the one laughing as they all went through the windshield and she stayed safely in her seat. That would teach them to make fun of her.

All of a sudden, the interior of the Tahoe was filled with clouds of black exhaust. Kimberly blinked as the acidic fumes stung her eyes, and waved a hand in front of her face, then peered through the windshield, looking for the culprit. The smoke was coming from a battered blue 1983 Mustang, which was riding the line in front of them. Even as she watched, the car backfired again, pumping out more smoke from its tailpipe. The thick, blinding fumes caused everyone in the car to cough and reach for the power window buttons.

"Gas it around this idiot," Frankie spluttered.

"Don't have to tell me twice," Kimberly replied. She flicked on her blinker, and then saw that the way around the Mustang was blocked by a Subaru station wagon, which was hanging in the fast lane. It was going just fast enough to prevent her passing, but was still moving maddeningly slowly.

Get out of the freaking way, Kimberly thought mildly. She glanced at it, irritated as it slowed down still further and pulled alongside her. In the front passenger seat of the station wagon was a seven year-old kid, who was smashing a toy semi into a red toy car with a look of rapt enjoyment on his face. He turned to stare out at her for a moment, a blank look on his face, and then went back to his game.

As the station wagon finally dropped back, Kimberly started to move over only to have a biker on a Japanese crotch rocket startle her back into the slow lane. The biker roared by in a shower of spray, weaving in and out between the larger, slower cars. Once the biker was gone, she found herself blocked in by, of all things, a Pacer.

Kimberly sighed. At this rate, they might just reach Daytona by the time they were fifty. She hoped that her pension plan would cover the amount of booze she was going to have to drink to make up for the last forty minutes, because if not, she was heading home right now.

In the leather-lined interior of the Pacer, Nora Carpenter glanced over at her son as the fifteen year-old drummed idly on the dashboard with two empty Deer Springs water bottles. "Tim, will you cut that out? I can't even hear myself think."

As Tim dropped the bottles obediently into his lap, Nora clicked on her blinker, falling into the lane beside a large red SUV full of hyperactive-looking teenagers. She pursed her lips and shook her head at the sight of them. They shouldn't be allowed to drive that thing. The girl at the wheel was practically a child, and the guys in the back didn't look much older. If it was up to her, all teens would be banned from the road until they reached a responsible driving age, which in her book would be about thirty.

Beside her, Tim winced, holding his jaw. "Damn, it really hurts, Mom."

"I know. We'll be at the dentist's soon, and please don't swear," said Nora, rolling up the window of her sensible beige Pacer.

Tim grinned to himself and went back to daydreaming about girls. As he shifted position in his seat, one of the water bottles fell to the floor, rolled round for a couple of moments, then finally settled, unnoticed, under the Pacer's brake pedal.

Kimberly sat up straight in her seat to stretch her aching back as she regarded the tight knot of vehicles surrounding her with a look of bewilderment. This was getting annoying. She just wanted to put her foot down and go, and all these idiots in her way were starting to piss her off.

Kimberly scowled as she checked her side and central rearview mirrors. No matter what she tried, she kept finding herself trapped behind the smoke-spewing Mustang. The SUV's windows were all closed now, but the air in the car tasted stale and bitter, and a thin stream of smoke continued to trickle in through the air vents, even though she had shut off the A/C unit.

No longer able to contain his irritation with the situation, Frankie rolled down his window and yelled at the car ahead. "Ever hear of the ozone layer, asshole?"

Oblivious to the pollution churning out of his aging Mustang, Rory Cunningham leaned over to snort a line of coke off a Def Leppard CD case, which was balanced precariously on the dashboard in front of him. After doing the line, he let himself drop back in the driver's seat and rubbed his nose briskly with his forefinger, then scraped his knuckles reflectively against the heavy stubble covering his upper lip and jaw, peering at himself in the rearview mirror. He hadn't shaved in a month, but the look still kinda worked, the stubble that covered his wiry Italian good looks set off by the unruly mop of black hair that flopped into his eyes at regular intervals. If his momma could see him she would slap him upside of the head and tell him to go get a haircut.

But she wasn't here, so he could do what he wanted.

Rory affectionately batted the furry red dice dangling from the rearview mirror and reached to turn up the volume on his stereo as the coke hit crashed through his brain with a dizzying blast. Loud rock music pumped out of what he laughingly called his sound system, and Rory started feeling like the world was on his side for once in his life. He may be a nothing, but right now, at this precise moment, he felt like a god. The rest of the world could go screw itself.

As he reached into his pocket for a second hit, a flash of red and blue caught his attention. Rory looked muzzily over at the lane beside him, and his eyes widened at the sight of a police car pulling up alongside him. His heart started pounding double-time. Reflexively, he tapped the Mustang's brakes to slow the car as he quickly removed the CD case from the dashboard and, after wiping it on his pants leg, slung it back in the wooden crate on the floor of the passenger side. Getting hauled in right now was not his idea of a good time, and if the pigs found his secret stash hidden in the spare tire in the trunk, he might as well kiss his ass goodbye.

He held his breath as the cruiser crept past him, but to his relief the cop didn't so much as glance in his direction. Rory mopped his forehead. Talk about a close call.

As the cop pulled ahead of both the Red Tahoe and the Mustang, Rory resumed his previous casual demeanor, leaning back so that his left leg was propped against the steering wheel. He puffed up his chest as the state trooper moved up and back over into the slow lane. It settled behind a semi tractor-trailer, which was loaded with logs.

"What?" he sneered at the cop car, now that it was safely out of earshot. "I'm wearin' a seat belt. You gonna bust me, bee-atch?"

Officer Burke muttered under his breath as he finally pulled out from behind the red Tahoe in front of him and into the passing lane, accelerating past the lumbering SUV and a smoke-belching black Mustang. His headache was subsiding slightly thanks to the two Tylenol he had just taken, but his skull was still tight and the queasiness in his stomach reminded him that he would be paying for last night for quite some time yet.

He flicked a glance in his rearview mirror at the Mustang, which was apparently running on coal, judging from the amount of black smoke billowing from its exhaust. He transferred his tired gaze to the driver, a cocky-looking young guy in a scruffy jacket, who would no doubt give him shit if he pulled him over for an emissions ticket.

Officer Burke chewed on the inside of his lip, considering the situation. He should probably pull the guy over, but his head really couldn't take that kind of abuse right now. His eyes swept the scene in front of him with a mechanical efficiency born of long years cruising the highways, looking for an easier target. The white van to his left was weaving about a bit, but he guessed from the pattern of its movements that the driver was just fiddling with their radio, trying to find a good station, and decided it was hardly worth his while.

Officer Burke's eyes suddenly locked in on a vehicle. Ah—there! The dirty, smelly semi directly in front of him had a loose rear license plate, which bumped and rattled with every dip in the road. The officer's eyebrows drew together in concern. If that plate came off at this speed it could cause a nasty accident, not to mention making the vehicle instantly illegal. It was practically textbook, not to mention happily lacking in paperwork.

Yawning again, Officer Burke gave his car a jolt of gas and surged forward.

One bust, coming right up...

Still trapped behind a wall of cars, Kimberly reduced her speed as the Mustang ahead of her put on its brakes, dropping as far back as possible from the cruising police car. She wondered what the driver was smoking to make him so spooked about the squad car. Judging by Dano's reaction to the cop, she guessed it was something pretty illegal. She watched as the driver in the Mustang flailed his arms around wildly, apparently conducting an imaginary conversation with the steering wheel in front of him.

"My God, who are these freaks?" Kimberly groaned to nobody in particular. "I can't wait to get off this highway, to the beach, meet some incredibly hot but wildly stupid guy and start having some fun."

In the back seat, Dano and Frankie's eyebrows shot to the tops of their foreheads. They looked at one another, sharing the same dirty thought, and did a silent high-five.

Oh yeah. This was gonna be such a great trip.

"Now that's what I'm talking about." Shaina gave a small laugh and clapped her hands together in delight. All right! That was the attitude! She tossed her head and gave Kimberly her best saucy look. "Look who's getting her swerve on."

Kimberly gazed through the front windshield as she listened to the others laughing and chattering animatedly around her, and for the first time in what felt like forever, she felt a warm glow start to steal over her. The terrible events of the last year began to fade away, to be replaced by a lingering sense of happiness and hope that she hadn't felt in a long time.

She sighed, stretching her arms out in front of her and wriggling into a more comfortable position in the driver's seat. Shaina was right, of course. She *was* going to be fine. Everything would work out okay, and they were about to go on vacation and have an incredible time. Once they got back from Daytona, she could resume her life—the life of an ordinary teenage girl, whose mother hadn't just died—and start enjoying herself again without feeling guilty.

Kimberly caught Shaina's eye and smiled warmly, hoping to convey her thanks to her friend. "You know, I'm glad you talked me into this trip, Shaina," she said.

"You're welcome." Shaina beamed. She knew that things had been tough for Kimberly, but there was no sense in living in the past. The future was where all the fun was at. She tossed her hair again and settled down in her seat, then reached out to touch Kimberly's arm. "It's about time you started living again."

In the patrol car, Officer Burke closed in on the semi, mechanically checking it out. It was a great beast that had obviously seen better days, smoke belching from the stack on its roof, rust and watermarks pock-marking its flanks. A huge stack of giant uncut tree trunks was tethered to the back with a great loop of chain, stacked lengthways in a pyramid fashion.

As Officer Burke got closer, he noticed a small spray of sparks coming from the road behind it. He frowned at the back of the vehicle, examining it closely. The semi was dragging a sizeable length of unsecured chain behind it, which had come loose from an anchor point at the back. It threw orange sparks up from the road as it whipped back and forth like an angry snake across the wet surface of the freeway.

Officer Burke mentally congratulated himself. That was a definite hazard, and he was glad he'd picked up on it in time. The driver was probably completely unaware of the state of his vehicle, only caring about getting his quota to the docks in time to pick up his weekly paycheck: easy prey.

It was time to move in for the kill.

Officer Burke reached for his police radio to report the driving hazard to dispatch. As he did so, his untouched coffee cup toppled forward off the dashboard of his cruiser and spilled hot coffee into his lap.

"Son of a *bitch*!"

The young Highway Patrol officer hissed in pain and made a grab for the paper napkins, which were still in the Dunkin' Donuts sack beside him.

As he did so, he took his eyes off the road for the briefest of moments.

That was all it took.

With a low creak, the rusty chain, securing the load of logs to the semi, suddenly gave way, stretched beyond capacity by the missing tether line. Corroded links pinged down the side of the cab like bullets as the extreme tension in the chain was released.

The loose logs started to roll.

*CRUMP!* The log nearest the edge flew off the unsecured side of the flatbed and landed in the fast lane. Such was its weight and speed that the half-ton log bounced once, twice, three times, before ricocheting into the slow lane, right in front of the police cruiser.

As Officer Thomas Burke looked up from mopping up the spilled coffee, the first and last thing he saw was the sawn-off end of a giant tree trunk heading straight for his windshield. His eyes widened in shock. He had enough time and presence of mind to gasp, but not to scream, as the log smashed through the windshield in a pile-driver blow, reducing his head to mush as it punched unhindered through the car and burst out through the back windshield in a spray of bright red blood.

The now-driverless police cruiser continued on its way, weaving crazily from side to side as the rest of the logs went the way of the first, spilling off the side of the semi and crashing down onto the freeway.

Oh, fuck!

The moment he saw the first log strike the road, Eugene slammed on the brakes of his motorcycle, but the asphalt was too slick from the morning's rain for the tires to grip. Eugene's stomach gave a sickening flip as he felt the back end of the bike start to slide out from beneath him. He remembered his Driver's Ed classes and tried to turn into the skid rather than fighting it, but the Kawasaki was going far too fast to maneuver.

Before he knew it, Eugene found himself flying through the air as the heavy bike laid itself down on the road at sixty miles per hour, a blaze of sparks curtaining up from beneath it. He hit the ground with a bruising thud and shot forward like a leather-clad puck on an air hockey table, sliding across the wet road and shattered safety glass from the demolished police cruiser. His back screamed in pain as he felt his leathers start to heat up and shred on the asphalt, but he knew that if he had not been wearing them, things would've been far worse.

Helplessly, he slid on down the road, closely followed by his toppled bike, his path taking him directly in front of the smoke-belching Mustang.

Rory yelled in panic as he braked and swerved to avoid the injured biker on the road in front of him. He had seen the logs burst free from the semi up ahead of him, but his drug-addled mind was too slow to respond to the sudden crisis. He needed to get out of the way of the log, but he didn't want to run this dude over…

Oh crap, he was going too fast to stop!

As an explosion of adrenaline rushed through him, he instinctively steered around the sliding bike. An instant later the wheels locked up and he lost control of the car. The engine howled as he shot off the tarmac, onto the grassy median that separated the divided highways, blowing his right front tire at fifty miles per hour. Rory was still yelling as the Mustang flipped, and rolled over and over in a storm of flying glass and metal, pinwheeling across the highway, before finally crashing down, upright across both lanes of oncoming traffic, on the other side of the highway.

Eugene flew across the rough surface of Route 23, completely unaware that he had narrowly avoided being hit by a car. The only thing resembling thought in his head was a frantic prayer of thanks to God that he'd suited up in full leathers that morning, including his helmet.

If he hadn't, he knew without a doubt that he'd be dead by now.

As he slid onwards toward the semi, he tried to shift his position, to direct his slide, but found that he couldn't move. He could already tell, in that funny way that happens during accidents when time seems to slow down and you go outside your body, that both his legs and arms were broken, although he couldn't actually feel any pain yet. Eugene was still in something resembling a seated position when his slide across the glass-studded asphalt came to a brutal halt as he slammed into one of the fallen logs, going from forty miles an hour to zero in a heartbeat, breaking his back on impact.

As he cried out in pain and struggled to move, he heard the screech of metal scraping against asphalt, and looked up to see a sight he really,

really didn't want to see — his motorcycle was skidding toward him on its side.

Eugene just had time for one final, anguished cry as the six hundred pound motorcycle smacked into him with a terrible finality, crushing him against the tree trunk. Blood sprayed out as the steering column of the bike embedded itself in the log, effectively chopping Eugene in half.

It killed him instantly.

Two lanes away, Rory sat sideways to the traffic in his demolished Mustang, his heart thundering as blood poured from his broken nose and split lower lip. He was too dazed to do anything but stare at the fuzzy red dice hanging from his rearview mirror. They were the only things in the car that weren't in some way broken or smashed.

He watched them bobbing back and forth comically while his scrambled brain rearranged itself. He licked the blood off his lip, took a deep breath, and wondered vaguely what he should do next. Shouldn't he, like, get out of the car in case it exploded or something? Or did that just happen in the movies?

Rory shifted in his seat, trying to assess the damage. His head hurt like a motherfucker, and there was something weird going on with his ribs, like they weren't attached right. The seatbelt had bruised his shoulder, but it'd stopped him from flying out of the smashed window and getting creamed like guacamole on the road, so he could forgive it that much.

Rory's hand drifted toward the door handle, and then he paused. What if getting out of the car just made things worse? Perhaps he should just stay here and wait for the paramedics to arrive. A ghost of a smile touched his bloodied lips. With any luck they would be hot female paramedics.

That would be kinda neat.

His mind was playing lazily with that image when the sound of screaming brakes intruded on his reverie. Rory muzzily raised his head to see a huge Mack garbage truck bearing down on him, its horn blaring. He had just enough time to scream once, futilely, before the vehicle plowed into the driver's side of the Mustang, pulverizing Rory with the remains of his car. Flames spurted up into the sky as the fuel tank ignited, turning the car into a giant fireball.

A hundred yards away, Kat O'Brian was still on the phone, oblivious to the metal-mashing carnage happening right in front of her. The only sounds in her top-of-the-range double-glazed Ford Expedition were the gentle hum of the A/C and the crackling scratch of her coworker's voice in her ear. "Forget it, I'll call the home office myself," she barked into her cellphone, no longer bothering to hide her irritation with her coworker. Jeez, what a crappy day, and it wasn't even breakfast time yet. Some days, she didn't know why she even bothered.

Kat hung up and squinted down at the keypad as she dialed the office number. When she looked back up again, she saw what looked like half a tree bouncing down the highway toward her. *What the...?* Kat dropped the phone and swerved into the next lane to try to avoid being hit by the runaway log. With a shock, she saw that the road ahead of her was completely blocked by fallen, bouncing logs, and that several vehicles had already struck the logs and were blazing away merrily by the side of the road. That was some heavy duty CNN news footage going on there, and she was heading right toward it.

Not for the first time in her life, Kat really, really regretted getting out of bed that morning.

But there was no time for regrets now. Kat had better things to do.

She screamed.

Back in the SUV, Kimberly stared in horror at the devastation unfolding on the road ahead of her. It didn't seem real, as though this was all happening on TV. She watched in disbelief as the fireball from the wrecked Mustang subsided, belching plumes of oily black smoke up into the atmosphere. Up ahead, the runaway garbage truck continued skidding along the road away from her, flaming wreckage and parts of the driver still wedged under its front wheels.

Frantically, Kimberly's eyes flew to the road ahead of her, calculating a path that would take her around the pile-up and allow her to miss the settling logs. This could be bad, but she could get them through this. She saw a clear path and guided the Tahoe toward it... then her head whipped forward as a Ford Expedition in the next lane sideswiped the SUV as it swerved to miss a huge log flying down the road toward it.

Kimberly could hear Shaina and the others screaming as she struggled to keep the Tahoe on the road. Its engine whined in complaint at the high-speed maneuver as she dragged it back onto the asphalt. For a moment it seemed that the SUV would fly off the highway, and then the tires gripped and crossed-up wheels righted themselves with a jerk and a shudder. Out of the corner of her eye she saw the Expedition bounce back into the fast lane, only to smash into one of the smaller logs that had come to rest half across the highway. It flipped the Expedition end over end, collapsing the roof like a closing accordion.

When the debris settled, the female driver was obviously, graphically, dead.

Kimberly gritted her teeth and silently cursed herself as she white-knuckled the wheel, flying past the wreckage. She just *knew* that she should've stopped at that service station.

Nora Carpenter heard the explosions and the sound of cars crashing a split second before she actually saw the collisions in the lanes ahead of her. Her worst nightmare came true as she found herself hurtling unstoppably toward a scene of fiery devastation, her innocent son strapped in the seat at her side.

"Oh God! Stop! Stop!" Tim screamed at his mother.

Nora didn't have to be told twice. She thumped the heel of her sensible flat shoes down on the brakes, but the fallen water bottle rolled up under the pedal and prevented it from depressing. There was nothing she could do but clutch at her son and scream as the Pacer hurtled toward the wreckage at top speed, then slammed into the back of an upside-down Expedition, folding the smaller car in on itself. Gasoline spurted, and a moment later both cars exploded violently, scattering flaming shrapnel in every direction.

Isabella Hudson steered around the flaming wreckage of the two cars and gave a yelp of fright as she saw one of the runaway logs come bouncing in the direction of her white delivery van. She jerked the wheel hard to the right to try to escape onto the shoulder, just as the front end of the log struck the rear door with a vibrating clang. The van rebounded away from the log, jumping and sparking on the asphalt as it nosedived off the side of the road and buried itself in the grass of the verge, smoke pouring from under its hood. Flames started to lick out from the gaping hole in its side, engulfing the flowers and wreaths from the Flight 180 memorial service, which were strewn on the grass all around it.

Kimberly fought desperately with the steering wheel as she jerked it to avoid the careening white van, praying she could keep the Tahoe out of danger. Her clear path was gone, and now she was barreling at high speed straight toward a deadly obstacle course strewn with flaming debris and giant logs. There was no time to downshift, no time to think, no time to do anything but grip the steering wheel and react as cars honked and screeched and spun around her like drunken dinosaurs, threatening to knock her off the road. She didn't dare hit the brake for fear of locking up the wheels again. If she spun off the road at this speed, she would be dead.

Further up the road, the driver of the log-haulage semi slammed on the air brakes of his rig. He glanced into his rearview mirror as the orange light of blazing vehicles flickered through his cab, and swore copiously and fluently. He'd been meaning to replace that rusted chain for days, but hadn't quite got around to it. Now it was too late. *Damn it!* His stomach turned to ice and he flinched at the sound of clashing metal and people screaming. Once word of the pile-up he'd just caused got around, his working days in this town were over.

The driver ground metal as he downshifted the lumbering semi, trying to kill his momentum enough to steer onto the side of the road. As he did so, the rest of the logs on the back of the flatbed were jolted off the platform by the sudden deceleration. They tumbled down onto the road in a noisy, bouncing heap. Suddenly freed from its load, the flatbed's wheels locked up as it jackknifed around like an angry scorpion, ending up broadside to the oncoming traffic.

The entire rig slid sideways, finally coming to a halt a hundred yards beyond the flaming wreckage that just sixty seconds ago had been a busy, rush-hour freeway.

As it juddered to a noisy halt, the last remaining log rolled off the edge of the flatbed as it whipped around, smashing down into the road—directly into the path of the Red Tahoe SUV that was speeding straight toward it.

"Look out!"

Kimberly saw the tree trunk launch itself off the back of the fishtailing semi as though in slow motion, and turned hard to the right to avoid it.

She was a fraction of a second too slow.

The Tahoe hit the log broadside at forty-five miles per hour, sending the SUV flipping over the top of the trunk and flying up into the air.

Time seemed to stop for Kimberly. Through a strangely calm fog she watched the world cartwheel around her, the horizon swinging around three hundred and sixty degrees as the Tahoe spun through the air in a graceful, deadly pirouette, rolling sickeningly like a whirligig ride at the fairground. Inside the vehicle, everything that was unsecured, including Shaina and Dano, went flying. Frankie had been ejected from the side window the moment the Tahoe hit the log, but the others didn't notice. They were far too busy screaming.

Metal and glass flew through the SUV, embedding itself in Kimberly's skin in small, stinging shards. The sunroof had been smashed when they had rolled over the log, and as the SUV flipped over a tenth and final time, Shaina screamed as she rolled across the roof and felt her head pop out of the top of the SUV, slicing her neck on the shattered glass.

The SUV spun one final time before finally crashing down on its side and skidding to a halt.

And then all was still.

Evan Lewis swore colorfully as he fought with the steering wheel of his brand new Firebird Trans-Am, using every last ounce of his Xbox slalom driving skills to avoid smashing his car into the twisted wreckage that littered Route 23. The Firebird's suspension rocked as the car bounced off the road into a drainage ditch and then rocketed up the other side.

A moment later it slammed back down onto the highway, sparks shooting from the underside of the car as it bottomed against the hard concrete. Evan yanked hard on the steering wheel and by some miracle of timing managed to get the car facing in the right direction. The car rocketed forward, flying over the burning cars onto the wet grass of the median and missing a cartwheeling red SUV by mere feet. Evan winced in distress as he watched the SUV thump down on its side ten meters away from him, bloody limbs dangling out of the smashed windows.

Evan once again congratulated himself on being the luckiest man on the planet as he spun the car back onto the road and prepared to brake. In his head he was already going over the story about how playing video games enabled him to survive a pile-up when the car to his left exploded, sending a cloud of thick, heavy smoke belching toward his car, blinding him. Flames flickered through the smoke in the darkness and Evan spun the wheel to avoid them as his vehicle sped forward, its engine still stuck in third gear. A second later the thick smoke in front of him parted to reveal a flatbed trailer completely blocking the road right in front of him.

He was heading straight toward the side-mounted gas tank.

Evan ducked down in his seat with idiot optimism as the gas tank came zooming up to meet him at head-height. A second later the Firebird struck the trailer's gas tank at thirty miles an hour, sheering its roof off. A massive explosion rocked the highway as the giant gas tank blew up on impact, sending a cloud of orange flame boiling toward the sky. Glass and flaming car parts rained down onto the highway like a firestorm in Hell. Moments later a second explosion tore the trailer from the semi as the Firebird's gas tank ruptured.

The Firebird, with Evan still inside it, started to burn.

\* \* \*

After what seemed like an eternity, Kimberly opened her eyes.

Right away, she wished that she hadn't. The Tahoe had come to rest on the driver's side, and since she was the only one wearing a safety belt, she was still in her seat, lying like a broken rag doll amid the shattered remains of her SUV. Shaina had been flung into the back seat with Dano, who she could hear whimpering behind her like a frightened child. Her head felt gray and fuzzy and her left arm was pinned against the buckled car door, while the shoulder strap of the safety belt was wrapped around her neck, keeping her from turning her head to either side. She was freezing cold and nauseous with shock. She felt broken safety glass grinding beneath her as she tried to move, and then stopped as a shooting pain stabbed deep in her side.

She lay still, trembling, trying to get her bearings.

"Shaina?" It hurt to breathe and it was all she could do to whisper her friend's name. "You okay?"

No reply.

Kimberly reached up with her free right hand and groped blindly toward the back seat. After a second she felt a slender hand, slick with blood, slip into her own and grip it tightly. Flames crackled nearby, and Kimberly could smell oily smoke and the sharp, pungent smell of spilled gasoline. She knew instinctively that she should get up, get out of the car in case it blew up, but it hurt too much to move. On the periphery of her hearing she could hear brakes screeching as cars the length of Route 23 spun onto the grass to avoid the pile-up.

After a couple of seconds, she became aware of a new and chilling sound—the sound of a man screaming in pain. Painfully rolling her head to the side, Kimberly looked blearily through her shattered windshield and saw the skeletal burning remains of the Trans-Am, minus its roof, rolling slowly out of a huge wall of fire. It coasted to a stop about fifty yards behind the Tahoe. There was something moving inside the car, and Kimberly saw with a fresh wave of horror that it was the driver.

He was still alive, trapped inside his blazing vehicle.

"Help me! Someone fuckin' help *me*!" Evan Lewis screamed as he rose up from his seat, battered and bloody, but still alive. As he struggled to free himself from his snarled seat belt, his skin began to blister and peel away from his flesh like the leaves of a book as his car continued to burn around him. Half his hair was gone and one side of his face was a charred, bleeding mess, but still Evan kept moving, thrashing around as he tried to escape. His leather jacket had already melted onto his skin in the intense heat, and smoke rose up from his jeans as the fire started to engulf him.

Kimberly wept. She was helpless to do anything but watch as the young man in front of her was roasted alive.

Then, she saw something far, far worse...

A huge out-of-control semi loomed through the curtain of fire pouring forth from the blazing log truck. Heavily laden with a double-decker trailer of new cars, there was no way the gargantuan vehicle could stop in time. Kimberly gasped as the semi smashed the Trans-Am out of the way, spinning it like a top. Its enormous front tire ran right over the driver's side of the car, brutally cutting off the burning driver's screams. With the back of the heavily-loaded rig sliding in at a ninety-degree angle, the semi kept on coming, tires thundering, bellowing like a gunshot stegosaurus.

It was heading right toward her.

The last thing Kimberly saw before she died was the semi bearing down on her, flaming chunks of twisted metal wrapped around its grill, as if the mouth of hell was rushing up to greet her. The rig's brakes screeched like banshees, matching her final scream of terror as the semi flew toward her.

# THREE

Kimberly's eyes flew open.

She jerked forward in her seat and stared around the cab of the Tahoe, the sound of her own death scream still echoing in her ears.

Then she froze, blinking wildly.

Impossibly, incredibly, she was suddenly sitting upright in the driver's seat of the intact Tahoe SUV, sitting at the stoplight waiting to merge onto the highway. The desecrated highway full of blazing wrecks was gone, and in its place was a normal, busy stretch of road just starting to fill up with early morning rush-hour traffic.

Sweating profusely, Kimberly spun her head to her left to see Shaina sitting in the passenger seat beside her, calmly filing her nails. She could hear Dano and Frankie laughing in the back seat as if nothing had happened.

Everything was normal again.

She looked down at her own hands, still gripping the steering wheel. Then she started trembling violently.

"Whoa! Easy, Kimmy," Dano said with a laugh as he pulled a silver lighter out of his jeans pocket and clicked it open. "This your first year of driving?"

"Want me to take over?" Shaina asked, glancing at Kimberly in concern.

Kimberly stared wide-eyed at her friend, struggling to control the surge of panic growing in the pit of her stomach. What the hell was going on? This was all wrong! She had just been here, done this! She had been here, then she had pulled onto the freeway, then the logs had fallen off the semi and they had all died.

Hadn't they?

Shaina saw the fear in Kimberly's eyes and frowned.

Suddenly a hand slapped against Kimberly's window, causing her to spin around, startled. Even before she turned around, she knew who would be staring back at her.

The old homeless woman met Kimberly's gaze steadily, a chilling look in her mad, faded eyes. Kimberly felt the knot of fear in her stomach pull tight and start to tear things inside her. She swallowed, her sense of reality stretched to capacity, unshed tears of panic starting to prickle behind her eyelids.

"*Ew*! Let's go!" Shaina pleaded.

"Get lost, you fucking freak!" Dano shouted at the old woman.

Kimberly stared, transfixed, as the old woman gazed back at her grimly. A terrible thought shot through her, and her eyes were dragged, unbidden, to the orange plastic bag full of empty cans the homeless woman gripped in her other hand, praying that what she knew was about to happen wouldn't come to pass.

On cue, the bag gave way, and the cans clattered to the ground.

The old woman's face fell, and she scurried off after the rolling cans.

Beside the SUV, the on-ramp merge signal turned from red to green.

Kimberly sat frozen in her seat, terrified, as her friends' laughter rang through the cab.

"Hey, Dano," Frankie said, leaning across the back seat to nudge his friend in the ribs. "Shouldn't we go back and help your mother?"

"Blow me," Dano sneered as he flipped him the bird. He sat back in his seat and yawned. "Hey, green means go, Kimmy."

Kimberly sat clutching the steering wheel with white-knuckled hands, hyperventilating as she struggled to understand what was happening to her. Her panicked gaze was drawn to her outside rearview, where she saw a lane of vehicles, including a cop car, backed up behind her. The cars started honking their horns. A moment later, a flash of yellow caught her eye. Kimberly turned her head to see a school bus chug past, a homemade banner reading: "DEMOLISH THE MUSTANGS—Smoke Their Butts!" draped over the side. As the bus passed by the entrance ramp, Kimberly could hear the high school football players inside the bus chanting in unison: "Pile-up! Pile-up! Pile-up!"

"Oh my God, oh my God," gasped Kimberly, suddenly realizing what was happening—or about to happen.

"What is it?" Shaina asked, confused.

Kimberly struggled to get the words out around the huge lump in her throat. "There's going to be a huge accident! We're all gonna die! I just saw it!" She pushed her sweat-streaked hair out of her face, staring around her in fear.

Frankie looked at Dano, who shrugged as if to say "hey—she's *your* friend."

"Okay, that's it," Dano said, a pissed look on his face. "It's my turn to drive."

"No, I'm serious!" Kimberly snapped back at him, trying to keep from bursting into tears. Why didn't he understand? They were all about to die, and she had to save them!

"Kimmy, what's wrong?" Shaina asked. Kimberly stared at her dumbly. Shaina was her best friend—but how could she explain to her what was about to happen without getting carted straight off to the loony bin? She knew what she was saying sounded crazy, but she also knew, without a doubt, that it was true.

If she drove out onto the freeway, they were all going to die.

And so were the people behind her on the entrance ramp.

She had to save them all—but how?

Precious seconds ticked past. The drivers stuck behind the Tahoe were now all leaning on their horns, adding to the confusion and jumble in her head. Was it true? Or was she dreaming? How could she find out?

With a sudden burst of desperate inspiration, Kimberly turned on the radio, frantically scanning the stations.

"What are you doing?" Shaina asked, baffled by her best friend's sudden weird behavior. She hadn't seen her take anything, but for her to be acting this messed up, she guessed that little Kimmy must have done some pretty serious drugs before leaving the house.

Shaina raised an eyebrow to herself. Wow—Little Miss Wholesome taking drugs. Wasn't that, like, the eighth sign of the apocalypse or something?

A newscaster's smooth, trained voice spilled from the car's speakers: "A candlelight vigil to mark the one year anniversary of the crash of Flight 180 will be held at 8pm tonight at the Mount Abraham Municipal Auditorium..."

Goosebumps sped down Kimberly's arms.

No. Oh God, no.

She stabbed at the search button, her expression frozen. "Highway to Hell. Highway to Hell," she muttered over and over.

"'Highway to Hell?'" Frankie frowned, clearly puzzled as to what that had to do with anything.

A moment later, the opening riff of AC/DC's "Highway to Hell" blasted through the cab of the Tahoe.

Kimberly turned to look pleadingly at Shaina as though this explained everything, hoping she would understand what she was trying to prove. Instead, all she saw was befuddlement and something like fear in her best friend's eyes. She knew then that she had lost her.

"Kimberly, you're scaring me," Shaina said gently.

That did it. There was only one thing left to do. Making a snap decision, Kimberly threw the Tahoe in gear and hit the gas. The others settled back in their seats, eager to be on their way, but to their surprise Kimberly hauled on the wheel, turning the SUV sideways so that it blocked off the entrance ramp. She hit the brakes, and the Tahoe rocked to a standstill, throwing them all forward. Then she sat back in her seat, staring fixedly out through the front windshield, shaking like a leaf. Her friends watched her in disbelief, their confusion quickly turning to anger.

"Have you lost your friggin' mind?" Dano yelled.

"Yeah, what the fuck's goin' on, Kimberly?" sputtered Frankie.

In response, Kimberly decisively switched off the engine and sat back in her seat.

Screw Daytona. They were staying right here.

\* \* \*

At the back of the entrance ramp, Officer Thomas Burke frowned as he saw the red Tahoe at the head of the line suddenly pull forward and cut across the entrance ramp's merge lane, as though it was doing a three-point turn in the middle of the road.

"What the fuck is this?" he muttered to himself, feeling his headache start to throb again. That maneuver was not only dangerous, it was also extremely illegal. Did the driver not see him sitting there in his police cruiser? It was obviously Crazy Day on the highway again.

Fine. All the more work for him.

He waited for the car to complete the turn, but to his surprise the Tahoe simply sat there, completely blocking the entrance to the highway. He glanced at the young girl behind the wheel, guessing that she'd simply stalled, but she didn't seem to be making any effort to restart the car.

As Officer Burke waited, he reached for more Tylenol, glancing queasily at the Dunkin' Donuts bag on the seat beside him. It was supposed to be his day off today, but he'd got a call at 6am telling him they had an officer down and they needed him to come in. He made a mental note to call HQ once he got going and find out how he'd gotten screwed, but right now he was tired, stressed, hung over and extremely cranky. He was in no mood for people messing him around.

When it became apparent that the SUV wasn't going to move any time soon, Officer Burke sighed and flicked on his blinker as he pulled out to investigate. He drove up the side of the entrance ramp, passing a Kawasaki ZZR1200, a white panel van, a beige Pacer, a white Ford Expedition, a black Trans-Am and a blue Mustang as he crept toward the head of the line to investigate.

"Kimberly, you've just gotta breathe," Shaina said, her tone identical to that of someone trying to talk a jumper down off a high building.

Dano shifted in his seat and saw a Highway Patrol car cruising up the shoulder of the on-ramp. His heart gave a nasty thud. "Oh shit! Shit!" he gasped, lifting his shirt and shoving his bag of weed and the joint he had been rolling down the front of his pants. "Five-Oh's coming! Let's fuckin' roll, man!"

"What?" Frankie's head whipped around in the direction of the approaching police vehicle.

"Oh my God!" Shaina moaned in disbelief, her eyes widening in alarm. Frankie wasn't the only one who'd brought drugs. She tried to focus, to think how to get them out of this one. If the cop decided to search their bags, they were all so, so screwed. Their vacation would be over before it had even begun.

"Do you know how much fuckin' weed I have on me? Huh?" Dano hissed to Shaina. "I *told* you she'd ruin everything!"

Shaina whipped around in her seat to fix Dano with a hard glare. "Okay, Dano. Just shut up." She turned back to Kimberly. "Stay cool, okay?" she ordered.

Kimberly stared down at the steering wheel, her heart racing. She knew that what she was doing was the right thing... but... but what if she was wrong? She glanced over her shoulder at the cop car as it pulled up behind them, its red and blue lights whirling. One thing she knew for sure, though, was that if she *was* wrong about this, Frankie and the others would never speak to her again.

As the police cruiser drew to a halt on the shoulder behind the Tahoe, Rory Cunningham scrambled to snatch up the transparent vial of cocaine sitting in plain sight on the passenger seat beside him, dropping it quickly into the inner pocket of his battered denim jacket. His Mustang was parked directly behind the red Tahoe that was annoyingly blocking the entrance ramp and holding everybody up, and as the Highway Police officer slid out from behind the steering wheel of his vehicle, Rory cursed his luck. If he had set off just ten seconds earlier, he would've been in line ahead of the red family wagon, and would be on his way right now down Route 23.

Now, he was blocked in behind some crazy lady, with a copper sniffing around just feet from him. If the cop decided to do a spot-check on his Mustang, he was *so* busted.

Rory pulled his jacket tightly closed and gave the officer an ingratiating smile as he passed, but to his relief the dude walked right past him, his beady peepers fixed on the red SUV. Rory hoped that the officer would get the driver to move the Tahoe out of the way quickly, because as soon as the way was clear, he was outta here.

Officer Burke gave the scruffy-looking guy in the Mustang a suspicious glance, but nothing more. The real issue at hand was finding out what the hell was up with the Tahoe so they could all be on their way. He was not in the mood for people to be pulling crazy shit with him today.

He jammed his patrolman's hat onto his throbbing head and approached the vehicle, idly noting the new condition of the Tahoe and the young age of the driver. All her passengers seemed equally young—and more than a little nervous. Kids on their first ever road trip in daddy's car, he guessed...

Great.

"Oh fuck. Oh fuck. I'm going to jail. I'm fuckin' going to jail," Dano moaned as he watched the officer stalk toward the SUV.

Officer Burke walked up to the Tahoe, pausing to fix the sweating, pudgy kid in the back seat with a hard look before focusing his attention on the driver.

"What's going on here?" he asked, using his patented Voice of Authority, making sure he let the others see that his right hand was resting on the radio holstered on his hip next to his gun. A little intimidation went a long way with kids this age. With any luck he'd have this girl booked and the line moving before his coffee got cold. Man, he couldn't wait to get back to the station for a long lie-down, maybe some calming tea, and then he'd have a nice relaxing morning sorting paperwork before—

"Look, there's going to be a huge pile-up!" cried the girl.

Officer Burke paused as the girl behind the wheel gazed up at him, her face pale. She looked about nineteen, maybe twenty, and had shoulder-length chestnut hair. Burke might have even described her as cute, if she hadn't clearly been having some kind of anxiety attack. As he gazed down at her in bemusement, the girl took a deep breath, trying to compose herself.

"There's gonna be a pile-up," she repeated urgently. "I saw it. There were bodies everywhere. There were logs! I saw it! It just happened!"

Burke glanced back at the chubby stoner in the back seat, who grinned nervously and spread his hands in an innocent shrug. The officer took a deep breath, noting the distinctive smell of marijuana in the air.

"Miss, I would like you to please step out of the vehicle," he said, with as much patience as he could muster.

Kimberly did as she was told, sniffling and wiping at the silent tears pouring down her face. The officer was staring at her as though she had just grown an extra head. In the back seat, Dano and Frankie were sitting up in their seats, ramrod straight, determinedly avoiding eye contact with her as though Kimberly was nothing to do with them.

Kimberly drew a deep, shuddering breath as she slammed the door behind her and leaned back on the cold metal of the car. As much as she dreaded what her friends would say and do later, and how badly her father would react to the news of her being arrested for blocking the traffic, she could not pretend what had just happened to her wasn't real. The lives of herself, her friends and the people in the assorted vehicles sitting behind them were at stake.

In the back seat, Frankie hung his head in despair. He knew he should've taken the train.

As the minutes rolled by with no sign of movement, the drivers blocked in behind the Tahoe were starting to lose patience. Evan Lewis honked the horn of his brand new Firebird Trans-Am, rolling his eyes in disgust. "Pull over," he bellowed at the Tahoe. The girlie driver stood beside the stopped vehicle, head in her hands, while the officer just stood beside her like a lemon.

Stupid bitch, getting in everyone's way, Evan grumbled to himself. It wasn't like he had to get to work, but he had never dealt with frustration well. Right now, as far as he was concerned, he had no reason to tolerate it at all.

In the cab of her white delivery van, Isabella Hudson rubbed her swollen belly pensively, feeling her unborn child kick and shift inside her. "I know, I know," she soothed. "Mama's hungry, too." She glanced back toward the line of stalled cars before her and sighed, drumming her fingers on the dashboard. "Come *on*..." she muttered.

Kat O'Brien glowered at the traffic jam in front of her and stabbed her cigarette out in the ashtray of her Ford Expedition.

"Jesus. C'mon!" she shouted in frustration. What with the rain and the traffic it was already shaping up to be a crappy day, and this unexpected jam wasn't helping her mood.

Eugene Hooper reached down to the miniature billiard ball keychain marked with the number thirteen and switched off the engine of his motorcycle. Taking off his helmet, he plunked it into his lap so he could get a better view of what was going on up ahead and gave a weary sigh. He rubbed the soul patch on his chin as he watched the cop order the white chick to get out of her vehicle. It looked like he was going to be late to class that morning...

Again.

"What's going on up there?" Nora Carpenter asked her son, craning her neck to see past the other cars in front of her. Beside her, her son Tim cradled his swollen jaw, looking miserable. He kind of hoped the girl would stay there a bit longer so he missed his dentist appointment. Bored already, he pulled two water bottles from the bag on the floor and started idly drumming on the dashboard with them.

Isabella Hudson shook her head in dismay and unfastened her seatbelt. "Fuck this," she muttered under her breath. "Let's get this show on the road, people." Removing her seatbelt, she carefully climbed out of her delivery van. As she set foot on the entrance ramp, the young male driver of the Trans-Am ahead of her got out of his vehicle too, slamming the driver's side door hard. He was wearing a brand new orange and red leather jacket, his angular, arrogant face twisted in a petulant scowl.

Isabella strode past him and approached the red SUV. "Excuse me? Sir?" she called, waving a hand to attract the officer's attention.

Officer Burke looked up from the weeping girl in front of him and saw that several drivers had gotten out of their vehicles and were headed in the direction of the Tahoe.

"Is there any way we could just drive around?" the pregnant woman asked, grimacing as she put a hand to her back to help support her swollen belly. "I have a delivery."

"I'm sorry, ma'am, but you and the others need to get back in your vehicles," Burke replied, trying to sound polite and authoritative at the same time, but succeeding only in sounding stressed and pissy.

"Just move it, okay?" snapped the young blond kid in the racing jacket. He jerked a thumb at the Tahoe driver girl. "Arrest this whack-job, wouldya? Some of us have lives, you know."

"Get back in your vehicle now," Burke replied, jabbing his finger in the direction of the Trans-Am.

As Isabella turned back toward her vehicle, throwing up her hands in despair, her cellphone rang. Her tense expression dissolved into a warm smile as she pulled her phone out of the pocket of the cardigan sweater she wore over her maternity clothes. "Hello?" She put a finger in her other ear to block out the noise of the freeway. "Yeah, I did. Why'd we get a message from Planned Parenthood on the machine? What's going on?"

Whatever the answer was, it definitely wasn't what she wanted to hear.

"You couldn't keep your dick in check for a month?" she screamed into the receiver, making the Trans-Am driver jump.

Nora watched the pregnant woman storm back to her van, pouring a stream of vitriol into her cellphone as she walked. She hopped up into the cab with surprising agility for somebody who was eight or nine months pregnant, and slammed the door behind her. Her raised voice was still clearly audible through her wound-down window.

"I wonder what's wrong with her," Nora said, to cover her embarrassment at the scorching profanities coming from the sweet-looking woman's mouth.

"What am I, psychic?" Tim paused in his drumming and took a swig from one of the water bottles. He winced as the cold water touched his aching tooth, sending a stab of pain through his jaw.

Nora raised an eyebrow at Tim, and then they both broke into smiles. She tousled his dirty blond hair.

"Okay, quit it already," Tim grinned. As his mother chuckled at him, he winced and tenderly placed his hand against his swollen jaw.

The teen's attention was soon diverted from his bad tooth by the sound of squealing tires. He looked over his shoulder just in time to see the white delivery van belonging to the psycho pregnant woman make an illegal U-turn out of the line of cars and speed back up the on-ramp.

Back at the SUV, Officer Burke glanced up tensely as the white van drove off, and then turned his attention back to the trembling, teary-eyed young woman in front of him. He wasn't quite sure what kind of insanity he was dealing with yet, whether it was organic or drug-induced. He was tending to believe it might be the latter, judging by the behavior of her fellow passengers and the sick, guilty look on the mug of the kid in the back seat. Every time he so much as glanced in the boy's direction the kid nearly had a seizure. It would have been funny if he hadn't been so tired.

Leaning against the door of the SUV, the young girl was still freaking out. "The radio played the same songs, the old lady's bag broke the exact way it did in my premonition," she babbled, gesticulating wildly as she spoke. Then her eyes widened in panic and she pointed a shaking finger at a big log truck as it sped past the ramp.

"That's it! That's the truck that's going to kill everyone!" she shouted, grabbing Officer Burke's elbow for emphasis. "You have to stop that truck!"

"All right, miss. Calm down" Officer Burke said patiently, as he tried to extract himself politely from the girl's panicked grip. In the passenger seat, he noticed that the girl's cute blonde friend was looking at her with a bewildered, pitying expression. He tried again, gently shaking the young girl to get her to focus. "I just need this lane open. I need you to pull your vehicle onto the shoulder."

But Kimberly wasn't listening. The whole of her attention was riveted on the semi log truck as it roared away from the entrance ramp, black smoke belching from the exhaust stack on top of the cab. There was a rusty chain dangling from the back of it, throwing a thin stream of sparks across the road as it dragged across the asphalt.

Kimberly's heart started pounding madly and she broke out in a cold sweat. She knew without a doubt that it was going to happen, that the logs were going to fall and people were going to die. Look, the chain was already coming off! That proved it, didn't it?

She whirled and seized the police officer by his lapels, cutting him off mid-lecture. "You're not listening! You have to stop that truck!" Kimberly gazed desperately into the car, seeking out Shaina for support. But her friend turned her head away, unable to meet her eyes. Judging by the expression on her face, she thought Kimberly had seriously lost the plot. The message was quite clear: Kimberly was on her own with this one.

Kimberly sagged, tears streaming down her face. "Why won't anyone *listen* to me?" she sobbed.

His patience maxed out and Burke sighed and reached for his cuffs. "I'm not going to tell you to calm down again—"

*Screeeeee!*

Officer Burke whipped around at the sound of an air-horn blaring in the near distance. It was swiftly followed by the shriek of brakes and the prolonged crash of metal on metal. The young police officer stared in stunned horror as multiple fireballs mushroomed along the eastbound lanes of Route 23, barely five hundred yards from where he was standing. He watched, frozen in shock, as the log semi jackknifed around, shedding the rest of its cargo of logs directly into the path of the oncoming traffic.

Kimberly's face crumpled as she saw the carnage unfold before her.

No! It was happening again! She hadn't been able to stop it!

She screamed in horror and collapsed against the SUV, one trembling hand covering her mouth.

Shaking off his stunned paralysis, Burke turned and sprinted back to his patrol car. Reaching in through the open window, he grabbed the handset of his police radio and stabbed the "call" button. "This is Unit Thirteen, requesting major medical assistance and emergency back-up for a major traffic accident on Route 23 eastbound, near the Mount Abraham Exit," he said.

Kimberly slumped back against the SUV, wide-eyed and shaking. As the gruesome, devastating events before her continued to play out, her attention was magnetically drawn to the flashing freeway sign at the entrance to the highway. It was frozen, displaying the message "NEXT 180 FEET."

Kimberly stared at the number 180, feeling her sense of reality start to tear.

Inside the Tahoe, Frankie, Dano and Shaina watched in dumbfounded horror as the traffic in the nearby lanes began to react to the accident, braking hard to avoid the wreckage scattered across the roadway. Metal crunched as dozens of cars slipped and spun on the wet road, some caroming off the road, others smacking into the steel divider rail separating the lanes.

Then, as one, the teens slowly turned to stare at Kimberly, who was still leaning against the hood of the SUV, weeping silently.

"Kimberly?" Shaina asked carefully. "What's going on?"

Kimberly didn't reply, staring fixedly at the spinning, exploding vehicles down the road as the accident continued to play out in front of her in graphic detail.

As flaming debris started to rain down less than fifty feet from the Tahoe, Shaina was the first to react. She leaned across the passenger seat and yelled at Kimberly, who was still standing at the foot of the ramp, apparently hypnotized by the carnage.

"Kimberly, get back in the car!"

Kimberly started, jerked back to the real world by the sound of Shaina's voice. Dazed, she moved back toward the driver's door of the Tahoe as though in a dream, only to find herself grabbed and yanked aside by a pair of strong hands.

Air brakes shrieked behind her, terrifyingly close, and an earsplitting crash echoed through the air as Officer Burke swung Kimberly around and flung her to the ground on the side of the road. She felt a blast of intense heat sear her back, and rolled over on the wet grass several times before sliding to a halt, bruised and dazed.

When she looked up, the Tahoe had gone.

Kimberly's heart stopped as she craned her neck around wildly to see an out-of-control semi pulling a double-decker trailer full of cars flying off down the road, the flaming remains of the Tahoe folded around its massive grill. As Kimberly's mouth fell open in shock, the SUV's gas tank exploded as the heat ignited the fuel line running from its engine, sending debris flying in all directions.

Kimberly pushed herself away from the shelter of the patrolman's arms and clambered mindlessly back onto the shoulder, screaming in horror at the sight of what was left of her car and her friends, wedged in between chunks of burning wreckage.

"No!" she screamed, tears pouring down her face. "Shaina, *no!*"

Burke crawled up out of the ditch. Instinctively, he grabbed the screaming girl and held her close, unsure as to whether he was trying to comfort her or keep her from rushing out into the chaos and confusion of the pile-up in the futile hope of saving her friends. The last thing he needed was an extra body to clean up.

The other drivers along the exit ramp, who had only moments before been eager to merge onto Route 23, now clambered out of their vehicles and stared in horror at the pile-up.

Eugene and Nora ran to help Officer Burke, sternly admonishing young Tim to stay put.

Rory clunked down the locks and hunkered down in the seat of his Mustang, freaking out at the thought of being taken to the cop shop for questioning about the accident.

Evan jumped back into his Firebird and slammed it into reverse, edging out of the lane and backing his brand new car as far away from the falling debris as possible.

In her Ford Expedition, Kat O'Brien took a deep drag of her smoke, ruefully eyeing the lanes full of snarled and smoking wreckage, as the distant wail of emergency vehicles grew steadily closer. "Great. Now I'm *really* gonna be late."

# FOUR

"Detective Suby, Sir?"

Detective Ron Suby paused in the crowded hall of the police station and turned to look at the young Highway Patrol officer who was walking briskly toward him down the corridor. Suby was in his late forties, wore a white dress shirt with the sleeves rolled up and a cheap brown tie, and had brown curly hair that had receded into a severe widow's peak. Although his fleshy pink face and potato-shaped nose made him look like a young WC Fields, the senior police officer was famous for his lack of humor.

Judging by the anxious look on Officer Burke's face, he was very aware of that fact. Suby looked the young officer up and down as he approached, taking in the smartly pressed gray shirt, the earnest, handsome face, the shiny black boots, the neatly fastened tie. He certainly looked the part, but if he wanted to shape up to be anything more than a two-bit traffic cop, he'd have to do something about his attitude. The kid was too damned serious, acting as though the world was one big conspiracy that it was his personal duty to solve.

This latest case was typical. Suby had already cautioned Burke twice this month for sticking his nose in where it wasn't wanted, but still, he seemed to feel a certain responsibility for the young girl at the center of the case.

Suby sniffed. He'd been that young and stupid once, believing every pretty young crazy who came up to him with a sob story to get out of a traffic ticket. The lad would grow out of it, and then he would finally get some peace.

He gave the young officer a suspicious glance as they set off down the hallway together. "What is it, Burke?"

Officer Burke licked his dry lips, hurrying to keep up with the Detective. "Look, sir, this girl is really freaked out. In fact, all of them are scared, as you can imagine."

"Scared? Shit, these people are the luckiest sons of bitches on the planet!" Suby rolled up his sleeves as he stalked through the bustling corridors of the police station, jammed with the usual lunch-time crowd of crazies, loonies and businessmen on their lunch breaks protesting about parking tickets. It made his head ache just to look at them. It was only 12pm and already the day was shaping up to be a real ball-buster, and that was without the case that had just come in. As far as he was concerned, Kimberly Corman and her bunch of freaks should be down in Trauma Counseling where they belonged, not up here cluttering up his main investigative offices, spouting off about premonitions and visions and whatnot.

For all Detective Suby cared, the lot of them could go take a running jump.

He grabbed a half-eaten bacon sandwich off the receptionist's desk as he pushed through the double doors that led to the main offices, and waved an impatient hand at Officer Burke. "Take this guy Evan Lewis—yesterday the kid wins the Lotto and today some loony bitch blocks traffic and he avoids the worst pile-up in years. *I* should be so damn unlucky." Suby yawned as he thumbed through the file in his hands, and gestured expansively with his bacon sandwich, dripping ketchup onto Kimberly's case file. "Go baby-sit the rest of 'em, will ya? I should be done with Lewis in a minute."

Suby stepped into the soundproofed interrogation room before Officer Burke could protest, firmly closing the door behind him.

Officer Burke gazed unhappily at the closed door for a moment. Then he squared his shoulders resolutely and opened the door to the adjacent meeting room.

The moment he crossed the threshold, the room exploded into movement as the motorists all rose from their seats as one and hurried toward him. A petite woman in a business suit was the first to buttonhole him, grabbing his arm as he tried to push past her.

"Not to sound insensitive, but how much longer is this going to take?" she asked.

"Yeah," chimed in the tall, well-groomed African-American man wearing biking pants and a pair of horn-rimmed glasses. "If I don't get to my classroom soon, the kids will tear the place apart!"

Officer Burke lifted his hands, waving for everyone to be quiet. "Please, just sit tight," he said, in what he hoped was a calm, authoritative voice. "I'll be with all of you in a minute, okay? We're doing the best we can. We're going to get you out of here as soon as possible."

As the hubbub subsided, his eyes went over to the end of the large wooden conference table where the motorists were seated, to where the young Tahoe driver was sitting a little distance apart from the others. Whereas the others were all chattering like agitated birds, trying to find out when and if they could leave, she was silent as a stone, staring down at her hands. It was as though an invisible bubble of silence surrounded her, isolating her from the rest of the room.

The guy in the biker pants saw him looking at the girl and shook his head in disgust. "I just think it's all a bunch of bullshit," he announced loudly.

Officer Burke frowned and waved a hand to silence him. Then he crossed the room and eased himself into the empty chair beside the girl. According to the paperwork on the wreck, her name was Kimberly Corman, and she was nineteen years old. He had done a little digging to look for any signs of mental disturbance or past drug abuse, but she had as clean a record as a college student could hope for.

Officer Burke studied her for a moment as she sat quietly, avoiding eye contact with the rest of the group, trying to get a sense of her mood. After everything she had been through that morning she should be a crying wreck, but Kimberly seemed to have shut herself off from everything and everyone, as though trying to comprehend what had happened to her. She gave not the slightest indication that she had seen him sit down next to her.

After a moment he cleared his throat. "Look, I know you've gone over all this with Detective Suby," he said gently, resting his hands on the desk in front of him, "but would you mind telling me what happened?"

Kimberly finally raised her eyes from her lap, quietly studying the young patrolman's face. It was an honest face, with a strong jaw and deep brown eyes. She got a strong sense that she could trust him, that he actually cared about her beyond what was necessary to get his little accident report out of her.

Still, she was defensive. She'd seen enough police movies to know the whole good cop/bad cop routine, but after the ear bashing that other fat detective had given her when she'd told him her story, it was almost a relief to have a sympathetic audience.

Her eyes flicked to his for a moment. Then she sighed, seeming to release something inside herself. When she spoke, her voice was no longer hysterical, but sad and tired. "It was like I was there... I knew something bad was going to happen, even before it did." Kimberly gnawed on a nail, her eyes distant, as though she was reliving the experience.

In the corner, Tim looked urgently at his mother as if to say, "I told you so!" Nora shook her head dismissively and sat back in her seat, arms folded. The girl was obviously on drugs, and the last thing she needed now was Tim getting his head filled with all this mumbo-jumbo "psychic" nonsense. She had enough difficulty getting him to focus on reality as it was.

Kimberly shifted in her seat, raising her worried eyes to meet Officer Burke's. "I remember *everything*. The sounds of the crash, the smell of burning flesh and spilt gasoline, the look on Shaina's face..." She fell silent, fresh tears springing to her eyes, and worked to keep the big lump in her throat from turning into a sob.

Shaina was dead...

"Do you remember what triggered the pile-up?" Officer Burke asked softly.

Kimberly took a deep breath, pushing aside her grief as she struggled to answer his question. "It was the log truck... and everybody, I guess. Everyone was driving like a maniac. I knew something horrible was going to happen."

Burke leaned forward, speaking calmly and clearly, like a lawyer leading a friendly witness on the stand. "You knew? You just mean a hunch, right? You got a bad vibe, maybe?"

"No," Kimberly said insistently, shaking her head. "It was more than that. All the songs on the radio were about car crashes. Some kid was banging toy cars together. This trucker was drinking and driving..."

Kimberly pointed to Kat O'Brien. "She was on her cellphone, not paying attention." She turned and pointed at Rory Cunningham. "And the exhaust from his car was choking me."

"Hey, don't be knockin' the 'Stang," Rory said defensively.

Kimberly kept talking as if she hadn't heard him. "There was a school bus full of kids yelling 'pile-up' for no good reason. It all felt... just wrong. Just like..."

She swallowed and looked to the others, all of whom were standing or sitting around her, watching her intently, clearly uncertain as to whether or not to believe her.

"Just like what?" Burke asked gently.

Kimberly sighed wearily and looked back down at her hands. "I know this sounds crazy... but you all heard about Flight 180, right? The kid who got off the plane? Well, that happened a year ago today. My premonition was just like his."

Officer Burke stared at Kimberly, his mouth going dry.

"What are you talking about?" Nora Carpenter asked as she nervously fingered the silver cross she wore on a chain around her neck.

Tim gazed at Kimberly rapt and wide-eyed. This shit was better than the Discovery Channel! Seeing as that was the only thing his mom allowed him to watch, he was eager to fill in the gaps in his education. Being in a police station with real live crazy people was the highlight of his year so far. He watched Kimberly eagerly, wondering what she would do next.

Eugene chuckled sarcastically as he stepped forward, his heavy biker boots clunking on the wooden flooring. "C'mon! Surely you must have read about the kid who had a dream about the plane crash, so he got his buddies off the plane? Then the thing blew up just like in the dream?"

"Maybe," Nora said weakly, although it was clear from her tone that she did not like where the conversation was going.

"Did you hear what happened after?"

Nora shook her head, seeming to grow a little paler.

Eugene smiled and removed his glasses, folding them and holding them in one hand like a baton, as he always did when he lectured his classes. He glanced around the room, ensuring he had their undivided attention. Kat O'Brian sat down primly in a chair, neatly crossing her legs beneath her miniskirt and very obviously trying to refrain from looking at the clock, as she had been doing constantly for the past two hours. Even Officer Burke was watching him, seeming to be as spooked as the rest of them were.

A captive audience, just what he liked.

Eugene started pacing the room, waving his glasses as he talked. "So a month goes by, right? Everything seems cool, but then the survivors start dying one by one, cause when your number's up, your number's up, right?"

He heard a sharp intake of breath from Tim and smiled to himself, wandering over behind the young boy and his mother, who were sitting on the edges of their seats across from the police officer, obviously wound up as tightly as springs. He dropped his voice and leaned in behind them. "Some people said Death Itself was stalking them, hunting down every last one... until they were all... dead."

As Nora made eye contact with her son and shook her head reassuringly, Eugene leaned forward between them and burst into a peal of loud, evil laughter, making the pair of them jump in their seats despite themselves.

As Nora glared at him disapprovingly, Eugene straightened up and gave Kimberly a mocking glance, dismissing her with a sneer. *"Please."*

Kimberly dropped her gaze, hanging her head.

"That's not exactly true," Officer Burke spoke up, breaking the uncomfortable silence. He wasn't exactly sure why he was defending Kimberly, but he felt that someone should. The poor thing seemed to be on the verge of tears again, and he was fast running out of Kleenex. He cleared his throat, somewhat surprised at how timorous his voice sounded, even to his own ears. "They didn't all die. Clear Rivers is up in a padded room at the Stonybrook Institution."

"Well, *that's* encouraging," said Rory with a snigger.

There was a ripple of nervous laughter amongst the group. Officer Burke saw Kimberly look to him for support. He held her gaze for a moment, and then looked away. He was in way over his head with this case, and the last thing he wanted to do was encourage the poor girl in her fantasies, if that was what they were.

Still, he couldn't help but feel that maybe, just maybe, there might be some truth in what Kimberly was saying. He sat back in his chair, staring at Kimberly thoughtfully. He'd always had a feeling that there was something else going on in this world; that a force beyond human understanding was somehow in control of events, shaping and guiding people's individual destinies on a level so complex they couldn't even begin to comprehend it. He'd avidly read everything he could get his hands on about the Flight 180 case, and while he knew that everything that had happened that day could easily be explained away as just a coincidence, a jest of fate, there was something in him that really wanted to believe that it was true. He knew that as a policeman this was possibly not the best attitude in the world for him to have, but screw it, it was his business.

He shifted his troubled gaze back to Kimberly. Whether she was telling the truth or not, this girl was also his problem now, because he knew sure as hell that Detective Suby wouldn't want anything more to do with her after hearing this little conversation.

In the soundproofed observation room next door, Detective Suby stood on the other side of the two-way mirror, arms folded, quietly studying the witnesses as they sat around the conference table. His half-digested bacon sandwich sat like a lump of lead in his stomach, which growled in complaint as he leaned back on the desk to take his not inconsiderable weight off his aching feet. All this eating on the run was playing merry hell with his digestion, and he knew exactly who to blame.

Suby stifled a burp with his fist, and then leaned forward and flicked on the intercom so he could overhear the conversation in the next room. He winced as he heard Officer Burke telling the young girl about that nut job from Flight 180, Clear Rivers.

Great, just what the girl needed to hear right now.

Suby sighed and reached into his pocket for an antacid. As soon as Burke had finished leading this little séance, he was going to have a very firm word with him.

The blond Lotto kid, Evan Lewis, shifted restlessly in the chair next to him. Suby felt his eyes on him as he watched the conversation next door through the two-way mirror. He was a nice-looking boy with his tousled blond hair and square jaw, and might have even been called handsome if it wasn't for the arrogant scowl he habitually seemed to wear. Suby had been in the interview room with him for two minutes and already he disliked him. So the kid had just won a ton of money. So what? Good manners cost nothing, but no one seemed to have informed Evan of this fact.

"I don't know why we're even here. What do you want from me?" Evan grumbled, folding his arms in frustration as he perched on the edge of the Detective's desk. "Some crazy chick blocked the highway with her car, said there'd be an accident, and there was one; big deal. Is that my fault?"

Suby shot Evan an irritated look and held up a hand, motioning for him to be quiet. There were more important things at stake here. The heavyset cop gazed ruminatively at Kimberly through the window, his face impassive. The girl was obviously two waves short of a shipwreck, but still, there was something very compelling about what she was saying.

Next door, the motorists were also getting restless. "Okay, you want me to believe that this is all true? That this is happening all over again? *Jesus*." Nora shook her head dismissively, pulling her beige cardigan a little tighter around her as a cold draft crept through the room.

"If I was never meant to pull over, then we all should have died in the pile-up," Kimberly insisted. She looked to the others, hoping to see mutual comprehension in their eyes. She saw only suspicion and irritation. Officer Burke sat quietly beside her, saying nothing.

"Which means... that Death could be coming for us," Tim said, getting into the swing of things, a crooked smile on his face.

"Yeah, what if we're all getting that *Diff'rent Strokes* curse or something?" Rory added in a hushed voice.

Kimberly glanced up at him hopefully, and then her face fell. They were making fun of her. Of course they were. Hell, if she had been in their position, she would be making fun of her too. She knew that what she was saying made her sound crazy, but at the same time, she knew with an unshakable conviction that she was right.

As she sat there pondering the situation, Nora abruptly got to her feet, tossing her long braid back over her shoulder. "You people are all certifiable, you know that?" she snapped. "I can't believe I've been listening to this crap. Come on, Tim, let's go."

"Jeez, Mom, stop trippin'. This is cool," Tim said with a laugh.

"Hey, lady, we were just yankin' your chain," Eugene said, realizing just how upset Nora seemed to be.

"Then you should be ashamed of yourselves. Come on, Tim." Nora grabbed her son by the arm, pulling him out of his chair.

"Mrs Carpenter, please!"

Officer Burke got to his feet to try to stop her from leaving, but he was a second too late. Nora had already reached the door, flinging it open and dragging her son out of the room. Burke hesitated, uncertain about whether he should go after the woman or stay with the other witnesses. He was painfully aware of Detective Suby's eyes on him from the other side of the glass, and was already dreading the lecture he would undoubtedly get for letting a witness go without permission.

As the door swung shut, the awkward silence amongst the remaining occupants of the room was broken by the sound of a man's voice.

"Kimberly!"

Kimberly looked up to see her father push open the door and enter the room, followed by Detective Suby and the young man who had been driving the Trans-Am. The moment she saw her father's face, his features haggard with worry, the wall of shock that had been keeping her from fully realizing the enormity of her loss crumbled. She leapt from her chair as if it was on fire.

"Daddy," she sobbed, dissolving into tears as her father caught her in his arms. He held her tightly to his chest.

"Oh, baby," he whispered, his voice tight with emotion. "Are you okay?"

"I'm so sorry, Daddy." Kimberly tried to say more, but all that came out were hiccupping sobs.

Mr Corman hushed his daughter, holding her tight and stroking her hair, much as he had when she was a little girl and had come to him for reassurance after falling off her bike. When he'd heard about the pile-up by the Mount Abraham exit on the lunchtime news, his heart had nearly stopped. That was the very road Kimberly and her friends had to take to get to Route 23! Like any parent, he had instantly imagined the worst.

The breaking news footage had been shot from a distance as the freeway had been immediately closed off in case of any more explosions, but the remains of a red SUV had been clearly visible in one shot, and the bottom had dropped out of Mr Corman's world. Receiving a phone call from the police station fifteen minutes later had nearly killed him. It had taken him a full ten seconds to get up the willpower to answer the ringing phone. The message that Kimberly was in fact alive and well and being held for questioning at the station was the best news he'd ever received in his entire life.

He squeezed his daughter tighter, kissing her hair and breathing in the scent of her, and he vowed to never let her out of his sight ever again.

As the pair of them embraced, Detective Suby shot Officer Burke a warning look, and held up his hand for attention from the group. "You can all go. Thank you for your time and patience."

"Good, I've been over this *X-Files* shit since the sixth season," Rory said with a yawn. He got up, scraping his chair loudly, and headed toward the door with the rest of the motorists. As he left the room, his hand went automatically to the inside pocket of his jacket to check on his coke vial. It was still there. He smiled to himself, imagining the look his friends were going to give him when he told them that he'd spent three hours at the cop shop, sitting ten feet from the NYPD's head honcho with a tube of class A drugs in his pocket. Thank God the detective hadn't seen fit to search him. True, he'd been shitting bricks for most of the time he'd been in that room, but still, it was an experience.

Rory sniffed, wondering vaguely if the police station had a men's room so he could go for a quick hit before he got back in his car. After all, if you were going to dance with the devil, you should do it properly, right?

Behind him, the room swiftly emptied. As she shouldered her purse, Kat paused on her way out the door to give the detective a quizzical look. "Is there any way this can get me out of jury duty?"

Suby didn't even bother to respond.

Kat shrugged and trotted out the door, her high heels clicking on the stone tiling.

Mr Corman placed a protective arm around his shaken daughter's shoulders as he led her out of the room. As she walked through the door, Kimberly took one glance back at Officer Burke, feeling a strange connection between the two of them. She saw that he was staring after her, a concerned look on his face.

As soon as the last of the witnesses were out the door, Suby turned to glower at Burke, who was standing awkwardly at the head of the empty conference table.

"Way to console the witnesses, Burke. Offering them coffee and donuts wasn't enough, huh? You had to go fill their heads with urban legends and other crap like that." Disgusted, the detective turned and stormed out of the room.

Burke sighed and turned to face the window, staring out at the afternoon sky. The American flag next to him moved slowly, as though stirred by some invisible breeze. In a weird way, he had never felt more alone. On one level he knew Suby was right—that he had unnecessarily frightened people who were already traumatized from witnessing the horrific events earlier that day.

Still, he couldn't put what the young girl Kimberly had said out of his mind. He had only been a police officer for three years, but you didn't stay on the job long if you couldn't develop a cop's instincts: the weird tingling at the back of your conscious mind that tells you that something isn't right, that despite your surroundings appearing normal, danger is lurking nearby. All his cop's instincts were telling him that something was wrong...

Very wrong...

# FIVE

As the afternoon shadows lengthened, Kimberly sat at the kitchen table in her parent's house, listening to her father clatter around in the kitchen. A small, sad smile lifted the corner of her mouth at the sound of him. Her mom had been dead a whole year and still her father hadn't quite got the hang of finding his way around the kitchen. Her mother had been a fantastic cook, constantly coming up with new and exciting recipes for their monthly dinner parties, and because of this their kitchen was stuffed with a wealth of unusual and expensive cooking implements that they would possibly never use again.

As a result, even a simple job like making a cup of tea would turn into a major expedition for her dad, involving a thorough search of the cupboards and repeated trips to the living room to ask Kimberly if the metal thing he'd found with the whisky bits was a coffee maker or a fruit juicer, or possibly even a wallpaper stripper. Several times Kimberly had gently suggested that he should have a bit of a clear out, but so far her pleas had been met with a polite yet firm refusal. Having his wife's things around the house comforted her dad, she knew, but even so, she was starting to get more than a little impatient with having to wait twenty minutes for a mug of tea.

She looked up gratefully as her dad finally hurried out of the kitchen, a mug of fresh herbal tea held proudly in his hands. Despite herself she glanced at her wristwatch.

Eight minutes. That had to be his personal best so far this year.

He placed the cup of tea on the table, and sat down opposite her.

She smiled up at him as she reached down to cup her hands around the steaming mug, feeling the warmth from the hot tea leach into her flesh, warming her cold fingers.

"Thanks, Dad," she said. She picked up the mug, took a tentative sip and put it down. She hesitated, staring up at the framed picture of her mom that sat on the mantelpiece behind him. There was something important she needed to ask her father, but she was uncertain how to broach the subject.

"Can... can I ask you something?" she said finally.

"Anything, honey," Mr Corman said, taking her hand in his and giving it a reassuring squeeze.

It was a while before Kimberly spoke. "Did mom ever have any... I don't know... weird feelings about anything?" Kimberly looked down at the floor, unwilling to meet her father's eyes when she spoke, for fear of seeing the same mix of confusion and disbelief that had been in Shaina's just before the semi-trailer had hit.

"What do you mean?"

"Like... visions, or premonitions, anything like that?" Kimberly lapsed into silence, staring down at her steaming mug of tea. Even to her own ears she sounded crazy and messed up, but she had to know.

Mr Corman took a deep breath, allowing his shoulders to drop as he exhaled. When he looked up at his daughter, his gaze was wistful, faraway. "I remember she always seemed to know when a storm was about to hit, even out of the brightest, bluest sky, and when you were a baby, she always seemed to be one step ahead of you, doing her best to make sure you didn't fall down and knock your head open or skin your knees. She said it was just her woman's intuition."

Mr Corman smiled at some memory, visible only to his inner eye, and for a moment he was there with his wife, wherever she was, if only for a few precious seconds. His wife was never far from his mind, but during his waking hours he did everything he could to shut her out, to turn away from thoughts of her soft warmth, her glowing smile, her glorious laugh. When he allowed himself to think of her in this way, even just for a moment, his loss seemed almost overwhelming to him, as though the very thought of her would rip his heart from his body and leave him lying alone, a bleeding, hollow shell, unable to do anything other than curl up in the darkness and let the tears flow until everything of her that was in him was cried out.

Mr Corman blinked as his eyes started to sting, forcing himself to focus. He shook his head at himself and smiled sadly, coming back to reality with a bump. "Your mother was an amazing woman, Kimberly, but she wasn't a psychic, if that's what you're asking." He looked at her closely, concerned. "Are you sure you're okay, sweetie?"

Kimberly sighed and pulled her hand free from her father's grasp. She wiped her eyes, feeling the moisture on the back of her hand. "Dad, I *know* it sounds crazy, but I'm really scared for the others. I've got this *really* bad feeling." She tapped her breastbone just over her heart for emphasis.

"Like what?"

"That... whatever this is, it's not over yet."

# SIX

Evan Lewis opened the downstairs entranceway to his apartment building, his muscular arms bulging under the weight of the huge pile of brightly wrapped packages he was carrying. As he fumbled to pull the key from the lock, a gust of wind pushed ahead of him, rifling through the piles of old newspapers and discarded Chinese take-out menus cluttering the foyer. He stepped quickly inside and kicked the door shut. He didn't want any of the riff-raff who hung on the street corner to see that he was carrying a double armload of high-class goodies back to his apartment.

Commonsense should have told him to put his packages down at the foot of the stairs and make a couple of trips, but he was in too big a hurry to get home and get started on his new life. Besides, he didn't trust the creeps he shared the building with enough to leave a brand new iMac sitting unattended, even for a nanosecond. He was a fortunate guy, but he didn't believe in pushing his luck, and he'd already pushed his luck in a big way earlier that day.

Renewing his grip on his burden, he began to climb the stairs leading to the second floor. As he did so, the shoebox atop the iMac slid back, effectively blocking his line of vision. At the same time, his shirt cuff caught on the nail sticking out of the end of a stair railing and pulled him slightly off-center. Grumbling, Evan threw his weight forward, hoping to free himself from the snare, but instead he ripped his shirt.

"Motherfucker," he spat. He stepped on one of the laminated menus that littered the stairwell, which caused him to slip and lose his balance as the packages he was carrying shifted forward. As he tried to compensate, he tripped over the flipped-up edge of the carpet runner. For a few seconds he pin-balled between the wall and the stairwell railing, trying to keep from dropping his purchases while not toppling over the banister to the foyer below. After finally regaining his balance with a stumble and a curse, he stepped onto the second floor landing.

The hallway was dark. It smelled of other people's cooking and the garbage left sitting outside the doors of their apartments in leaky trash bags. The floor of the hallway was fashioned from old dark wood, which had been scuffed and scarred from decades of foot traffic from the various tenants that crowded the building. Years ago, someone had installed oriental-style runners along the floor and the stairs in an attempt to upgrade the building's appearance. They were now even more threadbare and dirty than the floors they had supposedly decorated. The only purpose the runners seemed to serve, as far as Evan Lewis was able to ascertain, was as a means of tripping people going up and down the stairs, and as impromptu play mats for the Rodriguez brats when they were playing in the hall, which was damn near constantly. Evan wouldn't have minded that terribly much, if only the kids didn't leave their shit scattered everywhere. Jeez.

As he staggered down the hallway in the direction of his apartment, he narrowly avoided stepping on a toy ambulance, a handful of marbles and a basketball left in the middle of the walkway. As he approached his door, his foot landed on a rubber baby doll, which squealed like a wounded animal. Thrown off balance once again, his shoulder was slammed roughly into the doorjamb in a bruising impact that nearly caused him to drop his packages for the third time.

"Jesus Christ!" he yelped in genuine alarm, thinking he had stepped on a rat. When he saw the doll on the floor, its pink frock muddied from his boot, he rolled his eyes in disgust. "Fuckin' kids!"

Propping the bags and boxes he was carrying against the wall of the hallway for support, he reached into his tight-fitting jeans and fished out his lucky rabbit's foot key ring. The paint around the apartment door's handle and locks was smeared by generations of smudged fingerprints, and the doorjamb around the deadbolt boasted a half-assed patch job from when someone had attempted to kick the door open.

He slid the key into the lock and entered his apartment.

The first thing that greeted him upon entering the cheap, grimy, one bedroom apartment he called home was the reek of rotting food. The question of where the smell was coming from was another matter. Evan wrinkled his nose in distaste. At first he thought it might be coming from the trashcan that stood a couple of feet inside the front door and was full to overflowing with empty pizza boxes, discarded beer cans and old Chinese take-out containers, but as he put his packages onto the floor, he could tell the stench wasn't coming from there.

The first room upon entering the apartment was the kitchen, which opened onto the dining room and parlor area, beyond which was the tiny, closet-sized bedroom. Evan had lived in this apartment for five years, ever since he'd dropped out of high school, and the apartment was not so much his home as a place to sleep and refuel between his daily trips to work and the bar. The only attempt he'd made at customizing the place was the odd dying pot-plant and the Trans-Am decals slapped everywhere—on the fridge, on the kitchen units, even on the fire alarm stuck to the moldering ceiling. Against the far wall leading to the bedroom was a bookcase full of the model cars he had glued together as a kid, and where the wallpaper had started to peel off the living room wall, he had papered the bear plaster beneath with centerfolds pulled from *Car and Driver*.

The kitchen appliances that had come with the apartment consisted of a refrigerator, a gas range and a sink. Since the apartment building dated back before World War II, there was a surprising amount of counter and cabinet space in the kitchen, not that Evan used it to prepare elaborate home-cooked meals. A stained coffee maker sat on the counter top, and between the stove and the sink were his microwave and toaster. A couple of cases of Corona sat on top of the fridge, and the glass bottles would rattle merrily each time he opened and closed the door.

Evan deposited his newest purchases on the table, and stalked through the apartment, sniffing suspiciously. The source of the rotten smell turned out to be coming from what he laughingly called the dining area, which consisted of a cheap plastic dinette set with just one chair left positioned next to the window. Sitting on the tabletop amid a sea of empty Corona bottles was a battered skillet full of half-eaten spaghetti and meatballs. It was the meal he had been eating the other night, while watching the Lotto numbers being read by the bimbo from the New York State Lottery Commission. The sun had been shining through the window all day, encouraging the bacteria already living on the surface of the badly washed pan to multiply and feed on the remains of the meatballs, causing them to putrefy.

After shifting the smaller packages onto the counter next to the sink, ready for unpacking, Evan walked over and plucked the grease-filled frying pan off the table. He recoiled as a swarm of flies rose up to greet him. Holding his breath, he leaned over and slid the window open, then hurled the contents of the pan onto the sidewalk below. He'd be damned if he was going to have that lot stinking up his apartment by putting it into his trash.

As he turned back toward the kitchen, he glanced at the living room, the center of which was covered by a dingy, badly worn carpet. Against one wall was a butt-shot secondhand sofa. In between it and the old solid-state television set, currently resting on top of an improvised TV stand made from a palette of orange plastic milk crates, was a coffee table covered in nicks and cigarette burns. Hardly a home fit for a king.

Evan gave a grim smile as he gazed reflectively around the dingy hellhole he called home. In a few days he would get the fuck away from the shit-hole, never to return, except maybe to burn it to the ground.

He picked up a half-empty Corona and took a swig from it as he considered what a strange thing Fate could be. Less than forty-eight hours ago, he'd been a twenty-one year-old high school dropout working in the local Sav-U-Mor, pushing a broom, bagging groceries and stocking shelves. The closest he could have ever hoped to get to a Trans-Am was flicking through the automotive magazines as he restocked the wire units by the checkout lane. Now, thanks to his fifteen million dollar winning lottery ticket, he had the keys to one hanging from his lucky rabbit's foot keychain.

Outside of the bummer of a pile-up on Route 23, today had been pretty sweet, starting with him strolling into the Pontiac dealership first thing in the morning and buying the car of his wet dreams. After all, how could he shop for a really sweet crib without bitchin' wheels?

Then he had gone to his old job, dropped his pants, and told his boss to kiss his ass. Evan smiled at the memory. That had been *really* satisfying. Then he'd gone on the first of several shopping sprees he intended to treat himself to. He was going to spend like there was no tomorrow, giving himself everything he'd always wanted, but could never afford: a plasma flat screen television, a sixty gig iPod, a top-end digital hi-fi system, a home theater, two hundred dollar sneakers, snakeskin boots and enough bling-bling to sink a battleship.

All of it was for him.

Fuck his family getting their hands on any of it. His dad was a hard-ass son of a bitch who'd kicked him out of the house when he dropped out of school, and his mom had run off with some dude when he was ten. The way he looked at it, he didn't owe anybody anything. Fuck 'em all. He was the lucky one who'd won the lottery, not them. They could go and get their own winning ticket, as far as he was concerned.

Evan placed the empty frying pan onto the stove top, not even bothering to wash it, and gave the front burner knob a twist, causing the gas eye under the pan to burst into life. Hey, the heat would kill the bacteria in the pan, wouldn't it? His sink had been stopped up for days, and the last thing he wanted was for it to spring another leak, like it did last time he tried to turn on the rusted faucet.

He sloshed some cheap vegetable oil into the pan, and reached into the freezer to pull out a carton of frozen chicken nuggets. He bit the top off with his teeth and scattered them into the dirty frying pan: his kinda food. There would be plenty of time for caviar and lobster in drawn butter, or whatever the hell it was rich people ate, in the future. Right then, all he was interested in was fixing something to sustain him 'til the local cookhouse opened its doors at six.

As the pan he'd placed on the front burner started to heat up, Evan realized just how hot it had become in the apartment. He swiftly peeled off his jacket and Bill Wall Leathers T-shirt, revealing a pierced left nipple and a small butterfly-shaped tattoo on his left shoulder. His physique was muscular from hefting boxes in the back of the supermarket, although his waistline was starting to run to fat from all the fried crap he ate. Evan glanced at himself in the dented metal mirror above the sink, and made a mental note to buy one of those home-gym things. He already looked damn fine, but he wanted to look better, like Brad Pitt in *Fight Club*. Yeah. Once the ladies got a look at his new and improved body, he'd be fighting them off by the dozens.

The thought cheered him greatly, and Evan moved into the living room and turned on the oscillating fan positioned on top of the old television. He paused long enough to click on his CD player. As the thumping pound of nu metal filled the apartment, he returned to the kitchen again to check on his food. The chicken nuggets were starting to defrost in the pan, and Evan stared at them blearily for a couple moments before realizing that something was missing. What were the three food groups again? He was hungry, but eating nuggets by themselves like that was bound to do odd things to his stomach. He needed something to go with them.

Yawning, Evan opened up the yellowing fridge and scanned its sparse contents for a long moment. Leaking bottles of ketchup rattled in the door beside foul-smelling bottles of five-day-old milk. A hunk of dried-out cheddar cheese sat forlornly in a torn plastic wrapper on the center shelf. The bottom shelf was almost entirely taken up with old take-out pizza boxes, their leaking, wizened contents fossilized together in a variety of unappetizing food sculptures.

Evan's eye lit on the only semi-edible thing left in the fridge, a Chinese take-out box containing a half-eaten order of Moo Shu Pork. He plucked it from the shelf, and giving it a tentative sniff to check that it was still okay, placed the take-out box on the counter. As he removed a cold bottle of Corona from the fridge, he glanced at the colorful alphabet magnets, like those used by little kids, which spelled out "HEY E" on the side of the fridge. A girl he used to screw had put them there in a cheerful morning greeting, adding a touch of whimsy to his otherwise depressing kitchen.

Evan paused a moment. What was her name? Terry? Tawny? Whatever, she'd dumped him for some jerk working at the local Jiffy Lube, and he'd never gotten around to removing the stupid magnets. Why bother now? They'd been up so long he barely noticed them anymore. He'd be rid of them soon enough when he ditched that skanky fridge of his, and then he could start all over again.

As the chicken nuggets fizzled and spattered in the pan, Evan opened the fridge's freezer compartment and removed a box of frozen mozzarella sticks from the ice-encrusted box, setting them down next to the Chinese food. Perfect. The smell of burning reached his nostrils as the nuggets began to char, so he picked up the bottle of cooking oil and squirted an extra dash of oil into the waiting pan. As he did so he accidentally spilled some onto the range top, making the blue flame from the gas stove flare as it burnt off the extra oil.

As he was about to dump the mozzarella into the pan, Evan felt a sudden cold gust of wind play over him, strong enough to ruffle the hair on the back of his neck and send shivers up his spine. He paused, and then slowly turned to look behind him. The curtains around the apartment's windows were still, so where had the gust of air come from? Weird. Although he knew he was alone, he got a sudden, unsettling feeling that he was being watched.

The hairs stood up on the back of his neck as he slowly scanned the apartment, making sure that he was indeed alone. He knew that there was no way anyone else could've got into the apartment—his loser roommate had vanished three weeks ago, leaving him to pay the whole rent by himself, and he had promptly changed the locks when he'd come home one night to find his video recorder and a bunch of his new CDs gone. That asshole, he was much better off without him, and now that he had his millions, he'd never have to share a room with anyone ever again.

As Evan leaned back to peer out into the hallway, he didn't notice the cupboard door over the toaster swing slowly open. Inside the open cabinet, some silverware, which he had dumped on top of some poorly stacked plates, began to slide forward as if nudged by an unseen hand. Nor did he see the plastic magnet shaped liked an "H" drop off the fridge into the open Chinese take-out container directly below it, comically changing the message on the fridge so that it now read "EY E."

Satisfied that all was well, Evan turned back to his cooking, such as it was. He replaced the cooking oil atop the fridge and dumped the contents of the frozen food box into the frying pan. The mozzarella sticks instantly began to sizzle and pop on contact with the bubbling oil. Evan grabbed the cardboard Chinese food container and slung it in the microwave, oblivious to the fact it now contained a plastic-coated toy magnet.

Setting the microwave to "Reheat", he strolled over to the answering machine and telephone combo, which sat on the low wooden cabinet that separated the kitchen from the living area. The red call light was blinking like crazy. Evan raised an eyebrow and hit the play button on the machine, before turning his attention to the packages awaiting him on the counter next to the sink.

As he opened the bag from the swankiest jewelry store in the mall, a familiar voice floated out of the answering machine's speaker, sounding far sweeter than the last time he remembered hearing it. "Evan, it's Tawny! Sorry I haven't called... Hey! I heard about your lottery win. Let's hook up. Call me."

The next caller's voice sounded young, but definitely pretty, in a high school prom queen kind of way; the kind of chick who wouldn't normally have given him the time of day.

"Hi, Evan, it's Mikki—we met at Tucker's party last year? I know it's been a while, but I've been thinking of you. I just wanted to say congratulations. You can give me a call at 555-1223."

Barely twenty-four hours had passed since the news of his win had made the airwaves and local paper, and already the honies were calling him up, acting all hot and rubbing around his legs like hungry alley cats.

Life truly *was* sweet.

Evan grinned as he opened the velvet-lined watchcase, revealing a solid gold, diamond encrusted Rolex. He eagerly slid the oversized piece of jewelry onto his wrist, admiring how it sparkled as he turned it back and forth in order to catch the light, and continued to listen to his messages.

A young boy's voice came over the tinny speakers, which Evan swiftly identified as being Carlos, his floor-mopping buddy from over at the grocery store. "Evan, you suck. You buy one ticket in your whole life and hit the jackpot? We're going whoring in Prague, you know this. Shit, the boss is coming... Call ya later!"

Evan chuckled to himself as he removed a small clamshell box from the same bag as the watch. Inside was a gaudy twenty-four carat gold, diamond encrusted, horseshoe-shaped ring. He had always been a big believer in luck and its symbols, and that belief had finally paid off for him, big time.

As he held the ring up to the light, admiring it, there was a sudden, sharp, decidedly angry sounding buzz from the microwave, followed by a bright flash. Alarmed, Evan hurried over and peered in through the tempered glass front of the machine. He could see the container of Chinese food smoking, popping and fizzling as it sent out showers of sparks.

What the fuck?

As Evan quickly reached out to unplug the machine, a small internal explosion fizzed through the unit, cracking the microwave's glass door. Startled, Evan jumped back, the horseshoe ring flying from his hand and clattering noisily into the filthy sink. Evan watched in dismay as the ring rolled an entire revolution around the lip of the drain before dropping through the rubber collar that covered the sink's garbage disposal.

"You bastard!" Evan spat in frustration, the sparking microwave quickly forgotten. That was a three grand ring!

Man, it was always fuckin' something, wasn't it?

Grimacing, he quickly stuck his right hand into the garbage disposal, groping blindly around its slime-coated interior for the ring, with a look of extreme distaste on his face. His questing fingers located the ring, caught on a piece of orange rind that hadn't quite made it down as far as the processor blades. That was quite a piece of luck. Evan closed his hand on the ring with a sigh of relief, but when he tried to pull his hand back out, he discovered that the wristband of his brand new Rolex was caught on the rubber lip of the unit. Try as he might, he couldn't pull his hand back out without letting go of the ring.

As he yanked on his arm with growing annoyance, Evan was unaware of the knife atop the badly stacked plates in the cupboard next to his head, and didn't notice it as it lazily slid off the shelf into the toaster immediately below, falling so that its hilt protruded an inch and a half above the toaster slot.

"Come *on*!"

Evan pulled with all his might, grunting and cursing, but it was no use. His hand was stuck tight. As he glanced over his shoulder, he could see smoke starting to rise from the unattended frying pan sitting on the lit stove. He jumped as the microwave sparked again, cracking the already crazed glass still further, clearly heading for some kind of nuclear meltdown as the microwave radiation fizzed and sparked on the metal of the toy magnet. There was a sudden loud *WOOMPH* as the mozzarella sticks in the skillet, as well as the oil he had earlier spilled atop the range, caught fire, the licking flames spreading to the nearby Apple Jacks box still sitting on the counter next to the stove.

"Fuck!"

At the sight of the fire, Evan's irritation gave way to panic. He continued his fruitless yanking, but all that did was make his shoulder ache. He felt his wrist start to bleed as the sharp metal of his new Rolex scraped at his skin with each tug. He had to free himself so he could deal with the microwave and put the fire out before it spread any further, but how?

Looking around for something, anything that he could use to effect his escape, Evan's gaze fell upon a bottle of Palmolive dishwashing liquid sitting on the far side of the kitchen counter. He reached for the liquid soap with his free hand, but it was just outside his grasp. He tried again, straining to grab the bottle. This time his fingertips grazed it, knocking the bottle backward, where it came to rest against a pair of switches.

There was a shrill electronic shriek as the smoke alarm over the front door suddenly went off, making Evan jump. Then the phone began to ring, further adding to the din in the kitchen. The nu metal group on the stereo went into an eardrum-slamming rock breakdown as Evan scrabbled for the bottle, flames licking up hungrily behind him. As the wallpaper started to burn, he gave up trying to reach the bottle of Palmolive and turned his attention back to the telephone, only to discover that it too was just beyond his reach. He had no choice but to stand there, trapped and panicking, and listen as the answering machine picked up the incoming call.

"Dude, are you there?" The voice belonged to his ex-roommate, Rick. "Dude? Dude? Hey, are you the luckiest fucker in the world or what? You better be out, tossing back hundred year-old scotch with some fine ass bitches right now. Dude? Dude? If you're there, pick up."

"Help! Help me!" Evan shouted at the top of his lungs as he struggled to free himself, hoping his friend would somehow hear him, but it was no use.

"Anyway, now that you're loaded, man," Rick's voice continued on, oblivious to the danger his friend was in, "you better not forget about us little people, or you're gonna die alone. Call me, dude."

As the call ended, Evan lifted his leg and tried to use his foot to edge the Palmolive over to where he could reach it. The whole stove top behind him was now ablaze, three foot high oil-fueled flames leaping up from the pan and scorching the underside of the wooden kitchen cabinets. Evan scowled as he finally let the ring drop from his numb fingers and concentrated on pulling. He had to get his hand out, right now, or the whole damn kitchen was going to burn down with him inside it.

Hopping on one foot to maintain his balance, he tried to hook the bottle with his shoe, but missed and instead struck one of the two switches behind the sink. A look of horror crossed Evan's face and he froze, bracing himself for the sound of grinding metal and the agony of shredding flesh. But instead of his right hand being turned into hamburger meat, the light over the sink blinked on.

"Come on, come on," Evan chanted under his breath as he gritted his teeth and made one last push with his foot.

Suddenly the garbage disposal started to grind. Shrieking in horror, Evan convulsively leapt backward from the sink, miraculously freeing not only himself but his watch as well. It wasn't so much that he'd succeeded in pulling himself free as it was that the disposal seemed to have decided to finally let him go.

As he staggered backward, his arm brushed against the knife sticking out of the nearby toaster. He yelped in surprise as an intense electric shock went through his body, making his other hand flail out and knock the flaming frying pan onto the floor of the kitchen, sending burning grease sloshing onto the stack of empty pizza boxes piled high next to two weeks worth of garbage dumped near the door.

Within seconds, the entire kitchen was in flames, including the new iMac in its box, which was still blocking the door. Above the door, the fire alarm gurgled and cut out as the heat melted it into a shapeless lump of plastic. In the living room, a gust of wind made the windows suddenly all slam shut, causing the room to fill with smoke.

"Fuck! Jesus Christ!" Evan shouted, clutching his singed arm and staring in dumbfounded horror at the expensive disaster playing itself out right before his eyes. He had been home for less than ten minutes and already he had totaled his apartment. What in the name of holy fuck was going on?

As he stood there helplessly gaping at the flames, a sudden image slammed into his mind—he had a fire extinguisher! He remembered Rick pulling it out of the cabinet at their last apartment party and using it to ice the toilet seat. He was saved!

Evan's heart pounded madly as he ripped open the cabinet under the sink and grabbed the fire extinguisher. A look of triumph crossed his face as he shook it up and pointed the black nozzle at the fire, which had grown into a raging inferno as it feasted hungrily on the garbage strewn around the kitchen. He squeezed the handle to activate it, only to have a dribble of foam come out of the nozzle. He squeezed the handle again and again in a frenzy, but the fire extinguisher was empty.

Goddamn you, Rick!

Evan threw aside the useless extinguisher with a growl and began to cough as thick, white smoke filled the apartment.

Screw it all. He gave up. It was time to bail.

Evan sprinted into the living room and tried to open the grimy sash window behind the dinette that led to the fire escape. It refused to budge, the ancient pulleys fused by the heat.

A burst of adrenaline flooded through Evan.

He was trapped.

Panicking, he hurled the dinette table out of the way and grabbed a chair, using it to smash the window, which shattered in a shower of warped wood and spinning broken glass. The rush of fresh air from the open window helped clear his head, but it also added fuel to the inferno raging behind him.

With the heat from his merrily blazing kitchen searing his naked back, Evan dropped the fire extinguisher and went to boost himself over the windowsill and onto the waiting fire escape. Just as he was about to climb free, he heard a creaking sound, like fingernails on a chalkboard, and looked up to see the huge shard of jagged glass above his head start to detach from the frame. He jerked back just as the broken glass dropped free of the pane, shattering noisily on the floor.

Jesus! The whole place was trying to kill him!

Sweating, Evan looked back over his shoulder one last time and saw the entire apartment shrouded in flames, everything he owned going up in smoke right before his eyes.

What the fuck; let it burn. He'd replace it all, including his friends, with newer, better versions tomorrow.

Evan hopped athletically through the window and landed on the rusted metal of the fire escape, then clattered hurriedly down the metal steps that led to the street below, eager to put as much distance between him and his blazing former apartment as he could.

Just as his head dropped below the level of the main windows…

*WHOOOOMMMMPPHHH!!*

Evan yelled in fright and cringed back, hugging the brickwork as a huge explosion blew out what was left of the windows, showering him with broken glass, brick shrapnel and the atomized fragments of his personal belongings. His TV set and the remains of his iMac went whizzing over his head as though thrown by a giant hand, before dropping to the ground like vast, ungainly birds. The noise from the explosion made his ears ring, but the metal walkway shielded him from the fallout from the blast, leaving him shocked, but otherwise unscathed.

Once again, Evan thanked his lucky stars. If he'd left the apartment five seconds later, that explosion would in all likelihood have killed him.

As the debris tumbled and scraped its way down the ladder, Evan unfroze and continued determinedly making his way downward, his boots clanging on the metal stairway. He reached the foot of the first floor fire escape and tried to lower the sliding metal ladder that led to the sidewalk, but it was stuck, rusted into place by years of disuse. Frustrated, Evan climbed onto the ladder without thinking and bounced up and down on it, trying to use his bodyweight to dislodge it.

He was just about to give up when the ladder finally disengaged with a howl of sheering metal, shooting downward toward the ground with Evan clinging desperately onto it. It jerked to a halt ten feet above the ground and he reflexively let go, swinging his arms for balance as he plummeted the rest of the way to the sidewalk, miraculously landing on his feet with a thump, right beneath the fire escape.

Evan let out his breath in a gasp of relief as he checked himself over: he was okay. Fire alarms were ringing all around him. The fire department would be here soon. He craned his neck upwards to stare up at the flames licking from the windows of his apartment, then shook his head in amazement and allowed himself a sly grin.

"Shit, I'm lucky," he said with a small laugh.

Still looking upwards, Evan turned to walk away...

And slipped on the pile of rancid spaghetti he'd tossed out of the window minutes before.

His legs shot out from under him, and he landed on his back on the sidewalk, broken glass crunching beneath him. As he lay there, dazed and winded, staring up at the underside of the fire escape, the rusty ladder finally dislodged itself and shot downward, heading straight for his upturned face. Evan gasped and filled his lungs to scream as the ladder sliced down toward him.

It came to an abrupt halt, inches above his face.

"Jesus Christ!"

Lying on his back amid the broken glass, Evan began to laugh hysterically. He *was* the luckiest bastard on the face of the earth; there was no denying that.

Three seconds later, there was a single, awful groan of metal giving way.

Evan was still laughing as the heavy metal ladder suddenly dropped the final few inches and smacked into the sidewalk below, punching its way through Evan's left eye socket and cheekbone in a spurt of blood and ocular fluid, before finally coming to rest on the pavement beneath him, buried deeply in his brain.

Evan's body twitched once, and was still.

# SEVEN

It was coming up to 11pm, but Officer Thomas Burke was still at work, sitting at his desk in front of his computer. The door to his neat, carefully ordered office was shut, and the sounds of vacuuming and muted late-night chit-chat from the night cleaners reached his ears from the cubicle next door. The rest of his unit had gone home long ago, but still he sat at his desk, unwilling or unable to tear his mind from the events of the day.

Stifling a yawn, he sat forward in his creaking office chair and peered intently at the screen, the blue light from the computer monitor washing over his face. He had finished the last of the accident reports from the horrendous pile-up, and was focusing on researching what he told himself was a potential lead. Behind him, the pulled-down screens on his door and the shuttered window told a different story.

Burke hummed tunelessly to himself as he entered his password into the Police Database and pulled up the search function, which cross-referenced files from the Internet with legitimate police records. After a moment's hesitation he typed the name "ALEX BROWNING" into the box and hit "SEARCH."

Within seconds, listings for several dozen websites filled the search window. Burke scrolled through them, chewing on a thumbnail. Most of them seemed to have URLs like "secretsoftheunknown" and "planecrashsurvivors." Burke clicked on the first link on the page and a second window popped open on his computer, displaying a scan of a newspaper article.

The headline read: "MAN CRUSHED BY SIGN IN FREAK ACCIDENT." Underneath, in slightly smaller print, was the subheading "Coincidence?" Next to the headline was a picture of the "man," apparently taken from his high school yearbook. Burke winced as he realized just how young the victim had been at the time of his death. Hell, he was barely six years older than the poor kid.

Scrolling down the page, he saw a headline from *The Daily Gazette*. The print was set in the kind of type usually reserved for moon landings, declarations of war and presidential assassinations. It read: "FREAK ACCIDENT!" In a slightly less apocalyptic typeface was the subheading: "Another Flight 180 Survivor Dies In Accident."

Burke clicked on another link, this one supposedly involving actual police photos of the Flight 180 survivors' various "accidents." After spending the last three years of his life scraping drunks off the highway, he thought that he was prepared for what he might see, but even he recoiled when he saw the gruesome nature of the pictures on the display before him.

The first photo was simply titled "Terry after the bus accident," and showed a young Caucasian female with shoulder-length, curly hair, dressed in acid-washed pedal pushers, white sneakers and a long-sleeved shirt. Mercifully, she was face down on the pavement, her upper body lying on the sidewalk, while her lower body lay mostly in the gutter along the curb. Her left leg was horribly mangled, to the point of barely being attached to the rest of her body. Her left calf was turned so that it was lying on her back right hip, and the toe of her left sneaker—still immaculately white—was pointed skyward. There was considerable blood spatter and smearing along the pavement to the right of the corpse, suggesting the body had been pushed along the ground for a short distance by the front wheels of the bus that had struck her.

Next to the picture of the dead girl was a photo captioned "A nice shot before the coroner arrived." In it, a young, dark-haired man lay sprawled in a bathtub, his back pressed up against the tiles of the shower and his body turned toward the outer edge of the tub. The dead boy was hanging from a thin wire noose of some kind, his bloodied fingers still clutching at his own throat. The angle at which the picture was taken made it look as if the teenager's open eyes were staring up at the viewer, pleading for help.

Burke scrolled down a little farther and saw a third photo entitled "An officer investigates with Billy in body bag." Although far less grisly than the previous pictures, it sent a cold chill through him. A uniformed Highway Patrol officer was squatting down alongside some railroad tracks, his back to the camera and a retractable metal tape measure in one hand. The officer was measuring the distance between the railroad tie and the corpse, which was just to one side of him and was shrouded in a blue polyurethane body bag. The boy's head—minus its jawbone—lay a few feet away from the bag, tilted at an angle that made it look like it was staring at the officer.

At the bottom of the page were photos of the Flight 180 crash survivors, along with their names and how they died: Alex Browning: Killed by falling brick. Todd Waggner: Strangled/suicide. Terry Chaney: Hit by bus. Carter Horton: Crushed by sign. Billy Hitchcock: Decapitated by train. Ms Valerie Lewton: Burned in house fire.

Intrigued, Burke clicked on the picture of Alex Browning, which, like all the others, had been taken from the yearbook at Mt Abraham High, and showed him smiling out at the viewer without an apparent care or worry in the world.

The link took Burke to yet another newspaper article, this one with the headline: "FALLING

BRICK TAKES LIFE OF FLIGHT 180 SURVIVOR: Ironically, Victim Had Not Left House For Three Months Prior To Accident." Next to the headline was what he assumed was a more recent photo of the doomed young man, now looking considerably more haggard.

Glancing behind him to ensure he was not being watched, Officer Burke settled down to read the article:

> Mt Abraham, New York: A local mystery continues to evolve with the discovery last night that another survivor of Flight 180 died under strange circumstances. Alex Browning, 19, was found dead in an alley off Sycamore and Edinburgh, the victim of an apparent freak accident involving a falling brick. Police were called to the scene by local merchants, who heard screams from Browning's girlfriend, Clear Rivers, who was with him at the time of the accident. Although the official cause of death has yet to be determined by county officials, officers at the scene believe a brick from an adjacent building became dislodged and hit Browning in the face, killing him instantly.
>
> Clear Rivers was taken into custody for treatment for shock.
>
> Browning is the latest victim in a string of bizarre deaths that have stricken the small community of survivors from the tragic crash of Flight 180. So far, five people have died since the crash, in incidents ranging from suicide to

what authorities have labeled a "gas explosion." Although none of the deaths have been labeled suspicious, the irony that the people who escaped the plane crash would die so soon has not gone unnoticed. The whirlwind of speculation has even included the notion of a supernatural force at work to eliminate the survivors.

Authorities refuse to comment on any such conjecture and have ruled the deaths as accidental and thereby no longer under investigation.

Burke frowned and quickly closed the window, returning to the search engine. After a brief pause, he typed in the word "Premonition" and reached out for the mouse to hit the "SEARCH" button...

"Bwahhhh-haaaa-haaaa! Who knows what evil lurks in the hearts of men?"

Burke jumped in his seat and spun around. Then he relaxed, sagging down into his office chair. For such a big guy, his boss moved very quietly. He hadn't even heard him come in through the door.

Police Detective Suby fixed the young police officer with a hard stare as he perched on the edge of Burke's desk, polishing an apple on his vest. His hair was rumpled and his shirt was pulled out, and he gazed at the screen with tired, rheumy eyes. "You're not starting up on that Flight 180 shit again, are you?" Suby snorted. "I thought you were finished with this hoodoo-voodoo bullshit."

Burke frowned as he set his jaw, determined to make a stand in the face of the older man's skepticism. "Look, you weren't there. She said that log truck was gonna cause an accident, and it *did*. Isn't that just a little weird?"

Suby said nothing, but simply stared at him hard for a moment, shrugged noncommittally and took a bite out of the crisp apple he'd been cleaning. Burke sagged slightly. The look of utter disbelief in the detective's eyes was enough to make him surrender his attempt at arguing the matter.

"Never mind," he sighed, turning back to the computer and switching it off. "You've made your point."

"Good," Suby said, getting to his feet. "'Cause we just got some new info, and I don't need you getting freaky on me."

"What?"

"Evan Lewis is dead. Guess he wasn't as lucky as we thought."

With that, Suby walked casually away, contentedly munching on his apple, leaving Officer Burke staring after him.

Kat O'Brien was power walking her way through the evening, cradling the receiver of her telephone between her right ear and shoulder as she increased the speed of the Walking Machine set up in her apartment next to her thirty-two inch plasma TV. As she paced, she hit the volume button of the tiny silver phone headset tucked behind her right ear. "No, Mother," she said, her exasperation evident in her voice. "Just turn on *any* station, they've been playing it all day." She rolled her eyes in response to the barrage of questions pouring from the phone, taking a drag from her fifth French cigarette that evening. "Yes, Mother. Channel Four will do just fine. Here it is—gotta go."

Kat clicked a button on the side of her headset and hung up the phone, grateful for the respite from her mother's yammering, which usually centered on when and if Kat was going to find a nice man to settle down with and finally have kids. She glanced around her nicely furnished apartment, shuddering at the thought of small children crawling around the place, kicking up her sheepskin rugs and getting Oreo crumbs on her thousand-dollar carpets. She'd rather die than have a bunch of ankle biters mess up her apartment. She picked up the remote from the bedside table and pointed it at the TV, boosting the volume.

The newscaster, a pleasant-looking woman dressed in a bright yet tasteful blazer, spoke with a somber voice as aerial footage of a massive traffic jam played on the rear-projection screen behind her.

"To recap our top story: Route 23 was backed up for over nine hours today. A record breaking pile-up killed an estimated eighteen people…"

Nora Carpenter frowned in the direction of the television set as she placed the evening's meal on the dinner table—brown rice and steamed vegetables. Tim regarded his bland dinner with a sigh, and glanced up eagerly at the television set as the news report cut to a scene showing the twisted, smoking wreckage on Route 23. Although he wasn't normally interested in anything that didn't include monsters and the like, Tim had been glued to the screen for the last hour, watching the newscast with rapt fascination.

"Emergency crews spent hours sifting through the wreckage, hoping to recover any survivors from this tragic collision…"

Eugene Hooper looked up from the stack of bluebooks he was grading in time to see footage of a brigade of firemen armed with chemical fire extinguishers attempting to put out the fire that had reduced a VW Beetle to a husk of charred metal and melted glass. He removed his glasses, chewing the ends thoughtfully as he gazed at the screen, his grading momentarily forgotten. If it hadn't been for that crazy girl blocking the onramp, it could be *him* on the TV, being shoveled into that body bag.

Eugene shivered at the thought.

Onscreen, the news reporter went on. "So far, police are refusing to release the names of any of the victims until all the families have been notified…"

* * *

Ambrose Corman sat on the sofa in the darkness of his home's den, his arms folded across his chest, completely engrossed by the news coverage of the accident. He had been sitting in front of the television all evening since Kimberly had gone to bed, unable to tear his eyes away from the graphic images unfolding on the screen. The media was having a field day with this one, and for once, Mr Corman couldn't help but watch. Even the thought of Kimberly being anywhere near that pile-up made him sick with fear. He hoped that she'd been a long way away from the crash when it happened.

As he reached for his fifth cup of coffee that evening, the news reporter put a hand to her earpiece, and nodded to someone off-screen to roll a tape. "The camera of a Highway Patrol car managed to capture *this* shocking footage…"

The television screen was filled by a slightly grainy, off-center image of a large red SUV turned sideways in a lane of traffic. A young woman with dark hair in a blue jacket stood outside the driver's side door, staring at the pile-up just visible in the background.

Mr Corman froze with the untouched cup of coffee halfway to his lips. That was Kimberly! What was she doing on the news?

He waited, on the edge of his seat.

Then his mouth fell open in horror as a uniformed cop ran toward Kimberly, grabbed her, and pulled her out of the path of a fully-loaded, speeding semi, just moments before it smashed into the SUV, which erupted in a ball of flame as it was dragged off-screen by the truck. Although the video was not of the highest quality, Mr Corman could clearly see Shaina and Frankie staring through the side windows, throwing up their arms in a vain bid to protect themselves as the semi struck the Tahoe, reducing it to flaming rubble—with them still inside it.

"Oh my God," he muttered under his breath, his blood turning to ice. Kimberly had told him what had happened, but he hadn't realized that it had been *that* close. If the officer had reached Kimberly just two seconds later, they both would've been hit by the semi. He reeled as the ramifications hit him, setting his cup of coffee down quickly on the table before it fell from his suddenly numb hands.

On the screen, the newscaster went on, but Mr Corman was no longer listening, too fixated on the horror of what he had just seen. "As you at home can see, a semi comes careening across the roadway and smashes into a red SUV. The driver of the SUV was standing outside the vehicle, and the quick actions of a state trooper may well have saved her life…"

As Mr Corman stared blindly at the screen, he heard an intake of breath and a muffled sob from behind him. He spun around in his seat to see his daughter standing behind him, dressed in her nightshirt and jimmies, her face puffy from crying. He cringed, as if she had caught him doing something shameful. He hadn't even heard his daughter come into the room. He had no idea how long she'd been standing there, or how much she'd seen.

Quickly, he snatched up the remote and made to turn off the television, but Kimberly shook her head, wiping her eyes.

"No," she said quietly, struggling to keep her grief from overwhelming her. "It's okay. Leave it."

Kimberly stood quietly behind her dad and watched the replay of the SUV getting struck. She stared in mute horror at the images on the screen, her soul on overload. Tears came to her eyes, and she experienced a strange, dissonant feeling as she watched the event on the screen while simultaneously reliving the experience in her mind. The realization that she was witnessing the last few seconds of Shaina's life struck her hard and caused her to gasp with pain that went beyond any physical means of measurement.

Mr Corman sat back helplessly as the newscaster went on.

"The officer pulled her back at the last second just as the semi plowed into the vehicle. The passengers inside the SUV were not so fortunate, as all three were killed instantly…"

On the other side of town, in the dark, low-ceilinged living room of his bachelor pad, Rory Cunningham bent over the glass coffee table in front of him and snorted up the line of coke laid out along its surface, using the barrel of a disassembled ballpoint pen to make sure he got every last crystal. The air around him was thick with a heady mixture of marijuana smoke and burning joss sticks, and the rapid beat of his latest demo track thumped through the floor-mounted bass speakers, making the empty beer bottles strewn on top of the TV clatter. It was making him feel horny, for no particular reason.

But then, he was twenty-four. He always felt horny.

Sitting beside him on the sofa, jammed in between him and his bass player, three scantily clad honeys giggled coyly, batting their eyelashes at him. Judging by the lusty way the chick in the blue miniskirt and her blonde friend were looking at him and whispering to each other, he was getting more than lucky tonight.

Rory grinned to himself, wiping the light dusting of coke off the underside of his nose with the blue bandana wrapped around his wrist. Life was *so* fuckin' awesome right now.

As the coke rush hit him, he slumped back on the squashy sofa, wriggling his shoulder blades back between two of the honies. Comfortably settled, his blurry gaze locked in on the TV set, where he saw footage of the crazy bitch from the on-ramp getting yanked out of the way of the semi by the pig. He grinned as he felt the back of his throat go numb. As far as he could tell, he was the only person at the party even halfway paying attention to the TV.

"You see that shit?" Rory spluttered, waving a tingling hand at the screen. "I was right there, baby! Oh God, that's tight!"

The girl sitting beside him—he had no idea what her name was, and didn't really care—slipped a hand down the front of his pants and started to undo his zipper. Rory's head reeled from the overload of stimulants. Man, this was one *bitchin'* party.

"In other news: a freak accident took the life of a recent Lotto winner..."

Rory's grin froze as the picture on the screen behind the newscaster changed from a graphic showing the US highway Route 23 sign, to a DMV photo of a young blond guy.

A slow, stupid frown settled over Rory's drugged-out face.

Hey, wait a moment. He knew that guy!

Rory sniffed, then disentangled himself from the lusty attentions of the girls and leaned forward so that he could hear the news report, his manner suddenly sober, despite the dizzying mix of alcohol, testosterone and drugs rushing through his bloodstream.

"Friends say that Evan Lewis was on top of the world after recently winning a multi-million dollar lottery prize..."

"But in a tragic turn of events, Lewis died today while trying to escape a fire in his apartment..."

Unable to take her eyes off the newscast, Kat O'Brien stepped down off her treadmill and groped blindly with her right hand for her cigarettes and lighter, which were sitting on the bed stand beside the machine. She lit one of the smokes and brought it up to her lips with trembling hands.

Tim Carpenter turned away from the television to fix his mother with a worried look. Nora Carpenter looked away from her son and quickly drained her glass of Chablis, and then reached for the bottle to pour herself another. She had a strong feeling that she was going to need it.

Eugene Hooper stroked his soul patch, the term papers at his elbow forgotten, as he sat lost in thought, his attention focused entirely on the television screen as the newscaster went on.
"He managed to make it out of the burning building, but the ladder on the fire escape slipped and impaled him. Investigators believe that Lewis died instantly..."

Kimberly sat on the sofa, safe within the curl of her father's arm, and stared at the picture of the young man, the one who had been driving the Trans-Am earlier that day. Although the house was warm, she could not help but shiver. A chill started to spread through her, as though someone had injected liquid nitrogen into one of her veins. She felt it spread silently through her body, turning her blood to ice.

Kimberly turned away from her father so he would not see the look on her face as a terrible, unwanted thought wormed its way into her head.

It was beginning.

As the clock ticked up to midnight, Tim Carpenter lay stretched out in his bed, the latest Stephen King novel propped open on his chest. Normally he didn't have trouble getting to sleep, but the persistent tooth pain he'd been experiencing, along with the events from earlier that day, was making it difficult for him to relax.

Man. That was some super-creepy shit going down! First they had avoided the pile-up, which had been mind-blowing in itself, then the motorbike guy had told them the story about how the Flight 180 crash survivors had all been cursed or something... and now one of the Route 23 survivors was dead... Pretty freaky stuff...

Tim shivered and pulled the bedclothes higher up around him, wondering vaguely if it really was true and they really were all going to die. The thought of death had never really bothered him—at fourteen, it all seemed so remote and so far away—but after the events of today, he was starting to wonder if maybe this "curse" business was something that he should look into. If it all turned out to be true and they were all going to die, he had a pretty long list of girls he wanted to kiss first, just to be on the safe side.

He jumped as someone knocked lightly on his bedroom door. "Come in," he called, marking his place in his book and setting it aside.

The door swung open and his mother entered the room, dressed in a blue kimono-style robe, her long braid draped over her shoulder. She held a glass of water in one hand and couple of aspirin tablets in the other.

Nora Carpenter glanced around her son's room, taking in the collection of highly realistic McFarlane action figures—he got mad whenever she slipped up and called them "dolls"—modeled on famous movie monsters arrayed along the edges of his book shelves. The shelves were jammed to overflowing with books by Stephen King and Dean Koontz and the like. Horror movie posters hung from the walls, the faces of monsters and madmen staring down at young Tim. She wondered how he could ever sleep with all that nastiness going on around him.

Nora pulled her robe tighter around herself and gazed down at her son, tucked up safe in bed. "Here. I brought you these so you can sleep," she said with a smile, handing him the pills.

Tim took them, returning her smile. His mom must really be on another planet to be giving him pills. Drugs of all kinds were banned from his mom's house, even the most innocent of stomachache pills and vitamin tablets. His mom believed wholeheartedly in the healing power of nature, and so for her to give him an aspirin for anything short of a severed limb must mean that she was pretty freaked out about today.

"Thanks, Mom." Tim grabbed the pills before she could change her mind. He swallowed the aspirin and washed them down with a gulp of water from the glass, then slid down in bed, patting his stomach.

Nora eased herself onto the edge of her son's bed, absently brushing the hair from his forehead as she spoke. "We'll hit the dentist first thing in the morning, and I know how much you *love* that. Now, lights out, okay?"

Okay, Mom," Tim said, hunkering down in bed and nodding dutifully.

His mom smiled, kissed him on the forehead and got up to leave. As she headed toward the bedroom door, Tim was struck by a sudden thought. He clutched at the bedspread and called out to her.

"Mom?"

"Yeah?" Nora turned back to look at her son, already knowing what he was going to ask her. She gave an unconvincing smile and raised her eyebrows questioningly.

"You think... you think those guys were just yanking our chain today or what?" Tim had the same look on his face as he'd had when he was seven, and needed his mother to reassure him that no, sharks couldn't swim up the sewer system and come out in the bath tub and eat him.

"Oh, please," Nora said, with her best motherly laugh. "Some people just need some serious rewiring, that's all."

Tim smiled and looked somewhat relieved, but she could see that he wasn't entirely convinced. She watched him reach for his Steven King book and tuck it under his pillow, and sighed to herself. Ever since his father's death, he had become increasingly fascinated with fantasy scenarios—the more gruesome the better. His preoccupation with horror stories and scary movies concerned her, but this was certainly not the time or the place to lecture him about it. What he needed now was some serious shut-eye. In the morning, everything would seem better.

Or at least, she hoped it would, for her sake as much as his.

"Get some sleep," she said gently, blowing him a kiss as she turned off the lights and closed the door behind her.

Tim lay in the dark for a long moment. Then he threw aside his covers and reached under his bed for his old nightlight. He'd had it since before he could remember, but he hadn't used it since he was young.

He plugged the nightlight into the wall outlet next to his bed and lay back, gazing up at the ceiling as swirling pastel-colored stars and planets were projected there, chasing away the shadows that seemed to seethe and coil in the corners of his room. He knew it was babyish, but it brought back memories—happy memories—of when he was little and his dad would come home from work, tuck him into bed, and switch on this nightlight to keep him company as he went to sleep.

Now that his dad was gone, putting on the nightlight still made him feel safe, as if the last three years had just been a dream and any minute now, his dad would come tip-toeing through that door, alive and well, and laughingly tell him to switch the light off before he used up all the electricity in the house.

Tim sighed.

As he lay back on his bed, pulling the covers up to his neck, he could hear a roll of thunder coming from somewhere in the far distance. Tim felt a strange sense of—what was that word Steven King used all the time? Foreboding?

Yeah. That was it.

Tim lay back under the covers and listened to the storm approaching.

"You need anything to help you sleep?"

Kimberly looked up at her father, who was standing in the doorway of her bedroom, watching her get ready for bed. He was trying not to look too concerned, but she could see the worry in his eyes. He always had been bad at hiding his feelings, and now this gentle, honest man was having difficulty in reassuring her.

She would be okay. She would take care of both of them, just as her mother had before she'd—

Kimberly cut off that thought before it even began and affected a yawn, stretching her arms up above her head to ease the knots out of her shoulder blades. "Nah, I'm fine, okay?"

"Sorry," her dad said with an embarrassed smile. "Just being a dad. That's my job. I'm just so glad you're all right." He leaned forward and kissed Kimberly tenderly on the forehead, fighting to keep a smile on his face.

As he turned to leave the room, they both heard the sound of a car skidding on the rain-soaked road somewhere in the distance. The sound seemed to go on forever.

It was not what either of them needed to hear right now.

Kimberly watched her father freeze, tensing for the sound of the crash that was to follow, but it never came. Once it became clear there wasn't to be an accident, he let out the breath he'd been holding, smiled meekly at his daughter, and hurriedly left the room.

Kimberly let him go. After the events of today, it was clear that neither of them would be getting any sleep for quite some time.

As the night drew in, a light rain pattered against the windows of Kimberly's room as the approaching storm kicked up a squall. Kimberly lay in bed, unable to sleep, tossing and turning and listening to the rain drumming on the roof. A weird, sick sense of déjà vu went through her as her half-conscious mind flitted uneasily back to the previous night. She'd had trouble falling asleep then, too, but that was because she'd been so excited about her upcoming trip.

As things were now, she wished that she'd never booked the damned thing. She stared at the digital read-out on the alarm clock next to her bed; this time twenty-four hours ago Shaina, Frankie and Dano had still been alive.

Kimberly tried to clock this thought too, feeling the tears start to flow again, soaking the soft pillow beneath her. She was still trying to wrap her head around the enormity of her loss, but somehow, it hadn't quite sunk in yet. She couldn't believe that Shaina was dead. Now, every milestone, vacation and birthday would be a reminder of exactly how long her best friend had stopped being a part of her life. It was so weird to think of things that way, but she'd had plenty of experience with doing exactly that in the last year, after the death of her mother.

More things not to think about, Kimberly thought. She rolled over and buried her face in the pillow, wishing that the whole world would just end and be done with it.

As she reached for a tissue to wipe her eyes, a light breeze caused the papers on her desk to rustle, as if a spectral hand was rifling through them for information. The noise jolted Kimberly from her reverie. She blinked in the darkness for a couple of seconds, crumpled her tissue into a sodden ball and sleepily sat up in bed, craning her neck as she looked for the source of the breeze. She hadn't heard the window blow open, but the door was closed, so there was nowhere else the breeze could've come from.

Something fluttered downward from her dresser, catching her eye. Kimberly propped herself up on her elbows and gazed down at the floor. A picture of Shaina and herself at their high school graduation had come loose from her pin-board montage and fallen to the floor, their happy smiling faces visible in a blue slash of moonlight draped across her bedroom carpet. Frowning, Kimberly turned to look at the window, only for her frown to deepen even further as she saw that it was closed.

As she sat in her bed, trying to figure out the source of the strange breeze, the headlights from a passing car on the street outside cast eerie shadows on the ceiling and down the wall of her room. The shadows seemed to seethe and flow, like the liquid inside a lava lamp, at first taking on the shape of an airplane, then, to her surprise, something resembling two giant, skeletal hands, reaching out for her.

Gasping in fright, Kimberly leapt out of bed, her eyes huge with fear. Staring wildly around the room, her gaze fell on the VCR attached to the television set on the dresser in the corner of her bedroom. The digital readout on its face began to blink, the numbers projecting themselves onto the nearby wall in big glowing green letters.

The display read: "1:80."

Kimberly put a trembling hand to her mouth. She was too freaked to do anything other than stare, as the number of the doomed flight continued to flicker on the display. A bolt of mortal fear shot through her, and she made a sudden frantic dash for the door. She thumped on the light switch, and subsided, vibrating with fear, as light flooded the room, chasing the shadows back into their corners.

As she turned back toward the VCR, she noted that the display merely showed the blinking numerals "12:00." Outside the window, a clump of knotted, spindly branches creaked and tapped on her windowpane.

Kimberly swallowed, trying to calm her thumping heart. She was seriously, *seriously* wigging out here. She had to do something about it, or she would never be able to sleep.

She hesitated, gazing at the clock display, and then padded over to her brand new Apple computer and switched it on. Within moments she was logged onto the Internet and typing the name "Clear Rivers" into a search engine.

She clicked the top link, and waited.

As the page slowly loaded, Kimberly found herself staring at the picture of a pretty, albeit somewhat serious-looking young girl, about her own age. The girl had dark, shoulder-length hair. Kimberly thought she looked like the kind of high school student who would have been way into poetry and art class. She probably liked to hang on the Goth scene on the weekends. She was the kind of girl that Shaina would quite happily cross the street to make fun of.

Curious, she scrolled down the screen, reading the article that accompanied the picture, the headline of which read: "CLEAR RIVERS, SOLE SURVIVOR OF FLIGHT 180, COMMITTED."

The article continued:

> Mt Abraham, New York. The last survivor of the bizarre tale of Flight 180 has committed herself to the Stonybrook Institution, claiming that Death itself was trying to kill her. Nineteen year-old Clear Rivers of Mt Abraham, NY, checked herself into the renowned psychiatric facility two days ago, immediately following the violent death of her boyfriend, Alex Browning.

There was more to the piece, but most of it was simply a rehashing of the events that led up to the disaster of Flight 180, and the series of bizarre deaths that followed. Kimberly closed the search page and went to the AOL page for Map Quest. In the destination field prompt she hesitated, then typed the words: "Stonybrook Institution."

# EIGHT

The fog was closing in as Kimberly drove up the long, winding road that led from the front gates of the Stonybrook Institution the following morning. The weather was gray and cold, matching Kimberly's mood. She still couldn't believe that she was actually going through with this. She had got up early under the pretense of going for a long walk, but had borrowed a friend's car instead, a silver Beetle that had definitely seen better days, to make the two hour drive. Her father was concerned enough about her as it was; she didn't want to upset him any further by telling him about the curse of Flight 180 and asking to borrow her mom's car.

Kimberly peered nervously through the dusty windshield as she silently passed beneath the old, gnarled oak trees, which dotted the grounds like giants looming in the mist, guarding the institution from the world. The silhouettes of their wizened branches flowed across her windshield like liquid shadow, putting Kimberly uneasily in mind of the giant spindly "hands" she'd seen on her ceiling the night before.

The actual treatment center was situated high on a hill overlooking a nearby river, which was currently draped in a thick, shroud-like blanket of white fog. As Kimberly's car ghosted up the crushed gravel drive, she saw two white-clad doctors hurrying up the stone steps toward the tall columns of the center, their gowns flying out behind them like overworked specters.

In short, the place looked just like the spooky mental institution Kimberly had been picturing on her drive up here. She chewed on her lip as she passed under the main archway and pulled to a halt in front of the reception building. She only hoped that this Clear Rivers girl would be sane enough to give her the answers she needed, because as soon as she was done, she was outta here.

Twenty minutes later, Kimberly found herself sitting in the waiting room off the main foyer of the mental hospital, staring at the walls, which were painted in various pastel shades of blue and green, presumably to create a calming effect. All they succeeded in doing was making Kimberly feel like she was waiting to see the dentist, causing her to become even more nervous.

As she gazed around her anxiously, Clear Rivers's doctor entered the room.

Dr Blocker was a tall, well-kept woman in her late forties. She was wearing a cable-knit, turtleneck gray sweater and a pair of slacks under her white doctor's coat. A laminated picture ID was clipped to her breast pocket. She carried a clipboard in one hand and a small plastic tub, similar to those used by security guards at the X-ray stations in airports in the other, and her hair was tied back in a tight bun. She radiated an air of quiet, no-nonsense authority.

"Miss Corman?" she asked crisply.

"Yes, ma'am," Kimberly replied, getting to her feet a little too quickly.

"Follow me," Dr Blocker said, and started off toward the swinging double doors that led to the heart of the institution, her high heels clacking on the marble flooring.

Kimberly obediently followed the doctor through the doors and found herself walking down a long corridor. The walls were painted a stark, eggshell white, and the overhead florescent strip lights were so bright they hurt Kimberly's eyes. So this is what the inside of a mental institution looks like, Kimberly thought to herself. It was kind of creepy, in a clinical sort of way. She peered timorously through the windows of passing doors, half expecting to see crazy people in straight jackets blundering around their cells like you see in the movies, but saw nothing but darkened offices, their walls lined with neatly ordered paperwork.

Halfway down the hall was a series of large glass windows, through which a dayroom of some kind was visible. An old man with long, unruly hair stood in the first window, his face pressed against the glass. Kimberly couldn't help but stare at him, even though she knew she shouldn't. The man was dressed in a pair of pajamas and a terrycloth bathrobe, and although he didn't look dangerous, whatever his dark eyes were fixed on, it was far removed from the sterile corridor outside the solarium.

As they continued their way down the hall, Dr Blocker began to read off a prepared statement attached to the clipboard she was carrying. "At the request of the patient, you are to relinquish any sharp objects such as nail files, pencils, pens, safety pins, bobby pins, your necklace, matches, lighters, belts, belt buckles, earrings, chokers, shoelaces, paperclips, watches, money clips, pocket knives, food, drink, keys, poisons, pills and medications."

Kimberly glanced at the doctor in alarm. That was quite some list. Whoever this Clear Rivers person was, she had to be pretty psycho to warrant those kinds of safety procedures. She wondered for the tenth time that morning whether she was doing the right thing by coming here, but it was too late to turn back now. Shrugging, she removed her belt and necklace, the tie-cord to her raincoat and her earrings, and the keys to both her car and the house, and deposited them into the plastic bucket carried by

Dr Blocker, who logged each item on her clipboard.

They reached the end of the corridor. Dr Blocker paused in front of a large, metal door that was sealed by an alphanumeric keypad lock. She punched in a four digit code and the door opened inward with a soft *whoosh*, revealing yet another long white corridor. This one was lined with doors; each one had a number stenciled below a small Plexiglas observation window, which was set at eye level and double-barred with wire mesh.

As Kimberly moved to enter, Dr Blocker suddenly brought her arm down in front of her, blocking her way.

"Oh, I nearly forgot. Do you have a cellphone on you?"

"Yes," Kimberly replied meekly.

The physician held out the plastic container and shook it. Kimberly sighed, reached inside her raincoat pocket and dropped the cellphone in with her other restricted belongings.

"Great. Now, let me see your nails," Dr Blocker said.

Unsure as to how this was relevant, Kimberly held up her fingers and wriggled them.

Dr Blocker made one final tick on her clipboard. "I think we're all done."

"Wait, is she dangerous or something?" Kimberly asked, suddenly aware that potentially dangerous lunatics surrounded her on all sides. One of them might be the woman she was there to see.

"No, honey," the doctor said with a sigh, "but she expects *you* are."

She smiled and stepped forward, motioning for Kimberly to follow.

This was much more like the place Kimberly had pictured. The corridor was blindingly, oppressively white, and the air smelt sharply of antiseptic, tinged with the faint smell of vomit and air freshener. The walls were plain, featureless, with no sharp edges or loose objects. Overhead, the light bulbs were surrounded by balls of wire mesh, preventing them from being removed or from the inmates touching them. As they walked down the ward's hallway, Kimberly could hear voices, muted yet distinct, coming from the various padded rooms that lined the corridor.

"Help me!" cried the voice of an old woman, who sounded to be in genuine distress. "No! No! Nooooo!"

"Get them off me." This came from a man, who sounded both fearful and angry. "Get them off me. Get them off me!"

"Here we are," Dr Blocker said, with a genuine cheerfulness that seemed strangely out of place, considering their surroundings. They were standing in front of the door at the end of the hall. Like all the other rooms in the ward, the lock was operated by a magnetic card swipe, and had inch-thick glass protecting the viewing porthole, below which was mounted a metal communication grille. Above the top of the doorframe, a small viewing camera swiveled to face her, its red light blinking like a watchful eye.

Kimberly stared at the door, feeling a sudden surge of fear. She'd made eight phone calls, driven for two hours and filled out an entire legion of forms to get this far, but now that she was here, she was struck by a very definite urge not to go through with this. Visiting Clear had seemed like the most logical thing to do last night, from the warm safety of her bedroom, but right now, all she wanted to do was run.

She swallowed, staring hard at the door. "How long are you going to keep her locked up like this?" she asked in a small voice.

"Depends on her, I guess," Dr Blocker said with a shrug. "She's voluntary."

With that, the doctor swiped the magnetic key card through the lock and the door opened with a hiss. Voluntary? Kimberly had no time to process this. What kind of person would actually choose to live like this, locked up like a loony in a ward full of crazies? But it was too late to leave now. She took a deep breath and squared her shoulders, fighting the urge to flee as she resolutely stepped over the threshold into the room on the other side of the door.

"Room" wasn't truly accurate. It was actually a small cell, roughly ten feet square, with sterile, white, padded walls and floor. It was as stark and depressing as any federal penitentiary. The windows were little more than gun slits situated near the ceiling, which allowed sunlight to enter, but little else. The room was empty of all furnishings save a single mattress in the far corner, made of the same white padded material as the walls, with no pillow or bed linens to soften it.

The entire place was spotlessly clean, save for a section of one wall. Kimberly found her eyes drawn magnetically to it. The wall was covered with headlines clipped from newspapers, magazine articles, yearbook photos, diagrams of airline seating charts, printouts from websites, and autopsy photos, all of which seemed to hold some relation to Flight 180. The cuttings were stuck to the wall with soft adhesive and, where the sunlight touched them, their edges were starting to yellow and curl over, bearing testament to their age. There was an intricate spiderweb of thick, red Magic Marker arrows pointing to and from different photos, creating some kind of perverse flow chart.

The woman responsible for creating the demented shrine was standing in the farthest corner of the padded room. She was dressed in a pair of soft, loose-fitting pants and a white T-shirt, and her arms were firmly crossed, as if to protect herself. She was barefoot, with a white hospital number-tag around one wrist and dark circles under her eyes. There was a suspicious, defiant gleam in her eye, as though she had already made up her mind about Kimberly.

Kimberly had not been too sure of what to expect, but she was still startled to see how different the girl before her looked from the yearbook photo she had seen on the computer last night. In her picture, Clear had looked pensive, intelligent and somewhat vulnerable, and she had a softness to her face that had led Kimberly to believe she would be extremely shy. She had also had dark hair. The woman who was eyeing her warily seemed far older than her years could account for. There was no softness her. Her cheeks were hard, sculpted, her skin deathly white from lack of sunlight. The thoughtfulness Kimberly had glimpsed in the eyes of Clear's younger self was gone, to be replaced by a defensive, paranoid gleam in her ice-blue eyes, like those of a wild cat in captivity. Her hair had been dyed honey-blonde and hung in greasy, unwashed strands about her face. She was still a beautiful girl, fiercely so, although there was a hardness to her created by what Kimberly guessed was extreme stress.

"Clear Rivers?" Kimberly asked gently, taking a step forward.

"Don't come any closer," Clear, in a sharp, clipped voice.

Kimberly did as she was told, very much aware that she was alone in the room with this woman with nothing to defend herself. She had never felt more vulnerable. As the door swung closed behind her, she hooked her hands into the pockets of her raincoat as her eyes flicked up to the security camera, praying that whoever was watching her at the other end was paying attention.

As she stood there, breathing quietly, she saw Clear studying her carefully for a moment, as though trying to figure out exactly what kind of threat she posed.

"They told me you had something to do with the crash on Route 23."

Again, it was a harsh statement rather than an attempt at conversation.

Kimberly took a deep breath. "I thought... I thought you might be able to help me. I don't know who else I can talk to."

Clear raised a sarcastic eyebrow. "So what do you want from me?"

Kimberly dropped her gaze. "I can't explain it, but... but somehow I saw the pile-up before it happened I saved some people."

Unbidden, her eyes flitted to the Flight 180 shrine on the wall. She scanned the headlines with nervous interest.

"And now you think Death is after you," Clear said, her voice completely expressionless. Although she had a half-smile on her face, there was no hint of humor in her voice. "Nice work. If you're real lucky, you'll wind up in here with me." She sniffed, meeting Kimberly's gaze with a blank look, as though she were a boss at work wrapping up their meeting "Anything else?"

"Look, it's not just me." Kimberly took another step forward, hoping she could somehow get Clear to understand why she was here, so that she could—

"Stay where you are!" Clear shouted.

Kimberly jumped and dropped back, holding her hands up to show they were empty. "Okay, okay! You don't understand. One of the people I saved died last night in some freak accident. What if everyone else is in danger too?"

"Well, if you put them on the list, they're already dead," Clear said, her voice chillingly smug.

"What list?"

"*Death's* list," said Clear, as though that explained everything.

Seeing the confusion on Kimberly's face, Clear heaved a sigh and stepped out of the corner, pacing warily around the walls of the cell, keeping her distance from Kimberly at all times. "The survivors of Flight 180 died in the *exact order* they were originally meant to die in the plane crash," she said, in the manor of a teacher lecturing an exceptionally dumb student. She turned and tapped the elaborate collage of newsprint, photographs and diagrams affixed to the padded wall. "*That* was Death's original design: His list."

Kimberly's face tightened in fear. "Wait... You're telling me I was meant to die in that crash with my friends, so I'm next?"

"Hold on." Clear frowned, cocking her head to one side. "You said someone else died last night. Someone must have intervened. Sometime yesterday you must have nearly died, but someone saved you. That means Death skipped past you."

Kimberly's eyes widened as she made the connection between what had happened and what Clear was telling her "Of course! Officer Burke pulled me away from the crash that killed my friends."

"Congratulations, you'll be the last to go," Clear said, a rueful smile twisting her lips, "but don't worry, once the others are dead, it'll come back for you." Her eyes bored into Kimberly's, all traces of humor gone from her face. "It always does."

Kimberly shook her head, fighting down her panic even as she struggled to understand what Clear was telling her. "This still doesn't make sense. You said you die in the same order you were originally meant to. But Evan Lewis died last in my premonition, not first."

Clear's expression froze. "Wait. Died last? It's moving backward?" A look of surprise crossed the other girl's face. It was the first real emotion Kimberly had seen her express. She looked at Kimberly hard, narrowing her eyes as if fearful of trickery. "Are you sure?"

Kimberly nodded her assent. "Yes, I'm certain that's how it happened. In my premonition, that Nora woman and her kid died first, then Evan, and then... my friends." Kimberly's voice tailed off into silence as she realized what she was saying. Standing here in the corner of a padded cell, talking to this clearly deeply disturbed girl about Death's list and premonitions, Kimberly decided that she was starting to lose it. She had hoped that talking to Clear would make her feel better, but all she was succeeding in doing was making herself feel even more afraid. She wondered briefly whether insanity was catching; whether it really was all just a big coincidence.

After all, that made more sense than the alternative explanation.

As Kimberly stood there dithering, Clear spun abruptly on her heel to stare at the papers and charts on the wall, her eyes scanning back and forth rapidly, as if trying to decipher some kind of code hidden inside the welter of names, dates and times. "Backward... That's new." She stared at the wall, deep in thought. "What are you up to, you bastard?" she muttered, half to herself.

As the moments dragged by, Kimberly waited, glancing around the room. She noticed a small black and white TV screen set deeply back into the wall behind the door, which was hooked up to the video camera on the other side so that Clear could monitor her visitors. Kimberly's gaze went back to Clear, wondering what had compelled her to lock herself up and live like this for a whole nine months. As she watched, Clear reached out to touch a clipping stuck to the wall, muttering feverishly to herself under her breath. Kimberly wasn't sure if she even remembered that she had a visitor standing behind her.

She cleared her throat, hoping to get Clear's attention. The room was oppressively warm, and she was starting to sweat standing there in her thick raincoat and heavy-duty sweater. All she wanted right now was for this to be over, so she could go home and try figure out what to do next. She couldn't believe that this was her life. A week ago, her biggest worry had been her sliding score on her SATs, and whether or not Justin Martin was going to ask her to the end of semester dance. Now, suddenly, she had been plunged into this nightmarish alternative reality, and no matter how hard she tried, she just couldn't wake up.

"Why is this even happening to me?" she asked quietly, more to herself than in the hopes that Clear was actually still listening.

To her surprise, Clear stiffened, then turned and gave her a sympathetic look. "That's what Alex used to ask himself," she said softly.

"So what am I supposed to do?" Kimberly's voice was starting to waver as a knot of panic built up in her throat. She knew that there was a large chance that this could all be a load of bullshit, but there was something about the look that Clear had just given her... as though she was almost sorry for her. Kimberly realized with a startling clarity that Clear was telling her the truth... or at least, she thought she was.

She looked at Clear, desperately needing reassurance, and her heart fell as she saw the girl was once again staring off into the distance, lost in a world of her own.

"Clear!" she snapped.

"Watch out for the signs," Clear murmured dreamily, her eyes unfocused, as though repeating a mantra that someone had once told her.

"What?"

Clear's eyes suddenly snapped into an alert intensity. She stalked closer to Kimberly, fixing her with a piercing stare. "Have you ever seen anything creepy or ominous? An in-your-face-irony kinda thing?"

Kimberly thought for a second, her thoughts unavoidably dragged back to the events of the day before the pile-up had happened. She nodded slowly, unhappily. "The songs on the radio, yeah, and the guy in the beer truck, and everything on the road..."

"Well, don't ignore it. Those are signs, and recognizing them usually means the difference between life and death."

Kimberly felt her bottom lip start to tremble. She didn't want to die. There was still so much she wanted to do with her life. "Please, you have to help me."

"I don't *have* to do anything," Clear snapped. The softness vanished from her eyes like water vaporizing on a hot grill, to be replaced by her characteristic scowl. She turned away from Kimberly, folding her arms defiantly.

"But you beat it!"

Clear gave a bitter laugh and shook her head. Kimberly heard madness dancing with the cynicism in her voice as she waved her hands at the white, silent cell that made up her entire existence. "Take a look around! What exactly did I 'beat,' Kimberly?" Clear sniffed again, looking Kimberly up and down coldly. "If you were smart you'd forget about the others and save yourself."

"How can you say that?" Kimberly gasped, no longer trying to hide her distress. "You have a responsibility!"

"My friends are dead, that's how I can say that," Clear snapped back, her eyes flashing with barely restrained hostility. She abruptly turned her back on Kimberly and strode over to the collage on the wall. She plucked a Polaroid from the jumble of cuttings and thrust it toward Kimberly, apparently no longer concerned with keeping her distance. "And *this* is what happened to Alex when I was responsible for him."

Kimberly grimaced at the sight of the young man sprawled on the ground, a piece of brickwork jutting from the side of his face, the filthy pavement spattered with his brains and blood. He was violently and obviously dead.

"Get out," Clear said in a low, chilling monotone, "before you hurt me or yourself."

She turned away from Kimberly dismissively and punched the call button on the wall, disengaging the lock on the door of her cell.

Kimberly stared at Clear. Then she whirled and jerked open the door to the padded room, kicking herself for ever thinking that coming here and speaking to this person might make a difference. Fresh tears sprung to her eyes, but she held them in check as she paused on the threshold and glared back over her shoulder at Clear. The girl was standing in front of the shrine to her dead classmates, a smirk on her face.

"Know what?" Kimberly said coldly.

"What?"

"I think you're a coward. You hide out in here because you're too damn bitter and selfish to care about another living soul." Disgusted, Kimberly looked Clear right in the eye, fighting to keep her voice level. "In my opinion, you're *already* dead."

With that, she left, pulling the door shut behind her, leaving Clear Rivers sealed within her perfectly safe, antiseptic little world.

On the other side of the door, Clear stood and watched as Kimberly glared defiantly up at the camera, giving her the finger before turning and marching off down the corridor, her long jacket swirling as she vanished through the end doors.

Yeah, whatever, she thought irritably.

As the echoes of Kimberly's footsteps faded away, Clear stared at the door for a long moment, then sighed and turned back to the narrow mattress that was the only furnishing in the room. She looked down at it, a muscle twitching in her jaw, and then flopped down on it and propped herself up, back to the wall. She sat with her head in her hands for a while, her pulse still thumping from the heated exchange.

She should never have agreed to see the girl. Taking time out to talk to that silly little bitch had just antagonized her, not to mention knocking precious minutes off her ironclad daily schedule. She didn't know why she'd even bothered.

Overhead, the comforting background hum of the air conditioning unit mingled with the sounds of breakfast being served. Clear took a couple of deep breaths to steady herself.

Screw Kimberly. It was time to get back to work.

Rubbing a hand tiredly across her eyes, she scooted across the bed to lift the edge of the mattress. Reaching underneath, she removed a stack of newspapers and dropped them down onto the floor. Settling herself comfortably on the padded slab she called a bed, she thumbed through them with a speed born of daily practice until she came to the article she was looking for.

She glanced up at the hodgepodge of photos and graphs affixed to the wall, then back down at the newspaper, wondering if she should add it to her collection or not. That Kimberly girl had been pretty persuasive, and if she actually did have a vision, as she claimed, then perhaps it really was starting all over again.

And perhaps she needed to start on a new wall.

Clear meticulously tore the article out, then paused, studying the photograph of the young blond guy holding up the oversized lottery check, grinning at the camera as if he hadn't a care in the world. He was a nice-looking lad. The headline read: "LOTTO WINNER KILLED BY LADDER." Clear's gaze was drawn back up to the grisly collage on the wall. She looked at the cuttings, at the pictures, at the faces of her friends—so young and full of life in their yearbook photos that their death photos next to them seemed almost obscene.

A muscle twitched in Clear's jaw. Her friends were dead. Nothing she could say or do would bring them back, and in a way, her own incarceration was just putting off the inevitable. She was merely biding her time until she joined them. Even here, in this padded cell, disaster could still befall her. No matter how carefully she safeguarded herself, how many rules and regulations she made up to keep herself from coming to harm, the outside world would eventually work out a way to find her, to get through to her, to kill her.

Salmonella poisoning from her food.

A poisonous spider, creeping in through the tiny slit in the window.

An electrical fault in the asylum, making all the light switches live.

A malfunction in her TV monitor, blowing lethal shards of glass across the room.

All she was doing was killing time, until Time got around to killing her.

Clear rubbed her eyes and looked back down at the article, staring at the picture of the young man who had died. Evan Lewis beamed happily out at the camera, holding his check up high, with not the slightest clue that two days later he would be dead.

He wasn't much older than Alex had been.

There had been—how many more? Kimberly had mentioned a woman with a kid, and who else? Clear glanced fitfully at the door as she tried to force herself to remember. How many more had the girl saved?

As the moments ticked by, Clear gave a deep sigh.

Who was she trying to kid?

Carefully, she folded the article and put it down on the floor. She closed her eyes and swallowed, bile rising in her throat as she contemplated what she was about to do. Without glancing down at what she was doing, as though even looking would cause her to change her mind, Clear slipped her bitten nails down under the tag in her plastic hospital ID bracelet.

Slowly, with the expression of a condemned man walking of his own volition to the gallows, she began to ease it off her wrist.

# NINE

Kimberly pulled the borrowed silver Beetle into her driveway, still fuming to herself. What a waste of time! All that effort, and all that Rivers girl had done was make a bad situation worse. She was now convinced that she was going to die, that it was all hopeless, that there was no escape. If what Clear had told her was true, no matter how hard she tried, she would very soon be dead, along with everyone else she had saved from the on-ramp.

A small logical part of her mind was still trying to reason with her. See how ridiculous the whole thing sounds, she thought. I mean, come on! We're talking about visions and curses and omens of Death here! This is here and now, not the Middle Ages. What kind of a fool would I have to be to believe this whole thing?

A picture of herself lying dying amid the pile-up slammed into her mind with the strength and accuracy of a surgical drill, and she felt her mouth go dry as she tried in vain to blot out the graphic images, to shrug off the sense of black dread that had been rising in her ever since she had left the Stonybrook Institution.

But there was no escaping the way she felt. All her instincts were screaming at her, in the same way that your stomach gives a nasty lurch upon seeing a dark shadow move in an alleyway as you walk home alone at night. It wasn't logical; it was an animal instinct, plain and simple. She just felt *wrong*, as though just by being here, by driving this car and interacting with everything, she was somehow unavoidably changing the world in a way that it wasn't meant to be changed. She felt it in the closeness of the air, the tightness of her nerves, and in the tension in her body that seemed to grow worse with every passing hour since she had been discharged from the police station.

She knew that the most logical thing to do would be for her to just grit her teeth and bear it. She could ride out the storm and hope that when she woke up in the morning this terrible feeling would have dissipated like the storm clouds overhead. Then everything would be all right again, and she could carry on with her life without fear, without looking over her shoulder, without wondering if this was going to be the day that she would die.

The less logical part of her, the part most closely concerned with survival told her to run screaming into the night and hide, while she still had the chance.

Trying to shrug off the feeling, Kimberly turned down the familiar road and pulled into the drive outside her house. Glancing up the pathway, she was surprised to see a strange car parked where her father's would normally be. She looked toward the house and saw a man standing in front of it, facing away from her. He was about average height and build, with dark hair, and was dressed in a chocolate-colored corduroy jacket, stonewashed 501s and a pair of Timberland boots. He was peering through the window next to the front door, a cupped hand raised over his brow in order to get a better view.

Suddenly tense, she killed the engine, unclipped her seatbelt and got out of the car. News of the pile-up had only been in the paper for a day. She couldn't believe that she was getting stalkers already. Her sneakers crunched on the gravel driveway as she hurried up the pathway toward the house. "What do you want?" she called to the stranger, trying to keep the fear out of her voice.

As the man on the porch turned to face her, Kimberly realized he wasn't a stranger at all.

"I tried calling last night," Thomas Burke said, an apologetic smile on his face, "but your father said you were sleeping."

Kimberly walked up to him warily. eager to be inside the house. Her encounter with Clear Rivers had left her shaken and upset. She was in no mood to be dealing with the police right now. As far as she was concerned, Officer Burke's presence was just another reminder that all was not well with her life.

"Evan Lewis is dead," she said matter-of-factly as she climbed the steps of the front porch, reaching inside her purse for her house keys. If she could just get inside, then she could sit herself in front of the TV, stick on a movie and turn the volume up real high, and just for an hour or two she could pretend that everything was okay.

Thomas nodded thoughtfully and leaned against the large bay window that looked into the Cormans' living room. "Yeah, I've been getting calls all morning from everyone who was on the on-ramp." He paused, looking at Kimberly in a strange way. "We're all meeting at my apartment tonight. I can't risk doing it at the station."

Kimberly paused, her hand on the door, and turned to look at Officer Burke, seeing him properly for the first time. Dressed in his civilian clothes, he seemed much less intimidating than he had at the police station. He actually wasn't that bad looking, in a serious, grown-up kind of way. He gazed back at her intently, his brown eyes fixed on hers as though she had the secrets of the universe locked up behind her retinas. She realized with a shock that he was actually taking her seriously.

"Wait... then you believe all this Death stuff?" asked Kimberly, a look of surprise on her face.

Burke hesitated before he spoke, his eyes flicking anxiously to Kimberly's as though seeking reassurance. When he spoke, his voice was measured, unsure, as though even he didn't believe the words he was speaking. "I didn't, not at first. Then last year, I was dispatched to clean up one of the Flight 180 survivors."

"Clean up? I don't understand—" Kimberly broke off, distracted, as a strange sound came from behind her, a flapping noise, like the sound of numerous wings beating the air. A movement caught her eye. She glanced past Officer Burke to see a flock of hundreds of pigeons swooping down toward her from behind, clearly reflected in the glass of the big bay window.

Yelping in surprise, Kimberly ducked instinctively and lifted her arms to shield her head and face from the birds as they swarmed toward her. The wing beats got louder and she saw them swoop down toward her, their reflections buzzing across the windowpane. Straightening up, she glanced behind her to see...

Nothing.

The air behind her was empty.

She was alone on the porch, save for Burke. He was staring at her as if she'd suddenly lost her mind.

"Did you see that?" she gasped, too surprised to be embarrassed.

"See what?" Burke raised an eyebrow and glanced around, trying to figure out what she was talking about.

"The pigeons!" Kimberly replied in exasperation.

"Pigeons?" Officer Burke looked at her as though she had just sprouted wings herself.

"Pigeons," she replied solemnly. Then her eyebrows flew up and she gasped as it hit her. "It's a Sign!"

"A sign of what?" asked Burke, struggling to keep up with her.

Kimberly waved him aside impatiently. "If Clear's right about the order, then Nora and Tim are gonna be attacked by pigeons!" She frowned slightly, as if trying to make sense of what she'd just said.

Burke massaged his brow with one hand, trying his best to understand what Kimberly was talking about. "How do you kill someone with pigeons?" He leaned forward and touched Kimberly's arm, unsure of quite where all this was going, but swept up by it nonetheless. He thought she looked quite beautiful when she got all flustered. "I'm not following you."

Kimberly shook him off irritably. "They're next on Death's list. If we don't find them they're gonna die!"

Officer Burke looked at Kimberly solemnly, noticing how her eyes were perfectly almond shaped, and how she had a light smattering of faded freckles on her nose, as though she had spent the summer at the beach. He knew that here was a small chance that the girl might actually be crazy, but he was more than willing to take that risk. He couldn't risk losing more witnesses, and if Kimberly turned out to be right about this "pigeons" thing... well, it was shorts-eating time.

Reaching into his pocket, he pulled out his car keys and jerked his head toward his car.

It was time to put Kimberly's theory to the test.

At the dentist's office on the other side of town, Tim Carpenter stared intently at the fish swimming inside the large aquarium in the waiting room. They were mostly goldfish, although there were about a dozen fancy coldwater fish with bulbous eyes and impressive sweeping tails swimming around, kind of like the ones he used to keep when he was younger, before his mom had made him get rid of them. He knew all the species off by heart. In the dentist's tank he could see black mollies and bubble-eyes and fan-tails and speckled shubunkins and orandas, and mirror-plated ghost-carp, and even what looked like a baby koi, circling up near the surface feeding on a scrap of pond-weed. Tim watched it swim, wondering vaguely if the dentist knew that in a year or two the koi would grow to be over a foot long and would be too big for the tank. In his mind's eye, he pictured it bursting out of the aquarium and rampaging through the dentist's waiting room, terrorizing young girls waiting to have their teeth filled before kidnapping the screaming receptionist and climbing up the Empire State Building, helicopters buzzing round.

Tim grinned to himself. He really shouldn't have watched that *King Kong* DVD before coming here.

The centerpiece of the aquarium was a grinning fake skull, no doubt supposed to be that of a pirate who met his fate in Davy Jones's locker. The colorful fish swam placidly in and out of the fake empty eye sockets, unfazed by the gruesome décor, or by the sight of one of their fellow inmates, a small plain goldfish who had been sucked into the filter's intake valve and was now jammed inside the system. It wriggled weakly, stuck in the pump tube, mortally wounded.

Tim looked up from the fish's death throes and glanced nervously around the dentist's office. The office was situated on one of the upper floors of the Ellis Medical Complex, one of the more up-market clinics in town. Last time he had been here, the place had been deathly quiet, but on this visit they were building an annex next door, and the office rang with the sounds of drilling and banging, and the rattling of a jackhammer tearing up concrete. The view outside the window was spoiled by the lumbering cranes swinging building materials around, and by the ugly green scaffolding ringing the annex. The noise from the construction work was loud enough at times to drown out the office sound system, which was currently playing a Muzak version of John Denver's "Rocky Mountain High."

The dentist's assistant, a pretty young Asian woman dressed in a white dental hygienist's smock, stepped out from behind the reception desk and opened the door that led to the examination area. She beamed brightly, undeterred by the sounds of loud and noisy construction echoing through the office. "Tim? The doctor's ready for you now."

Tim stood up from in front of the aquarium, fighting down the traditional attack of nerves, and turned to fix his mother with a mock-serious look. "If he gives me the gas and I wake up with my pants unbuttoned, we ain't payin'."

Nora's jaw dropped and she quickly raised the *Reader's Digest* compendium she was reading to mask her rather shocked laugh. "What? Tim!"

Her son gave her a wink and turned to walk toward the open door that led to the suite of examination rooms beyond the reception area. The sooner this was over and done with, the better. His tooth had been giving him gyp all month, and it was only last week that the pain had gotten so bad he had dared to tell his mother about it, knowing that he'd be whisked straight off to see the dreaded dentist. In Tim's head the guy was waiting in his office right now, sharpening his tools and laughing evilly, ready to rip out the offending tooth and add it to the tooth necklace he traditionally wore in Tim's fevered imaginings. Tim tried to breathe, imagining how much fun his father would make of him if he knew he was scared of a little thing like the dentist.

As he passed the fish tank his gaze was drawn to the window, to one of the cranes, which was lifting large metal panels to and from the construction side. He stared at it for a moment, a strange feeling of unease washing over him that he attributed to the fact that he was just about to go and have a tooth filled. He was jolted back to reality when he accidentally bumped into the side of the aquarium, causing a precariously perched canister of fish food to spill onto the carpeted floor. He glanced guiltily back at his mother, but she was reading an article in one of the magazines from the coffee table. Then he looked over at the receptionist, but she hadn't seemed to notice either.

He shrugged and hurried toward the waiting door: no harm, no foul.

As Tim entered the examination room, his dentist rose to greet him. Dr Lees was in his early fifties. He wore horn-rimmed glasses and had graying hair and a penchant for Madras shirts and Dockers. Tim secretly thought he looked like an older version of Barney Rubble. "There you are, Tim!" he said, flashing a mouth full of professionally cleaned and maintained teeth. "What happened to you yesterday? We missed you here." He patted the seat of the examination chair.

"We got hung up by that accident on Route 23," Tim explained as he crawled into the dentist's chair, his spiked-up blond hair brushing the fish mobile that hung directly overhead. He hated it when the dentist tried to be friendly with him. He always did this, acting like they were best buddies just minutes before he started sticking sharp things into Tim's mouth and hurting him, and then over-charging his mom for the honor.

Tim shivered at the thought.

"Good Lord," Dr Lees exclaimed, a look of genuine surprise on his face. "How lucky that you're okay."

"Yeah," Tim replied, smiling weakly.

"Your mother says you've been having some pain lately?" Dr Lees continued, pulling on a pair of latex surgeon's gloves.

"Not really," Tim mumbled. His eye was drawn to the large tray of glinting implements lined up beside the chair. Suddenly, he really wished that he hadn't come here today. If his tooth was really that bad, it would fall out by itself eventually, right? And then everything would be okay again and he could get on with his life.

He lay back in the chair and watched as the cranes whirled and swung outside the window.

In the waiting room next door, Nora Cunningham finished her article in the Reader's Digest and put the magazine aside with a sigh. The article had been entitled "Coping With Loss," and although diligently and sympathetically written, she thought it was basically a load of old garbage.

It wasn't that the writer had been insensitive in any way. It was just that he had never gone through what she had gone through, so how could he possibly know what she was feeling?

There wasn't a day that went by that Nora didn't wish that her husband was still alive. He had died unexpectedly, three years ago, and Nora was still picking up the pieces. One day he seemed perfectly fine, the next he suffered a grand mal seizure while in the middle of a conference call at his office. By the time the doctors had diagnosed the tumor, it was already the size of a golf ball, with roots extending so far into his gray matter that to try and excise it would be the equivalent of a pre-frontal lobotomy. Six months, twenty-five radiation treatments and five bouts of chemo later, he was dead.

The loss of the love of her life had been devastating, but she told herself she had to keep soldiering on for the sake of their son. Tim had always meant everything to her, but now that she no longer had her husband, he had become everything to her, too. If Tim had not existed, she wouldn't have had a reason to get out of bed during those first few horrible months following her husband's death. He had kept her sane when the rest of the world seemed to be going crazy, and had been there for her during those times when it seemed like she, too, would slip off the edge. Every day she thanked her lucky stars for him.

It wasn't easy being both mother and father to a growing boy, especially one as precocious as Tim. He had always been advanced for his age, but since his father's death he seemed to be taking this to an extreme. Sometimes she worried that he was growing up too fast. She could see that he was eager to become the "man" of the household, but at the same time, she wished that he would stay her little boy for just a few years longer. She worried that she might be encouraging him, at least on an unconscious level, by relying on him excessively and giving him so many chores around the house. After reading that other *Reader's Digest* article last month, she was also becoming increasingly concerned that he was sublimating his anger and resentment at being cheated out of a "normal" childhood—one with a two-parent home—by burying himself in the unreality of horror novels, monster movies and sick websites.

She sat back in her chair, gazing uneasily out the window. What was that one she had found him on the other day? Some *Buffy* chat-site about vampires? To her, that just summed up everything that she thought was wrong with the Internet. What kind of perverted person would log onto a computer specifically to talk to a fourteen year-old boy on the other side of the country about vampires?

Still, she wasn't comfortable with putting her foot down and telling her son what he could and could not do. Her own parents had been particularly strict, resulting in a great load of tearful teenage angst on her behalf when she was his age. She had sworn to herself that she would never treat a child of her own like her parents had treated her, and she had to keep reminding herself that Tim was no longer a little boy, but a young adult. He was making the rocky transition to manhood without the guidance of a father, and she had to walk a fine line between being protective and being controlling, especially with the bad influences that seemed to come from every possible direction. She had to prepare her son to live in a very scary world, no matter how badly she wanted to seal him behind a wall of glass, safely removed from the repetitive pain and hurt that she knew would come as an unavoidable part of his life.

As she sat there, gazing blankly out of the window at the swinging cranes, the dental assistant came back into the room. Nora looked up as the pretty woman made a perfunctory circuit of the room, straightening the magazines on the coffee table and tossing an abandoned paper cup into the trash. She noticed the spilled fish food next to the aquarium and sighed to herself. Then she walked over to the nearby broom closet and pulled out an upright vacuum cleaner. Plugging it into the wall outlet below the fish tank, she began to run the vacuum back and forth over the dried fish flakes, whistling tunelessly along with the PA as she vacuumed up the mess.

There was a sharp grinding noise that caused Nora to blink and look away from the window, her train of thought abruptly derailed. The assistant frowned at the vacuum and gave it a hard shake, forcing it to cough up a bent carpet nail.

She shook her head in disgust and proceeded to continue vacuuming around Nora's feet.

Unseen and unnoticed by either woman, the water filter inside the aquarium sputtered and conked out, the intake valve now completely blocked by the body of the dead fish that had been sucked inside it minutes before. The unit hummed under the strain, then one of the small tubes running around the back of the tank popped off its connecting block under the pressure. Water spurted out, spraying against the whitewashed wall and trickling down toward the electrical socket.

On the other side of the room, the dental assistant finished vacuuming up the spilled fish food and glanced around the room, deciding to give the carpet a bit of a clean while she was at it. Nora absently lifted her legs as the woman vacuumed under the coffee table, unaware that just yards from her, water was trickling down toward the plug of the vacuum cleaner. The water pooled on the linoleum, forming a large puddle. Then it started flowing quietly across the floor, heading unerringly for Nora's unsuspecting feet.

Tim glanced away nervously from the tray full of carefully arranged dental instruments which Dr Lees kept next to the chair as he worked. A bead of sweat appeared on his brow as he refocused his attention on the nearby construction work, which he could see through the window directly in front of him. As he watched, he saw the monstrous crane swing a stack of plate glass the size of a wall of sheetrock toward the waiting workers standing down below the annex. To his mind, it looked like the head and neck of a giant brontosaurus, carrying its burden of goods like the big dinosaur in the opening titles of the Flintstones. Although the window was closed, he could hear the drone of the crane's motor clearly, along with the shouts of the construction crew and the constant noise of the jackhammers down below.

He flinched as Dr Lees took a pick and mirror and started examining his mouth, drawing him from his reverie. After a couple of moments, he saw the dentist's forehead furrow in a frown.

"I'm disappointed, Tim. Does your mom know that you've been smoking?"

"Uh-huh," Tim grunted around the sharp utensils in his mouth, afraid to nod his head for fear of getting a pick embedded in his gum.

Dr Lees gave him a doubtful look, and returned to probing around his back molars with the explorer. Tim suddenly gripped the arms of the chair and hissed in pain.

"Yeah, that'll have to be filled," the dentist muttered, more to himself than Tim. Cleaning his mirror on his surgically clean paper bib, he reached toward Tim's mouth once more to get a better look at the tooth.

*BLAM!*

The dentist's hand jerked reflexively as he was startled by the noise, but luckily the pick was already out of Tim's mouth. Dr Lees turned around in time to see a pigeon fluttering dazedly away from the large window behind him. A big crack spider-webbed its way across the glass from where the bird had thumped into the window.

Dr Lees threw down his pick in frustration. "Jesus. How many times am I gonna have to replace these damn windows?" He waved a hand at the window. "Ever since they started work next door, it's driven the damn birds crazy."

Heaving an aggravated sigh, Dr Lees picked up a syringe from the instrument tray at his elbow and turned back to Tim, holding the loaded hypodermic in one steady hand. Tim's eyes widened at the sight of the giant needle. This was worse than he had expected.

"Now, this will only sting for a moment."

Dr Lees stuck a gloved finger in the boy's mouth, pulling down his lower lip in order to better expose the gum line. "There we go. Open big for me. Wider... Wider..."

Tim reluctantly opened his mouth while nervously eyeing the approaching syringe. He quickly looked away, only to see another pigeon headed straight for the window.

*BLAM!*

Dr Lees jumped in his seat as the second bird slammed into the window, nearly jabbing Tim's tongue with the syringe and making him squirm uncomfortably. He looked toward the window angrily. "How the hell do they expect me to—?" He took a deep breath and put the syringe on the instrument tray, turning back to his patient, flustered and irritable. "Would you rather have the laughing gas, Tim?"

Tim nodded his head vigorously.

"Okay," the dentist said, pushing himself away from the chair. He turned his head in the direction of the door. "Jean! I'm going to need you in here. Jean?"

There was no reply. Through the half-open door he could hear the faint sounds of vacuuming.

Dr Lees frowned, wondering where on earth his assistant had got to. Glancing back at Tim, he made a snap decision. What the hell, he'd do it without her. He was overrunning his schedule as it was because of this blasted disruption from the construction crew. If he didn't hurry things up he was going to be seriously cutting into his afternoon slots before he was even halfway through the day.

Leaning over, he switched on the compressors that ran the oxygen and nitrous oxide feeds in the two tanks behind his dentist's chair. "Okay, Tim, I'm going to get you started here," he said as he placed a gas mask over the boy's face. "You'll be awake and a little groggy, but you're not going to be able to move much. I'm going to be inserting a dental speculum to keep your jaws propped open while I work."

Tim inhaled deeply through his nose. The laughing gas mixture smelled vaguely of bubblegum. Within a few seconds he began to feel his arms and legs growing heavy. His body seemed to be drifting on a current of cool air. He barely felt any discomfort as Dr Lees placed a plastic device in his mouth and dialed it open so that he had an unobstructed view of the tooth he was going to be filling.

Dr Lees lowered the speeding drill into Tim's open mouth. "Very good, now open big. Wider…"

Tim closed his eyes and tried to ignore the sound of the dentist's drill biting through the enamel of his tooth. As much as he disliked having his teeth worked on, he was more worried about Dr Lees talking to his mom about his smoking. He knew the dentist hadn't fallen for his claiming she knew about the cigarettes. This meant that he was going to get chewed out in the car on the ride home. He'd rather have every tooth in his head filled than deal with that.

Tim breathed steadily through his nose, feeling the creeping numbness spread through his body. He wished his mom would lighten up a bit. She worried about him too much for her own good—much less his. She'd always been something of a worrywart, but she'd gotten worse since his father's death. He knew if his dad was still around he'd tell his mom not to worry about his "development" so much, and just let him alone to make his own mistakes. He wouldn't have worried about his son's interest in monsters and demons and crap like that. He would have realized it was just a stage his son was going through—one most boys go through at one time or another, no different than his obsession with dinosaurs when he'd been in kindergarten. So he liked monster movies and scary books, big deal. So did every other kid his age. It didn't mean that there was anything wrong with him.

Personally, Tim blamed all the self-help books and articles his mother had buried herself in for the last three years. There had to be something screwed up with that. She had dozens of them, given to her by well-meaning friends and family members, and he would find them everywhere, lying around the house—on the sofa, half-hidden under yesterday's newspapers, in the kitchen face-down beside the stove, beside the toilet in the bathroom. He was getting sick of picking them up all the time. He'd tried to read one once and had got bored after the first couple of pages. How could a book tell you how to live your life? She thought that she was helping herself, but all she was doing was stirring herself up, looking for someone to tell her what to do and how to think because she didn't know anymore.

Although he was only fourteen, Tim knew the difference between what was real and what was not. He knew monsters didn't really exist, although he thought it would be cool if they did. What was real was him, and the other people in his mother's life—the countless friends who had been there to lend a shoulder or an ear when his mother had been going through the worst of her grieving. Instead of burying herself in her books, locked away in her dark, stuffy room, she should be out helping him fix his bike, or paint the house, or make a barbeque for the people next door. His dad may be dead, but that didn't mean that she was, too.

As the dentist's drill whirred away above him, Tim wondered if his mother was even trying to make conversation with the female receptionist next door, or whether she was just sitting there, nose buried in her book. As much as Tim missed his dad, he knew his mom was lonely. She needed to start dating and living her own life again. Maybe if she had something in her life besides worrying about him, she might not spend all her spare time at home, sitting in front of the television set and drinking white wine.

The drinking, in particular, concerned him. Before his dad got sick and finally died, his mom would have one, maybe two glasses of wine at dinner over the course of the week. Now it was at least three glasses every night, and that was just what he saw her drink before he went to bed. His mother was a wonderful woman. She had done everything she could to make sure he was cared for and prepared for life, but what was she going to do with herself once he was gone? He'd be out of school and out of the house in five years, when he went off to college. As hard as it might be for his mom to accept , he wasn't going to be hanging around here forever. Some time or another she was going to have to get used to the idea of him not being around.

As Tim sat in the dentist's chair and wondered about his future as a college student, the stopped-up aquarium pipe next door finally gave way, sending a gush of water splattering against the wall. The plug socket was drenched, and overloaded with a bang, shorting out the vacuum cleaner Joan was using to clean the waiting room carpet. The explosion was masked by the sounds of the jackhammer from next door.

"What the...?" The dental assistant frowned as the vacuum sparked and died. She shook it, but it remained dead. As she turned toward the wall socket to check the plug, there was the sound of breaking glass, and a large gray pigeon suddenly crashed through the plate glass window of the reception area.

Startled by the unexpected intrusion, Jean gave a shrill scream at the sight of the wounded bird fluttering on the floor at her feet. She had lived in London before she came here, and had a mortal fear of pigeons, those damned disease-ridden, winged rats. This was a rodent bird from her worst nightmares—all flapping, dirty wings and scratching claws, a scrawny body caked in mud from the recent rain, and crazy, beady little black eyes. She kicked at it convulsively as it fluttered weakly toward her, and dropped the vacuum cleaner with a loud thud as she backed away from it in disgust.

Nora jumped to her feet as the bird flapped into the waiting area, stepping away from the creeping puddle of electrified water a second before it touched her shoes. Putting down her magazine, she went to help the assistant capture the bird.

In the treatment room, Dr Lees halted his drilling at the alarming sounds coming from his waiting room. There had been a crash, then a scream, and then a thump. In his mind, that was never a good equation. "Goddamn it already!" he snapped, snatching the protective paper bib away from his neck. It was just one thing after another today, and it wasn't even lunchtime yet. He marched out of the room to investigate, leaving the drowsy Tim in the chair.

Next door there was chaos. As Dr Lees warily pushed open the door, the first thing he saw was his assistant Jean and Tim's mother, both yelping and shrieking and crawling around on the floor of the reception area, which was for some reason sopping wet. They were trying their best to capture a badly injured pigeon, which was flopping around frantically, spreading feathers and blood wherever it went.

"Oh, great, not again," he groaned.

Back in the treatment room, Tim stared up at the exotic fish mobile hanging over his head, his jaws opened as wide as they could go. His mouth was starting to ache, but he was too sleepy to really care much about it. Beside his head, the gas hissed away quietly.

*SssssssssssSSsssssssSSSsssssss...*

Unseen and unnoticed, there was another quick, quiet electrical surge from the shorted-out wall socket. The compressor, which was supplying oxygen to the unattended anesthesia machine Tim was hooked up to, fluttered off, while the nitrous flow remained strong. The oxygen dial spun down to zero. If Dr Lees had been there he would've noticed the warning light come on on the side of the machine, and quickly turned off the nitrous.

But Dr Lees wasn't there. He was next door, trying to help his assistant catch the pigeon.

Tim was vaguely aware that something was wrong, but as his consciousness started to slip away from him, he couldn't quite pin down what it was. Every time he thought he had a grip on what was happening, the world just slipped away from him, like a slippery bar of soap in the bathtub. The harder he tried to concentrate, the further the world seemed to recede.

As he sat dozing in the chair, eyes half closed, he was dimly aware of a cool breeze entering the room. He watched blearily as the fish mobile overheard started to rotate, like the mobile above a baby's crib. One of the toys fixed to the mobile, shaped like a small, round puffer fish, wobbled alarmingly. A moment later it detached from the line and fell directly into Tim's wide-open mouth with a soft plop. Tim felt it enter his mouth and tried to spit the thing out, but his jaws had been propped open, which prevented him from doing so. In fact, his head was at such an angle that his attempts to dislodge the rubber fish from his mouth seemed to move it even further down his throat. Tim struggled to raise his hand to his face, but his vision had suddenly gone blurry and it felt as if someone had tied anchors to his arms and legs.

He tried to call out for help, but all that emerged was a choked, gurgling sound. As his consciousness slipped even further away from him, he tried to push the thing out with his tongue, but only succeeded in somehow drawing the fish to the very back of his throat, cutting off his air supply.

With the nitrous mask still clamped over his nose, Tim instantly found himself growing dizzy from lack of oxygen. His eyes were still open, but as he coughed and gagged quietly, they rolled up, exposing the whites. He was suffocating, and he couldn't do a thing about it. Marshalling all his strength, he forced one hand to rise from the armrest, only to have it drop back in his lap, as limp as a wet sock. The sounds from the commotion in the next room seemed to fade away, as if someone had turned the volume down on the world around him. His eyes began to fill with tears, which ran down over his cheeks and into his ears, as he continued to choke.

He was just starting to think about what his schoolmates would say when they heard that he'd been killed in a dentist's chair by a rubber fish, when someone blurry and dressed in white appeared in the periphery of his vision and quickly moved toward him. Although tears and the anesthesia blurred his vision, he could tell it was Dr Lees's assistant.

The receptionist turned off the valve on the nitrous tank and speedily removed the rubber puffer fish from Tim's gaping mouth. She shoved the offending toy into the pocket of her smock and looked around quickly to make sure no one else, especially not Mrs Carpenter, had seen what had transpired. As far as she could tell, no one had any idea how close Tim had come to dying in the dentist's chair.

She shook her head ruefully. It had just been one of those days.

Kimberly gnawed on her thumbnail as she stared out of the passenger side window of Burke's Jeep Cherokee, the rainy streets flying by her in a blur. Time was ticking away for Nora and Tim; she could feel it as surely as she could sense the pulse in her throat. They had already wasted time driving to the Carpenters' home in the hope of finding them there, before they set out into the world or had a chance to put themselves in any proximity to pigeons. They were met only by the cleaning lady, who informed them that Nora had taken her son to see a dentist at the Ellis Medical Complex over on Fourteenth Street.

"I hope they're still okay," Kimberly muttered, more to herself than anyone else. She wished that Officer Burke would drive faster, but being a police officer, she knew that a request to hit the gas and to hell with the speed limit might not go down too well.

"We're only a couple of blocks away," Burke said, trying to sound as positive as he possibly could. "Don't worry, we'll get there."

Kimberly turned her worried brown eyes up toward him. "Yeah, but will we be in time?"

Tim and Nora strolled through the foyer of the Ellis Medical Complex arm in arm. Tim was visibly relieved, not just because his teeth no longer hurt, but because it was clear from his mom's behavior toward him that Dr Lees had not seen fit to mention his smoking to his mother.

That was a blessing, if nothing else.

As they exited the building through the big revolving doors, the constant din of the construction grew exponentially louder. Directly in front of the medical complex was a large flatbed truck, the bed of which contained huge sheets of plate-glass. Next to the truck was a crane they had seen out of the window of the dentist's office, which was busy raising the payload up to the waiting construction workers overhead, one giant pane at a time.

"So, what did the doctor say about your tooth?" Nora asked casually, as they started to walk across the scaffolding-strewn yard toward the parking lot.

"I honestly can't remember much after he gave me the gas," Tim said with a shrug.

"Tim! Nora!"

Nora glanced up in surprise at the sound of a man shouting her name. She saw two figures running toward her, coming up from the parking lot, one of whom appeared to be the young patrolman who had been at the crash site the other day. As they got closer, she saw that the strange young girl who claimed to have foreseen the horrible accident was with him.

They pelted across the grass toward her and her son, yelling and waving their hands frantically.

Nora frowned. She could've sworn the young woman had just yelled, "The pigeons!" at her.

"What are they doing here, Mom?" Tim asked, pulling his arm free of his mother's grasp, "and why are they yelling 'pigeons'?"

"I don't know, honey," Nora replied. This day was just getting weirder and weirder. She couldn't wait to get home so she could have a glass of wine and relax. She hoped that she hadn't gotten anything nasty by touching that bird up in the waiting room. Last thing she wanted right now was for Tim to come down with something.

As Tim and Nora walked curiously toward the approaching pair, Tim spied a giant cluster of pigeons that had gathered on the sidewalk of the complex, pecking at the crumbs left by the construction workers after they'd finished their brown bag lunches. He gave a sudden grin as he made the connection. Yeah, pigeons! The dirty little vermin. With a jubilant cry he ran at the flock, yelling and stamping his feet to drive them off. Taking fright, the pigeons rose in a great, filthy cloud, flying straight for the operator of the nearby crane, who instinctively turned away in his cab to protect his face and eyes from the birds' wings and claws.

# FINAL DESTINATION 2

As he did so, he inadvertently knocked a lever.

It was a very bad lever for him to knock.

The sound of a heavy metal chain uncoiling rapidly filled the air.

"Lady! Watch out!" A construction worker suddenly grabbed Nora by the elbow, yanking her clear of where her son was standing.

"Tim!" Nora screamed. It would be the last thing she ever said to him.

Tim looked up, still grinning, in time to see a giant pane of reinforced plate glass hurtling down toward him. By the time his brain had registered what he was looking at, it was too late. The heavy pane of glass struck him dead centre and crashed down on top of him, snapping his neck and killing him instantly.

*"Noooooooooooo!"* screamed Kimberly.

Fragments of glass and blood erupted in a fountain-like spray as the force of the impacting glass sheet shattered every bone in Tim's upper body, causing the violently displaced body fluids and viscera to spurt from his ruptured stomach cavity. The whole lot hit the ground with a crash, reducing what was left of Tim to jelly. Spinning glass rained down in a shining, tumbling cloud, scattering across the sidewalk.

Kimberly stared in horror, her trembling hand covering her mouth. What had just moments before been a fourteen year-old boy, was now cruelly reduced to something barely recognizable as human.

Nora crumpled in the construction worker's strong arms, and screamed and screamed and screamed.

Red and blue police lights whirled as Kimberly leaned back against one of the four police cars that now filled the parking lot, staring at the roped off section of the sidewalk, now surrounded by a ring of gawping onlookers. Half an hour had passed since Tim had been crushed, but still people lingered around the accident site; passing shoppers and construction workers in red checked lumberjack jackets, and gray-suited employees from the office complex next door. Kimberly tried to ignore them, barely noticing the warmth of Officer Burke's arm draped around her shoulders, as he tried in vain to comfort her. Through the whirling fog of her shock and confusion, one thought stood out.

It was all true.

She had cheated Death, and now he was coming for her.

They really were all going to die.

She gazed numbly over at Nora as Officer Burke excused himself and went over to talk to her. The poor woman was standing beside an ambulance, staring in crazed grief as her son's remains were literally shoveled into an open body bag, just a few dozen feet away from her.

Kimberly watched as Officer Burke approached her. He touched her arm gently and began to speak, looking earnestly into her eyes. After a minute, Nora shook her head and, turning away from him, went back to staring at Tim's gruesome remains.

A moment later, Officer Burke was back at Kimberly's side. "It's no good. Nora's not coming," he said grimly. "She won't leave her son."

"But she's in danger! Didn't you tell her she's next?" Kimberly roused herself and started walking toward Nora, but Burke grabbed Kimberly's arm, holding her back. Their eyes met and the Officer shook his head, motioning in the direction of the grieving mother. Kimberly followed his gaze, and got his meaning at once. The coroner's men had finally succeeded in getting what was left of Tim into the body bag, and were transporting it over to the waiting ambulance. Nora stopped the gurney before it was loaded into the back of the vehicle, staring at the blue polyurethane shroud for a long moment before collapsing into tears again.

Officer Burke watched her quietly, feeling a chill pass through him. "Right now, I don't think she cares."

# TEN

Thomas Burke pulled his black SUV into the driveway of the Corman home and killed the engine. During the whole drive back from downtown, neither he nor Kimberly had said a word.

As the roar of the engine died away, Kimberly held up her hands and watched them tremble like those of the old woman she'd seen picking up cans from the side of the road the day before. She felt weirdly detached from her body, as if she was floating in the deadly black winds of her own oblivion. Her whole being was vibrating, from the top of her head to the tips of her shoes. "Look at me. I can't stop." She turned in her seat to fix Thomas with a look of utter despair. She'd stopped thinking of him as Officer Burke a while back. "This is really happening again, isn't it?"

It was a statement, not a question.

Thomas didn't need to reply. The look on his face said it all.

Kimberly took a shaky breath, realizing how keyed up she was. She turned back to stare out of the front windshield, clenching her fists in her lap. Her mind was fragmented, her entire worldview exploded, the pieces still drifting back downward, choking her thoughts like the clinging ash of a volcano. "I hoped we'd get there and they'd be okay... that Clear Rivers was full of shit and Evan's death was just a freak accident..." She turned frightened, liquid brown eyes up to Thomas. "But we're all going to die, aren't we?" Kimberly swallowed, feeling fear settle in the pit of her stomach like a ball of cold hard lead. "I'm so scared."

Thomas reached over and took one of her hands in his own, giving it a gentle, reassuring squeeze. Ever since he had saved her from the runaway semi back on the on-ramp, he'd felt an overwhelming sense of responsibility for her, as well as a great deal of gratitude. If she hadn't blocked the traffic like that, he knew that there was a good chance that he would've wound up among the dead in that pile-up.

Because of her, he was alive.

And because of him, so was she.

Now Death was out to get them, to fix both of those "mistakes." and there was nothing he could do to stop it.

His mind was still reeling from what had happened, but he knew he had to keep it together enough to help Kimberly. The last thing she needed was the big tough police officer falling apart on her too. "Look, I'm scared too, but you can use that fear. It'll sharpen your instincts. Maybe keep some of us alive."

Kimberly pulled her hand back, a look of consternation on her face. Thomas could easily see that the young girl before him was bewildered and distraught by all that had happened to her in the last twenty-four hours. She looked like she was on the verge of being completely overwhelmed. She was so young, and she had been through so much. He wished that he could help her, maybe take some of her pain away, but he knew that there was a limit to what he could do. He was just a traffic cop. How could he possibly help her?

"I know you didn't ask for any of this," he continued, trying to keep his voice as soothing as possible, "but I don't think you have it in you to quit, either."

Kimberly stared quietly ahead as Thomas spoke. Part of her was listening to what he had to say, but another part was silently raging at the unfairness of having to shoulder the weight of not only her world, but the worlds of so many others as well. She had saved the lives of seven people, and now, not more than forty-eight hours later, two of them were already dead. How many more would have to die before she figured out how to help them? Would they all end up locked away in the bowels of the Stonybrook Institution?

If not, how long would it be before they were all dead?

And what would happen to her? If Clear was right, she would be the last to die. So what, she was supposed to sit around and watch them all get picked off by Death, one by one, utterly powerless to do anything to help them? Did she have any control over her fate at all, or was it really all hopeless?

Kimberly had so many questions that she desperately needed answers, but for once in her life, she had nobody to turn to. She thought that she had never felt so alone.

As she wiped a stray teardrop from her eye, the vanity mirror on the passenger side sun visor abruptly dropped down, and she caught a brief glimpse of a shadowy figure moving behind the vehicle.

Kimberly jumped and then spun around in her seat just as Clear Rivers stepped into view from behind Thomas's car, dressed warmly in a fashionable brown leather jacket and jeans. Maybe it was simply that she was dressed in street clothes, as opposed to shapeless institutional-issue pajamas, but the young blonde woman seemed to possess a determined, powerful presence she had lacked earlier. The two women stared at one another for a long moment, before Clear's eyes flickered over to Thomas and then back to Kimberly.

"Clear, this is Thomas Burke," Kimberly said uneasily, tilting her head toward the police officer. "Thomas, I'd like you to meet Clear Rivers."

Clear nodded absently to Thomas, her attention still focused on Kimberly, her blue-eyed gaze as intense as a laser scalpel.

Kimberly looked Clear up and down guardedly, and realized that an explanation was required for her distressed condition. She took a deep breath to calm herself, trying to keep the barely-suppressed hostility and resentment out of her voice. "The second one just died: a thirteen year-old kid."

To her surprise, Clear simply folded her arms and nodded, completely unfazed. "I hope you're ready for this."

"Ready for what?" asked Thomas.

The Bludworth Funeral Home and Crematorium was a huge Gothic building made of ancient gray stone, located just outside Mount Abraham, New York. It sat brooding on the hill, watching over the town like a giant, sullen caretaker. It had taken them over an hour to drive there in Thomas's SUV, and by the time they arrived, the sun had long since set. The funeral home was located directly next to an old cemetery, which was already shrouded in a light mist, tinged a pale, shadowy blue by the rising moon. The parking lot was partially filled with a wide array of cars attending an evening cremation, most of which had placards on their dashboards that said in big block letters: "FUNERAL."

Clear was the first out of the vehicle, and motioned for the others to follow her around the side of the building, skirting the front door and the party of mourners milling about on the porch.

"It's this way."

Thomas dubiously eyed the moss-encrusted angels and obelisks that lined the pathway. Going with Kimberly to try to save Nora and Tim had been a big leap of faith for him, and now he was blindly following her and the Flight 180 girl to a cemetery to look for some guy who apparently had the inside scoop on all this Death stuff. Call him old-fashioned, but wasn't this fast getting to be more than a little unbelievable? He wasn't one to call it all bullshit, especially not after the experience he'd had last year and what he'd seen over the past two days, but still, he was more than a little wary of all this.

"How is this guy going to help us, anyway?" Thomas asked, following Clear as she left the paved pathway and struck out sure-footedly across the grass toward the back entrance to the crematorium. He wondered a little guiltily if this counted as trespassing.

"He seemed to know a hell of a lot more about death than he ever told us," Clear replied mysteriously.

The side entrance was accessible via a short set of worn granite steps that led down to a heavy oak door with thick metal hinges. It looked more like the portal to a medieval dungeon than the basement of a modern building.

Thomas gazed at it doubtfully as the three of them stood in a half circle before the door. "Should we knock?"

Clear glanced over her shoulder at Thomas as if he'd just asked the stupidest question in the world. "He probably already knows we're coming," she said darkly.

Thomas and Kimberly exchanged looks.

Clear yanked open the door, leaving Kimberly and Thomas to shift about uncomfortably at the top of the stairs before cautiously following after her.

They found themselves in a passageway that looked more like a tunnel than a corridor, as it appeared to have been carved out of natural rock. The rough-hewn walls were dirty and slick with moisture, and they could hear the echo of something dripping up ahead. There was an open doorway at the end of the corridor that was outlined by a flickering orange light, like that of an open flame.

Thomas thought that it was a little like being in a Freddy Kruger movie. All he needed now were some rusty copper pipes and the sound of a girl screaming, and he'd be done.

"This is cheery," Kimberly whispered over her shoulder to Thomas, who nodded his head vigorously in agreement, and went back to concentrating on not slipping on the damp, slick stone steps.

As they neared the doorway, the shadow of a man appeared on the wall, and then just as quickly disappeared, like a phantom in the darkness. Thomas's heart sped up, and he instinctively reached back under his brown suede jacket, brushing his fingers reassuringly across the hilt of the .45 revolver he kept in the rear holster fixed to his belt, even when he was off duty.

Just in case.

Marshalling their collective nerves, the trio stepped inside the room.

The first thing Thomas noticed was the oppressive heat. The room was sweltering hot, the far wall shimmering as though in a delirium of heat haze.

The second thing he noticed was a large stainless steel cremation system, which stood ten feet high, eight feet wide, and over twelve feet deep. The door to the cremator was open, and he saw what looked like a series of metal rollers, like the tray return cart at the police cafeteria. As he stared into the open furnace, the gas jets lining the walls of the cremator abruptly ignited and orange-yellow flames belched out, making them all flinch back as the blast of intense heat singed their faces. It takes a temperature of 2,500 degrees to incinerate a body, Thomas remembered, not from his police training, but from all those late nights he'd spent in front of the Discovery Channel, soothing the distress from his mind after an evening sweeping up bits of drunk drivers from the length and breadth of the freeway.

That wasn't an image he wanted in his mind right now. He quickly banished it.

At the far end of the room, next to an industrial galvanized double-sink, a large stainless steel door had been propped open. The light from the room beyond the steel door was reddish, and what looked like smoke or steam poured out into the cremation area. Clear stepped cautiously toward it, the spokesperson for their unauthorized party. As she approached, peering through the door, the mist parted and a metal gurney bearing a dead body emerged from the cold room.

Clear jumped back in horror, and then glanced around quickly to check that the others hadn't seen her freak. She was lucky. They were too busy freaking out themselves to have noticed.

Pushing the gurney was the man they had traveled so far to see. Mr Bludworth was an African-American male, well over six feet tall, with a long, lean face and tightly clipped hair. He had a high forehead, chiseled cheekbones and a wide, expressive mouth. He was dressed in a pair of dark gray overalls with a protective rubber apron over the top, as well as a pair of latex gloves. His eyes were so dark that they were almost black.

"Hello, Clear," the mortician said, favoring her with a grin that would put a skull to shame. "I've been expecting you."

With scarcely a glance at the group, he pushed the gurney into the room and wheeled it past them, stopping it directly in front of the yawning mouth of the fire pit. He locked down the brakes and punched a button beside the hatch, turning the flames up still higher.

Although she didn't want to look, Kimberly couldn't help but stare at the corpse on the gurney. She had never seen a dead body this close before. The body was that of a young man in his very early twenties with short blond hair. His skin was deathly white, and mottled dark veins stood out on the lower portion of his body, where his blood had congealed in his arteries. Except for the gaping, bloody hole, the size and shape of a soda can where his left eye used to be, he seemed otherwise unharmed. Kimberly blinked and moved around the gurney to look at the untouched side of the dead man's face. She recognized him instantly.

"Oh my God!" she gasped, putting a hand to her mouth.

Thomas stepped forward and looked over Kimberly's shoulder. He seemed equally surprised. "That's Evan Lewis!"

"Come to pick my brain?" Bludworth asked mildly as he turned to close the cold room's insulated door.

"Just a simple question and we'll leave you alone with your new friend," Clear said levelly, trying her best to control her disgust. The stiff on the trolley was wigging her out big time, and she wanted nothing more than to get some answers so she could be outta there. This setup was far too familiar to her for comfort, and after nearly a year locked in a padded cell, being paranoid about rusty staples in her magazines, getting this close to an open furnace and a disease-ridden corpse was pushing her nerves about as far as she wanted them to go.

As Bludworth walked around the gurney, releasing the clamps on the side, he paused to look down at Kimberly, frowning slightly as if there was something about her that was familiar. Kimberly drew back nervously as the mortician leaned in toward her and inhaled, as though drawing in the scent of her.

"Dead, but still *fresh*," he said with a humorless chuckle.

Kimberly shuddered and quickly looked away. The sooner they got what they needed from this creep, the sooner they could leave, and it couldn't be too soon, as far as she was concerned.

"Look, we drove a long way to get here," Clear said firmly, planting her hands on her hips. Even Kimberly could see that she meant business. "So if you know how to stop death, it sure would be swell if you told us."

Bludworth picked up a pair of pliers from a nearby table, shaking his head ruefully as he spoke. "For what purpose? You seek a back way out of a room with but one door. You can't cheat Death. There are no escapes."

"Bullshit!" Clear snapped back, her eyes flashing angrily. "You *told* me that Death has a distinct design, but Alex and I cheated Death not once, but *dozens* of times." She tilted her chin defiantly, her eyes flashing in the dim red light. "If the design is flawed, it can be beaten."

The mortician sighed as he clamped the pliers onto the surgical steel nipple ring piercing Evan Lewis's left nipple. He glanced up to make sure he had his audience's complete attention, and then yanked the ring off, along with Evan's nipple. He held up the pliers, turning them so that the overhead light bounced off the ring, before dropping the piece of body jewelry—along with the mangled nub of flesh it was still attached to—into a small steel bowl.

Kimberly closed her eyes, feeling a surge of nausea at the mortician's little display. Even Thomas turned his head in revulsion, but Clear remained unmoved. She simply stood and glowered at Bludworth, waiting for him to continue.

The mortician stared at the young woman in front of him for a long moment, and then a small smile cracked his lips. He reached out to cup her chin with the tip of his fingers. Clear jerked her head away, her control slipping at his touch. Unremitting hatred flashed briefly in her eyes before being quickly smothered. She took a firm step back, glaring at the mortician.

"There's such *fire* in you now!" Bludworth said with something resembling pride. "People are always most *alive* just before they die, don't you think?"

Without waiting for a reply, the mortician rolled the gurney over to the waiting cremator, and with a single push, sent the body of the late Evan Lewis sliding across the rollers into the machine's fiery heart. The smell of burning hair and sizzling fat was already filling the room as the mortician closed the insulated door to the cremator.

His point made, Bludworth pulled the latex gloves from his hands with a snap and started to stroll toward the door, whistling tunelessly to himself under his breath.

Kimberly's fists clenched in fear and anger. Without even looking at Thomas, she knew what he was thinking: how long would it be before the same fate befell them?

She pictured herself lying naked on that slab, Mr Bludworth staring down at her, pliers in hand, and something in her mind rebelled. As the mortician strolled past her, she forced herself to reach out and grab his arm, preventing him from leaving. Mr Bludworth froze and turned to look down at the dark-haired girl with something like contempt in his eyes, which quickly turned to amusement as he saw the desperate, fearful look on her face.

Kimberly dropped her gaze quickly as the creepy mortician guy turned to face her, his eyes narrowing like a rattlesnake coiling to strike. "Please. If there's anything that might help... What harm could it do?"

Mr Bludworth didn't reply right away, and Kimberly looked up at him to find him staring at her intently, unmoving. She swallowed, hoping against hope that she might somehow be able to reach whatever shred of humanity might still be alive within this strange and frightening man.

Then the corners of Bludworth's mouth twitched, and for a moment Kimberly was afraid he was going to laugh at her. Instead, his face seemed to momentarily soften, and something like kindness seemed to flicker deep within his eyes.

*"Solus novus anima licet evinco mortis,"* he said, in a deep, sepulchral voice.

Kimberly exchanged baffled looks with Thomas and Clear, both of whom shrugged.

Bludworth sighed and rolled his eyes. "Only new life can defeat Death," he translated.

"What the hell does that mean?" Thomas grunted, still staring at the closed door to the furnace.

Bludworth rocked back on his heels and took a deep breath, clearly irritated by the ignorance of his visitors. "Some say that there is a balance to everything, an equilibrium that is the connective tissue of the universe." He looked from one to the next, holding eye contact with each of them for long enough to cause discomfort, before moving on. "For every life there is a death, and for every death a life. The introduction of a life that was not meant to be, a soul forbidden to roam the earth... that could invalidate the list...and force Death to start anew."

"Is that why Death is working backward this time?" Kimberly asked, suddenly feeling brave.

The mortician stepped forward until he was looming directly over her. He sucked on a tooth, considering her question, and then let his hand drop to the necklace and the locket she wore round her neck, a Christmas gift from her mother.

Kimberly tensed uncomfortably as Mr Bludworth critically examined the locket, turning it back and forth as though he was debating over a purchase at a convenience store. He stroked his fingers possessively over the chain, his eyes gleaming oddly. "To figure that out, you'll have to follow the signs... Kimberly. But be warned. To disrupt the grand design is to unravel the tapestry of the universe. When you pull the threads apart, you may find yourself hanging from them."

Kimberly stepped away from him, profoundly unnerved. "How—how did you know my name?"

Bludworth shook his head and flashed a distinctly evil grin as he glanced down at the oversized, solid-gold Rolex encrusted with diamonds adorning his wrist. There were a couple of light scratches from the garbage disposal on the wristband, but otherwise it was as good as the day Evan Lewis bought it.

"Sorry," he said. "Time's up."

# ELEVEN

Clear watched cautiously as Thomas filled up his SUV at Kimberly's local gas station, her hand poised over the emergency shut-off switch the whole time. She had been outside of the safety of her cell for less than five hours, and already she was getting twitchy. She glanced toward the entrance of the store, nervously tapping her foot as she waited for Kimberly to return to the car. She had been in there for what Clear deemed to be an unnecessarily long period of time. She sucked in a breath of the cold, damp air, trying to keep calm, to keep her mind on the job.

Come on... Come on...

Losing patience, Clear stepped back as far as she dared, peering in through the plate glass window of the store, while keeping an eye out for passing cars or anything else in the vicinity that might be dangerous. She could clearly see Kimberly standing at the back of the store, dithering between two different types of soda at the drinks cabinet, completely unaware that she was being watched.

Clear snorted. What was the girl playing at? People's lives were at stake, including hers. She was supposed to be paying for gas, not shopping for snacks.

The sun stung her eyes, and she brought up a hand to wipe them. It was cold outside, and she wished she'd brought more clothes than the light jacket and cotton top she was wearing. She'd been indoors so long in her centrally heated box that she'd lost track of the seasons. She was painfully aware that she was back out in the real world again, the world she had tried so hard for so long to avoid. On every side she was surrounded by an impossible myriad of colors, smells, sights, sounds, tastes, sensations... a whole universe of sensory input that her danger-sensitized mind was currently trying in vain to process. Her head ached with the overload. It had been so long since she had been outside, the wind whipping her hair, the sunlight warming her skin. She wanted so badly to feel free.

Instead, she just felt dangerously exposed.

As Clear stepped back further from the gas pump, anxiously skirting a discarded and rusty thumbtack on the concrete floor, the doors finally opened and a couple of teenagers came bouncing out, dressed in baggy pants and oversized sweatshirts, custom skateboards tucked under their arms. Kimberly followed them, carrying a brown paper bag and giving them a cursory glance as she passed. Clear saw the younger kid glance appreciatively at Kimberly's backside and make a suggestive gesture to his two scraggy-haired friends. The three of them shared a laugh.

Some things never change, Clear thought, glaring at the kids.

"New life defeats Death? Follow the signs?" Thomas said sarcastically, as Kimberly rejoined the trio. "Where the hell did you find that guy?"

"Yeah, I thought he was supposed to be helpful, not freak us out," Kimberly agreed as she deposited her paper bag of supplies into the back seat and handed each of her companions a can of Red Bull.

Clear took the can without thinking and shook her head irritably. "He was. If we can use your ability to see the signs, we can cheat Death long enough to figure out what 'new life' means." She gave a small, humorless laugh as she saw the guarded looks on her companion's faces. "I know. It worries me that I understand him, too."

As Thomas topped off the tank, some gas spilled from the nozzle onto the ground as he returned the pump to its cradle. A moment later, one of the skate punks—a tall, skinny kid of about eighteen, with a backwards baseball cap on his head and a golden ring in one ear—strolled between the SUV and the pumps, a Camel clamped between his lips. He was absent-mindedly striking a Zippo lighter as he walked. His T-Shirt bore the words "NO FEAR." The slogan was surrounded by stylized leaping flames.

Without realizing it, all three exchanged quick glances. Before the kid could light the cigarette, Clear slapped him on the back of his head, rudely jolting him from his reverie.

"What the *fuck* are you thinking?" she snapped, gesturing at the gas pumps and the still-open gas tank on the SUV.

The teenager quickly glanced over at his buddies, who were looking at him with smirks on their faces, waiting to see how he responded, and then back at Clear. A slow, cocky grin spread across his face. "I'm thinking suck on my junk, bee-atch!" he replied, grabbing the crotch of his oversized pants.

"You little punk!" Clear gasped.

Thomas chuckled to himself, amused by Clear being taken down a peg. He looked over at Kimberly to share the joke, only to find her pale and glassy-eyed.

"Kimberly?"

Kimberly was no longer listening. Her legs buckled and she slumped back against the SUV, staring blindly at nothing as the images poured into her brain and rolled before her eyes.

*Hands... Bloody hands... A woman's hands... Clutching a steering wheel, but to what? A white van... A white van speeding out of control... There's a guardrail up ahead. A bruising jolt as the white van crashes through the rail and splashes down into a lake. Water! Water pouring in from everywhere! The van is sinking... with her still inside it. A shock of cold as water pours through the windows, the doors, filling the interior, rushing into her mouth as she screams and struggles to escape, smashing her bloody fists against the broken windshield. It's no good. The icy lake water swallows the van with frightening speed. The water closes over her head and she gasps reflexively from the cold. But there is no air, only cold, dark water, filling her lungs, drowning her...*

"Kimberly!"

Kimberly snapped back to reality with a jolt to find herself propped against the rear bumper of Thomas's car. She couldn't breathe. She doubled over, clutching her throat and gasping like a landed fish as her burning lungs kicked back to life and sucked in the cool, clear air.

"What is it?" Thomas asked, genuinely alarmed.

"What is it? What did you see?" Clear leaned forward urgently, staring hard into Kimberly's faced as if trying to see through her eyes and into her head. Kimberly struggled to speak, but all she could do was choke and gasp as if she'd just been pulled out of a swimming pool. She shook her head weakly, gesturing toward the road.

Clear felt her paranoia going into overdrive. This was no good. The girl had obviously just had a vision, just like Alex used to, which meant that they were probably all in danger, right now. She lurched to her feet and stared around them like a hyper-alert Doberman, scanning the perimeter of the gas stop for possible danger.

What she saw made her feel anything but safe. Directly across the street from the convenience store, a ConEd repairman in a cherry picker was repairing a transformer that was crackling like a Fourth of July sparkler, throwing sparks out in random bursts over passing cars, which slewed to avoid them. Clear flinched back as a red Corvette nearly rear-ended a silver Nissan, whose driver had been spooked by the sparks. Over to one side of the convenience store, a man in a red pickup truck was attempting to swap out propane tanks for his barbeque grill, and accidentally dropped one onto the pavement of the parking lot. Clear's panicked gaze swung around and she saw that, right next to the entrance of the parking lot, an employee was standing on a fifteen-foot ladder in order to change the gas price numbers on the store's signage. A young woman was coming up the sidewalk, walking a collection of dogs, ranging from a Great Dane to a Cairn terrier, all of whom seemed determined to run directly under the ladder.

A whole world of danger, surrounding her on all sides, pressing in on her as it closed in for the kill.

"You have to tell us *now*," Clear snapped, putting an urgent hand on Kimberly's shoulder.

"I... I..."

Clear grabbed Kimberly by the shoulders and gave her a hard shake. "You're strong, you hear me? Nothing scares you! Look at me! Now, what did you see?"

Kimberly took a deep breath and swallowed; she meekly met Clear's gaze and held it. "I-I was driving a white van, it must've gone out of control because it crashed into a lake and I... I drowned."

"You were *there*?" Thomas asked incredulously.

"I can practically taste the water in my mouth!" Kimberly ground out. She shook her head again, struggling to compose herself. "And there was something else... the smell of flowers."

"Then it wasn't just a sign," Clear said ominously.

"It was a premonition?" asked Kimberly, struggling to understand what was happening to her.

Thomas paced back and forth for a moment, his brow knitted. "Remember the on-ramp? There was a pregnant woman in a white delivery van."

"Holy shit!" said Clear, staring at him as she made the connection. "He said 'only new life can defeat death.' If she gives birth to a baby that was never meant to be born—a brand new soul that was never part of Death's Design..."

"It throws the entire list out of whack," Kimberly said as she straightened up, her own eyes beginning to gleam like Clear's, "and we all start over with a clean slate!"

The two girls stared at one another, feeling a connection spark between them for the first time.

"Come on, guys—that one seems like a reach, don't you think?" Thomas said, although it was clear from his tone of voice that he was already more than half convinced.

Clear spun to face him. "What else could it mean?"

"We need the pregnant lady's number," Kimberly said, feeling a surge of excitement flow through her. "We've got to warn her about the lake so she'll live long enough to have the baby!"

"Well, *that'll* be an easy conversation to have," Thomas said sarcastically. His half-smile suddenly disappeared and he struck the center of his forehead with his balled fist. "Shit! I don't have her number! She never came to the station."

"How are we going to find her? There must be *thousands* of white vans in this state," Clear groaned. Kimberly shook her head in despair. Then the two of them realized that Thomas was smiling. Wordlessly, they turned to stare at him.

"Hey," Thomas said with a crooked grin. "I'm a *cop*, remember?"

# TWELVE

Thomas sat at his workstation at the police station, Clear and Kimberly on either side of him as he searched the tape from his dash-mounted recorder on a VCR. He calmly scanned through the video footage of the crash from his patrol car camera.

"The tape hasn't been rewound since I filed my accident report," he explained. "We'll have to watch it in reverse, if that's okay."

He punched the control on the face of the VCR deck and the monitor suddenly jumped to life, showing the jack-knifed semi that had plowed into Kimberly's Tahoe. As they watched it suddenly righted itself in a burst of fire and leaped back out of the frame, leaving the red SUV unharmed and the three passengers inside it alive.

"Oh, God," Kimberly said as she stared at the image. She could clearly see Shaina and Dano's heads moving back and forth as they talked.

"Sorry," Thomas said as he quickly flicked off the monitor.

Kimberly took a deep breath and squared her shoulders. "No, I'm okay. Put it back on."

Thomas turned the monitor back on and Kimberly silently watched as the patrol car slowly crept its way backward up the on-ramp.

"There it is," said Kimberly, leaning forward to tap the image of the white delivery van as it appeared on the screen.

"Got it!" said Thomas. He hit the pause button as the cruiser moved back past the van. The freeze frame clearly showed the vehicle's license plate. "Jackpot!" he said with a grin, sliding his chair over to a nearby computer and typing the plate number into the DMV database.

The pause function on the VCR shut off and the tape began to roll once more. Kimberly could not help but stare at the monitor as the camera showed first Evan Lewis's Trans-Am, and then Nora Carpenter's Pacer. She could see the drivers of each vehicle in surprising detail. Although both Evan and Nora seemed irritated by the delay they were being forced to endure, neither seemed at all aware of the horrors that awaited them.

"What I don't understand is why everything is happening so fast," Clear said, puzzled. "After Flight 180, a month went by before anyone died, but now two people are dead in less than a day."

"Maybe Death is through fucking around," Kimberly replied with a shrug.

Clear visibly gulped, seeming to grow smaller as she turned her hunted eyes to the room around her. This was clearly not something she wanted to think about.

"Here we go," said Thomas as the computer pulled up the DMV's information on the vehicle. "With the plate number I can put out an APB. The vehicle is a delivery van registered to Marcus and Isabella Hudson." He scanned the files and gave a low whistle. "Christ! There are almost a dozen domestic disturbance complaints on those two! The last time she went to the hospital for a week."

Clear grabbed her jacket and stood up. "Then let's get outta here."

The outside of the Hudson house looked disconcertingly normal, given what they knew about the couple's violent history with the police. Kimberly had expected a trailer, maybe a shotgun shack, with broken-down cars in the front yard and a washing machine on the porch. Instead, their home was an impeccably kept two-bedroom Shaker with frilly curtains in the windows and nicely maintained rose bushes flanking the sides of the house. A blue Armed Response card was planted firmly in the neatly clipped grass of the front lawn. Although the white van was nowhere to be seen, there was a Toyota Camry parked in the driveway.

Thomas climbed the front stairs, followed by Clear and Kimberly. "Let's lay this on her gently. The stress alone could upset the pregnancy."

As he knocked on the door, they could hear the sound of a large dog barking inside the house. Thomas glanced at his wristwatch and knocked again, this time harder. There was still no reply. Glancing back at the others, Thomas was stepping forward to peer through the mottled glass of the side window, when—*slam!* The door flew open and a huge rottweiler lunged forward, foam dripping from its snapping jaws.

Kimberly and Clear jumped back in alarm, while Thomas instinctively reached for the gun holstered at his hip. Before he could draw, the massive animal gave a yelp as it was yanked back inside the house by its spiked collar. A pair of heavy boots clumped into the doorway, attached to a tall, heavyset, scowling man.

"Get back, damn it!" Marcus Hudson snarled at the dog, hurling it back into the hallway behind him. Marcus was in his late thirties, with dark, curly hair and a neatly trimmed goatee. He was dressed in nothing but a pair of slate-gray jogging pants, displaying his muscled, tattooed arms and barrel-like chest to their best advantage. He fixed the strangers on his front porch with eyes as dark and cold as those of a cobra. "What is it?"

Thomas cleared his throat and held up his badge so the other man could clearly see it. "I'm Officer Burke. I'm looking for an Isabella Hudson."

Upon seeing the stranger lift his arm to his owner, the rottweiler suddenly renewed its frenzied barking. Hudson turned and gave the dog an unexpectedly swift and vicious kick to the hindquarters. "Shut *up!*" he shouted, spittle flying from his mouth. The dog cowered in the face of its master's rage, backed off into the house and fearfully trotted away. Marcus turned back to the others, a barely-hidden sneer on his lips.

"Are you Marcus Hudson?"

"Maybe," sniffed the man, crossing his arms suspiciously. "What's this about?"

Thomas peered around Marcus into the house. "May we come in?"

"No." Marcus's stare got even colder. He gazed steadily back at Thomas, making it clear that he was not intimidated by the presence of a police officer on his front porch. "What's this about?" he repeated.

"It's about your wife, Isabella. Is she here?"

Hudson's eyes flickered behind him. Thomas looked over the other man's shoulders in time to see the figure of a blonde, naked woman, a bath towel clutched to her chest, hurrying toward the back of the house.

"No, and I'm a little busy, so if you could—"

"Look, pal," Thomas said, raising his voice slightly as he took a step forward. "It's probably nothing, but I need to see—"

Hudson moved to block the doorway. "Forget it. You'll need a warrant. I know; I'm a lawyer."

Clear bristled, incensed by the man's pompous tone. She shoved herself forward, getting between Thomas and Hudson. "Where's Isabella? Did you finally *kill* her, you fucking wife-beater?"

Marcus's eyes flared and he moved to shut the door, but Thomas had used Clear's distraction to wedge his foot in the jamb. The door thunked on the end of his steel-capped police-issue boot and rebounded. "We can do this here or at the station, makes no difference to me."

Marcus glowered for a moment, and sighed, letting his folded arms drop to his sides. Shooting a wary look at Clear, he turned to face Thomas, eyeballing him as though daring him to make a move. "Fuck it. We had a fight. Some things got broken. The dog went crazy. She left me. Wouldn't say where she was going."

"What was the fight about?" Thomas asked, pulling out a small notepad to write this down.

"Take a guess," Marcus replied acidly, flicking a glance over his shoulder.

"Does she have a cellphone? A way we can contact her?"

"Nope. She wasn't giving answers, and I wasn't asking questions."

"We're wasting time with this piece of shit!" Clear snapped, disgusted by the man's utter disregard for the whereabouts and wellbeing of his wife and unborn child. "Let's just get to the meeting." Impetuously, she turned her back on Marcus and flounced back down the steps toward the SUV, followed a moment later by Kimberly.

Thomas put away his notebook, and after fixing Marcus with a hard look, he turned to follow the two girls.

As Marcus began to close the door, he paused and shouted after the retreating trio. "Hey, when you find her, tell her the kid's half mine!"

Clear spun around and gave the man an angry middle finger. "Then I guess he's gonna be taking the short bus to school."

Hudson's face darkened with rage and he slammed the door shut. Somewhere in the house the dog was barking again.

"I said shut up!"

# THIRTEEN

Rory Cunningham held the key to his apartment up to his nose and gave a quick snort, inhaling the line of cocaine precariously balanced on top of the piece of metal. He wiped his nostrils free of any telltale residue, blinking as the hit buzzed its way up his nostrils, through the mucus membranes and into his bloodstream. If he was going to have to go to some pig's loft for a pow-wow, the least he could do was get a buzz on.

As he glanced around the foyer of the condo, he saw a man in his early thirties, dressed in a gray wool blazer and slacks, a newspaper folded under his arm, standing in front of the elevator. The elevator doors made a pinging sound as they opened, and the man with the newspaper stepped inside the waiting car. Rory sprinted after him, calling out as he ran.

"Hey! Hold the door!"

The doors were more than half-closed as Rory jumped between the safety bumpers into the elevator. The heavy sliding metal doors slid shut, clamping onto Rory's battered lace-up boot, trapping him with his right leg extended to one side. Instead of triggering the doors to reopen, however, the servos merely whined sullenly. A clicking sound came from the door's motor as the flywheel spun over, trying its best to close the door with Rory's foot still stuck in it.

"Hey! Let go of my shoe!" Rory yelled, hopping on one foot to maintain his balance. He pulled on his foot as hard as he could, but the elevator refused to relinquish its grip.

The man in the wool blazer hit the "doors open" button on the car station panel in an effort to help him, but to no effect.

"Gimme back my shoe!" Rory snarled as the elevator began to rise. As he yanked a second time, the laces on his boot came loose and sent both him and his footwear flying backward. Rory staggered slightly as he bent to pick up his boot, and peered down at it sadly.

"Jesus Christ! I wrote to management two weeks ago about these friggin' doors!" the man in the wool blazer said, smiling apologetically at Rory.

Rory ignored him, turning the shoe around in his hands, inspecting the tread. The hit was starting to kick in now, swamping his brain with a dizzying rush of pleasure. He blinked myopically at the man who had just said something to him, and turned his attention back to his shoe. He frowned at something wedged deep within the boot's waffled sole.

"Damn! Is that dog shit, dude?" Rory leaned forward unsteadily, thrusting the soiled boot into the other man's face so that it was less than an inch from his nose.

The man in the wool blazer recoiled, a look of polite revulsion on his face. This young man was obviously drunk, or on drugs, or possibly both. He turned away, discretely pressing the button to the next floor rather than the sixth floor, where he'd originally been heading. The last thing he wanted was to be vomited on by some junkie, right before going home to his wife. He'd never hear the end of it.

As he stood there, staring fixedly up at the ceiling, he felt the guy's eyes on him. He turned to see that the young man was openly staring at him, his pupils hugely dilated.

Definitely drugs, he decided to himself with a shudder.

Rory stared at the stiff in the suit, blinking furiously to crank him into focus. There was something weird on the dude's face. By his mouth there was a thing... A thing that wasn't supposed to be there.

It looked kind of silly.

Suppressing a sudden giggle, Rory cleared his throat; the noise sounding hugely amplified to his own ears, and he waved to the man to get his attention. His arms seemed to be moving in slow motion, like they were underwater or something, and he watched them for a moment with great interest before realizing that there was something he was supposed to be doing. He blinked again, a memory sparking in his brain, and he turned his attention back to Suit Guy, peering at him closely. "Um... you got a little somethin' on your face."

The man pulled a pained expression, and reached up to brush quickly at the corner of his mouth before turning away again.

Rory peered at him closely. Through his drug-fuelled haze, he saw that not only had the thing not gone, but it seemed to have grown. He shook his head determinedly, struggling to focus. "It's still there, bro. Here, I can get it for you." Rory noisily licked his fingers, finding his mouth on the third attempt, and reached toward the cowering man's face.

"No, it's all right." the man said with an unconvincing smile, pressing again at the next floor button.

Rory sighed to himself. *Jesus!* Some people were just so uptight! He shrugged to himself and shot the guy a quick glance. What was it? It was like... a bit of meat or something. This guy was about to go home to his family with half a fuckin' turkey stuck to his chops. Rory's mouth twitched as a second wave of hilarity swept through him, but he controlled it with an effort. They were in an elevator. It was rude to laugh at people when you were in an elevator. He had to be polite.

Trying again, he flashed Suit Guy his best polite look. It came out more like a lecherous leer. "I'll do it for you if you want me to," he persisted.

The man shrank away from him, glancing fixedly down at the elevator's progress button.

Rory sighed dramatically, and then paused as comprehension dawned. The guy was just trying to be polite too, right? He beamed at Suit Guy warmly, suddenly understanding what his deal was. "Just let me do it!" He licked his fingers noisily and stepped toward the man.

Just then the doors to the elevator slid open with a ding, and the man in the wool blazer gratefully hurried out.

"What?" Rory frowned as he slid his shoe back on, watching the other man speed-walk down the hall as fast as his legs could go. His wife was SO gonna yell at him for coming home with food on his face. It served him right. That's what he'd get for being so damn *polite*.

Rory grinned to himself as the doors slid shut.

Thomas Burke's apartment was a one-bedroom loft with natural brick walls and exposed wooden beams and lintels. It boasted a large central living area, with an ultra-modern kitchen in one corner, and an open stairway that led to a lofted work area. It was prime living space, and his measly salary barely covered it, but it wasn't like he had any other expenses. He didn't smoke, he didn't drink much, his car was leased to him from work, and, well, yeah. He had no other expenses. He lived a good, if dull, life.

Thomas stood in the kitchen area, surrounded by gleaming stainless steel fixtures, on the phone to his mobile call-out unit. He had called in several years' worth of favors on this little job, but considering what was at stake, he felt it was more than worth it. "Hey, man, how ya doing? Listen, any word on that white van yet?" He listened for a moment and sighed. "Okay... well, keep checking."

Hanging up the phone, he turned to look out at his assembled guests. Part of him felt a little weird at having so many people in his apartment, but he knew that this was a tactical necessity. There was nowhere else as safe as his place, and the last thing he wanted to do was to lose any more of his witnesses. Losing Nora's kid yesterday had been bad enough, but if he was going to keep the rest of them alive, he had a heck of a lot of talking to do. He hoped that they'd be receptive to what he had to say.

He ran a practiced eye over the group, trying to get a sense of their mood. The cokehead kid, Rory, had been the last to arrive, of course. He was now sprawled on the sofa next to Kat. Still clad in her top-dollar business suit, she was looking faintly disgusted and was trying to sit as far away from him as humanly possible. Next to her sat the hunched, rocking form of poor Mrs Carpenter, who looked positively shell-shocked, as well she should. She didn't seem to be paying attention to anyone, sitting there staring sightlessly at the small patch of carpet in front of her. Clear Rivers was pacing around the kitchen island like a hungry jungle cat, checking to make sure all the knives and other cooking utensils were safely stowed away, while Kimberly was seated in a leather easy chair in front of the group, her back to the flat-screen television set. The only member of the group that was keeping his distance was the schoolteacher, Eugene Hooper, who was leaning against the far wall, clearly trying to separate himself from the others as much as he could while still being in the same room.

"Does anyone have a valium?" asked Nora, her voice hoarse from hours of sobbing.

Kat opened her purse and pulled out a prescription pill bottle, shaking a single blue pill into the palm of her hand. "You'll want to take—"

Nora snatched the proffered medication up and popped it in her mouth, swallowing it dry.

"—half of that," Kat finished weakly.

In the corner of the room, Kimberly covered her ear with a hand as she listened to her silver cellphone. "I'm sorry, Dad... it's just that we're having a hard time with Shaina's eulogy. I'm just going to stay at Tonya's tonight and I'll see you tomorrow. I love you too."

She folded up her phone and returned it to her pocket, glancing grimly around the room at the assembled on-ramp survivors. This was important. She kept telling herself that she had no reason to feel guilty for lying to her father under these circumstances. If her dad knew the truth about what was going on, it would only frighten and worry him, and she had no desire to make things any harder for him than they already were.

Over on the sofa, Nora wiped her nose with the wadded ball of tissue she held clenched in her fist, and seemed to come back to life. Her red-eyed gaze focused in on Clear as she came back into the room and stood before the group, arms folded like a drill sergeant.

"If what you're saying is true," Nora said slowly, between sniffs, "that would mean... I'm next."

"This is crazy," Eugene interrupted, shaking his head in disgust. "First Death's stalking us, and now premonitions? Come *on,* people."

Clear shot Eugene a sharp look, and turned to speak to the distraught woman seated on the couch who, up until a few hours ago, had been the mother of a healthy, happy teenage boy. "You're not next, Nora. Nobody *has* to be next— that's the point. We need to help each other in order to get through this."

"This can't be happening," Kat said, the panic she was fighting to keep under control causing her voice to flutter. "My career's at a peak. I finally met a quality guy. I just bought a new house."

Nora turned to stare at her blankly. Judging by her expression, she thought that Kat's "quality guy" could go take a flying leap.

"So, maybe if you shut the fuck up you'll live, huh?" Rory muttered under his breath.

"Yeah, like I'm going to take advice from you," Kat retorted, giving him a disgusted look.

Nora stared down at the carpet again, fresh tears starting to well in her eyes.

Kimberly sighed and pushed herself out of the easy chair. "Look, as long as you know what to look for, you have a fighting chance." She picked up a small cardboard box and reached inside, pulling out a prepaid cellphone, which she handed to Nora. She repeated the same action with Kat and Rory, providing each of them with their own cellphone. She gazed down at the assembled group, looking them each in the eye in turn. "If I call you and say 'subway,' get to a high rise fast."

Rory looked at her, confused.

"A place where no subway could possibly go—get it?" Kimberly explained, rolling her eyes. She hoped that Thomas would have some luck in finding the white van soon, because if she ended up in a padded cell with this Rory guy, she might as well just shoot herself right now and be done with it.

On the outskirts of the city, Isabella Hudson scowled as blue cop lights suddenly appeared in her rearview mirror. What the hell? She glanced at her speedometer. She wasn't speeding, so what was going on? After everything that had happened to her today, did she have to be pulled over on the way to her sister's mountain cabin as well? Did the world really hate her that much?

The police car behind her let go with a menacing series of whoops, leaving her with no doubt that hers was the vehicle the cop was gunning for. Cursing under her breath, Isabella pulled the unmarked delivery van over to the shoulder of the road.

Deputy Steve Adams, a tall, square-faced man in his early thirties, stepped out of his patrol car and advanced on the white van, his gun holster unsnapped and a large flashlight held in his left hand. The plates of the van matched the APB for the stolen vehicle he'd received earlier in the evening. He approached the driver's window cautiously, and was surprised to find a heavily pregnant woman behind the wheel. Still, his years on the job had taught him that appearances were often deceiving, so he kept his gun hand close to his holstered weapon.

"I need you to step out of the car, ma'am."

"Are you *kidding* me?" Isabella groaned. "What did I do?"

"This vehicle has been reported as stolen, miss."

Isabella glared at the cop. She unfastened her seat belt and eased herself out of the driver's side door. Something told her that bastard Marcus probably had something to do with all this.

Back at Thomas's apartment, Clear stood up to address the group, strolling back and forth in front of them as she talked. "Remember, everyone, just because Kimberly's got the power doesn't mean we're not all capable of seeing signs to some extent."

There was a muffled cough from the corner. Clear raised an eyebrow and looked over to where Eugene was standing, shaking his head to himself.

"Sorry, but I gotta call bullshit on this," Eugene said, rolling his eyes in disbelief. He had endured enough foolishness for one night, if not for an entire lifetime, listening to these crazy bitches go on about Death and lists and the order of deaths, as if the Grim Reaper was not only a real person, but one afflicted with Obsessive Compulsive Disorder. "I've listened to all your arguments and theories, and its *all* bullshit."

"Call it what you want," Clear said. "But it'll keep your ass alive."

"My ass *is* alive!" Eugene snapped as he stood up from his seat and reached for his leather jacket. "And it has been *all day*. There's no one after us but you, trying to make us *all* crazy."

As Eugene picked up his jacket, the key ring for his motorcycle, the one shaped like a miniature billiard ball, fell from one of its pockets. Upon landing on the ground, the tiny replica thirteen-ball broke free and rolled across the loft's hardwood floor into the waiting jaws of a loaded mousetrap, which promptly snapped closed. The ball was sent sailing into the air—where it was soundly smacked by one of the spinning blades of the overhead ceiling fan, sending the orange-and-white striped sphere whizzing across the room, straight at Clear's head.

The young blonde, showing the instincts of a combat-hardened veteran, dropped to the floor as the ball whizzed by. The ball struck the pulley-and-winch system that held the young Police Officer's canoe suspended off the ground, balanced out of harm's way on an overhead beam. The pulley snapped as the ball ricocheted away, putting the full weight of the old-fashioned canoe onto the supporting brackets, which twisted downward and gave way. With a low groan, the heavy fiberglass canoe tipped off the beam and tumbled downward, only to be pulled up short about five feet above the ground as the rope it was tied to pulled tight. Kimberly screamed as the canoe swung down through the room in a tight arc like a pendulum, whistling past Clear's head, missing her by mere inches. There was a crash as the point of the canoe buried itself in the living room window.

In the ensuing stunned silence, the sound of broken glass tinkling on the ground outside seemed unnaturally loud.

"I should've seen that coming," Clear said dryly as she nonchalantly dusted herself off. Huddled on the sofa, Rory, Kat and Nora stared at her.

"Well, if death has got such a hard-on for you, maybe you should get the hell away from us," Eugene blurted, as Kimberly and Thomas moved to grab the fallen canoe and pull it out of the window before its rope gave way entirely.

"We *need* her!" Kimberly told him. "She's the only one who's dealt with this before!"

Clear glared at Eugene, and turned back to the three frightened people on the sofa. "We're going to have to look out for each other from now on. Sleep in shifts." Clear looked around the apartment, shaking her head in dismay. "And we have to danger-proof this deathtrap."

It was late. Nerves were starting to fray. Kat pulled a length of gray duct tape off its roll, tearing it free with her teeth, and slapped it across one of the wall outlets in the kitchen. As she tried to repeat her action, she accidentally folded the tape onto itself. She tried to pull the duct tape apart, but all it did was become even more snarled, sticking messily to her fingers. She yanked it off with a rip, and grimaced as she saw that the industrial-strength tape had pulled all the nail varnish off one of her newly French-manicured fingers.

Frustrated, Kat balled the tape up in her fist and hurled it irritably across the room. "Screw this. I'm going outside for a smoke."

"It's not safe out there," Thomas said as he removed a mirror from a nearby wall, placing it safely down on the floor ready to be put away.

"So? Nora's gonna bite it before me anyway, right?" said Kat with a small titter.

Thomas simply lifted an eyebrow at her and returned to what he was doing.

"God! You people have *no* sense of humor." Popping a cigarette into her mouth, Kat brushed past Thomas, heading for the door.

Nora sat on the sofa and numbly watched as the others busied themselves with making the loft area what Clear called "danger-proof.". The biker schoolteacher guy was pouring liquor down the drain. The young man in the dirty denim jacket who smelled bad and was in dire need of a haircut was putting a collection of kitchen knives into a shoebox. The brunette girl, Kimberly, the one who said she'd foreseen the accident on the freeway, was unscrewing light bulbs from all but one or two fixtures. Nora wondered if she should get up and help them, but she felt as if she was moving underwater and just didn't have the strength.

Maybe it was the Valium, or maybe it was just the sad truth of it all, but she really couldn't find it in herself to care much about dying right now. She looked down at the tiny teddy bear key ring she clutched in her left hand. Tim had given it to her as a Mother's Day present when he was ten years old. Back then her husband had been alive and healthy, and her family whole. It seemed like an impossibly long time ago now, like something she had read in a storybook instead of actually lived.

Closing her fist on the teddy bear, she picked up the cellphone Kimberly had given her and looked at it for a moment. She pursed her lips sadly and placed it aside on the end table. These people were asking her to believe the unbelievable at a time when she could barely remember her own name. Whatever the truth may be, she wasn't going to find it here. She'd had enough. It was time to go home.

Shouldering her purse, she stood up and moved unsteadily toward the door. As Nora struggled to put on her jacket, Kimberly stepped forward, a concerned look on her face as she eyed the bereaved mother. She looked pale and haggard, as though she was about to collapse, and Kimberly's heart went out to her. Her showing up at the meeting had been a big surprise, but now she could see that the woman was in definite need of some rest.

"Nora? You okay?" Kimberly asked gently.

Nora took a deep, shuddering breath, her eyes brimming with unshed tears. When she spoke, it sounded like the words were being dragged from the innermost depths of her soul. "Nearly three years ago, my husband died, and now Tim." She shook her head, glancing with empty eyes around the room. "There's nothing left for me."

Nora fought to put her arm through her jacket sleeve, but her hands were shaking so badly it took her several attempts. She was painfully aware that everyone in the room had stopped what they were doing to watch her.

"Don't say that. Once you lose hope, it's already too late," Kimberly insisted.

"If it's my time to go, to be in heaven with my family, then I can accept that," Nora said evenly, pulling her long braid out from the collar of her jacket so that it hung down her back. She dropped her gaze, staring blankly at the floor.

Kimberly reached out and touched her arm. "You can't give up! Trust me, we can fight this! If we stick together until that baby is born we can..."

Her voice tailed off as she saw the look on Nora's face. Even she could see that Nora wasn't buying it. She opened her mouth to argue, to try to reason with the woman, but Nora shook her head and held up her hand, silencing Kimberly's protests. "If you'll excuse me, I have a funeral to prepare for," she said tiredly, pushing past the younger woman.

As Nora headed toward the door, Eugene put aside what he was doing and moved to pick up his jacket, following Nora across the room.

"Hey! What do you think you're doing?" Kimberly asked, grabbing the schoolteacher's arm.

"I'm outta here." Eugene cocked his head at Clear, who was still hard at work in the bathroom, pouring Domestos down the drain. "I mean, why am I listening to a girl who just got out of the nut house?"

Kimberly stepped in front of Eugene, blocking his way to the door. "Seeing you die once was enough for me."

"Look, *I* control my life, not some crazy list that Death's put together," said Eugene with infuriating calmness.

"I'll be sure to carve that on your headstone," Clear remarked acidly from the bathroom.

"Whatever! Maybe you scare these people, but I'm not buying that shit!" Eugene shot back over his shoulder as he pulled on his jacket.

"Be careful, dude," Rory called after him.

As Eugene moved to leave, Thomas stepped out of the bathroom, where he had been helping Clear remove such potential dangers as prescription medicines and shaving equipment. "Eugene..."

"What?" the schoolteacher asked, no longer bothering to hide his exasperation.

"Even if *you* don't believe—give this to Nora," Thomas said, holding up a silver cellphone.

Eugene stared at Thomas for a moment, then snorted derisively and snatched the phone, dropping it into the pocket of his jacket. Goddamn crazy cop. Then he turned and opened the door of the apartment, ushering Nora out into the hallway. The door slammed behind him.

As the door swung shut, Rory broke the tense silence, as he removed Thomas's framed Police Academy diploma from its place of honor on the wall.

"Hey, dude—where you want this?" he called out to Thomas.

"Just put it in the closet," Thomas said, pointing toward the large walk-in just off the foyer.

Rory opened the closet and felt for the light switch inside the door. When the lights came on, Rory raised an eyebrow in bewilderment. Oh, man. Why me?

The closet was filled with an alarming number of potentially lethal items: a daunting jumble of sports and camping equipment, including kayak paddles, spiked metal soccer cleats, a hacksaw, a mountaineer's pickaxe and pitons, hockey skates, and, to top it all off, a bowling ball precariously balanced at the very edge of the upper shelf. Rory swallowed hard as he looked for a safe place to put the diploma tucked under his arm. It kind of figured that the cop would be a jock, but did he have to be such a fucking cliché about it?

Okay. Breathe. He was strong. It was just a closet. He could do this.

Wary of danger, Rory hugged the side of the closet as he bent over to place the diploma against the wall. As he did so, his butt knocked into an acoustic guitar, which scraped along the wall and slid to the floor with a loud twang. His nerves frayed to snapping point, Rory cried out and stumbled backward, accidentally knocking down the kayak paddle, which swung around and swept everything off the top shelf. Rory's eyes went wide with fear as he saw the entire pile coming down on top of him. Mindlessly, he flung himself backward, yelling in fright.

"Help! Help me!"

In his mind's eye he could see his throat being sliced open by the blades on the hockey skates, his eyes being gouged out by the soccer cleats, his skull crushed like a ripe melon by the bowling ball.

Rory fell backward out of the closet and onto his ass, landing in a screaming, thrashing heap on the floor. He flung his hands up to cover his head as a multitude of dark and spectacularly noisy objects tumbled down around him, waiting for the end...

Which never came. A couple of seconds ticked by, and then Rory screwed up his nerves and opened his eyes again, fully expecting to see blood and his own internal organs lying merrily strewn all over the hallway. His gaze ticked left, then right. Then he relaxed with a sigh. All that had fallen on him were several dozen wire coat hangers, three empty camping backpacks and a fallen volleyball trophy. He risked a peek into the closet and was relieved to see that the skates, cleats and bowling ball had all remained in their respective places. He was safe.

"Whoa," he breathed, unable to believe his good luck. He glanced up to see the rest of the room standing and staring at him, wondering what the hell he was yelling about. Kimberly stared at him accusingly, and rolled her eyes as she saw the mess he'd made.

"Sorry," Rory said lamely.

As he sat up, Rory's eye was drawn to the volleyball trophy, which was cast in the shape of a man with his hands held out, ready to return a serve. The trophy had landed upright and was surrounded by a jumble of wire coat hangers. The light from the closet shone through the jumble of items, throwing a weird shadow on the littered floor. Rory blinked dazedly, squinting down at it. Seen from this particular angle, the shadow looked like a surreal caricature of a man with hooks coming out of his hands.

Thomas approached Rory to help him up and noticed him staring owlishly at the floor as though hypnotized. He followed Rory's gaze, and frowned at the sight of the strange shadow.

Down on the floor, Rory felt a strange kind of panic shoot through him. That Clear girl was always going on about signs, wasn't she? Could this possibly be a sign? "Man with hooks. I see a man with hooks!" Rory looked around frantically, hoping someone would believe him. "Someone?"

"Yeah, yeah, I see it." Thomas agreed, tilting his head as he peered down at the shadow. Behind him, the others murmured in agreement.

"Is that a sign? Do you guys see that?" Now Rory was starting to scare himself, and his anxiety quickly transferred itself to the group. Kimberly turned to Clear, a look of sudden fear in her eyes as she made the next logical leap.

"Nora's going to be killed by a man with hooks!"

"Get the phone."

As Clear whirled and ran for the door, Thomas and Kimberly dashed for the telephone. Rory remained crouched on the floor, staring in dumbstruck horror at the twisted shadow before him.

Eugene pushed the call button on the elevator down the hall from Thomas's apartment and glanced over at Nora as she dabbed at her tear-swollen eyes with a wad of tissue. He wondered what in the name of hell had possessed him to attend such a loser-fest. It was bad enough those psycho bimbos were making everybody crazy, but to try and pull a guilt trip on this poor woman and attempt to talk her into postponing her own son's funeral? Man, that was as harsh as it was nuts. Even the cop seemed to be in on it. What kind of police officer would believe that kind of bull?

The elevator made a cheerful pinging noise as its doors slid open, revealing the car's sole occupant, a tall, gaunt, balding man dressed in a rust-colored polyester leisure suit. He was carrying a large wire basket filled with a selection of prosthetic arms. Some of the artificial limbs had rubbery-looking hands, while others boasted stainless steel hooks.

"Going down?" Eugene asked.

The gaunt man didn't reply, seemingly lost in a little reverie of his own.

Eugene and Nora exchanged looks and then stepped inside the elevator, turning their backs to the strange man and his even stranger cargo. Just as the doors to the elevator finally slid shut, Eugene thought he saw Clear running down the hall in their direction. He heaved a small sigh of relief as the elevator began to move downward. He'd had enough of that crazy chick to last a lifetime, and Nora certainly didn't need to hear any more of that foolishness.

Outside in the hallway, Clear arrived at the elevator just as the doors slammed closed.

"Shit!"

She slapped her hand on the Call button, hoping that the doors would reopen, but the elevator had already started its slow trip downward.

She glanced up at the flashing red numbers above the elevator, but it was already on the next floor. There was no time for this! Nora was in danger, and it was vital that they stopped her from leaving the building. She would head them off in the lobby.

Spinning on a dime, Clear hared back down the hallway and headed for the stairs.

Behind her, the call button glowed brightly, casting a red glow over the darkened hallway.

The elevator hummed as it made its way down past the fifth floor, then the fourth, then the third. Eugene idly lifted his eyes from the floor of the elevator to check out the concave mirror mounted in the upper corner of the car. As he did so, he could see the warped reflection of the gaunt man standing in the back of the elevator. As Eugene watched, the man glanced in his direction to make sure he wasn't looking. Then leaned forward and delicately sniffed Nora's braided hair, a perverse look of pleasure on his wrinkled face. Nora was still too distracted by her grief and the Valium she'd taken earlier to even notice.

Eugene looked over his shoulder and fixed the weirdo with a hard stare, clearing his throat pointedly. The gaunt man's eyes flew open and he quickly stepped back, shooting Eugene an affronted look as his cheeks flamed red with shame for having been caught in the act, whatever the hell that was. Eugene looked back over at Nora, but the poor woman seemed oblivious to her surroundings. He thought that it was probably just as well. She'd been through enough today without the added trauma of knowing she was getting perved on by some crusty old freak.

As the elevator reached the third floor, the cellphone Thomas had given to Eugene to give to Nora gave a sudden, piercing ring.

Startled, she dropped it to the floor.

As the phone continued to ring, Nora glanced apprehensively back at Eugene, then carefully knelt down to pick it up. She pressed it to her ear, tossing her braid back over her shoulder. There was a great deal of static on the line, but she could just make out Officer Burke's voice on the other end. "Hello? Officer Burke? I can't hear... what?"

"What is it? What's wrong?" Eugene asked anxiously, hovering behind her.

Nora could just make out the police officer's voice through the torrent of static.

"A man with hooks is going to kill you."

Nora's face turned gray. Slowly, she turned to stare at the clawed hooks of the prosthetic limbs in the basket the gaunt man was holding, mere inches from her face. An unholy terror filled her eyes as the cellphone slid from her suddenly numb fingers.

"Nora... Crrrrrrrrrkkkkkk... hello?"

Eugene grabbed the squawking cellphone from the elevator floor and put it to his ear, but all he could hear was a squeal of feedback and static. Whatever those douche-bags had said to

Nora, it had clearly upset her. Christ, how long were they gonna keep this up? He *knew* he should've thrown that phone in the can while he'd had the chance.

Before him, Nora slowly rose to her feet; her eyes squeezed shut as she mouthed the Lord's Prayer under her breath. Oh, dear God. It was all true! There was no way that Officer Burke could have known about the hook man before he called. It was all true, and now she was going to die, right here in this elevator.

Her grief-stricken lethargy seemed to shatter like ice and she felt her heart start to pound violently in her chest, almost choking her. All of a sudden she was gripped by a fierce resolve.

She didn't want to die.

She wanted to live!

As she stood up, shaking in panic, one of the hooks protruding from the basket snagged the end of her waist-length braid, just above the elastic hair-band that bound the separate sections together. Nora lurched forward, only to be brought up short like a dog on a leash, her head yanked backward by her captured braid.

"Let me go! Let me go!" Nora wailed frantically.

"Wait, Nora! Wait! You've caught your braid," Eugene said, trying to calm the panicking woman. He stepped forward to try and free Nora's hair from the stainless steel hook, only to collide with the old man, who was trying to do the same thing.

"Goodness gracious, darling!" the gaunt man said, his voice almost grandfatherly. "Let me help you with that."

"Stay away from me!" Nora screamed. She desperately spun around, flailing at the man in a vain bid to keep him away from her. In her mind he had grabbed her hair and was even now reaching into his pocket for a knife, ready to slit her throat. She had to get away from him.

*Ping!* The doors of the elevator opened onto the ground floor lobby. Nora gratefully lunged through the still-opening doors, desperate to escape the man with the hooks, but the prosthetic arm refused to relinquish its grip on her hair. Nora spun around on the end of her hair, reaching up to tug her braid away from the man, when...

*WHAM!* The elevator doors suddenly slammed shut on her neck. Nora yelled in pain and reached up to try to pull the doors apart, but to no avail. Although she was blocking the safety bumpers, the doors did not bounce back open, but remained clamped shut. Nora started choking as the heavy metal doors squeezed her neck in a grip like a boa constrictor's, trying their best to close with her head still inside the elevator.

Slowly, Nora started to strangle.

Having finished her cigarette, Kat strolled into the lobby from the street, where she was greeted by a very strange sight. Nora was standing outside the elevator leaning forward, with her head somehow caught in the doors. The older woman was screaming and sobbing at the top of her lungs.

What the...?

Kat dropped her bag and raced toward Nora.

Inside the elevator, Eugene leaned on the "Doors Open" button, only to have a shower of sparks arc out from inside the control panel, singeing his hand. He whipped it back in pain as though stung, and scrambled to help Nora, grabbing the edges of the door and heaving. The door-closing mechanism snarled and whirred as though chewing on Nora's head, the ancient motors unwilling to give up their prize.

"Oh, God! Get me out of this! Help!" Nora screamed as she clawed at the metal doors, digging deep gouges in the crumbling paintwork. She felt a sudden pain as the sharp edges of the steel doors cut into the delicate skin of her throat. She tried to pull them away from her neck, but her scrambling fingers couldn't get a grip on the slick metal.

There was another cheerful *ping* as the up button on the control panel suddenly lit up and the elevator began to rise. Someone had obviously pressed the call button on one of the floors above. Eugene watched in horror as Nora's head abruptly dropped to the level of the floor. He shouted incoherently as he pounded on the shorted out Emergency Stop button, trying to halt the car's relentless progress upwards.

Outside the elevator, Kat stared, dumbstruck, as Nora's wildly struggling body was lifted upward toward the ceiling, her kicking feet no longer touching the floor. While Kat had always prided herself on being a no-nonsense junior executive capable of thinking on her feet, nothing she had encountered in the business world had prepared her for something like this. As she stood there, frozen, the sound of running feet echoed in the hallway and Clear burst out of the stairwell door and ran to the elevator.

"Help me, damn it!" Clear yelled over her shoulder as she fought to pry to doors apart.

Kat came back to life with a jolt. She rushed forward and grabbed one of Nora's flailing legs, trying to pull her back down. The elevator lurched upward again as the car tried to ascend, only to jam again as Nora's struggling body hit the ceiling. There was a loud clanking sound as the ratchets on either side of the elevator's cable tightened, trying to draw the car upwards.

Inside the car, Nora looked pleadingly up at Eugene, as he pulled valiantly on one of the sliding metal doors in an attempt to open it wide enough for her to be freed. It was like trying to pull apart solid stone.

"I don't want to die," Nora moaned, blood starting to trickle from her mouth onto the floor of the elevator. Then her eyes flew open as the car jerked upwards another few inches, the elevator's motor growling under the strain. The trickle of blood coming from Nora's mouth became a flood of dark crimson as vital blood vessels inside her neck and throat burst, and her neck was further crushed between the floor of the elevator and the ceiling of the lobby.

Outside, Kat and Clear yelled in panic as the elevator jerked upward a third and final time, grabbing Nora's flailing legs to try to pull her out. Her head was right at the top of the doors, and the sounds of choking and frantic yelling came from the tiny slit of light at the top of the doors.

Suddenly, there was a loud, sickening crunch, like that of a stalk of celery being twisted apart, and Nora's body finally came free of the elevator, falling back so rapidly that Kat and Clear were knocked to the floor.

Kat hit the ground hard and rolled over, winding up facing away from the elevator. She could feel something warm on her face. Dazed, she opened her eyes and saw Nora's body lying on the lobby floor alongside her. The woman's arms and legs were still flailing, as if somehow trying to escape her fate, and geysers of bright red blood pumped from her neck. But there was something wrong here, something so fundamental it took Kat's stunned brain a second to fully comprehend what she was looking at.

Nora's head was missing.

Kat made a choking noise and scuttled away on her heels and the palms of her hands as fast as she could.

Inside the elevator, the gaunt man screamed like a high school girl as Eugene, spattered in blood, collapsed in the far corner, sobbing in terror as Nora's severed head rolled forward and rested against his foot, gazing up at him accusingly.

# FOURTEEN

Thomas slammed the phone down into its cradle, no longer bothering to hide his agitation. "Damn! It keeps going to voicemail!"

Rory was pacing back and forth behind him, his eyes bugging from his skull. "Oh shit, oh shit," he moaned as he chewed at his thumbnail. He really needed another hit right now, but was too terrified to leave the apartment.

They all jumped at the sound of the phone ringing. Thomas grabbed the receiver up, not bothering to check the caller ID. "Nora? Nora, is that you?"

Kimberly came up behind him and leaned in close, trying to hear what was coming in over the receiver. "Is she okay?"

Thomas motioned for Kimberly to be quiet, his brows knitted together as he listened intently.

"Okay... okay, thanks." He hung up and looked at the others, his eyes flashing with excitement and relief. "They found the van! Isabella's being held at the Greenwood Lake Sheriff's station."

Kimberly and Rory both let out their breath at the same time and exchanged glances, a hopeful look on their faces. Isabella was safe, which meant that they were, too.

Finally, things were looking up.

*KA-BOOM!* The door to Thomas's apartment suddenly flew open, rebounding noisily off its stopper. Eugene came staggering in, his eyes wild, ranting like a madman. "No escape my ass!" he howled, tears flowing down his cheeks. He barreled into Thomas's living room, staring around him wildly, and then spun around and shook his fist at the ceiling as though addressing an invisible tormenter. "*I* control my fate! I die on *my* terms, you hear me, you Grim Reaper cocksucker?"

Thomas glanced at the others and then cautiously approached the ranting schoolteacher, trying his best to regain control of the situation. As he got closer he saw what looked like fresh blood splashed across the other man's leather jacket. He recoiled, his heart starting to pound wildly. He didn't want to think about what that might mean. "What happened, Eugene?" he asked carefully, taking a step toward him.

With a sudden burst of energy, Eugene lunged forward and snatched Thomas's service revolver from the holster clipped in the small of his back.

Shaking violently, he smacked off the safety catch and straight-armed the gun, aiming the wavering tip directly at Thomas's head. "Back off! Back the *fuck* off!" he bawled.

Thomas immediately froze, holding his hands up.

"Whoa! Take it easy." yelped Rory. "What's wrong, man? Just tell us what happened."

"I ain't going out like that!" Eugene sobbed hysterically, waving the loaded gun wildly back and forth at the others.

Rory and Kimberly started slowly backing away from Eugene. Thomas stood completely still, holding his hands up, palms out. He tried not to let his own fear show in his voice as he addressed the crazed man, trying to keep him calm. "Just give me the gun, Eugene. Give me the gun."

"No! Fuck, no!"

"Eugene. Give me the gun."

A twisted, insane smile crossed Eugene's face and he turned the muzzle of the revolver away from the others and placed it to his own temple.

Rory quickly stepped forward, putting himself directly between Eugene and Thomas. "Chill, bro, this is me now. Don't do it, man. Don't do it."

"On MY terms!" Eugene howled at the ceiling.

"Eugene, don't do it!"

Eugene shook his head, tears squeezing out from his closed eyelids as he took a final breath and firmly pulled the trigger.

Kimberly screamed. Rory cowered. Thomas flinched, bracing himself for the sound of gunfire, followed by a shower of bone, blood and brains.

Instead, there was the hollow metallic sound of the firing hammer falling on an empty chamber.

*Click.*

Eugene's face crumpled as he found that he was still alive. Tears started to flow unchecked down his cheeks as he pulled the trigger again and again and again, each time rewarded with nothing but the sound of the pistol dry firing. He slumped to his knees, sobbing in frustration and fear, his burst of suicidal resolve exhausted.

Thomas quickly wrested the firearm from the shaken man while Rory knelt beside Eugene and put an arm around his trembling shoulders as he broke down in tears.

Kimberly breathed a sigh of relief, shaking her head in disbelief as she cautiously approached Thomas. "You don't keep it loaded?"

Thomas gave her a strange look and broke open the revolver with a twist of his wrist, exposing the cylinder full of copper-jacketed bullets. The silver center cap at the end of each bullet was dented, indicating that the hammer had struck each one in turn.

"They were all duds?" Rory said hopefully.

"Six in a row? Never, that's impossible!" Thomas breathed.

Eugene started to laugh hysterically between sobs.

"It wasn't his turn to die."

Kimberly, Thomas and the others turned to see Clear and Kat standing in the open door of the apartment. Clear stood with her arms folded, looking grim. Kat was standing with her arms held stiffly away from her body, white as a sheet and trembling uncontrollably. Both women were completely drenched in blood.

"Can we find the pregnant woman now, please?" Kat asked meekly.

# FIFTEEN

Since Greenwood Lake was several hours away, and only accessible via a two-lane highway that wound its way through the mountains, it was decided that they would sleep in shifts and leave come first light, rather than risk traveling at night, with all its associated hazards. Shortly after dawn, the six survivors left in Kat's Ford Expedition, with Kat behind the wheel and Thomas serving as her navigator. Kimberly, Eugene and Rory were packed three abreast into the back seat, while Clear rode in the cargo area, her legs folded into the lotus position as she looked out of the rear window, scanning their surroundings for signs of danger.

The early morning sunlight flickered through the trees as Kat's SUV roared down the road, tirelessly eating up mile after mile of wet asphalt.

The road was clear, the air cold and damp. They drove past miles of crisp green forest, the looming trees seeming unnaturally quiet for this time of day. There was no birdsong, no traffic noise, nothing but the purr of the Explorer's engine and the splash of its tires as it drove relentlessly onward toward their destination. The inside of the car was silent, each person alone with their own thoughts.

Clear sat calmly, gazing straight ahead. They were in uncharted territory now, making up their own history as they went along. The winds of Fate were behind them, and they were running with them rather than running from them. If Mr Bludworth was right about this "new life" thing, they should all be safe at this moment. She only hoped that Kimberly's premonition didn't come to pass before they reached Isabella.

Kimberly sat quietly next to Rory, trying to organize her thoughts and control the black pit of fear that had been in her from the minute she'd had her first premonition. It had been growing stronger by the minute since they had left the house, and now it was getting to a point where it was nearly unbearable. Back in the apartment, high on the knowledge that Isabella was safe and sound, making this trip had seemed so logical. Here, in the cramped confines of this steel and glass box hurtling along the road at eighty miles per hour, a full tank of gasoline sloshing around not more than three feet away from her, she was starting to doubt the sanity of their decision to go and see Isabella together. If something happened to the car or they crashed, they would all die at once, still all in the same order as they were originally "meant" to die, but perhaps seconds or even milliseconds apart. She wondered if it worked that way, and if so, what kind of a sick son of a bitch Death had to be to have come up with a design like that in the first place. Everyone died sooner or later. What possible difference could it make what order they died in?

Kat gripped the wheel tightly, chewing anxiously on the inside of her lip. She gazed out of the windshield, watching the road rush by in a series of streaked blurs, trying to concentrate on her breathing to calm her shattered nerves.

In... out...

In... and out...

In...

Oh, fuck it, who was she kidding? She had just seen a woman get her head pulled off by an elevator. She needed drugs, not freakin' yoga.

Thomas shifted in his seat, darting the occasional little glance into the rearview mirror at Clear, who appeared not to notice, preoccupied with her own thoughts, whatever they were. He felt kind of exhilarated, but also kind of scared. At first he had been a little unnerved by his readiness to believe Kimberly and Clear about all this premonition stuff, but after the events of the last two days had conclusively proven to him that there really was some kind of evil Grim Reaper mojo going on, he suddenly felt very afraid. If

Death really was out to get them, they needed cold hard facts and a carefully thought through plan of action. Right now, at best, they were working on guesswork, based on supposition, based on the word of a woman who had spent the last nine months locked up in a padded box in a loony bin. How safe could they really be when the very person who was purporting to be able to help them had voluntarily locked herself up in a Mental Asylum rather than do just what they were doing now? Why had she not gone to Mr Bludworth in the first place and found out about this "new life" thing before?

It made no sense. As a cop, Tomas needed sense.

Eugene tapped his fingers restlessly on his knee, beating out a nervous drum solo as the long minutes of silence ticked by. He didn't want to die. He didn't want to die. He didn't want to…

Rory wriggled deeper into his seat, thoroughly enjoying the feeling of being sandwiched next to Kimberly. True, she was kind of weird, but she was really warm and she smelt *so* good. He wondered vaguely if she would make out with him if they survived all this "Death" stuff.

As they left the city limits, Rory anxiously looked around the interior of the vehicle, voicing a concern he knew that they were all sharing. "Is this safe, guys? I mean, someone in this car is about to get whacked; do the rest of you *really* feel like sitting next to him? Or her?" He glanced over at Kimberly and pointed at the back of Kat's head. "Hopefully her," he mouthed in a stage whisper, and then grinned.

Kat caught Rory's little performance in the rearview mirror and favored him with a disdainful curl of her lip.

"Guys, let's not panic. Isabella's safe," Thomas said, using his best self-assured cop voice. He knew that eighty percent of what people heard when you spoke was not what you said, but how you said it. Using The Voice had kept accident victims calm, made criminals confess, and made ordinary people get the heck out of his way when he was in a hurry to get someplace, but right now he wished only that he felt as sure as he sounded.

"How do you know?" Kimberly asked. Judging by her tone of voice she really wanted to believe him, but was wary about getting her hopes up.

Thomas twisted around to look over his shoulder into the back seat and gave her a confident, reassuring smile. "You said she was going to drive into a lake, right? How can she when she's in protective custody?"

The floorboards creaked as Isabella paced back and forth inside the solitary holding cell at the Greenwood Lake sheriff's station. The three walls around her were fashioned from twelve-inch thick cinderblocks, while the fourth was composed of closely spaced metal bars painted institutional green. There were a couple of metal benches jutting from the wall that also served as beds and a seatless toilet with a cracked pedestal in the far corner.

It figured. This was just a perfect end to her day.

Isabella paused in her pacing to swear colorfully at the ceiling, and then resumed her impatient march. This was all Marcus's doing, she was sure of it. It was just like the narcissistic son of a bitch to accuse her of stealing the van. It was her van, for crying out loud. He might have bought it for her, but it was hers. She used it in her florist business—any one of her regular customers could testify to that. He wasn't satisfied with cheating on her while she was pregnant with his child. Oh no. He had to see to it that she ended up with an arrest record as well. No doubt he planned to use that against her in the divorce court. He'd made it clear as she stormed out of the house the other day that he sure as hell didn't intend to pay alimony, much less child support.

Isabella paused at the back of her cell, staring down at the warped metal bench. It was all so unfair! Her parents had warned her about Marcus, but she had been too much in love to hear what they were trying to say. Marcus might have been a handsome man and a promising law clerk when she'd first met him ten years ago, but he was also manipulative, controlling and incredibly self-centered. She'd caught him cheating on her before their marriage, but had chosen to look the other way. She thought that once they were married Marcus would settle down and become a good husband and father. Now she realized she had been kidding herself. Marcus was interested in one thing and one thing only: Marcus. All a wife was to him was someone to wash his clothes, clean his house, and tell him he was the greatest lover, smartest lawyer and handsomest man on the face of the Earth, twenty-four hours a day, three hundred and sixty five days a year.

True. She should've seen this coming. Most of her friends had, but she had always brushed aside their concerns, reassuring them that she was fine and that she was on top of the situation. The concerned comments had started when she had been a freshman in college, and had chosen to drop out in order to marry him. Over the years she had regularly bitched to her friends about how he used that fact to try and keep her down, often ridiculing her lack of higher education. Whenever they got into a dispute over finances—such as his spending too much of his paycheck on dinners for his clients—he would try to shut her up by calling her stupid and ignorant in the ways of the business world. And for the longest time she had allowed him to browbeat her into acquiescence.

Then her parents had died a few years back and left her and her sister with a sizeable inheritance. Isabella had ignored Marcus's complaints and used her half to start her flower shop. She had become moderately successful at it, too. Marcus resented her working outside the home and, more importantly, he resented her having something besides him in her life. That's when the calls to the police started becoming a regular part of their domestic life. The battles over money and her increasing independence of him had become more and more volatile over the years, until the night she found herself in the Emergency Room with a black eye and busted lip, and a police woman asking if she wanted to file charges against Marcus for Assault and Battery. She was tempted, but she also knew what that would do to Marcus professionally. First of all, he'd probably lose his job at the law firm, and she was in no position to try to support herself and a fledgling business.

After that, Marcus seemed to straighten up and fly right—or rather he gave the impression that that's what he was doing. When she found out she was pregnant, he was less than thrilled, but seemed at least willing to go along with it. Isabella knew that new fathers were often nervous about the idea of a baby, and then kicked into Super Dad overdrive once they held their child in their arms for the first time.

Now she realized that Marcus had simply been playing along in order to keep her from filing charges against him. What a sneaky, manipulative, two-faced bastard he was. He might have supplied the genetic material for the child she carried, but she would be damned if she was going to allow her baby to grow up around such a person. As far as she was concerned, Marcus Hudson was nothing more than a sperm donor. From here on in she would figure out how to survive on her own, without such a negative influence in her life. She owed that much to her baby. The last thing she wanted was for any child of hers to grow up like Marcus.

Glancing up, Isabella looked through the bars of the holding cell and saw the deputy who'd arrested her seated behind his desk, cleaning his service revolver with gun oil and a red felt rag. He was young, and looked kind of wet behind the ears. Maybe she could work the sympathy angle on him. It had to be worth a try. What else did she have to lose?

"Hey!" she said, approaching the cell door. "Look at me—does it look like I'm in any condition to commit grand theft auto? This is insane!"

Deputy Steve Adams turned his swivel-back chair to face his prisoner, swinging his gun in her direction. "Hopefully the district judge can straighten it all out by Monday morning." Dropping his head as though uncomfortable with the situation, he resumed cleaning his gun, polishing the barrel with an oily rag.

"Marcus!" Isabella said as she rested her forehead against the cool metal of the holding cell's bars. A very small ray of brightness began to shine through the seething red murk in her mind. The district judge was a woman, and based on what she had read about her, Isabella knew that she might have a very good chance of actually winning this case. All she had to do was to stand there on the plinth with one hand on her nine-months-pregnant belly and the other holding up a report card from the STD clinic, and her name was as good as cleared. "When I get outta here, I'm going to sue his cheating ass off!"

As she fumed over the injustice of it all, she was suddenly aware of a short, sharp twinge in her lower abdomen, followed immediately by warmth between her legs and the sound of fluid splashing onto the cell's concrete floor. As she stared at the mess covering her shoes, it took her a moment to realize what was happening.

"Oh my God!" she gasped.

"What? What now?" Deputy Adams groaned. He hated having to play jail keeper to yuppies from the city. They always acted as if the rules of law were written for everyone but themselves, and this woman was certainly no exception.

"My water—it just broke! I'm going to have my baby!"

Deputy Adams was out of his chair as fast if it had suddenly been set on fire. He stared at Isabella in horror. "No. No! Not here! You can not do this to me!"

"Don't just stand there—get me to a hospital!" Isabella shouted.

"Just give me a second to think!" Deputy Adams blurted, his mask of authority slipping to reveal a young man who was suddenly very much in over his head. Greenwood Lake was a small mountain community, so small, in fact, that there was only one police cruiser for the entire force—which consisted of himself and Sheriff Perry. Whenever one of them made an arrest, they would come back to the station to handle the booking while the other took the car and went back out on patrol. Right now, Sheriff Perry was out answering a report of a rabid raccoon going through the Hendersons' garbage cans.

Now this crazy lady was about to have her baby, right there in front of him, and he was stranded here with her, with no car and nobody to tell him what to do. So Deputy Adams did the only thing he could think of to do.

He started to panic.

Isabella grabbed the bars of the cell and pushed her face against them, baring her teeth in a fierce grimace as she spoke. "I'm not gonna have my baby in a jail cell. Get me to the hospital!"

The same thought was simultaneously occurring to Deputy Adams. Spinning around, he grabbed up the walkie-talkie from his desk and hit the send button. "Sheriff Perry this is Deputy Adams. Come back!" A look of mortal fear crossed his face as the walkie-talkie remained silent. "God. I *need* the car. Sheriff Perry, do you read?"

More silence. Perry was probably down at the Dog and Duck again, chatting with that bar girl. Goddamn him. He was always hanging around, snooping in his business until the one time he really, really needed to have him here. Oh, this was bad. This was very, very bad.

Adams hurled the walkie-talkie down in frustration and stared at his prisoner. She was doubled over, clutching at her stomach, obviously in some distress. Without the car, they were stuck here.

But what could he do? The station didn't even have hot running water, and the only towel in the building had been thrown out last Saturday after a drunken kid had thrown up in the cell and he'd used it to clean up. He had undergone first aid training as part of his job, but delivering a baby was a long way from splinting a broken finger or applying a tourniquet.

"My van! Take my van!" Isabella panted, pointing to the keys to her vehicle, which he had confiscated earlier and placed atop his desk.

"Right!" said Adams, grabbing the car keys with a gasp of relief. "Right, we'll go. Okay." He was saved. Thank Christ for that. Grabbing his jacket and gun, he snatched the cell keys off their hook and ran around to unlock the door and let Isabella out. "C'mon, let's go."

As Kat's SUV crossed the city limits border, the strip malls and gleaming plazas of the city and its surrounding suburbs had finally given way to rolling farmlands, horse farms, granaries and forested hills. As Kimberly looked out of the window at the picture-postcard farmhouses and dairy barns, she couldn't help but read menace into everything she saw, even the folksy signs advertising homemade fudge and natural apple cider at the roadside produce stands. She wondered how Clear was feeling right now, having lived with this feeling for a year. She'd been doing it for just three days, and already she was a nervous wreck.

Kimberly glanced quickly over her shoulder, pretending to be trying to read a sign that had just passed them, but really taking a quick, hard look at Clear. She was sitting calmly in the back of the SUV, gazing out of the window, her posture relaxed, but every particle of her being radiating alertness. She looked like a trained hunting dog, always on the alert even when she was supposedly resting. Her unblinking gaze was currently locked in on the flow of traffic behind them, on the lookout for anything that might resemble danger. The jut of her jaw and the tilt of her head indicated to Kimberly that should any driver behind them do anything as stupid as talk on their cellphone or try to change their radio station while driving, she would somehow make them regret it.

Kimberly turned back around and chewed on a fingernail. Clear may be a little abrasive and hard to get on with, but considering what she'd been through, somehow she couldn't find it in herself to blame her.

As the Ford Expedition rounded a bend in the narrow, winding road, Kat hissed in irritation. There was a large, slow-moving tractor directly ahead of them. Kat hit the gas and swung the wheel, passing the tractor on the shoulder. As they sped past the farmer, the SUV hit a large pothole. Unknown to anyone inside the Expedition, the force of the impact bent a piece of metal trim upward into the front driver's side wheel well, where its sharp metal edge proceeded to grind against the rubber of the tire.

Eugene had been staring out of the window at the passing scenery for some time. His fit of hysteria had passed and he now seemed almost preternaturally calm. When he finally elected to talk, his words broke the anxious silence like a gunshot.

"Wanna hear something crazy? This isn't the first time I've cheated death."

Everyone in the car turned their heads to listen to him, intrigued.

Eugene rubbed his forefinger on his upper lip, his gaze fixed on a point beyond the passing scenery outside his window. "Some punk kid brought a knife to school and killed his teacher," he said slowly. "Would've been me, but I got transferred to another school two days before."

"Fucking weird, man," Rory said, nodding his head in agreement.

"You want weird?" Thomas said, glancing in the rearview mirror at Rory. "Last year, my partner and I were heading out when a call comes in about a train wreck. Frank decides to let me handle it alone." Thomas paused, then sighed and went on. "He died that night in a shoot-out. If that call had come in just ten seconds later, I'd be dead too."

"Please. I got that beat," Kat said with a roll of her eyes, completely unaware of her utter lack of tact. "So, last May I was supposed to stay at this cheesy little bed and breakfast in Pennsylvania, right? Well, there was a major gas leak no one knew about and all the guests suffocated during the night."

"So what happened?" Eugene asked, not sure where all of this was going.

"Duh! I never made it! The bus I was on splattered some chick all over the road and we had to stop."

"Was that in Mount Abraham?" Clear interjected, suddenly sitting bolt upright.

"Yes," Kat replied, looking spooked. "How did you know that?"

"That bus you were on killed Terry Chaney. She was supposed to die on Flight 180."

Kat turned a little paler.

Eugene leaned forward, his eyes gleaming with sudden comprehension. "The teacher I replaced was Valerie Lewton at Mount Abraham. She died in an explosion."

Thomas turned around in his seat and stared at Clear. "Shit! The call about the train wreck that saved my life came in the night I scraped up Billy Hitchcock."

"Wait a minute—who are these people?" Rory asked, puzzled by the connections the others appeared to be making.

"The people who got off of Flight 180," Kimberly explained.

"They were my friends," Clear added quietly.

Deputy Adams sat behind the wheel of Isabella's white delivery van, speeding up the narrow winding road toward the Greenwood Lake Hospital. Isabella sat beside him, breathing Lamaze-style through clenched teeth. He still couldn't believe he was doing this. He was driving a vehicle that was reported as stolen, going over the speed limit to get this quite clearly insane woman to a hospital, leaving the main station unguarded and unmanned. He couldn't even begin to think about what Sheriff Perry was going to say when he got back from patrol in an hour and found the hastily posted note he'd taped to the window to explain why the station was closed in the middle of the day.

The white van's engine whined in protest as he urged it up a steep hill. There was a Volkswagen mini-bus chugging along ahead of them, which at this speed was about to be seriously in his way. Deputy Adams reached for the switch that would throw on his lights and siren, only to be reminded he was driving a civilian vehicle, not his police cruiser. He tried to pull around the laboring vehicle, but had to duck quickly back into his lane of traffic to avoid being struck by oncoming cars.

"Get around it!" Isabella growled between clenched teeth, squeezing the handle of the door hard enough to cause the plastic to crack audibly.

Deputy Adams took a deep breath, steeling himself to commit his fourth traffic offense in as many minutes, and then leaned on the horn as he floored the gas pedal, passing the VW on the shoulder.

It's an emergency. Keep telling yourself it's an emergency, he thought to himself.

Back in the Expedition, comprehension was beginning to steal over the group. Rory sat forward in his seat, waving his hands excitedly. "Remember that theater in Paris that collapsed last year, killing everyone inside?" he asked, his face lighting up. "I had tickets to go, but that night, I'm trippin' my brains out on acid, sippin' lattes and such, and I see this dude get *whacked* by a falling sign." He punched his open right palm with his balled-up fist for emphasis.

"That was Carter," Clear said, her eyes clouding as she remembered that night in Paris. It had been less than a year since that fateful night, but it might as well have been a lifetime ago.

Rory shook his head in amazement. "Freaked me out so bad I hid in a shopping cart for four hours. Course, I missed the show."

"What about you, Kimberly?" Clear said, trying to keep her voice as gentle as possible. Kimberly was the hub of all this. She had to have a story, too. "Tell us what happened."

Kimberly looked out at the horse farms and pastureland rolling past her window, and then dropped her gaze to the floor. She took a deep breath, as if preparing to push a heavy weight off her chest. When she finally spoke her voice was distant, measured, as though she was repeating something that even she knew sounded crazy.

"About a year ago, my mother and I went to the mall. I was supposed to meet her outside, but I got caught up watching some news report about some kid who committed suicide." She gave a small, sad smile. "I kept thinking, 'How can you strangle yourself in a bathtub? That's stupid.' It felt... wrong."

Thomas glanced over at Clear and mouthed the name "Todd?" Clear nodded, her face expressionless, as she continued to listen to Kimberly's story.

"There were gunshots outside and I ran…" Kimberly fell silent for a moment as she swallowed the lump that was forming in her throat. "Some kids tried to steal her car. She fought them off—she was a fighter—and they killed her." Kimberly turned to look at Clear, her eyes bright with unshed tears. "After the funeral, I had this feeling it should have been me. I figured that's how everyone must feel." Kimberly looked quickly away as her lower lip started to tremble, not wanting to show weakness to this tough, strong woman. "But I guess I was right."

Clear stared at the back of Kimberly's head for a long moment. Then reached over and took her hand, giving it a small squeeze.

Half a mile away, a young boy stood in the field at the bottom of a hill. Brian Gibbons was fifteen, American, and male. Therefore the last thing on earth he wanted to do was load bales of hay into the back of his family's pickup truck. He would much rather have been two townships over, hanging with his friends at the Stonecrest Mall, which was the only enclosed shopping environment in the county. While there was plenty to do at home, very little of it qualified as fun, as least not as far as Brian was concerned. At least at the mall they had a multiplex cinema, a food court and a skate shop, which was where he'd bought the black Limp Bizkit T-shirt he was wearing. His mom had bawled him out about wearing what she called "Gangster Rap" clothing around the house, despite his many patient attempts to explain to her that Gangsta Rap actually meant something else these days, but that hadn't put him off wearing it. If anything it had just made him more determined to pick up that Marilyn Manson baseball cap the next time he was there, just for the hell of it.

Although he had spent virtually all of his young life on the farm, Brian dreamed of one day getting to go to New York City. More than anything, he wanted to be able to go hang around outside the MTV studios and try to see famous rock stars and other celebrities go in and out, like they showed all the time on MTV and MTV2. Of course, his folks would have multiple fits if they knew that's what he wanted to do. They couldn't understand what he saw in the city. Their idea of a great time was going to church and attending ice cream socials with their blue-rinsed friends from the Book Club. They were constantly worried he was going to run off and get himself hooked on drugs, join a band like the ones he idolized, or catch a social disease. They couldn't figure out what he had to be bored about. After all, he had plenty of chores to keep him busy. And there was the lake with all its outdoor recreational and camping facilities, and the surrounding fields with all those great old trees to climb and barns to play in...

heck, Greenwood Lake was a perfect place to grow up in—a nice, sleepy, safe little town.

But, damn it, that was the problem. Nothing ever happened around here!

In the distance there was the quiet swish of an approaching car. Brian sighed to himself as he leaned on his hayfork and peered up the hill through the trees. Hey, there was a car coming! That was probably the most exciting thing that was going to happen all day.

With a sigh, Brian picked up his pitchfork and got back to work.

In the back of the Expedition, Clear looked at her fellow passengers, a light of new understanding in her eyes; suddenly the months of collecting news clippings, studying airliner seating schematics and poring over crime scene photos finally and unexpectedly paid off for her. She had always known there *had* to be a pattern. Just because she couldn't see it didn't mean it wasn't there. She thought that it was a bit like one of those Magic Pictures from kindergarten. At first glance it looked like a bunch of unrelated items jumbled together, but if you kept looking long enough, and hard enough, and from the right angles, you could see the wild animals hiding in the background. If you were too close or too far away, you couldn't see the big picture, but there had to be a pattern to it all. For it was the nature of chaos to produce patterns.

And what could be more natural than dying?

No, not dying, Death...

...Death himself.

Clear shifted in her seat, her eyes snapping back into focus with a new intensity. She panned her gaze back and forth between the other passengers, connecting with them each in turn. "When we got off Flight 180, it didn't just change our lives. It affected *everyone* and *everything* we've come into contact with ever since."

"I'm not sure I'm understanding you," Eugene frowned.

Clear turned to look at him. "Being alive after we were supposed to die caused an outward ripple—some kind of defect in Death's design."

Eugene nodded his head, his jaw dropping as he made the connection. "So if *you* had never gotten off the plane, none of *us* would be alive in the first place."

"*That's* why Death is working backward!" Clear said animatedly. "It's trying to tie up all the loose ends, sealing the rift once and for all."

A stunned silence once again fell over the passengers of the Expedition as they all processed this new information.

Thomas glanced over at Kat, who was biting her lip as she stared through the front windshield, blinking rapidly. She looked extremely nervous and more than a little exhausted, which didn't surprise him considering the day she'd just been through. She hadn't slept at all that night, endlessly chain-smoking hour after hour since she had emerged from the bathroom after showering to get Nora's blood out of her hair. He wondered if he should volunteer to take over the wheel. They weren't that far from their destination, and since he was the one with the police connections, it would probably look better if he was the one seen driving up to the sheriff's station. As it was, he was going to have a hell of a time explaining to all concerned why he'd put out an APB on a heavily pregnant woman.

Just then, the piece of trim that had been bent toward the wheel well sheared off a thick piece of its tread. The Expedition's front left tire blew out with a muffled bang, sending fragments of rubber flying everywhere.

Inside the car, Kat gave a surprised shriek as the entire SUV pulled hard to the left, spinning out of control and crossing into the oncoming lane of traffic—right toward the white delivery van that was flying up the road toward them, on a collision course.

# SIXTEEN

"Look out!"

In the cab of the white delivery van, Isabella screamed as a Ford Expedition suddenly swerved out of its lane directly toward them.

"Hang on!" Deputy Adams shouted. Gripping the wheel tightly, he jerked it to the left, narrowly avoiding the SUV.

Isabella screamed, more in pain than fear, as the van lurched off the edge of the asphalt and started jolting over the uneven, pitted ground of the grass siding. She was bounced up and down in the cab as the van's loose suspension dealt with several large potholes, and branches clattered across the windshield as the speeding van made short work of several waist-high saplings that had been planted along the edge of the road in an optimistic attempt to re-wood the area. But the officer held the van steady, and a moment later he eased off the gas and carefully nosed the vehicle back onto the road.

"We're okay, we're okay," The Deputy gasped, as he straightened out the wheel. He felt the van's tires grip the road soundly, and breathed a sigh of relief as he reached over to pat his passenger/prisoner reassuringly on her bulging belly.

Then he glanced into the rearview mirror and swore softly to himself. The same could not be said for the Expedition, which had sailed off the other side of the road, smashed through a split-rail fence and bulldozed its way into a nearby pasture.

Downshifting, Deputy Adams hit his blinker and slammed on the brakes, guiding the vehicle over to the side of the road. He stared into the rearview mirror, a sick look on his pale face.

Could this day possibly get any worse?

At the bottom of the hill, Brian Gibbons looked up at the sound of screeching tires—not an uncommon sound on the winding stretch of two-lane highway that bordered the family farm—and to his amazement saw a large sports utility vehicle barreling toward him at top speed. He barely had time to leap to safety as the Expedition plowed through the hay he had been loading into the pickup truck, sending bales flying in all directions like so many bowling pins.

Kat screamed at the top of her lungs as the vehicle continued its plunge down the side of the hilly pasture. As petite as she was, it was all she could do to keep the SUV upright. Her mouth dropped open as she saw a large propane tank looming in her path, and she yanked desperately on the wheel, seeing in her mind the car striking the tank and them all being burned alive as the resultant explosion ripped though the car.

"Oh, shit!"

Kat slammed on the brakes and the Expedition missed the propane tank by inches as it crashed instead through a temporary fence, smashing it to matchsticks. *Crump!* One of the wooden crossrails stabbed through the driver's side door, piercing the tough metal as easily as a pencil poking through a Styrofoam cup. The rail snapped off as the car continued on its way, its wheels slipping and spinning in the mud. Everyone in the car yelled in panic as the Expedition's momentum sent it careening toward a construction site, plowing past earth movers, crashing through irrigation ditches and pipes, all the while sending debris flying in its wake.

"Jesus Christ!"

A giant stack of sawn-off metal pipes loomed directly in their path. Kat closed her eyes and screamed again as she stood on the brakes and yanked as hard as she could on the steering wheel, sending the vehicle into a one hundred and eighty degree spin. The back of the Expedition slammed into a pile of rebar with finality, abruptly halting the car's progress and sending the longest bar of metal rocketing through the rear window. Miraculously, it missed Clear and

Rory before striking the front seat and bursting out through the front of Kat's headrest. It was lucky for her that the force of the impact had thrown her forward against the steering wheel, or the length of rebar would have punched its way through her skull as easily as it had the rear windshield.

The stack of pipes collapsed with a thunder of falling metal, strewing them liberally over the surrounding ground and piling them up against the back of the crashed SUV.

Up on the road above the hill, Deputy Adams stared in dismay at the distant wreckage of the silver Expedition in the van's rearview mirror, a sick look on his face. Oh man, he'd really done it this time. He could just imagine Officer Perry's joy at finally having a reason to fire him, besides his current and rather flimsy argument that he used the office computer to surf Internet porn whenever he wasn't in the office.

But damn it, it was not only his job, but also his nature to try to help others in such situations. Without thinking, Deputy Adams put the white van into park and reached for the handle of the door. Isabella reached over and grabbed his arm, squeezing until her knuckles turned white.

"Please! It's not going to wait!" she moaned, clutching at his shoulder.

"But I've got to go help those people!"

"Do you want to deliver this baby?" Isabella replied between gritted teeth.

Deputy Adams looked at the pregnant woman beside him, then back at the wreck in his rearview mirror. His brows knitted in an agony of indecision.

She had a point, and he very definitely had a problem.

At that moment, he saw red Volvo pull onto the shoulder by the crash site. A couple of people got out and hurried across the pasture toward the car.

"Those people can help," panted Isabella. "Let's go."

Deputy Adams breathed a secret sigh of relief and picked up his walkie-talkie. "Officer Adams reporting a vehicle collision off Nine A at the one-eighty mile marker, send all emergency vehicles to the scene."

"*Go!*" Isabella shouted as her voice rose into a scream with the first wave of contractions. "*Go!*"

"Okay! Okay!" the deputy said, throwing the van back into drive and stomping on the gas. He'd done all he could for the crash victims. Or so he hoped.

Glass tinkled and steam hissed as the inside of the crashed Expedition came slowly back to life.

"Is everybody alright?" Thomas asked, hauling himself upright and shakily turning to check on the others.

Kat slowly sat back up, dazed from being bounced against the steering column. As she did so, the back of her head grazed the two feet of snapped-off rebar jutting from her headrest. She froze, turning to look at it, then jerked away, crying out in horror at seeing how close she'd come to being impaled through the head. In the back seat, Rory held his trembling hands before his eyes as if amazed that he could still see them. Kimberly shook her hair, spilling busted safety glass onto the floor like dandruff.

In the back of the SUV, Clear looked around carefully, still dazed from the impact. Her eyes lit on the giant metal spike that had skewered the vehicle like a shish kebab and she swallowed carefully, unable to believe their luck that they were all still alive. If she and Rory had been sitting just four inches to the left and Kat hadn't been flung forward like that, Death could've easily taken out all three of them in one easy move. They were all unbelievably lucky to be alive.

Suddenly a bloody hand reached from the back of the vehicle, grabbing at Clear's shoulder. Clear spun around to see Eugene writhing around in the back seat, opening and closing his mouth like a landed fish. The schoolteacher clutched his ribcage and made a thick wheezing noise as a deep red stain slowly spread across his shirt, where a broken rib had pierced his skin.

"Oh my God. Eugene?"

"He can't breathe! He can't breathe!" Kimberly said, panicking.

"Help me get him out of the car," Thomas snapped.

Kat tried to move to open the driver's side door, and then winced in pain. "Oh, my leg!" she cried, as a sudden bolt of oddly numb pain shot through her. Looking down at her lap, she clapped her hand over her mouth, shocked to see a ten-inch thick wooden fence post protruding through the side of the car. It had punctured the door, shooting across the top of her left leg as neatly as a deadbolt. Although it had merely grazed her leg, the wooden shaft had effectively jammed the door shut and pinned her to her seat.

"Not my time. Amazing..." Kat whispered as she lowered her trembling hand from her face. She sat and watched helplessly as the others removed Eugene from the back of the Expedition and placed him gently on the ground next to the SUV.

"Take it easy now. Keep his head up." Thomas warned. The last thing he wanted was for Eugene to choke on his own blood before they could even get him to the hospital.

Rory nodded and took off his denim jacket, folding it into a pillow and placing it underneath Eugene's head. Eugene's face was gray from shock as he stared up into the cloud-filled sky, his breath coming in whistling gasps.

"I think his lung's collapsed," Kimberly said.

No shit, thought the ice-cold part of Eugene's mind that was still quietly, bizarrely logical. The rest of his mind was a white-noise scream of paralyzing fear as he felt his life draining away, drop by precious drop. His chest was in agony, and every breath was like a red-hot lance stabbing deep inside his body.

He didn't want to die. He didn't want to...

Clear looked up and saw a couple of men sprinting toward them from the direction of the road, as well as an older man dressed in dungarees and work boots who looked like he might be one of the construction workers. There was a gangly-looking teenage boy striding over in their direction, looking concerned.

"Is everyone all right?" one of the men yelled.

"Help! We need help over here! Call an ambulance!" Clear shouted back.

The guy in the work boots pulled out his phone and started dialing 911 as he ran.

Brian Gibbons skidded to a halt beside the crashed SUV and stared down at the bleeding man sprawled on the ground. He'd never seen anyone hurt and bleeding like that before, at least not in real life, anyway. He'd seen hundreds, if not thousands, of deaths and bloody injuries on television and in the movies, not to mention spectacularly wicked car wrecks, but it was totally different in person. For one thing, it was a lot more scary than exciting. The noise coming from the man's lungs were horrible, like a kind of wet rattle, as if he was drowning from the inside or something. He looked terrified. Brian unconsciously took a couple of steps backward, staring down at the man in fear.

"Hey, you! Kid! Help me!"

Brian whipped around in the direction of the voice and saw the woman who had been driving the Expedition. She was still sitting behind the wheel of her wrecked vehicle, trapped by a chunk of fence post that was sticking out of the side of her car. She waved frantically at him, signaling for him to come closer.

"I can't move my leg! You gotta get me out of here before this thing explodes!"

Brian's eyes widened at the mention of a possible explosion. Clicking over into Super-Sleuth mode, he sniffed the air and dropped down on his hands and knees, quickly scanning the ground underneath the SUV. In movies, cars always seemed to blow up the minute something went wrong, but he knew enough about automobiles to know most were better built than that.

"It's okay, lady," he said as he stood back up. "I don't smell gas. And none's dripping either."

"Okay, hurry! Get this thing off me; just pull it off, okay?" Kat said breathlessly, trying not to succumb to complete panic. "Be careful!"

The teenager stuck his head through the open driver's side window and peered down at the woman's trapped leg. He couldn't see any blood, which was something of a miracle, given how big the post was and how far it had gone inside the car, but that was cool, because now he could rescue the pretty woman and be a hero.

Reaching down, he took a firm grip on the post. Bracing his feet in the mud, he tugged with all his might. Kat immediately cried out in pain, swatting at her would-be rescuer.

"What the fuck are you doing, Jethro? I still need this foot, thank you!"

"I'm sorry!"

Brian stepped back, flustered by the lady lashing out at him when all he was doing was trying to help her. He'd always heard his father talk about how all big city people were rude. It had never occurred to him that his dad might actually have known what he was talking about.

Boy. That had to be a first.

"Dad!" he yelled, and then looked up at the sound of approaching sirens and heaved a sigh of relief. He was definitely out of his league here. Better to stand back, out of harm's way, and let the professionals take over.

A police cruiser left the road and bumped down the steep bank as Officer Adams's police backup arrived. Clear hovered nearby, watching anxiously as a pair of Emergency Medical Technicians quickly assessed Eugene's injuries. While one of them readied the gurney, the other placed a tube down the schoolteacher's throat and began manually working the respirator bag, forcing air into his deflated lungs.

"Get a move on! If this guy doesn't get on a respirator soon, he's not gonna make it!" the EMT yelled at the driver.

As the paramedics hurried Eugene toward the back of the waiting ambulance, Clear stepped forward, leaning in so that she could see her as she spoke. The EMT handling the manual respirator rolled his eyes in exasperation as Clear kept pace with the stretcher. Last thing he needed was some grief-crazed girlfriend getting in his way and cluttering up the place.

"Eugene, everything's going to be okay. I'm going to be right here! We're going to get you to the hospital," Clear reassured Eugene.

The paramedics loaded Eugene into the back of the ambulance, accidentally hitting his IV stand against one of the doors. Clear's eyes flashed in alarm. "Be careful with that! Check the gauges on the regulator and be mindful of overdoses. Oh, and watch for potholes and puddles!"

As Clear tried to climb inside the ambulance after Eugene, one of the paramedics pushed her back out. "You can't come in here, Miss!" he said firmly as he reached for the door handle.

"Look, I made him a promise…"

"And if you don't let me do my job, lady, he's dead, okay?" the EMT replied, slamming the ambulance door closed in her face, leaving her to stare at the "Lakeview Memorial Hospital" emblazoned across the back of the emergency vehicle.

Some thanks, she thought.

The ambulance's lights sprang to life, followed by the banshee wail of its siren as it sped off, spraying gravel as it left.

"Watch out for power lines!" Clear shouted hopefully after the retreating vehicle.

A rescue worker brushed by Clear, his biceps bulging as he carried the Jaws of Life toward the SUV. "Excuse me, ma'am—hot soup coming through," the firefighter said with a crooked grin. Clear raised an eyebrow at him.

As he passed by, the big hydraulic hose that connected the Jaws of Life to its power unit wrapped itself around Clear's leg. The hose tightened. Clear looked down and realized for the first time that she was surrounded on all sides by shards of broken glass and broken metal from the rebar and the pipes. A breeze kicked up, making the broken shards of pipe clatter together. Clear's heart sped up, and she quickly disentangled herself from the hose and walked briskly over to where Thomas was talking to some fellow law enforcement officers. She stood in the middle of the most inoffensive-looking patch of ground she could find, crossing her arms and shifting from foot to foot impatiently. The sooner they all got away from this death trap of a crash site, the better.

Over on the other side of the wrecked car, Brian stared as the firefighters and other emergency response techs bustled back and forth around the Expedition. The rude city lady behind the wheel was still stuck there, although the rescue response team was bringing out something that look like a giant pair of pliers attached to an air hose to try and force the door off its hinges.

Brian felt sick to his stomach, not from the sight of the blood so much as from feeling bad for wishing something exciting would happen to him. True, this *was* kind of exciting, but he'd been hoping for something good, like getting laid or going to a rock concert, not something bad, where people were all hurt and stuff. That was just typical of his luck lately.

Preoccupied with his own thoughts, Brian stepped out onto the dirt driveway that led from the main road to his family's farm, unaware of the WWED news van that was currently hurtling in the direction of the crash scene.

Suddenly he felt someone grab him by the back of his shirt and spin him around, off balance, throwing him to the ground. Something large and fast whizzed by.

"Watch it, dude!" Rory shouted as he yanked the boy out of the path of the speeding van, hitting the dirt with him a second later. A horn blared behind them as Rory scrambled to his feet, yanking Brian upright by the scruff of his neck. The kid was trembling and ashen-faced from his close call. "Are you tryin' to get yourself killed, little boy?"

"Uh, no... thanks," Brian mumbled, his cheeks flushing bright red.

"Use your head, little man," Rory said with a crooked smile, slapping the kid amiably on the shoulder.

Brian glanced up at the guy who had just saved his life, and risked a cautious grin. He was kind of cool-looking in a scruffy sorta way, like a guitarist from some indie rock band. He had a skull on his neck chain and everything. He felt pleased to have been saved by such a person. Wow, would he have some stories to tell the other kids in his class on Monday morning!

Brushing himself off, Brian nodded amiably to the guitarist dude as he turned and walked off, then turned to watch the news van that had nearly killed him as it tried to pull up alongside the wrecked SUV.

However, as it approached the scene, a State Trooper walked up, shaking his head, and sternly waved the van away. Annoyed, the driver of the WWED news van threw the vehicle into reverse and backed up until he was on the other side of a three-strand barbed wire fence that separated the Gibbons's pasture from the construction site for their new dairy barn. In doing so, the driver inadvertently backed over some large, sharp rocks, one of which punctured the van's gas tank.

Unseen by the camera crew, who were too busy scrambling to get their gear together in order to catch the action in time for the six o'clock news, gasoline started pouring out of the ruptured gas tank, slowly at first, and then faster as the settling weight of the news van sinking in the mud enlarged the hole. The coffee-colored gasoline poured over the rocks, then trickled down the hill onto a piece of old, rusty corrugated tin roof. Pooling at the bottom, the gas spread through the wet grass and trickled over the edge of a hillock into a broken length of PVC irrigation pipe unearthed by the Expedition's wild ride through the Gibbons' field. The flood of inflammable fluid ran under several hundred feet of loose dirt, before coming out just to one side of the wrecked Ford Expedition.

Still trapped in the driver's seat of the Ford, Kat feverishly dug through her purse, and then heaved a sigh of relief as her hands closed upon her cigarettes and her lighter. She knocked one of the smokes free of the pack and quickly lit it with trembling hands. She took a deep breath, savoring the taste of the tobacco.

God, she was a wreck! Normally Kat prided herself on being pretty together, but the events of the last couple of days had really done a number on her nerves. While she had a reputation for being a cut-throat competitor in the boardroom, the metaphorical blood spilled in the office cubicles where she worked was nothing like what she had seen spurting from poor Nora's neck as she'd flopped about on the floor like a fish. Oh, God—she could still smell it on her clothes and in her hair and on her hands and...

She closed her eyes and tried to push the image of Nora's headless body out of her mind. Things were bad enough already. She didn't need to make them worse by working herself up. She was a strong woman. She'd had to be to get where she'd gotten in a man's world. Sure, a lot of people saw her as a bitch—including most of the on-ramp survivors she was now stuck hanging around with—but she preferred to think of herself as tough-willed and unafraid to speak her mind. It was not in her nature to back down when confronted with problems, whether it was in her professional or private life. She was determined to get over on this Death thing, somehow. She'd dealt with hostile takeovers and backstabbing office personnel before, and she'd be damned if something as stupid as a curse was going to interfere with her plans.

After all, she was on the fast track, with everything to live for. She was up for a promotion at work, she'd just finished closing on a nice two bedroom Tudor in a Toney suburb, and she was dating a guy who looked like he might actually be worth settling down with. If she played her cards right, she might even have time to knock out a couple of kids before the biological clock stopped ticking. At least that would get her mother off her back. A career, a house, a husband and kids was all she really wanted, and she was so close, so very close to finally having it all. Was that really too much to ask for? Life owed her that much at least.

She took a long drag on her cigarette, watching the embers burn cherry red. As soon as she was out of this car, she could really start living again.

Kimberly, Clear and Rory stood at a safe distance and watched as the rescue personnel used the Jaws of Life to try to pry open Kat's door.

Kimberly peeled off from the group and moved in to talk to Kat, "You doing all right in there?"

Kat grimaced as she lit a new cigarette off the smoldering butt of her old one. "My legs are starting to cramp up. And God, why am I so thirsty? Does anyone have any bottled water?"

"I'll go ask."

As Kimberly trotted off, the rescue worker kneeling beside the driver's side door fired up the Jaws of Life, which roared like a chainsaw, and wedged the spreader's tip in the space between the hinge and the body of the car. There was a loud *ka-chunk* as the extrication tool began bending the jammed metal backward.

Kat flinched; her head already throbbed from banging it against the dashboard, and the noise made by the hydraulic machine was making her headache even worse. "Christ! You wanna give me a heads-up next time, pal?" she snapped.

Moments later, Brian and his father, the older man in work clothes who had come from the direction of the construction site, approached the Expedition. Mr Gibbons held a dented tin cup full of tap water in one hand.

"Here you go, ma'am," he said, leaning into the car in order to pass the water to Kat.

Kat took the offered water and sniffed it suspiciously, a scowl on her face. God, she hated being stuck in the boonies. She glanced up at the farmer and his son, who were watching her from across the dented hood of her car, and raised the tin cup in a mocking salute before drinking it.

Over by the parked police cruisers, Kimberly was standing by herself, her arms crossed over her chest, watching the rescue workers as they attempted to extricate Kat from the remains of her SUV. She was dimly aware of Rory hanging on the periphery of her vision, but was too focused on what was going on in front of her to pay him much attention. As it was, most of what he'd said to her up 'til this point consisted of callous jokes at someone else's expense or drug-related humor. In a way, he reminded her of a far grungier, more burned-out version of Dano. Maybe that's why she tried to ignore him whenever she could.

Rory cleared his throat and coughed into his fist, forcing Kimberly to look in his direction.

"Is—is she gonna be okay?" he asked, nodding in the direction of Kat.

"Yeah, I think so," Kimberly replied distractedly, without taking her eyes off the Expedition.

"Can I ask you a question?" Rory's demeanor was unusually serious.

Kimberly glanced up at him and saw that sweat was running down his face. "Sure."

"When I die... is it gonna hurt?" asked Rory, a pleading look on his face.

Kimberly was taken aback, surprised by the vulnerability she saw in Rory's eyes. She turned to look at him properly, watching as he stood and twitched and sniffed, his unwashed hair hanging down in greasy ringlets around his face. He actually wasn't that bad looking, she thought, if only he would get a haircut and a shave, and maybe take a shower every once in a while. Right at that moment he needed some kind of reassurance, if only the promise of a swift and painless death. It broke her heart that she had no comforting words to offer the guy. She could tell him a lie, but this was his own death they were talking about here. It wouldn't be right for her to bullshit him over this.

"I... I don't know," she said softly.

Rory swallowed hard and dropped his gaze to the ground as he nodded his understanding. A beat went by as they both watched the emergency rescue workers fussing around Kat. Then Rory reached into the front pocket of his jeans and fished out his driver's license and the keys to his apartment. He stared at them for a moment, and then looked back up at Kimberly.

"And you're gonna die after me, right?"

"I guess so," Kimberly shrugged, not sure where he was going with his line of questioning. Her own voice rang in her ears, and she swallowed and felt goose bumps break out all over her at the thought of what she had just said.

She was going to die...

"Would you take these?" Rory asked, handing her his keys. "And if I die..." Tears welled up in his eyes and he had to swallow what felt like a golf ball wedged in his throat in order to continue. "Could you throw all my drugs out? Paraphernalia, porno, you know... anything that would break my mom's heart."

Kimberly gave Rory a guarded look, waiting for the wisecrack or the sneer that was so much a part of his character, but all she saw in his eyes was tired resignation. For once in Rory's life, he was being serious.

"Please?" Rory added.

She gazed at him wordlessly for a long moment. She nodded silently and closed her fingers around the keys and the driver's license, transferring them to her jacket pocket.

The two of them stood side by side in companionable silence, watching the rescue workers cut Kat out of the SUV.

Rory took a deep breath and blew it back out through his teeth, relieved to have at least one worry taken off his shoulders. He stuck his hand into his other pocket, only to frown as his fingers brushed against something smooth and cylindrical in shape. He pulled it out and stared down at the half-empty vial of coke lying in his cupped palm. He smiled sadly, and then glanced around. If he was going to die soon anyway, what the hell difference did it make? All he needed was a little privacy... like that pasture on the other side of the barbed wire fence, just beyond the dead oak tree.

Nodding a goodbye to Kimberly, Rory set out across the field.

Kat was on her fourth cigarette and counting. The ear-splitting racket created by the Jaws of Life made her jump yet again, this time hard enough for her to lose her grip on her cigarette. It dropped to the floor of the vehicle and rolled onto the mat.

"Damn, can't you be quieter with that thing?" she hissed as she replaced her dropped smoke with yet another cigarette, squinting down past the log to awkwardly stamp out the fallen cigarette with the one leg that hadn't yet gone completely numb.

"Sure, I'll just set it to 'quiet' mode," the rescue worker grinned.

"Yeah, thanks, that'd be nice," said Kimberly, completely missing his sarcasm as she pulled her cellphone out of her belt-clip to check the time.

As she peered down at the dial, there was another loud *ka-chunk* as the rescue worker slammed the Jaws of Life into the side of the car again. Kat jumped in her seat yet again, but managed to maintain her composure, shooting the worker a filthy glare. He responded with a wink and a saucy grin. Kat looked at him again, automatically checking him off on her points system. Blue eyes, good skin, great smile, fit bod... Hey, he was actually kinda cute.

Maybe her day was looking up, after all.

Ten feet from her, Thomas paced back and forth, anxiously eyeing his watch. Every minute they were delayed here meant Isabella Hudson had time to slip out of their grasp. All it would take would be for her to post bail, and it would be beyond his power to track her down before it was too late.

They *had* to keep Isabella safe. It didn't even occur to him to question all this any more. This was his life now—finding out about and cracking this Flight 180 "curse" thing. He would worry about little things like the total disruption of his worldview later, when they'd saved Isabella and he had time to sit down and think things through a bit.

Making a snap decision, Thomas flipped open his cellphone and called the Lake Greenwood sheriff's station to make sure Isabella was still in custody.

"Sheriff Perry? Officer Burke here, I'm trying to get some information on Isabella Hudson..." A look of alarm came over his face as he listened to the Sheriff's response. "She did? Okay. Thanks."

He snapped his phone shut and ran to where Kimberly and Clear were standing, watching Kat's rescue operation. "Isabella's at Lakeview Memorial just down the road! They're prepping her for delivery! We gotta go now!"

The girls exchanged wary looks.

"What about Kat?" Kimberly asked.

"I'll go check," Clear said, sprinting toward the SUV.

Kat was still chain smoking, a worried look on her face that was only slightly softened by the great view of the cute rescue worker's ass she was getting by leaning forward in her seat to watch him work on the door. Rather than pull the fence post out—along with all the skin off the top of her legs—the theory seemed to be to remove the door and lift the whole lot up off her. She liked that plan very much, but it was just taking so freakin' long.

"How're you doing over here, hero?" Clear asked, trying to sound as upbeat as she could. She'd heard that was a good thing to be around accident victims.

"I could be worse," Kat said, gesturing to the rebar behind her head with her cigarette. "Just find Isabella and end this thing, okay?"

"Are you sure?"

"Yeah, go on. I'll be fine," Kat said with a weak smile that suggested she didn't believe a word she'd just said.

Thomas stepped up behind her. "Let's go. Where the hell is Rory?"

As he scanned the area, he could see the cokehead standing in a field several hundred yards away, on the other side of a barbed wire fence. Damn it. Leave it to that drug-addled burnout to go wandering off. This was more precious time that none of them could afford to be wasting right now. Thomas pocketed his cellphone and began striding purposefully in the direction of the dead oak tree Rory was standing behind.

It wasn't supposed to end this way.

Rory looked around him at the empty, windswept pastureland. He sniffed and nodded to himself in weary resignation. He wasn't exactly sure how he had planned his life to end, but he was pretty sure it involved being old and in a bed somewhere. Or young and in a bed somewhere surrounded by dozens of beautiful naked women, too blissed-out to notice that the cyanide his twelfth ex-wife had slipped into his double mocha decaff that morning was finally taking effect.

That would've been cool with him.

Then again, nothing else had gone to plan, so he really shouldn't be surprised that his death was to be as fucked up as the rest of his life.

Back when he was a kid, he'd figured that he'd be a famous rock star by now. He'd left home for the big city with every intention of making it big as a musician. He was going to be the next Kurt Cobain, dude! Nothing was going to stop him.

Nothing, it turned out, but himself.

So here he was, ten years later, and the only thing he had in common with Cobain was a monumentally dumb and freakishly expensive drug habit. Getting into a band had been easy enough, but actually getting anywhere had proven far more difficult than he'd ever imagined. After a few years, several failed bands and several dozen failed relationships, he'd learned that it was easier to party like a rock star than to actually be one. Somewhere along the line, he wasn't exactly sure when, the partying had become more important than the music. He couldn't remember the last time he'd actually played guitar. Not that it mattered, since he'd hocked his Stratocaster to get cash for some blow some time back and his smackhead ex-roommate had stolen his Randell amp.

Now here he was—standing in some hick's forty acre field, in the ass-crack of nowhere, stuck with a bunch of straights and suits, waiting for his number to come up. He probably wasn't even going to get the chance to tell his mom or anyone else that mattered to him goodbye and that he loved them, and that he was sorry for being such a sorry-ass fuck-up.

Rory sighed and shrugged to himself. Screw it all. Maybe the next life would be better.

And in the meantime…

Making sure he had his back turned to the group gathered around the SUV, Rory opened the vial of cocaine, delicately tapping some onto the back of his hand. Shit, since he was probably going to bite the big one soon, he might as well make sure he wasn't feeling any pain when it happened. If nothing else, he definitely needed some help pulling himself together.

On the other side of the barbed-wire fence, Kimberly lifted her head as a strong breeze blew past her, ruffling her hair. As she looked around, her gaze fell on the side passenger window of one of the nearby emergency response vehicles. In its reflective surface she saw what looked like a man dressed in dungarees sitting on the hood of the Expedition, mopping his brow with a blood-red handkerchief. Kimberly frowned and turned back around to face the SUV-only to discover that no one was anywhere near the hood of the vehicle.

That was weird.

Right at that moment there was a final ka-chunk as the driver's side door was pulled off its hinges. A couple of firemen hurried forward and carefully maneuvered the door, along with the huge piece of timber jutting from it, away from the Expedition. Finally freed, Kat leaned forward, resting her forehead on the steering wheel as she heaved a great sigh of relief. She began to feel the damage now in great throbs of black pins and needles, as the trapped blood began to flow back into her legs. She figured she'd sit here for a moment 'til the feeling subsided. Then she'd get out and start to figure out what the heck she'd tell her insurance company about all this. She hoped that it wouldn't raise her premium too much.

Mr Gibbons pulled the red work rag he kept in his back pocket out and used it to wipe his brow. This was far more excitement than he was used to. He moved towards the front of the SUV.

Kimberly's eyes registered the red handkerchief and hot-wired her mouth before her brain had a chance to kick in.

"Wait!" Kimberly screamed, but it was already too late.

Overcome by stress, the farmer sat down on the front bumper of the Expedition, his weight jostling the front of the car, which bounced downwards and struck a rock beneath the front bumper. There was a sound like a champagne bottle being uncorked, and the airbag packed into the steering wheel of the SUV abruptly deployed, sending Kat's head flying backward at one hundred and fifty miles per hour.

Everybody froze.

As the white vinyl bag slowly deflated, Kimberly and the others could see Kat sitting upright behind the steering wheel, her body held in place by the rebar that had speared her skull as neatly as a martini olive on a cocktail stick. The back of the headrest was soaked in blood, which dripped from the length of metal that protruded from between Kat's eyes like a perverse unicorn's horn.

Clear turned away, sickened.

Another one down... Four to go...

As rescue workers rushed pointlessly to her side, Kat's dead, limp hand dropped to her side, and her last cigarette fell from her fingers onto the ground, landing amidst churned dirt and busted safety glass. A stiff breeze kicked up, rolling the still-smoldering cigarette toward the broken irrigation pipe filled with gasoline that lay directly under the Expedition. Within seconds the bluish flames were invisibly shooting back up the buried irrigation pipes and over rocky terrain, headed back towards the source of the fuel.

As Kimberly turned away in grief from the sight of Kat's dead body, she saw Thomas climb over the three-strand barbed wire fence next to the oak tree, headed in Rory's direction.

"Rory!" yelled Thomas.

As Rory turned around to face him, Thomas felt a strong breeze at his back and heard a loud cracking sound coming from overhead. He glanced up just in time to see one of the larger branches on the dead oak tree he was passing under suddenly break loose and drop down toward him.

Thomas cried out and instinctively threw himself onto the wet mud of the ground, narrowly avoiding being struck by the falling tree limb.

Just than the finger of fire found its way to the news van's ruptured gas tank.

*WHOOMPH!* Behind him, the news van erupted in a blossom of orange fire as the gas tank exploded, the concussion from the explosion blowing the fence next to the vehicle out of the ground and across the nearby field at seventy miles per hour. Thomas heard a loud thrumming sound and looked up from his prone position on the ground as two fence posts went flying right over his head, the barbed wire stretched taut between them like an egg-slice.

Over by the trunk of the tree, Rory saw the barbed wire fence flying toward him a split second before it struck. There wasn't enough time to run, duck, scream or even say the traditional "oh, shit!" By the time his brain had processed what was happening, the speeding barbed wire was already several feet behind him.

Rory swallowed, feeling a weird, cold sensation spread through his body like seeping poison. He could see the cop, Thomas, lying on the ground a few yards away, peeking out at him from behind a big-ass fallen branch. The girls, Kimberly and Clear, were standing on the other side of the road, their hands over their mouths, wide-eyed with shock. He couldn't see Kat anywhere. She must still be in the car. Judging from the looks on everyone's faces, he must be hurt or something.

Funny, he didn't *feel* hurt. Hell, he couldn't really feel anything, good or bad.

Rory tried to raise his hand to let the others know he was okay. As he did so, his left arm dropped away in two pieces, having been severed above the elbow and at the wrist by the flying barbed wire.

Fuck. That couldn't be good.

And weirdly, there was no pain.

As Rory struggled to take a step forward, be became abruptly aware that he couldn't move his legs at exactly the same time that he seemed to be falling down. As he toppled to his right, Rory was alarmed to see what appeared to be a good chunk of his midsection falling to the left, trailing a length of intestine behind it as it went.

Still... no pain...

As his head struck the surface of the freshly mown pasture, Rory found himself staring up at what appeared to be his own legs—yep, that was them alright; he recognized the bong-water and ketchup stains on the pants leg—still standing upright. As he watched, the knees buckled and his lower torso joined the rest of his body on the ground.

And now, there was pain...

Lots of it.

Fuck.

As Rory lay dying, surrounded on all sides by pieces of his own disarticulated body, the last thing that went through his head as the blackness claimed him was: So much for being comfortably numb.

The Gibbons' pasture was in even more turmoil than it had been before, as one group of rescue workers abandoned the SUV to try and put out the fires caused by the flaming debris from the news van, and the rest ran toward the bloody chunks of meat that just a few moments before had been a living, breathing human being.

Kimberly marched toward Thomas, where he was still standing staring in shock at Rory's remains. She wanted to cry and scream, to rant at the sky about the unfairness and horror of it all, but there was no time left for such outbursts. Grief and shock were luxuries that none of them could afford, not when any one of them could be the next to die.

Reaching the old oak tree, Kimberly stared down at the fallen branch, the one that had caused Thomas to move out of the path of the deadly flying fence wire.

"It wasn't his turn... and it's not my turn," she whispered under her breath. She turned as though in a dream and saw Mr Gibbons standing behind her. She hadn't even heard him approach. The farmer's skin was the color of old oatmeal and he was trembling and weeping, clearly distraught by the part he had played in the death of another human being.

"I'm so sorry... I didn't... it just..."

Kimberly set her jaw, pushing aside her own pain. There would be time enough for tears and sorrow if she and the others survived the day. Squaring her shoulders, she stepped forward and stuck out her hand.

"Give me the keys to your truck... Now!"

# SEVENTEEN

Kimberly sped along the dangerously twisty two-lane black top in the direction of the hospital, her knuckles white as she gripped the wheel of Mr Gibbons's aged Ford F-150. She had blown the speed limit wide open, and only the fact that they had their own personal traffic cop sitting in the passenger seat urging her on was giving her any confidence to keep up this kind of speed. The ancient truck's engine rose to a scream as they hit its top speed, but Kimberly kept her foot on the gas, milking the Ford for every last drop of power it had.

"Hurry up! There's no time! She's about to give birth!" Thomas cried as he pulled his seatbelt on and buckled himself up, checking in the rearview mirror for any sign of police attention. Luckily for him, there was none.

Kimberly glanced at the truck's speedometer, then back at the road. Taking a deep breath, she reached over with one hand and unbuckled her safety belt, letting it slide back into the holster. Then she slammed the accelerator to the floor.

"What are you doing?" Clear yelped. "You're gonna kill us!"

"No. If anyone dies from a crash now, it'll be me," said Kimberly firmly, "but I can't die if Eugene and Isabella are still alive. I'm last on Death's list."

"Are you crazy? What makes you think you'd survive a crash?" Clear said, nervously gripping the dashboard in an attempt to brace herself as the farm truck bounced over potholes at breakneck speed.

"What happened when Eugene tried to kill himself out of turn?"

"Six duds in a row," Thomas said, comprehension slowly rising in his eyes.

"And when it was Rory's turn to die—that branch fell and saved Thomas's life," Kimberly added.

"Death's maintaining the order," Clear said softly, nodding her head in understanding.

"That makes no sense!" said Thomas. "Isabella was supposed to crash her van into a lake. Could we have... I don't know, altered her destiny or something when we had her arrested?"

"I don't think so," Clear replied. "Alex's premonitions happened exactly as he saw them, no matter how much we tried to change it." She shook her head to herself, the whole twisted paradox of Fate spinning out inside her head like wire wool wrapping around her brain. She had spent the last twelve months with all the time in the world to think things through, to try to work it out, and even she hadn't been able to even begin to get a handle on all of it: Fate, Death, the premonitions—all of it. Because Alex had seen the future, he and their friends had gone to great, elaborate lengths to try to avoid it—and the very steps they had taken to avoid it had actively caused their deaths on more than one occasion, in exactly the same way as Alex had seen in his premonition. It was like their free will hadn't made a blind bit of difference.

So what did that mean? People were just puppets, living out their lives in accordance with someone else's script? That made no sense at all. Who was this "someone else?" And why would they write a script? What was the purpose? It gave her a headache just thinking about it all.

Clear rolled her eyes, wishing that life would just be simple for once. What was that old saying? Forewarned is forearmed? More like forewarned is no freakin' good 'cause you're gonna die anyway.

"We *have* to make sure the baby is born!" Kimberly said, her eyes gleaming with the steely determination of a zealot. She clicked on the blinker as the truck sped around the side of a red import Mini, the move making straw blow off the back and litter the road behind them.

Suddenly the road ahead of her grew gray and foggy around the edges, as if all the color and focus had been drained from her surroundings. Her vision faded out, becoming a dark void. She opened her mouth to cry out, but no air would enter her lungs. She instinctively clawed at her throat, letting go of the steering wheel as she did so.

*She can't breathe. There is a strange woman leaning over her. She can't see much of her face, but she has the impression of an older, somewhat austere woman with an unsmiling face. The older woman is dressed in a white lab coat. There is a nameplate pinned to her lapel that reads "KALARJIAN."*

*Now she is in a hospital corridor. The walls are painted a pale blue and there is a large number two on the wall at the end of the hall. There are people hurrying back and forth, most of them dressed in pale green scrubs. The woman in the lab coat—Kalarjian—is up ahead, ducking into an open door.*

*Now she is strangling again, fighting desperately for oxygen. Her lungs feel as if they are filled with molten lead. She can hear a woman screaming in the background and the sound of an EKG monitor going faster and faster and faster. The woman Kalarjian is once more standing over her, her hands around her throat...*

"Kimberly! Kimberly, watch out!"

Startled, Kimberly snapped back to reality just in time to see a mini-van heading right toward the truck. Before she could react, Clear grabbed the steering wheel from her and yanked on it, bringing the truck back into the correct lane of traffic. The mini-van's horn blared loudly, making them all jump.

"What did you see? What am I looking for?" Thomas asked anxiously, checking the road ahead of them for danger.

Kimberly rubbed her throat with one hand as she took the wheel back from Clear, dizzy with disorientation, trying her best to shake off the persistent feeling that she couldn't breathe. "No... it's not here." She glanced over at Thomas, panting heavily. "This one was different, more like the pile-up and the van going into the lake. It wasn't just a sign, I was there."

"Was it another premonition?" Clear asked, carefully scanning Kimberly's face for any hint that she might succumb to another attack. She wondered whether having Kimberly drive was the sanest choice she'd made that day.

"Yeah... I was in a hospital... There was screaming... a nurse was choking me. I couldn't see her face, but I could see her nametag—Kalarjian.

"Kalarjian?" echoed Thomas, raising an eyebrow.

Kimberly nodded her head, a grim look on her face. "I think a nurse named Kalarjian is going to choke Isabella to death."

# EIGHTEEN

Eugene lay flat on his back, staring up at the ceiling over his head. It was a cheap cork ceiling that had been painted white, and the two industrial-strength strip lights blazing away above him were giving him a headache.

Well, this pretty much sucked.

He wasn't sure where he was or what had happened, but he knew that he was in a hospital, and that he was in pain. The last thing he remembered was being thrown around inside the SUV as it careened off the road, followed by a sharp pain inside his chest and the sudden, distressing inability to breathe. He had a dim recollection of being carried out of the vehicle and placed on the ground, and of Clear's face hovering over him, telling him he was going to be all right. Then everything had mercifully gone dark for a while.

When he came to he was here, in this bed, being stuck full of needles by a blurry nurse. Whatever particular combination of drugs they had pumped into him had done a reasonable job of dulling the pain, at the expense of his almost total inability to move. Even rolling his head to the side was a major effort, and when he tried to wriggle his toes or move his hands, it was as though he was moving them through thick, clinging glue. He couldn't move his head very well, nor could he speak, thanks to the oxygen tube down his throat and the drainage tube inserted in his nose, but he could see enough to either side to know he was hooked up to an artificial respiration machine. He could hear it as it pumped tirelessly up and down, forcing air through the tube snaking down his throat. There was no sign of Clear, Kimberly, or any of the others in the room, nor could he hear their voices in the hall. That meant there was nobody aware of his situation, and no one to watch his back.

The realization that he was on his own made Eugene's heart constrict nastily, as if it was clamped in a vise. The heart monitor next to his bed began to make a chirping sound like a distressed bird as Eugene's pulse raced in panic.

At the sound, a nurse entered the room. She was dressed in pastel pink stretch pants and short-sleeved scrubs depicting Mr Potato Head as a doctor. She picked up the clipboard affixed to the foot of his bed and studied it for a long moment. Her brow creased and she reached down to Eugene's neck, giving the tube a shake to make sure it was stable.

Eugene winced, his body jerking convulsively.

"Sorry." The nurse said in a clipped voice. "Can you feel that in your trachea?" Eugene rolled his eyes to indicate what a stupid question that one was.

"Ah, quit complaining," the nurse breezed matter-of-factly. "I got burnt babies in the Children's Ward braver than you."

She bent over and brusquely stuck an electronic thermometer in his ear. Eugene opened his mouth to speak, but only a pained, dry rattle came out. The nurse gave him a grim smile as she removed the thermometer and peered at the digital readout. "Don't bother. You won't be talking for at least a month. Think you can handle that, jabber-jaw?"

Eugene had never felt so helpless and alone in his life, and this woman was doing nothing to help the matter. She almost seemed to be enjoying his suffering. He wanted to tell her to shut the fuck up and to go get a real nurse, but he couldn't even do that. All he could think of were those news stories he'd seen on TV about "Angels of Death"—medical workers who would put those patients they considered troublesome or beyond hope out of their misery by shooting overdoses into their IV lines.

Seeing the look of sudden fear in his eyes, the nurse's lips tightened and she perched on the edge of the bed, jarring Eugene and making him wince yet again. As she leaned over and patted his hand, he could see that her nametag read "HARAHAN."

"Don't worry," she said with a crooked smile. "Everyone learns to love me once they get used to my sense of humor."

Eugene blinked back the tears welling in his eyes, grateful to see a human side to this creature that had the power of life and death over him. Maybe he would be all right after all.

Thomas held on tightly as Kimberly steered around a slow-moving tractor-trailer, slowing down only enough to allow them to safely pass the vehicle before hitting the gas again, sending the pickup surging forward. He thought that considering how many drivers they had nearly hit so far, they were lucky that they hadn't been pulled over yet.

But luck, as Thomas was fast becoming aware, had a very nasty habit of running out.

As the ancient Ford shot past a small row of stores, a squad car in front of the barber shop abruptly switched on its lights and pulled out in pursuit.

"Shit!" Kimberly looked first at the blue lights flashing in her rearview mirror, and then at Thomas, hoping he could tell her what to do.

"Keep going!" said Thomas, making an executive decision he knew he would probably pay for later on. He glanced over his shoulder at the police cruiser on their tail, and uttered a silent prayer up to whatever Gods might still be on his side at this point. "I wouldn't know how to explain any of this anyway!"

Kimberly flicked an anxious glance in the rearview mirror at the cops chasing her. She had been raised to always observe the law, drive at a safe speed, and make sure she always wore her safety belt, but if she was a good girl and did all those things, she would not have much of a life left to her.

Rounding a corner, she looked up the road and saw a busy six-lane intersection ahead. Unconsciously she glanced over at Clear, almost as though she were asking permission to do what she was about to do.

"Speed up," Clear said, egging her new friend on.

"Yeah, fuck 'em!" Kimberly said with a grim chuckle, checking her rearview mirror. "No offense," she added, looking quickly over at Thomas, who was hastily buckling his safety belt. He gave her a cockeyed grin and rolled his eyes at her.

The little pickup's engine redlined as Kimberly sped toward the intersection, steering with one hand while pulling her seatbelt completely aside; making sure it offered her zero protection. Out of the corner of her eye she could see Thomas pressing himself back in his seat, his face as white as a sheet.

"Be alive, Isabella, please be alive," Kimberly whispered under her breath as she rammed the pickup's gas pedal to the floor.

Kimberly's eyes widened in fear as she saw the rapidly approaching street light turn from green to yellow to red; it took all her concentration to keep her right foot away from the brake as the truck blazed through the intersection. Her body went stiff with tension. She could hear car horns blaring to all sides of her and saw vehicles swerving wildly to avoid colliding with the pick-up, but she forced herself to remain focused on reaching the hospital at all costs. As she reached the far side, she saw the police car that was pursuing them fishtail into a ninety degree turn, slewing around in a wild arc as smoke poured from its rear tires. It barely avoided the intersection.

"Nice try, motherfucker!" Kimberly yelled at the dwindling reflection in her rearview mirror.

"That's it. I'm officially on the 1:00AM," Thomas sighed, shaking his head in dismay.

Eugene lay in bed and tried to swallow, wincing at the unpleasant sensation of drool seeping out of the corner of his mouth. Oh yeah, that was real attractive. He was glad that nobody from his department could see him now, but he had to do something. He had been here forty minutes and already he was bored. He wanted nothing more than to rip the tubes from his body and walk out of the door. There was grading to do, errands to run, enquiries into the price of locked-and-sealed nuclear bunkers to make. If he survived all this—and he knew that was a very big if—he was *so* asking Miss Ferro out.

A small tear began to slip down the side of Eugene's cheek.

How did he end up like this? He had worked hard all his life—from as early as he could remember—to try to build a real future for himself. He'd studied hard in school, kept out of trouble, and spent his adult life trying to bring knowledge and hope to a younger generation. As a professional educator, his entire life had centered on science, rationality and facts. Now here he was, laying in a hospital, bleeding like a stuck hog, the victim of a curse that was right out of a horror flick. To make matters even worse, he could no longer tell himself it was bullshit, because he'd seen with his own two eyes that it wasn't.

As Eugene lay in his hospital bed, he could feel Death's presence all around him. His eyes traveled nervously around the room, assessing each object in the near vicinity for its danger potential. A cold chill crept over him as he took in the trays full of needles, the oxygen tanks, and the metal implements hanging from the walls. Although he couldn't see the Grim Reaper, he knew that it... he... was lurking nearby, in much the same way that a gazelle can feel the eyes of the lion hidden in the tall grass of the veldt.

This was no good. He was going to go crazy if he kept thinking like this. Eugene's eyes flickered up toward the television set mounted near the ceiling at the foot of his bed, hoping to find something to take his mind off his worries. The local news was already in progress, with a perky blonde woman, dressed in a subdued pinstripe jacket and dark blouse two sizes too small for her, seated in front of a backdrop that read *"WWED-3 NEWS."*

"A bizarre accident has left two people dead: one of them killed by a safety device meant to protect us. Ironically, the woman was impaled through the head after her emergency airbag deployed. She was trapped in her vehicle after it crashed in a field near Greenwood Lake. The airbag somehow deployed, forcing the woman's head back onto a metal pipe that had penetrated the vehicle." Here a tape rolled, showing blurry footage of the accident as it happened in the background of the dark-haired reporter's interview. "A man traveling with the woman was also killed in a separate freak incident involving an explosion and WWED's own Action Report van. Police have speculated that one of the deaths may have been narcotics related and urge children to stay away from drugs."

The camera cut back to the anchorman, who smiled at the camera with a blank cheerfulness that indicated his mind was on anything but the words coming out of his mouth. "Good advice, Sue, and stay in school, kids! Up next, Johnny Showers has the weather…"

Eugene began to sob soundlessly. Although he was far from their next of kin, he had shared in these people's lives for nearly three days, and despite his initial dislike of them all, they had come to mean something to him.

Now Kat was dead, and from the narcotics reference he guessed that Rory was too.

Where would it ever end?

As he stared in mute horror at the television set, a dark shadow fell across the foot of his bed. Eugene jerked, startled as a large, heavy-set orderly pushed a housekeeping cart through the open door into the room, blocking his view of the television screen.

"Sorry, man," the orderly rumbled as he went about emptying the wastebasket and swapping out the bath towels and water carafe. As the orderly turned back around, Eugene lifted his hands and frantically pantomimed writing. The big man saw him and nodded.

"Need a pen? Sure. If you like, I'll bring crosswords for you, too."

Eugene tried to nod a "thank you", but the tube in his throat hampered his movement.

The orderly pushed his cart back out of the door, only to pause at the threshold and give a little shiver that seemed oddly delicate, given his size.

"Jeez, it's freezing in here!" The orderly leaned over and flicked the thermostat next to the door, causing the vents just below the ceiling to close.

As the two sets of vents slammed closed, the last burst of air from the bottom of the closing vent blew over the medical equipment on the stainless steel cart beside the bed, knocking over the clipboard placed there earlier by the nurse, which in turn knocked into the oxygen hose, causing one of the three feed-tubes to pop off the top of the tank. Oblivious to the situation, the orderly left the room, closing the door behind him as he left so Eugene could have some privacy. The door shut slowly with a soft sucking sound, effectively sealing and soundproofing the room.

Unable to speak or move, Eugene lay and stared in silent terror at the closed door as the sound of the leaking oxygen hissed softly in the background.

Outside the room, the orderly pulled the door shut behind him and stared down at the housekeeping cart in front of him. His feet were one big ache, and all he wanted was for this shift to go quickly so he could get to the cafeteria and have a bit of a sit-down with his friends from D-Shift for half an hour. He would probably have to do a quick drive-by the candy machine on his way down to the next ward and pick up a Baby Ruth to boost his flagging blood sugar, and then—

"What are you doing here?" a voice snapped.

The orderly looked up from his musings to see the ward's administrator glowering up at him. The administrator was a deeply unpleasant little man with pebble glasses and a face that looked like he was sucking on a sour pickle.

"The Henzels are still waiting for you in the Children's Ward."

The orderly stared at him for a moment. Then he smacked his head with the palm of his hand. "Shit! I *totally* forgot! Right, right, right! It's Gregory's big day."

"And Mrs Dempsey in hydrotherapy can't feel her legs," the administrator added, but the orderly was already halfway down the hall.

The administrator shook his head in disgust and walked past the housekeeping cart blocking Eugene's doorway without giving it a second glance.

Dust billowed as Mr Gibbons's Ford pickup truck bounced up the ramp into the hospital parking lot and skidded to a halt in front of the main entrance. Kimberly and the others were out of the truck before it came to a full stop. Luck had continued to smile on them, or so it seemed, as there had been no further sign of pursuit after they had ditched the cops during their near miss at the intersection.

As they hurried inside the hospital, Clear lost no time in zeroing in on the admitting desk. She sprinted over to the desk and slapped her hands down on top of it. An older woman dressed in a paisley-print smock top sat behind a computer terminal, hooked up to a hands-free telephone headset. She glanced up at Clear with a frown.

"Isabella Hudson. What room is she in?" Clear asked breathlessly.

The receptionist shook her head. "I'm sorry; I can't give out that information unless you're a relative."

"I'm her sister," Clear blurted.

Clear's response had been a little too quick and a little too frantic for the receptionist's taste. She eyed the strange girl with the wild blue eyes and unruly blonde hair dubiously. "I'll have to see your ID, Ms Hudson."

Clear took a deep breath and gave the receptionist a wide smile. She turned away, as if to reach for a wallet or a purse, then, without warning, vaulted over the counter. Before the surprised receptionist could protest, Clear straight-armed the woman out of her chair onto the floor and seized control of the computer. With a few quick keystrokes she had the information they needed.

"Delivery room six: upstairs. I'll find Eugene and catch up with you."

Kimberly and Thomas nodded their understanding and dashed off in the direction of the elevators, while Clear jumped back over the reception desk and headed in the direction of Ward B.

The receptionist got up off the floor and grabbed the telephone next to her desk. Her fingers trembled as she stabbed the buttons that would put her in contact with hospital security.

"This is Reception. We need Security on Level Two, Stat!"

Inside the hospital room, Eugene's eyes darted frantically about as a commercial for Captain Crunchy's Flash-Fried Chicken was replaced by another news report.

The dignified-looking anchorman was back, and behind him was a graphic that read "ROUTE 23 TRAGEDY."

"More tears were shed this morning in the wake of the tragic pile-up that rocked the Tri-State area," the newscaster said over a quick montage of emergency crews pulling mangled cars apart, grieving families, and makeshift shrines of yellow ribbons, cut flowers, balloons and teddy bears clustered along the shoulder of the scorched length of highway.

Suddenly the sound and image on the television began to flutter and roll. Eugene looked back to the oxygen hose, which was still hissing softly. The beeps on the EEG machine began to increase. Eugene's hand crept over the blanket, inch by agonizing inch, as he reached for the nurse call button—only to discover it was just of reach.

Over on the medical cart, the second hose feed popped off the machine. The hiss of escaping oxygen grew louder.

Lakeview Memorial's on-call obstetrician frowned down at her newest patient, one Isabella Hudson. She wasn't exactly sure what the story was with the mother-to-be, but judging by the nervous-looking deputy hovering at her side, it promised to be interesting. The patient had come in through the emergency room, presenting what she claimed was an early labor. Although it had been difficult getting a coherent history out of the panicked woman, it had finally been discovered that Isabella was two weeks early. That in itself wasn't too big a problem, but what she had just discovered going on inside Isabella was.

"Listen to me, Isabella—I need you to stop pushing," the obstetrician said slowly and distinctly, making sure her patient understood what was being asked of her.

"What's wrong?" Isabella asked, trying to peer down between her knees, her hair plastered to her face by rivulets of sweat. "Is the baby all right?"

"The cord is around the neck; it's causing fetal distress," the obstetrician replied matter-of-factly. "If I can't turn it, we may need to do a caesarian." She turned to one of the nurses standing nearby and gave her a curt nod. "Get Dr Kalarjian up here—now!"

Deputy Adams glanced down at the obstetrician, who was busy trying to maneuver Isabella's baby safely through the birth canal, then quickly looked away. He had never seen a baby being born before, and was unprepared for all the blood, fluids and screaming that was involved. The diagrams in the first aid books had seen fit to leave out all the gross stuff, and right now, he was kind of glad. He would've never come in here if he'd known it would be like this.

He wiped at his neck with a discarded towel, blinking quickly as the world started to swim a little in front of his eyes. Oh, Christ, he was going to faint. "Uh... maybe I should step outside? I'm just kinda in the way here..." he said, smiling queasily at the crazy pregnant lady, who was sitting on a birthing table in one of the hospital's delivery suites, her feet up in the stirrups, her entire face and upper torso drenched in sweat.

Isabella turned to stare at him. She had always envisioned the birth of her baby being a family affair, with her sister and husband there to provide support, understanding and peeled grapes for her during the hours of labor. Now she was having her baby in a strange hospital, attended by strange doctors, and under police custody. She was so, so glad that her mother couldn't see her now, or she'd be hearing this story circulated around their neighborhood for years.

Then again, she had to admit that the country bumpkin deputy, as freaked out as he might be, was more genuinely concerned for her wellbeing and that of her baby than Marcus would be, if he were here.

Husband or not, she was damned if she was going to have this baby by herself.

She grabbed the deputy by the front of his shirt and yanked him forward so that their noses almost touched.

"Don't you dare leave me!" she growled between clenched teeth.

"Dr Kalarjian: Code Blue in Delivery Room Six. Dr Kalarjian to Delivery Room Six: Code Blue."

"Did you hear that?" Kimberly hissed, as the nurse's voice echoed through the halls via the hospital's intercom system.

"Where're the friggin' elevators in this place?" Thomas growled, his head swiveling about like a radar dish.

Kimberly gave him a look, sharing a thought.

As one, they turned and ran for the stairwell.

Two floors above them, Eugene scratched at the top sheet of the hospital bed, trying desperately to inch the call button closer to his hand. As he reeled the sheet in, he was unable to see that the cord had managed to become tangled with the power cord of the EEG machine, pulling the plug slightly out of the socket.

After what felt like an eternity, Eugene was finally able to grip the call button with his fingertips. As he inched it closer toward his palm, there was a muted buzz from the wall socket near his bed. Eugene's eyes widened and he froze, struggling to keep his trembling fingertips from moving the call button one way or another. The last thing he needed was a stray spark igniting the pure oxygen leaking into the room.

Terrified, yet still determined, he carefully reached out with his free hand and began rapping on the side rails of his bed, hoping that someone outside might hear the noise and come to investigate. He had never wanted to scream so badly in his life, but the respirator tube funneled down his throat kept him from so much as moaning.

Suddenly, the brakes on the respirator cart parked beside his bed, loosened by Nurse Harahan's brisk jostle a little earlier, gave way, and the machine began to slowly roll toward the door.

Eugene could feel the tube inserted in his trachea stretch and then pull tight. He managed to quickly clamp his teeth down on it to stop it pulling out altogether, but it had already been pulled halfway out. The pain was excruciating, but there was nothing he could do but watch the door and pray for intervention. In the background, he could hear the EEG machine climb off the charts as his heart rate increased tenfold.

Eugene had never considered himself a particularly religious person, but he closed his eyes and silently began to pray.

Please. Please, let someone find him before it was too late.

After a couple of false starts, Kimberly and Thomas turned down a long corridor on the second floor that led toward a bank of elevators.

"Finally!" gasped Thomas in relief.

As they hurried forward, they saw a young intern step out of an elevator, and then turn and hold the door open for an older, dark haired woman dressed in a white doctor's coat over blood-red scrubs.

"Dr Kalarjian! Here you go," the intern said genially.

"Thanks," the doctor said, nodding curtly as she stepped inside the elevator.

Kimberly and Thomas exchanged a look of dread, and broke into a dead run.

"Dr Kalarjian, stop!" Kimberly shouted, but it as too late. She and Thomas arrived at the elevator just as the doors slid shut. Before they closed all the way, Kimberly caught a glimpse of a tall, authoritative-looking woman in her early forties, her dark hair pulled into an austere bun, staring back at her.

As the doors thumped shut, Thomas instinctively hit the call button on the elevator panel, but it was too late. The doors remained obstinately closed.

Kimberly and Thomas whirled around and headed back down the corridor toward the stairwell. The pair thundered up the stairs at breakneck speed, popping out onto the next floor just in time to see the elevator continuing upward.

"Shit!" Kimberly managed to gasp between gulps of air. "Come on!"

With that they re-entered the stairwell and continued climbing upwards.

Clear walked up and down the corridors of the hospital, scanning the room numbers like a hawk hunting for its prey: B-168, B-171, B-173...

"B-187... B-187..." she whispered to herself, sounding like a retiree trying to coax out the winning number at Bingo.

A hand suddenly grabbed Clear and shoved her against the nearest wall, knocking the breath out of her. A heavy-set security guard, built like a high school football player gone to seed, bent

Clear's arm behind her back. Clear winced in pain.

"Hold still!" he shouted in her ear, as he reached down to his belt and pulled out a pair of jangling handcuffs, pulling her closer to him as he did so. He smelled like spearmint gum and greasy fried chicken. Clear's nostrils twitched in disgust.

As the guard fumbled with the handcuffs, Clear struggled frantically to free herself, but she was at a distinct disadvantage, as the security guard pinning her to the wall had at least six inches and seventy pounds on her. Kicking and bucking in the guard's iron grip, she glanced to one side and saw an old man dressed in a hospital gown, standing staring in an open doorway across the hall, watching the unfolding events with puzzled interest. It was probably the most exciting thing he'd seen all week. The old man was extremely thin with mottled skin from liver disease.

"No point in fighting, girlie," the man said with a sad smile. "It'll all be over soon enough."

Fuck that! I don't want it to be over, Clear thought desperately. She allowed her body to go limp, hoping it would cause the security guard to loosen his grip somewhat. "Please, you don't know what's happening!"

"Shut the fuck up," the security guard snarled, giving her a small shake to underscore his orders. Giving up on trying to open the handcuffs with just one free hand, he reached over and pulled his walkie-talkie from its holster on his hip and brought it up to his face. "Larry, I've got the woman down near Recovery. Don't worry; I've got her under control…"

Suddenly, Clear's elbow came flying back, smashing the walkie-talkie into the security guard's face hard enough to loosen a front tooth and make his nose bleed. As the guard howled in pain, she spun out of his grip and brought her knee into his groin. The security guard clutched at his crotch and collapsed onto the floor like a sack of wet laundry.

Clear stepped over him and sprinted down the hall as fast as she could go.

The old man stood in the doorway of his room and watched her go, and then turned his attention to the security guard, who was gagging and groaning on the floor at his feet. The old man shook his head and chuckled. Turning, he went back to bed, the loose ends of his hospital robe flapping behind him in the breeze.

"What's happening to my baby?"

Standing at the end of the delivery bed, the obstetrician grimaced as she shone her torch around. It was as she feared—the baby's shoulder had become caught behind the mother's pelvic bone, resulting in a failure to progress. If something wasn't done soon, the baby ran a real risk of cerebral palsy or some other brain injury related to lack of oxygen. She knew that while a newborn infant's blood is specially equipped to compensate for low levels of oxygen, the ability was not infinite. If there was a placental abruption, resulting in internal hemorrhaging, both mother and child could very well die.

"Contractions have stopped. Arrest in descent halfway through the birth canal," she announced to the OR team.

"Induce labor?" the anesthesiologist asked.

"No time," she replied, shaking her head. "The cord's compressed. The child's in fetal distress."

The anesthesiologist checked the fetal heart monitor at his elbow. Although a surgical mask hid the lower portion of his face, his eyes spoke for themselves. "Variable decelerations, it's losing oxygen."

"Oh, God! What's happening?" Isabella wailed, struggling to sit up before collapsing, exhausted, back onto the sweat-sodden pillow.

"Where the hell is Kalarjian?" the obstetrician snarled at the nurse.

Dr Kalarjian strode briskly out of the elevator and headed down the hallway in the direction of Delivery Room Six. She had been preparing to leave for the day, only to have this last minute emergency dropped in her lap. She sighed as she thought about her dinner plans with her husband. This weekend was their anniversary, and they had made reservations for a romantic getaway in the nearby Catskills. Still, if it turned out to be something relatively simple, she might be able to get out in time to salvage something of the evening.

She was twenty feet from the delivery room when the door to the stairwell slammed open and a man and a woman thundered out into the hall. The man was in his late twenties with dark hair and a day's growth of beard, while the woman was somewhat younger, but looked equally disheveled. While both were well dressed, there was wildness in their eyes that spoke of extreme desperation. With a small start, Dr Kalarjian recognized the dark-haired girl as the woman who had called her name and tried to stop the elevator a few floors down.

"You! Stop!" the man yelled, pointing at the baffled doctor.

"What's the problem?"

The dark-haired man grabbed Kalarjian by the left elbow, roughly thrusting her up against the corridor wall hard enough to make her wince. The girl ran on past them with a nod to the man and sprinted toward the swinging doors of the delivery room.

"Jesus! Let me go!" Kalarjian spat, struggling to free herself from the strange man's grasp. "You mind telling me what the hell is going on?"

The dark-haired stranger thrust a badge in the angry doctor's face. "Police business, doc," he said sternly.

In room B-187, Eugene clamped his teeth down tighter on the tube leading to his trachea, feeling the muscles in his jaw start to lock up from the tension. Sweat ran down his forehead and his shoulders shook silently with sobs of terror as he fumbled for the call button, trying to press it without causing the intertwined power cables to come loose.

His trembling fingers reached out for it, moving closer, closer, closer...

As Eugene's fingers touched the call button, the wire gave a sudden coil as it rolled over a fold in the sheet. Abruptly, the unit slithered backward, dropping off the edge of the bed. As it fell, the small yet significant weight of it tugged on the power cable that connected the respirator unit to the wall, pulling it half out of the socket.

Eugene tensed, waiting for the explosion.

But nothing happened, except for something far, far worse.

The respirator switched itself off.

Eugene's eyes flew open as the air stopped flowing into his lungs. He tried to take a breath, but there was no air. Gagging, he tried to reach up to pull the respirator tube from his trachea, but his drug-numbed limbs seemed to be welded to the spot. He couldn't even get up the energy to move his fingers. His eyes bulged from his head as he fought to take a breath around the thick plastic tube that was blocking his windpipe.

As the TV above his head began rolling a cheery trailer for a John Denver CD compilation album, Eugene started to suffocate.

Kimberly burst through the doors of the delivery room, staring around her frantically. She saw that

Isabella was lying on an elevated metal examination table, her head and shoulders propped up by big blue hospital pillows. An anesthesiologist was standing just behind the laboring mother, bracing her shoulders as she pushed down. Crouched between Isabella's spread thighs at the opposite end of the table was an obstetrician, who didn't even look up on hearing the door bang, so completely focused was she on the task at hand. A nurse was both assisting the obstetrician and trying her best to soothe the patient. On the other side of the table, holding Isabella's hand as she struggled mightily to deliver her child into the world, was a young, rather anxious-looking deputy, who was watching the proceedings with a look of horrified fascination on his pale, sweaty face.

"Isabella! Is the baby okay?" Kimberly burst out.

Everyone stopped what they were doing for a heartbeat to look up at the young, wild-eyed girl dressed in street clothes standing just inside the door of the delivery room.

Isabella gave her a confused look. Kimberly realized that they had spent so much time and energy tracking her down, that they had all forgotten that Isabella not only didn't know what was going on and how big a role she and her baby played in the lives of so many others, but she also hadn't actually met any of them face-to-face.

It was something of an oversight, but right now, that didn't matter. The only thing that was important was the baby.

The nurse moved to block Kimberly's way. "What are you doing here?" she snapped. She looked down at Kimberly's shoes, still soaking wet and caked in mud from walking in the Gibbons' pasture, and gave a shudder. This was supposed to be a sterile environment. Graphic images of germs and diseases and—more importantly—of herself having to spend the rest of her shift scrubbing and disinfecting the entire wing, swam before her horrified eyes, and she made a convulsive shooing gesture toward Kimberly.

"Get the hell out of here right now!" she cried.

"You don't understand! Is the baby all right?" Kimberly shouted as she grappled with the nurse, trying to shove her way past her. She had come too far, and seen far too much horror and suffering to be turned aside now. "Is the baby okay?"

Just then Thomas burst through the door, police badge in hand. "Police business, ma'am," he explained breathlessly.

Everyone turned to look at him, utterly confused.

The tension in the delivery room was suddenly broken by the thin, high-pitched wail of a newborn baby. The nurse gave Kimberly and Thomas a sharp look, as though to say "I'll deal with you later," then hurried back to the delivery table to check on the baby.

The obstetrician grinned as she triumphantly lifted the eight pound, six ounce baby, still slick with blood and birthing fluids, up high enough for Isabella to see.

"Congratulations—you have a healthy baby boy!" she announced.

Kimberly squealed in delight at the news. Throwing her arms around Thomas's neck, she hugged him tight as he wrapped his arms around her waist and picked her up off the floor, twirling her around in a tight circle.

"Oh my God! It's finally over!" Kimberly laughed, tears of joy glinting in her eyes. She broke free of Thomas's embrace and raced over to Isabella, patting the weary new mother on the hand. "Thank you! And congratulations!" she cried.

With that, she and Thomas joined hands and hurried out of the delivery room to find Clear.

Isabella watched the door bang shut behind them, and then looked over at Deputy Adams, who was still clutching her hand.

"Who the hell are they?" Isabella asked.

On the next floor, Eugene choked and gagged mindlessly, trying to draw air into his collapsed lungs around the edge of the thick plastic tube currently lodged in his trachea. Tears leaked from the corners of his eyes and dripped down onto the pillow as he prepared to release his hold on the tube with his teeth, letting the rolling respirator cart pull it out. He knew that there was no way he could breathe by himself unaided—they'd told him his lungs had totally collapsed—but anything was better than this feeling of having something lodged in his airway, choking him to death.

Squeezing his eyes tight shut, his head swimming with lack of oxygen, Eugene got ready to let go of the tube, sending a silent prayer speeding in the direction of his dear mother. She had no idea that he was here, in this hospital, and he knew that she would be devastated by the loss of her only son. He only wished that he could see her one last time to explain to her why he had to leave her like this. He prayed that she could forgive him.

Then... *Beep*.

*Beep... beep...*

Eugene's eyes flew open as a series of beeps filled the room. And then—oh thank holy Christ—air suddenly whooshed into his lungs as the emergency battery power clicked on, restarting the respirator.

Eugene thought that air had never tasted so sweet.

As he glanced over at the respirator, he felt the pressure diminish from the tube as the machine rolled a final quarter inch and its front wheel hit a snaking power cable, halting its roll. He realized instinctively that something had happened. He could feel it in his blood. Somehow the others had gotten to Isabella in time and made sure her baby was born.

A wave of intense relief washed over him, and Eugene began to weep. It was over. He was going to make it. He had once again cheated Death.

\* \* \*

Clear was hurrying down the hall, away from the moaning heap of the security guard, when she heard the elevator doors chime. She looked up and saw Kimberly and Thomas strolling out of the car, linked arm in arm, and laughing like a couple of giddy school kids. She hurried up to them, a panicked look in her crystal blue eyes.

"A guard grabbed me before I could find Eugene—I haven't been able to locate him!" she started urgently.

Thomas grinned and scooped Clear up, spinning on his heels as he gave the surprised girl a huge bear hug. At that moment he had never been happier in his life—a life that now promised to be considerably longer.

"It's okay! She had the baby!" he laughed.

"We've done it! We're safe! It's over!" Kimberly added, wiping tears of happiness from her cheeks.

Clear stared at Thomas then Kimberly, stunned at the news. Up until that moment, she had never truly believed they would be able to beat Death. The best she had thought they might be able to do was prolong the inevitable, just as she and Alex had managed to do, less than a year before. She had lived with the constant threat of death for so long that she had surrendered any hope of anything resembling a normal life, much less a lengthy one. Now she had been given a reprieve from Death—one that had been won at the cost of the pain and suffering of so many others, both friends and strangers alike.

For the first time in over a year, Clear Rivers didn't smirk, sneer, or grimace: she actually smiled.

Kimberly smiled back at her warmly. She put her arms around Clear's neck to give her a hug.

Then she froze. She staggered backward as though she'd just been hit in the stomach by a full swing from a baseball bat. She felt as if the world surrounding her was falling away, as though she was dropping backward at high speed down a long, dark tunnel. She had only experienced the strange sensation a couple of times before, each time associated with a premonition of some kind. Surely that was impossible—Isabella's baby had been born and Death's list had been erased.

Hadn't it?

*She is back at the scene of the pile-up on Route 23. Flames flicker, metal crunches, voices scream. Now she is inside the cab of Isabella Hudson's delivery van. Isabella is behind the wheel, staring out at the flames and spinning vehicles up ahead of her in shock. She hits the brakes and quickly swerves out of the path of the destruction that has already claimed the lives of so many other motorists. Safely on the shoulder, she lets the van coast to a stop, rolling past the blazing ruins of Evan Lewis's Trans-Am. She stares in horror at the driver's charred and smoking body, still trapped behind the steering wheel. Then she gets out of the van, covering her mouth in a vain attempt to hide her revulsion at the sight of the burning chunk of twisted metal that had once been a red Tahoe full of teenagers...*

"Kimberly! Are you okay? What's wrong?"

Kimberly opened her eyes to find Thomas kneeling over her. She was lying on the floor of the hospital corridor. She was freezing cold, and although she could not see herself, she would not have been surprised to find out that her lips had turned blue.

"Are you okay?" Clear's carefree smile had been replaced by the same worried frown she had worn since Kimberly had first met her. She reached down and grabbed Kimberly's hands, briskly rubbing them between her own to warm them.

"I... I know how it feels to be dead," Kimberly muttered thickly.

"What did you see?" Clear asked.

Kimberly grunted, rolled over, and tried to sit up. Clear grabbed her arm and helped her back on her feet.

"Where's Eugene?" Kimberly swayed on her feet, trying to chase the clinging fog from her mind.

Thomas looked at her unhappily. "But it's over! Isabella's baby was the key. You saw her die and everything, right?"

"What if I made a mistake?"

Thomas shook his head firmly. "Impossible. She was on the on-ramp..."

"I'm not sure..." She turned her tear-filled eyes up to Thomas. "I don't think Isabella was ever destined to die in the pile-up." Kimberly swallowed, trying to fight down the bitter ball of panic rising in her throat.

Thomas groaned in dismay. "Then what's the premonition of the lake supposed to mean?"

"Can you remember anything else about it?" Clear pleaded, grabbing Kimberly by the arm.

Feeling pressured on all sides, Kimberly took a deep, shuddery breath and shut her eyes again, forcing herself to remember the lightning fast visions that had flickered across her mind like St Elmo's fire.

*A small forest of pine-tree shaped air fresheners swing violently back and forth from the rearview mirror of a big van as it bounces its way toward a large body of water, the surface of which shines like a silver shield.*

*The driver is woman, even though Kimberly cannot see her face. She knows the person behind the wheel is a woman because she can see her hands. They are a woman's hands, and they are scored by numerous deep cuts. Blood oozes from the wounds and makes the steering wheel slick and sticky.*

*The van is headed right for the lake, bouncing along a paved footpath past poured concrete picnic benches. The vehicle flies into the water off the shore, sending a wave over the hood. The van sinks like a stone, the tires settling against the bottom of the rocky lakeshore.*

*Cracks appear like cobwebs across the windshield, letting in cold, green water. The sun is a rapidly diminishing silver disc, soon to be extinguished forever by the lake water pouring into the van. The woman raises her hands as if to try to grab at the fading light, but becomes entangled in the collection of air fresheners.*

*Panic...*

*And then darkness...*

*A heavy, numb feeling spreads through her. She feels as if she is trying to crawl from the bottom of a deep, dark well. Suddenly Dr Kalarjian is peering down at her as if from an impossible height. An EEG machine screams out a flat-line. Dr Kalarjian is back again, this time pushing a cart loaded down with medical equipment. The cart looks very big and very heavy, and the doctor is pushing it with all her strength, as if trying to get it up a hill.*

*The bloodied hands return, filling her mind's eye as they clutch the steering wheel of the runaway van...*

Kimberly was suddenly back in her own body, staring at her own trembling hands, held before her eyes.

"Bloody hands... someone with bloody hands..." she muttered, trying desperately to piece together the snatches of imagery and decipher their meaning.

Clear's eyes widened as she jumped to the logical conclusion. "Eugene! We've got to find Eugene!" Before either Thomas or Kimberly could say anything further, Clear spun around and dashed off down the hallway.

Kimberly watched her go, shaking her head as she pondered things through to herself. "Only new life defeats Death... only new life defeats Death... What is that supposed to mean?"

Thomas put an arm around Kimberly's shoulders as they hurried off after Clear.

Clear sprinted ahead of Thomas and Kimberly, her eyes scanning the room numbers on the passing doors, looking desperately for B-187. She had promised him she'd stay with him, and although it had not been her fault that she hadn't been able to keep her word, it pained her deeply that she had not been able to follow through on her promise. Although they had not gotten off on the best of footing, she had come to view Eugene as a friend; someone whose safety and wellbeing she cared about as much as her own. It had been a long time since she had felt that way about anyone else.

The day Alex died, half of his face smashed into jelly by a falling brick, she had shut herself down emotionally. In less than a year she had lost everyone who had meant anything to her. The pain from the loss of first her friends, and then her lover had wounded her so deeply, she feared letting anyone or anything get close to her ever again. She simply couldn't stand going through the emotional agony that came with surviving the loss of a loved one. Better to live the rest of her life, such as it was, insulated from others. It was safer that way.

But it was unnatural for humans to exist in such a manner. What good was life if you couldn't share it with family and friends?

Kimberly had changed all of that when she had come to the Stonybrook Institution. It had been Clear's decision to leave the institution in order to help her, but if it had not been for her visit, Clear knew she would still be there, locked up in that awful cramped cell, the tang of disinfectant in her nostrils, and the screams and rants and half-articulated cries of the other inmates ringing in her ears twenty-four hours a day.

Although Clear knew she was in very real danger with every breath she took and every step she'd made since leaving the sterile cocoon of the Stonybrook Institution, she had not felt so alive, so connected to herself and the world since the day she'd followed Alex Browning off Flight 180.

Even if she died tomorrow, in a strange, twisted way, Kimberly had saved her life.

For that much, Clear was grateful.

Redoubling her pace, she darted on up the hallway, turning a corner and jogging past a bank of elevators. As she started down the next hallway, she paused as she realized the room number on a nearby door was identical to that of the doomed flight that had so radically changed her life.

Room B-180.

Logically, that meant that Eugene's room should be on the opposite side of the hall! She looked up the corridor and saw a large housekeeping cart parked in front of B-187, partially blocking the door.

Grinning despite herself, she sprinted up the hall.

"Eugene? Are you in there?" she called out as she pushed the cart away from the door.

Inside his oxygen-saturated room, Eugene blinked back tears of joy. As much as he had wanted to wring that crazy bitch's neck when he'd first met her, he had to admit he'd never heard a sweeter sound than her voice calling his name.

Down at the end of the hallway, Kimberly froze mid-step as she heard Clear shout out Eugene's name. Something felt wrong. She could feel it deep inside her, although she couldn't put her finger on exactly what was up.

"Make way. Make way, love-birds!"

Kimberly blinked, startled as a tall, heavyset African American orderly shouldered past her and Thomas. The orderly was carrying a ballpoint pen and a small notebook in one hand, and a three-layer birthday cake in the other. The cake had blue and green icing that read "Happy Birthday Gregory." It was topped by thirteen sparkling novelty candles.

As the orderly strode toward Eugene's room, the birthday cake held aloft in his hand, the candles atop the cake seemed to frame Clear's head, ringing it in a halo of fire.

"Wait," Kimberly whispered, trying to piece together the half-forgotten fragments of vision, but it felt as if her brain was full of fog.

"So, in your vision, what else did you see? An EEG machine and...?" Thomas asked, trying not to let his fear get the better of him as he continued to prod Kimberly for more info. It was bad enough that they had spent the better part of two days, at the cost of two people's lives, on what had proved to be a wild goose chase, but now Kimberly seemed to be flaking out on them in a big way. Like right now. Instead of looking at him while he was trying to talk to her, she was staring over his shoulder, in the direction of Clear.

"Can you hold that open for me, please?" the orderly asked Clear as he walked toward Eugene's room.

"Sure," Clear smiled, pushing opening the door to Room B-187 so he could enter ahead of her.

The look of relief on Eugene's face quickly dissolved as he saw the sparkling candles decorating the birthday cake. His eyebrows drew together in alarm. An instant later there was a muffled *whoosh* as the flames from the birthday cake ignited the escaped gas trapped within the sealed hospital room, filling it with fire from floor to ceiling. The oxygen tank next to Eugene's bed exploded, sending chunks of shrapnel the size of a man's fist tearing through his body.

Eugene was killed instantly.

The wall of flame struck Clear and the orderly like a burning fist, peeling them apart like oranges as their skin and muscles instantly blistered and charred.

Clear's mind seemed to detach as the remains of her body were blasted backward through the air by the force of the explosion. Time stretched as she watched the green hospital corridor fly past her at high speed as darkness crowded the edge of her dying vision. There was no time for regret, or sadness, or fear, just an oddly calm feeling as her mind separated from her body. It seemed to arc upwards toward the ceiling even as her charred mortal remains thudded down onto the ground, driving the air and the life from her body. There was a moment of searing pain as Clear reflexively took her final breath, drawing the superheated air into her lungs, and then everything mercifully faded away to black.

There was barely half a heartbeat between the explosion and the end of Clear River's young, tormented life, but it was long enough for one last thought:

I can finally rest now. Thank God.

# NINETEEN

*WHOOMPH!*

As the wall of fire blazed down the long corridor toward them, Kimberly threw herself at Thomas, knocking him to the floor. An instant later, the housekeeping cart that had been parked in front of Eugene's room sailed overhead, propelled down the hall by the force of the explosion, sending burning rolls of toilet tissue and smoldering towels in every direction. Kimberly buried her head in Thomas's shoulder as the intense heat of the explosion roared by overhead, scorching her hair and stinging her exposed skin.

And then it was over.

The pair of them lay there on the ground for a moment, winded and shaken. Then Kimberly cautiously lifted her head, staring with watering eyes down the corridor. At first she thought her ears were still ringing from the blast, but as she blearily looked around, she realized what she was hearing was the sound of the hospital's fire alarm system, triggered by the smoke pouring into the hallway from the blasted open remains of Eugene's room. There was smoke and debris everywhere along the corridor, and several small fires had started up in adjacent doorways. In the near distance she could hear people coughing and shouting in panic at the sounds of the explosion.

As the smoke cleared, the first thing Kimberly saw was Clear's body, lying less than thirty feet away. The crisped body of the orderly lay a short distance from her, unmoving. The only way she was able to identify the first body as being that of Clear's were the clothes; her brown leather jacket and jeans, which were scorched all down her front, but otherwise intact. Her long blonde hair was gone, reduced to black stubble, and the skin of her face and torso had been burned away, leaving the raw muscle and bone exposed.

Kimberly gasped. Clear Rivers was dead.

"No!'

Kimberly lurched to her feet and started scrambling down the corridor toward the body, only to feel a surprisingly strong arm go around her shoulders and hold her back. Kimberly tried to push Thomas away, but he held onto her tightly, pulling her back down the corridor and away from the grisly sight of the charred corpse lying smoking in the hallway.

Kimberly finally subsided in Thomas's arms, all the fight going out of her. Her whole body shook as muffled sobs wracked her, and the world swam before her eyes as she stared at the crisped body of what she'd been certain, until about twenty seconds ago, would have been her new best friend. She was amazed by the deep sense of loss she felt at Clear's death. She had barely known the woman forty-eight hours, but the pain she was feeling right now was as sharp as what she'd felt when she'd seen poor Shaina die before her very eyes. It had only been two days, but it seemed like a lifetime ago that she had sat down at her computer and typed the name "Clear Rivers" into the search engine, those eleven tiny keystrokes unwittingly sealing Clear's doom. During their very brief time together, the two girls had shared a unique bond, one now severed by the very thing that had brought them together: Death.

Thomas followed Kimberly's stare. A muscle in his jaw twitched, but he remained otherwise under control.

"Guess I'm last now, huh?" he said grimly, as he helped Kimberly back onto her feet. He tried a small smile, but he was only fooling himself. He gazed down at Kimberly, pleading her with his eyes to say something to reassure him. Being a cop, death had never been very far away, but now standing here in the burning corridor of the Lakeview Hospital, it was quite literally all around him. His nostrils wrinkled at the stench of burning flesh, and he turned away from Clear's body, sickened.

As Thomas gently released her, Kimberly was suddenly aware of a strange tingling feeling in her hands. She looked down and saw that the top of both hands were covered with deep cuts where flying broken glass had sliced them open, and that blood was dripping from the wounds. Strangely enough, she felt no pain.

"Bloody hands!" she croaked, turning her trembling hands back and forth as if she'd never seen them before. She turned to face Thomas, a wild look in her eyes. "It's me! The premonitions are about me!"

"What?"

Kimberly turned, still in a daze, and looked down the corridor. As though in a dream, she saw Dr Kalarjian hurrying in her direction, pushing a large cart full of emergency medical equipment ahead of her, orange firelight flickering all around her.

"Crash cart! Let's go! Move it!" she yelled at a young intern, who grabbed onto one end of the cart and helped her maneuver it through the debris littering the floor. Dr Kalarjian saw Kimberly and Thomas, and frowned disapprovingly at them, but continued pushing the heavy crash cart futilely toward Eugene's room, hoping that there would be a life left in there to save.

Kimberly's eyes widened as the doctor hurried by, as if she was finally seeing things clearly for the first time in her life.

"Oh my God," she muttered aloud. "That's it! Dr Kalarjian... the EEG machine..."

Moving as if she was in a trance, Kimberly turned in the direction of the sliding glass doors that led to Emergency Admittance. She could plainly see a large, gray body of water lapping at the grassy shores of the bank that led up to the Lakeview Hospital.

"The lake..." she whispered.

Suddenly a white-and-blue ambulance pulled up outside the doors to the ER and two paramedics leapt from the cab. They hurried inside to try to help the wounded inside the hospital.

"The van."

Thomas frowned, worried by Kimberly's detached behavior. He stepped forward, putting himself between her and the doors to the emergency room.

"What are you talking about?" he demanded, grabbing her by the elbows so that she had to look into his face as he spoke.

Kimberly's gaze went over Thomas's shoulder and fell onto the staff bulletin board hanging on the wall directly behind him. Her mouth fell open. Amongst the Xeroxed work-related notices and hand-printed fliers for used cars and free kittens, there was a news clipping with the headline: "LAKEVIEW HOSPITAL EMT BREATHES NEW LIFE INTO DROWNING VICTIM."

"New life," Kimberly breathed, biting her lip as the final piece of the puzzle fell into place before her. Of course! Suddenly, everything seemed clear to her. All the whirling confusion in her head stopped, crystallizing into a single, crystal clear vision of her own. She knew what she had to do.

She didn't want to do it, but if her theory was correct, it was the only way they could finally cheat Death, once and for all.

"What is it?" Thomas asked. Taking hold of her shoulders gently, he looked deeply into her eyes, as though trying to see her very thoughts.

"You can't cheat destiny," Kimberly said with a sad smile. "I know what I have to do to save us." She looked up at Thomas, a single tear sparkling in her eye. "I have to die."

"That's... that's crazy!" Thomas said. He leaned forward and took hold of Kimberly's hand, his voice low, insistent. "You *can't* give up now! We've *got* to fight this thing."

Kimberly shook her head sadly, and leaned forward to plant a solitary kiss on the policeman's right cheek. Brushing her face softly against the stubble on his jaw, she heaved a deep sigh, squeezing her eyes tight shut as she resigned herself to the inevitable.

Then she whispered in his ear: "Get Kalarjian."

Before Thomas could stop her, Kimberly whirled and ran toward the automatic door, jumping through just as the paramedics opened the one-way door from the outside. The doors hissed shut behind her with a metallic *clump*.

"Kimberly, wait!" Thomas yelled, sprinting after her. As he reached the emergency room doors, there was a crackling sound accompanied by a shower of sparks, and the glass doors abruptly slammed shut. Thomas banged his palms against the glass in frustration, and then tried to pry the doors apart with his bear hands, but they refused to budge.

Ignoring his cries, Kimberly ran over the long, wet grass outside toward the waiting ambulance. Although a blue stripe ran down the side of the vehicle, the ambulance's hood was otherwise solid white.

The white van...

As she yanked open the driver's side door, the sight of six multicolored pine tree shaped air fresheners hanging from the rearview mirror greeted her. A chill went through her. It was indeed the van from her vision—and the key was in the ignition and its motor was running.

Kimberly felt the bleak winds of Destiny sweep up behind her as she put a foot in the cab, and hesitated. She glanced up one last time at Thomas, who stared back at her through the jammed doors, the look on his face pleading her not to do what she was about to do. It was too late—and there was no denying fate. This was something that had to be done, and she was the only one who could do it.

Taking a deep breath, she threw the ambulance into gear, turning around in a screaming one-eighty and sending gravel flying out from under the rear wheels.

As the ambulance peeled out, Thomas grabbed the edges of the frozen sliding door and braced himself, then pulled them apart with a growl. When the gap was wide enough he squeezed through, scraping his forearms raw on the metal edging. He scarcely felt the pain, so determined was he to get to Kimberly. As he stumbled out into the open air, he was joined by the paramedic who had arrived in the now-stolen ambulance.

"What the fuck?" the driver yelped, as he watched his van—with all his gear in it—disappear off across the grass. "Hey! Bring that back."

Ignoring him, Thomas started sprinting after the speeding van. He knew he couldn't outrun it on foot, but he was damn well going to try.

Kimberly tried to ignore the dwindling figures jumping up and down and waving at her in the rearview mirror as she drove down the gravel road that led from the back of the hospital toward the lake. She shifted up a gear, glancing anxiously around her. To the left was a stand of tall, dark trees; to the right was a series of short, squat fence posts linked together by low-hanging chains. Beyond the fencing were picnic tables, free-standing barbeque grills set into cement, open-air pavilions and a children's playground, all of it leading to a fishing dock that jutted twenty-five feet into the lake.

Kimberly felt her blood raging through her body as she steered the ambulance toward the water, busting through the dangling chain between a couple of posts. Links sprayed down the side of the van with a clatter.

As she drove, she glanced downward.

*Bloody hands... A steering wheel... Tree-shaped air-fresheners dangling...*

A wave of déjà vu swept through her with such power that her head reeled. She had been here before, but this was only just happening. She couldn't even begin to get her mind around all of this, but the reality of it was undeniable. It all looked right, it all felt right. She had to go through with this, so that she and Thomas could live.

If she was right about this, they might just make it.

If she was wrong... Well that didn't bear thinking about.

As the ambulance bounced its way though the picnic area at top speed, smacking aside plastic deckchairs and plowing down landscaped bushes, Kimberly was glad it was early in the season and the weather was still too raw for families to be out enjoying a day at the lake.

The dock loomed straight ahead, and beyond it lay the lake, waiting patiently for Kimberly to keep her rendezvous with Death. And beyond Death waited... what? Their Salvation? A new life? Or was Death really the end?

The wheels rattled loudly as the ambulance rolled along the wooden planking of the dock, heading at high speed toward the water. A thrill of fear shot through Kimberly as the reality of what she was doing suddenly hit home, leaving a bitter, metallic tang of adrenaline in her mouth.

This was it.

All this talk of curses and premonitions and of doing what was right to cheat Death was all very well, but actually doing it, actually sitting here in this van with her foot to the floor, shooting toward a lake with the sole intention of drowning herself... it was another thing altogether.

She was about to kill herself.

A picture of her father slammed into her head with frightening force, and Kimberly tightened her grip on the wheel and breathed a silent prayer for forgiveness. A dozen scenarios flashed through her mind, all of them ending with her dead and buried and her father leaning on her tombstone and weeping.

All but one.

Kimberly held onto that vision with everything in her. For her Father's sake, if not hers, she only hoped that she and Clear and Bludworth were right.

There was a lurching sensation in the pit of her stomach as the ambulance shot over the lip of the dock, and then the large, heavy vehicle was airborne. Kimberly instinctively cried out as the ambulance shot off the end of the dock. Such was its momentum that the ambulance sailed nearly thirty feet across the surface of the lake before gravity took over from velocity and the nose of the van dipped sharply toward the water. The van splashed down hard, the hood of the vehicle crumpling as a tidal wave of lake water smashed against the windshield with enough force to crack it like an egg. The ambulance bobbed like cork for a couple of seconds, then began to sink quickly, nose first, into the lake.

Kimberly was thrown back against the driver's seat as the ice-cold lake water flooded into the cab of the ambulance, pouring through the air vents, the door seals and the window frames. There was a drawn-out cracking sound as the windshield bowed inwards under the pressure of the rising water, crazing with a myriad of cracks that swiftly joined up and began leaking water, slowly at first, and then with greater pressure as the cracks split open with the crunch of splintering glass. An instant later the windshield buckled and detached from its frame. Icy green water sprayed into the cab, swiftly rising toward Kimberly's head.

On the shore, Thomas ran through the empty park toward the dock, his heart pounding like a trip-hammer as he saw the ambulance start to sink below the surface of the lake. His lungs ached from running so fast, but he was in no position to stop and catch his breath. He ran down the dock and dived into the chilly water without pausing to remove his jacket or kick off his shoes. He prayed he could reach Kimberly in time.

Although dazed by the impact, Kimberly was still conscious and otherwise unhurt as the van began to sink. Within seconds of hitting the lake, the water rushing in through the cracked windshield was already up to her chin. It was so cold it took her breath away. Fighting against the wave of claustrophobic panic that was threatening to claim her, Kimberly forced herself to remain calm. Every survival instinct in her was screaming at her to reach out and wind down the window, to grab the door handle and open the van's door while she still had a chance.

But she didn't. Instead, she took a deep breath as the ambulance tilted sharply. Its rear axle pointed toward the sky, and then slid swiftly below the lake's watery surface. Kimberly pushed her chin up into the little pocket of air that remained in the van's cab as the vehicle went down... down... down... until it settled upright on the rocky lake bed, twenty feet below the surface of the lake.

"Kimberly!"

Thomas took a deep breath and dived down deep at the spot where he'd seen the ambulance sink. Although the water was murky, he could just make out the ambulance's white outline against the lakebed below. The cold, muddy water stung his eyes, but he forced himself to keep them open, peering frantically through the green gloom.

As Thomas pulled himself along the side of the submerged ambulance, he hoped against hope that there was still an air pocket near the roof of the vehicle, so Kimberly could still breathe. But as he reached the driver's side door, he was dismayed to find the entire interior was flooded. He could plainly see Kimberly seated behind the wheel of the stolen ambulance, her hair floating about her face as if she were some kind of mermaid. He couldn't see any kind of detail, but he could see color, and as far as he could make out there was no blood. He hoped that she wasn't too badly injured from the van's splashdown into the water.

Now, all he had to do was get her out of there.

Thomas reached out and yanked on the door handle, but because the pressure inside the vehicle had yet to equalize, it refused to budge. He looked back at Kimberly, to find her watching him sadly through the window. She lifted her hand and touched the glass. Suddenly a burst of air bubbles rushed from her mouth, as her taxed lungs, aching for air, emptied themselves and water rushed into her respiratory system.

Thomas was helpless to do anything but watch, as Kimberly started to drown.

Trapped inside the van, Kimberly clutched her throat as water rushed into her lungs, snorting and gagging at the terrifying sensation. Out of the corner of her eye she was vaguely aware of a series of dull underwater concussions as Thomas drew his revolver and slammed its butt repeatedly against the glass in a vain bid to smash the glass and save her.

It was no use. Within seconds, her head began to ache as if it was being split down the middle from the inside out. Her lungs burned horribly, as if they were on fire. The dirty lake water had flooded both lungs, overwhelming the tiny sacs inside that made breathing possible. Her brain screamed for oxygen. She instinctively opened her mouth to try and breathe, but there was no air, only more water. Her head swam, and she realized that she was about to pass out.

As she drowned, she was aware not only of a terrifying feeling, not only of the physical pain and distress of it, but also of a sense of utter hopelessness. Bit by bit, fighting it all the way, Kimberly began to slip into unconsciousness. She felt the welcome gray oblivion start to claim her, and the terror was replaced by a strangely peaceful state. Images—fragments of memory—flittered across her mind's eye as her oxygen-starved body began to shut down.

*At first the images are pleasant ones, almost happy. Her father stands at the foot of the drive, waving goodbye as she heads off on a great adventure. Shaina gives her a saucy wink as she turns in the passenger seat to make a wisecrack. It's so good to see her again; she misses her so much. Evan Lewis, alive and still in possession of both eyes, grins at her from the seat of his Trans-Am; he seems so cocky and self-assured. Dano and Frankie snicker as they pass a joint back and forth, mindlessly unaware of anything besides their own pleasure and the imminent possibility of getting laid.*

*Then, suddenly, everything becomes increasingly darker and more violent. A flying log pitches out of nowhere and smashes into an SUV, sending the hood flying off as the vehicle literally stands on its nose, spinning around and around with a howl of tortured metal. Then the flatbed semi smashes into the Tahoe, killing Shaina and her friends, while Thomas grabs her and throws her to the ground, out of harm's way.*

*Her first glimpse of Clear, huddled away in her padded cell, both frightened and intrigued by the stranger who has intruded into her refuge.*

*Tim Carpenter is squashed like a bug before his mother's horrified eyes.*

*Mr Bludworth's face, distorted by the shadows thrown from the roaring furnace, laughing as he yanks the nipple ring from Evan Lewis's mutilated body.*

*Nora's grief-stricken face floats up at her, to be quickly replaced by the sight of Clear and Kat covered in Nora's blood.*

*Eugene puts the gun to his head and pulls the trigger... and pulls the trigger... and pulls the trigger.*

*Kat, trapped behind the wheel of her Expedition, stares in horror at the length of rebar jutting from her head rest, unaware that her own death is staring her right in the face.*

*Rory rubs his nose as he turns to face her, a stupefied look on his face microseconds before he's sliced up like a deli ham.*

*Isabella's baby, still wet from the womb, cries in angry defiance at the brave new world he has found himself delivered into. Dr Kalarjian pushes the crash-cart through the smoke and chaos of the devastated hospital. The ambulance pulls up to the doors of the emergency unit, like the magical steed told of in fairy tales, come to take her away to a distant shore.*

*And then Death itself, an endless black abyss of nothingness, sensed by every living being, but unimaginable to all but the most desolate of souls, trading cards with Fate and its own bastard cousin Destiny as it twists back on itself like a snake, consuming and devouring everything in its path.*

*Now she has come full circle, watching the water of the lake surge over the hood of the ambulance as she sinks to the bottom like a stone. And somewhere Thomas is still pounding... and pounding... and pounding against the glass.*

She could hear someone whispering in her ear. As she tried to listen, she realized that there were a multitude of voices, all blending together, all of them familiar to her.

"Only new life defeats Death."

"If it is my time to go and be with my family in Heaven, I can accept that."

"I know what I have to do to save us: I have to die."

And that's when Kimberly's heart stopped beating.

# TWENTY

She was somewhere far away. She couldn't see where she was because there was no light, although it was not dark, either. It was like a gray fog surrounded her. She was neither warm nor cold, up nor down, sad nor happy—she simply was.

She was vaguely aware of muffled and indistinct sounds around her. The noises reminded her of voices heard from the bottom of a swimming pool.

Suddenly there was pain, as if someone had struck her full in the chest with a hammer. She couldn't breathe.

Then the fog lifted and she could hear the keening of an electronic alarm of some sort, and see the figure of a woman hovering over her. Although she couldn't focus, she had the feeling that she knew the person leaning over her.

"Ready again and... clear!"

There was a second jolt as the defibrillator paddles in Dr Kalarjian's hands sent a short, sharp surge of voltage into Kimberly's body. The fist-sized muscle in her chest suddenly kicked itself back into play, sending blood rushing back through her icy cold limbs.

Kimberly coughed violently, and Dr Kalarjian reached for the young woman's neck, turning her head as she cleared her airway so that the lake water she vomited out would not be re-aspirated. The EEG monitor next to the gurney switched from the incessant scream of a flat line to the reassuring beeps of a steady heartbeat.

"She's back!" The nurse monitoring Kimberly's vital signs shook her head in amazement. You saw some incredible things in this job, and saving a young teenager's life had to rank pretty high up on that list.

"Five CC's of narcodon! I want her stabilized and prepped for ICU," Dr Kalarjian said as she stripped the rubber gloves from her hands and tossed them into a nearby trash can.

Kimberly turned her head, weakly, looking around at the controlled insanity of the Emergency Room. People were still running around, trying to deal with the chaos created by the explosion of the oxygen canister in Eugene's room. She felt weird, detached. She had just died and been brought back to life, and only twenty minutes or so had passed. She couldn't believe that such a thing could happen.

But it had, and she was still alive. There was only one burning question in her mind now.

Had it worked?

She was alive, so that was a start.

Then a terrible thought hit her. "Thomas?" she whispered, suddenly fearful that perhaps she had not been quick enough. What if he drowned trying to save her? Was that to be Death's final cruel jest?

Suddenly Thomas stepped into her limited field of vision. Kimberly sagged with relief. The young policeman was soaking wet and had a blue blanket draped around his shoulders, his dark hair spiky and wet. He looked adorable. A huge smile was plastered across his handsome face.

She knew then that they had won.

"Welcome back. We lost you for a minute there," Thomas said, taking her cold hand into his own and giving it a squeeze. He beamed down at her with a softness in his eyes that made Kimberly's bruised heart melt.

And there was something different here. Kimberly could feel it in her bones. The black pit of fatalistic despair that had filled her for the last two days was gone, and in its place was a warm, contented feeling. Something had changed, and Kimberly was willing to bet her life that she knew what it was.

"Yeah, and next time you intentionally drive into a lake, I'll kill you myself," Dr Kalarjian remarked acidly as she pulled a blanket up to Kimberly's chin. With that, she turned and walked off to help someone who really needed her.

Kimberly stared up at Thomas, tears of relief welling up in her eyes. "Can you feel it?" she asked, her voice little more than a hoarse whisper. "We did it... for real."

"I know," Thomas said, tightening his grip on her hand. "I feel it, too. Thanks to you, we cheated Death."

Kimberly felt so weak, weaker than even Isabella's newborn baby. She couldn't lift so much as her hand, but it didn't matter. She was alive. Thomas was alive. That was all that mattered.

She took a cautious breath, wincing as her battered lungs complained, but that was good. Pain was good.

Pain meant that she was alive.

Then the tears came. After her mother had died in the carjacking last year, she had felt so guilty for surviving—for living when her mother had died. She had thought that it should've been her who had died so her mother could've lived. Every day for the last three hundred and sixty days she had lived with that terrible secret, burning her up from the inside out like a ball of napalm in her heart. Now, she had never felt happier to be alive, and she would never feel bad about being so for the rest of her days.

Kimberly looked up at Thomas as he rested a hand on her forehead, stroking her hair gently.

She knew she didn't need to say a word to him to explain any of this.

He knew.

Suddenly, the gray clouds over Lakeview Memorial parted, and a single, blinding shaft of sunlight stabbed down, flooding the windows of the Emergency Room, bathing everything in a golden light. Kimberly blinked as the warm light suffused the ward, offering up a silent, heartfelt prayer of thanks to God.

It was a sign; she knew that now; a sign that the shadow of the angel of Death had been lifted.

She had done it.

It was over.

They were free.

# EPILOGUE

Kimberly leaned back in her lawn chair, savoring the warmth of the late summer sun on her skin. It was truly a beautiful day. The sky was blue, the sun was high in the sky, and the fresh summer breeze gently tousled her hair as she reached for a second helping of Mrs Gibbons's delicious homemade coleslaw.

It was hard to believe that five months had passed since the day she had plunged the ambulance into Greenwood Lake. Now here she was, whole and healthy, sitting in the Gibbons family's spacious backyard, enjoying a barbeque and the company of people who, with the exception of her father, had been absolute strangers until that fateful day on Route 23.

Following her daring rescue from what should have been a watery grave, she had been forced to stay at Lakeview Memorial for nearly a week as she recuperated. During that time, she had become friendly with the Gibbons family, whose farm had been the unfortunate site of the wreck that took the lives of Kat and Rory. Once she had recovered, there was then the matter of the ambulance she stole and drove into the lake. Mr Corman managed to find a lawyer who was able explain to the authorities that Kimberly's actions had been those of an emotionally fragile young woman who, moments after seeing her good friends blown to smithereens, had panicked and tried to flee the scene of the carnage in the first vehicle she could find... which just happened to be an unlocked ambulance with its keys in the ignition. The reason the ambulance ended up in the lake was not a deliberate decision on her part, but the result of clouded thinking brought on by the emotional trauma of seeing her friend's chargrilled corpse up close.

At least that was what Kimberly had told her attorney. Since her lawyer was expecting her to lie about her reasons anyway, she decided it was wiser to go with a believable untruth than try to explain what had actually happened. The ambulance company wisely decided to drop the criminal charges, and the Corman family's insurance company settled the whole thing.

Kimberly smiled as she glanced over at Thomas, who was seated beside her father at the picnic table, which was covered in a red and white checkered cloth and heaped with condiments, an enormous bowl of home made potato salad, and big chunks of juicy fresh watermelon. Thomas caught her eye and smiled back. His bosses had not been nearly as forgiving of his peculiar behavior, especially his blatant abuse of authority. Shortly after getting out of the hospital with her new baby, Isabella Hudson had filed a civil suit citing unlawful arrest and harassment by a police officer. That, along with Dr Kalarjian's complaint of police brutality, resulted in Thomas being placed on administrative leave until the higher ups finished their investigation. Then he was demoted and reassigned.

Quite frankly, Thomas didn't give a flying rat's ass about any of that. He was alive, and Kimberly was alive.

That was all that mattered.

Meanwhile, Isabella had taken her civil settlement from the police department and was doing very well, enjoying the company of both her new baby and her new boyfriend, Deputy Steve Adams.

Despite the tribulations they had faced, and largely due to the consequences of their actions, neither Kimberly nor Thomas regretted doing what they'd had to do. After all, everything they'd done had led them to this very moment. To them, being able to live out their lives without the constant fear of Death hanging over them made everything worthwhile.

If they felt any sadness, it was that they were the only two people sitting around the table who fully appreciated that.

Kimberly picked up the shish-kebab skewer on her paper plate and took a bite, relishing the taste. She couldn't begin to put a price tag on being able to eat something like this, and not have to worry about whether a jostled elbow or errant sneeze might send the metal skewer through her eye or the roof of her mouth to spear her brain.

"God, this is good!" she said between bites. "Big props to you and Brian, Mrs Gibbons."

"Props?" Mrs Gibbons looked a bit puzzled by Kimberly's terminology as she put a platter of hot dogs on the picnic table. "Our... pleasure," she hazarded with a smile, on the off-hand chance that she had just been paid a compliment.

Mr Gibbons smiled back at his wife, then turned and looked at Kimberly. "You ready to head back to college?"

"Three short glorious weeks away," Kimberly said, as she helped herself to some more mashed potato.

"Can I go too?" Thomas asked with a lopsided grin. "My new partner doesn't brush his teeth in the morning. Makes patrol a living hell."

"I guess things are pretty much getting back to normal," said Kimberly with a laugh, and then her face softened as she saw the look on Thomas's face. She touched his arm gently under the table, and was rewarded with a brief, rueful smile. It would be a while before either of them would be able to forget the fateful events of the last year, but at least it was all over now.

Mr Gibbons turned to Mr Corman, giving him a conspiratorial dig in the ribs. "You may want to think twice about letting Kimberly live off-campus. Our eldest daughter did, and she came back with piercings all over her face." He dropped his voice and gave Mr Corman a grimace. "Amongst... other places."

Brian raced over to the table and deposited a plateful of cooked veg'n'meat kebabs on the table in front of his father. He had been given the honor of tending to the propane grill, and was making the most of the responsibility. "He used to call her the Pincushion, like from Hellraiser," he said with a grin, before turning back to his father and wiping his greasy fingers on his bright red barbeque apron. "You got the spatula, Dad?"

"Sure, here."

As Brian reached across the table to grab the spatula from his father, he accidentally bumped Thomas's arm, just as he was about to put the shish kebab skewer into his mouth. Thomas quickly put down the skewer and cocked an eyebrow at the young teen. It had been five months, true, but he was still kinda jumpy.

"Careful, son!" warned Mr Corman. He picked up his own shish kebab and examined it, eyeing the sharp metal skewer. "Jeez, these things are dangerous!"

"Trust me, I've been through closer calls," Thomas said with a wry smile.

"So have I!" Brian said excitedly. "Tell 'em about the news van, dad!" With that, he turned and happily jogged back to get the last of the kebabs from the gas grill, which was set up about fifty feet away from the picnic area.

"What's that?" Kimberly asked, curious.

Mr Gibbons sat back in his chair, glancing affectionately at his son as he tended the barbeque. "Well... Brian was nearly hit by a news van that day out in the field... but your friend Rory pulled him back at the last second. He saved his life for sure."

"You never told me that, Peter," said Mrs Gibbons, genuine surprise in her voice. "Boy... that was certainly *lucky*."

As the Gibbons and Mr Corman continued with their small talk, the smiles froze on Kimberly and Thomas's faces. As their gazes locked over the picnic table, each saw the return of an old, familiar fear in the eyes of the other. As one, they quickly glanced over to where Brian stood tending the barbeque in front of his family's rickety old gas grill, which was powered by a large tank of propane. Flames were leaping from the surface of the grill, whipped up by a stiff breeze that seemed to have sprung up out of nowhere.

Kimberly's eyebrows shot up in concern.

Gee, that looked kind of—

*BOOOOOOM!*

A loud explosion rocked the pasture and a fireball shot up into the air, as the twenty-pound